Hawaiian Embers

SHERI LYNNE

DORRANCE PUBLISHING CO
EST. 1920
PITTSBURGH, PENNSYLVANIA 15238

The contents of this work, including, but not limited to, the accuracy of events, people, and places depicted; opinions expressed; permission to use previously published materials included; and any advice given or actions advocated are solely the responsibility of the author, who assumes all liability for said work and indemnifies the publisher against any claims stemming from publication of the work.

This is a work of fiction. Names, characters, places and incidents are either the product of the author's imagination or are used fictitiously, and any resemblance to actual persons, living or dead, business establishments, events or locales is entirely coincidental.

All Rights Reserved
Copyright © 2024 by Sheri Lynne

No part of this book may be reproduced or transmitted, downloaded, distributed, reverse engineered, or stored in or introduced into any information storage and retrieval system, in any form or by any means, including photocopying and recording, whether electronic or mechanical, now known or hereinafter invented without permission in writing from the publisher.

Dorrance Publishing Co
585 Alpha Drive
Pittsburgh, PA 15238
Visit our website at *www.dorrancebookstore.com*

ISBN: 979-8-89027-216-4
eISBN: 979-8-89027-714-5

BOOKS BY SHERI LYNNE

HAWAIIAN SERIES:
Hawaiian Dreams
Hawaiian Flames
Hawaiian Embers

Hawaiian Dreams and *Hawaiian Flames*…I liked how the author combined love, humor, suspense, thrills, and so much more in both books! Page turners for sure! Highly recommend them to all the romance suspense lovers out there! Can't wait to have Hawaiian Embers in my hands!

-AUDREY, HILLSDALE, MICHIGAN

Hawaiian Dreams…It reads like a Hallmark movie…great read!!

-PAM, CEMENT CITY, MICHIGAN

Hawaiian Flames…Impossible to put down! It grabs you right from the start!

-DONNA, CEMENT CITY, MICHIGAN

Hawaiian Dreams…Very detailed and brought each character to life. I couldn't put the book down!

-CAITLIN, COLDWATER, MICHIGAN

Hawaiian Dreams…I found this book to be suspenseful and entertaining. The writer brings humor along with a strong faith within the characters.

-KAREN L., FLORIDA

Hawaiian Flames…I found this book to be a fun easy read. I was so intrigued by the plot I could hardly put it down. Can't wait to see what the author has up her sleeve on her next book!

-KATHY, HANOVER, MICHIGAN

ACKNOWLEDGEMENTS

This book was written in memory of my brother-in-law, Gil Ross, who passed away in November of 2022. His identical twin brother, Gordon, who passed away in 2013, shared many escapades through-out their time in the US Air Force with some of those memories living on through-out the pages of my books. Although this book is fictional, Gil, and his lovely wife Kathy shared some of their early events when they first met, and her journey to become a social worker. I have weaved some of their events into the lives of the characters in my book. Kathy is now retired and lives in Minnesota, close to her family.

A special thank you goes out to the Michigan State Commercial Vehicle Officers, who helped me to understand what happens in the world of human trafficking.

Thank you, Melissa and Karen, for reading my manuscript and keeping me on track. Also, I would like to thank all my friends and family who have supported me through-out the writing of my Hawaiian series. I couldn't have done it without you. Thank you to my daughter Wendy, her husband Joe, and my darling little granddaughter who brings such joy to my life. I love you all!

Hawaiian Embers is the third book in the trilogy. Mark, identical twin to his brother Mike, finds himself tangled up in the middle of a human trafficking ring involving one of his waitresses and her daughter. As you read Mark and Tammy's story, my hope is that you will become more aware of what a victim might go through when they are sold or kidnapped. Human trafficking is fast becoming the number one crime in America and across the globe, surpassing drug trafficking. When you are out, if you see anything suspicious in a parking lot or city, please report it.

CHAPTER 1

MARKUS JOHN TREVAINE, co-owner of the Hawaiian Lanai, a successful restaurant located on the island of Oahu with his identical twin brother Mike, was sitting at his desk, trying to get through the reports he needed to go over, and file, before the end of the week. But his mind kept wandering back to the day he had taken Cameron, his seven-year-old son, to the ice cream parlor in downtown Honolulu. He had just dropped his brother Mike, and his wife Jenna, off at the airport for their flight to Paris for their honeymoon. He had driven downtown and parked his car near the ice cream parlor. When he and his son came out of the car, he saw Zack, a detective from the police department, and Tammy, one of his waitresses, come flying towards them, yelling out his name. He'll never forget the frightened look on her face as she tried to explain what had happened. Her little girl was missing. When they heard screams in a parking lot across the street, Zack and he went flying over and caught a man trying to get the little girl in his van. He smiled, remembering the little girl kicking the jerk in the shins, which gave them time to catch the guy and get him cuffed. She was one brave little girl. After the incident, he invited them to the ice cream parlor, where he was able to get to know Tammy and her little girl, Bethany, a little better. He hadn't realized what a pretty woman Tammy was. He remembered she was wearing light blue jeans and a dark green tank top that day that hugged her body. The outfit showed off her petite figure perfectly. Her long light brown hair flowing softly around her shoulders brought out her liquid amber eyes that changed to gray-green when she laughed, complimenting her soft facial features beautifully. Whenever she met his eyes while they talked, she'd smile, and something deep inside of him seemed to ignite. Funny, he never really noticed her before that day.

He shook his head. He needed to get these thoughts out of his head. He and his brother Mike had set up rules regarding the dating of their employees when they first opened their restaurant. He was married at the time, so he didn't care one way or the other. But now that he was divorced, he didn't know what he wanted. His divorce was final a month ago, and it still stung.

It took almost a year to get through the emotional trauma of living apart, splitting up their time with Cameron, and helping him adjust to living with one parent separately. For the most part, Cameron seemed to be handling it. There were times when he would act out, but they would work it out, and he would be fine. He was also a little gun shy about getting into another relationship. It would be too painful if it didn't work out, not only for him, but for Cameron should he get attached.

His only focus should be on his son and the restaurant business. And yet… He had felt something, sitting there in the ice cream parlor with her, while the kids were off playing video games not too far from their table. He hadn't spoken to her since then, other than the occasional times when he needed her to check on a customer.

After their time together at the ice cream parlor, she probably thought he was ignoring her, which in a sense he had. He couldn't let himself be caught up in these feelings he was starting to have for her. He shook his head again and focused back on the reports. He would soon need to be out on the floor. Jenna and Mike were due back on Sunday. It will be a relief to have them back. Even with their new general manager, Jack Fleming, handling the front of the house, and he overseeing the whole operation along with the financial end, it had taken its toll on him. Maybe he would take a few days and relax. Just to get his head together, just him, and no one else. He smiled. He could only hope.

By the time he was able to get out on the floor, there was a lineup at the door. He jumped in and began seating customers along with Jack. When the restaurant slowed down it was well after eight. He noticed Zack had come in and was seated at the bar. Sergeant Zack Williams was a detective for the HPD. He and his brothers, along with the police department and the state police out of LA, stopped a drug heist and were able to arrest all who were involved except the drug lord who had set up the drug deal. He got away. As far as he knew, they hadn't found him yet.

He walked up to Zack and took a seat beside him at the bar. "Hey, Zack. How's it going? Have you and the police department had any luck finding Manchez and his wife?" he asked.

Marco Manchez and his wife Millie were frequent customers at their restaurant, and unbeknown to him and his brother, ran a loan shark and drug-trafficking ring under the cover of his legit businesses in downtown Honolulu.

Zack turned to him. "Hey, Mark. Unfortunately, no. We thought we had a lead, but it came up dry. We're still working on it. Is Tammy working tonight?" Zack looked concerned.

"Yes, she's working in the lanai tonight."

"Would it be possible for me to speak with her?"

"Yes, but what is this about?" he returned with his own concern in his voice, wondering what he could possibly want to discuss with Tammy.

Zack hesitated, "Actually, Mark, it concerns you as well. If you have some time, I would like to speak to both of you. It has to do with the guy who tried to take her little girl."

Mark's heart started to beat a little faster as he thought back to that day. *The guy was in jail. Could he have gotten out already?* Mark's thoughts turned back to Zack. "Have you eaten dinner yet?"

"No, I was waiting to see if I would be able to sit down with you both."

"Listen, I haven't eaten yet either, and there's a corner booth available, which will give us more privacy. Let's head over there, and I will see how Tammy's doing with her customers. See when she will be available to talk."

Zack nodded, grabbed his drink, and went over to the booth while Mark went to check on Tammy.

When Mark entered the lanai, he found Tammy taking an order from some customers at one of her tables. He waited by the waitress station until she was finished.

Tammy turned to see Mark, standing tall and handsome, with those deep blue eyes staring directly at her. Her heart leaped as she caught his eyes. She tried to fight the attraction that happened within her every time she came near him. Since the incident where he and Zack saved her daughter, Bethany, from a human trafficker, he'd hardly spoken to her. Just goes to show he only felt sorry for her and Bethany. There was no attraction on his part. Even if there was, he wouldn't date her, due to the rules he and Mike set at the beginning when they first opened the restaurant: No dating employees! Such a stupid rule!

Nervously, she came up to him. With her eyes still focused on his, she noticed that his eyes had an intensity she hadn't seen before, changing them to an even deeper blue. She felt the warm liquid sensation coursing throughout her body. Was there something there? As she searched his eyes, suddenly, it was gone.

Mark, watching Tammy with their customers, smiled. She was a great waitress. Gazing at her body when she turned and walked towards him gave him a rush. He felt the same feeling deep down inside of him start to ignite again. Her hair was pulled up into a ponytail, and bounced with every step she took. She hardly wore any makeup, but it didn't matter. She was pretty without it. Her small breasts showed in the snug fitting t-shirt with "The Hawaiian Lanai" printed across the front of them. In a short black skirt, he couldn't get enough of seeing her beautiful long legs walking toward him.

He took a deep breath and shook himself as she approached him. With curious eyes meeting his, she asked, "Mark, is there something you needed to see me about?" she asked nervously.

Mark quickly switched his eyes from admiration to business. "Yes," he stated. "Tammy, Detective Williams is here, and he needs to talk to you about the attempted kidnapping involving your daughter, Bethany. I see you have just taken an order for one of your tables. Do you have any more customers that need to be waited on besides this one order that you need to place?" he asked.

Tammy's heart began to race. "No, my other customers are just finishing up. I just need to place this one. Can... Can you tell me what he needs from me?" she stammered as she felt her body start to shake.

Mark could see what he just told her had affected her. He gently placed his hands on her upper arms, which was not what he should have done, as he could feel the energy radiating from her to him! "I'm sure it's nothing to worry about. He actually needs to talk to both of us. When you are finished with closing out your customers, I'll have one of the other waitresses take over for this one that you are placing. Then join Detective Williams and I in the bar lounge."

He suddenly realized that he still held her, with his hands on her arms, his thumbs gently going back and forth as if they had a mind of their own. He dropped them. Tammy felt the warmth of his hands calming her nerves. When he released her, she felt that warmth leaving her. She tried to ignore it, but she couldn't help the feelings flowing through her. She turned away from him. She didn't want him to see in her eyes how much he affected her.

"Yes, sir," she replied. Her eyes turned back to him when he left to speak to Carol. As she watched him go back into the bar lounge, she blew out a breath. *You better get ahold of yourself, Tammy*, she disciplined herself. *You will only get hurt in the end.* And that is something she did not want to go through again. She had already been burned once. She swore never again!

Mark went to check with Jack, to make sure he was able to handle the rest of the evening. When he confirmed, he went and joined Zack in the bar lounge. He slid into the booth. He could still feel the energy when he placed his hands on her arms. He needed to get a grip. This cannot happen!

Zack could see something was going on with Mark; he seemed nerved up. "Are you okay, Mark? I didn't mean to upset you. I just need to make you and Tammy aware of some information we received. I'm hoping that Tammy might be able to answer some questions that may clear some things up pertinent to the case."

Mark glanced over at the entrance door to the lanai, then he turned back to Zack. "I'm fine, Zack. I'm just concerned about Tammy. She was a little shook up when I told her you wanted to see her." He wasn't going to let anyone know of his attraction for her. "She should be out soon. Do you know what you would like to order for dinner? I'm starving." He waved Megan over.

"Yes, I think I will have a cheeseburger and some fries," he returned.

"You read my mind." He smiled.

Megan came up to the booth and they each gave her their order. Mark ordered coffee with cream with his meal.

"Zack, would you like another beer?" asked Megan.

"No thanks, Megan, but I will have a black coffee."

"You bet. I'll be right back with your coffees."

When she left, Zack turned and asked, "How're Peyton and Stacy doing? Are they getting adjusted living on the big island together?"

Peyton was Mark and Mike's older brother. He was just discharged from the army in May, after serving our country for a little over twelve years. He had spent time in the special ops division, with his last tour in search and rescue. Stacy Rayland was a detective for the state police out of LA, working on a case here on the island when they met. Looking back, the case started out with liquor being taken out of their restaurant by two of their employees, and blew into a massive case of loansharking and drug smuggling. Peyton, Mike, and he, along with three detectives out of LA, the local police department, and a special agent out of Waco, Texas, were able to capture and arrest the drug ring, all except for one: Marco Manchez. Peyton fell madly in love with Stacy while working on the case. When Peyton landed the job with the hospital on the island of Kona as a helicopter pilot, Stacy transferred out of the LA State Police Department to the local KPD, so she could be closer to Peyton. Last he heard, Peyton had closed on a small farm outside the city and was fixing it up for him and Stacy to move into.

"Mark?"

Mark came out of his trance. "Sorry, Zack. Peyton and Stacy are doing fine. He loves his job, and Stacy seems to be kept busy with homicides within the city. Justice, his dog, loves running around the farm when they are there. He seems to be adjusting nicely to civilian life after serving in the military as a rescue dog."

"That's good to hear. When are Mike and Jenna due back?" he asked.

"On Sunday, and I am not afraid to tell you that I will be glad when they are back! It's been a long two weeks."

Megan brought over their coffee and placed them on the table.

"They've sent some pictures back to me on some of the tourist attractions in Paris. Looks like they're having a good time."

Zack nodded. Mark looked worn out. "What about you, Mark?" he asked, concerned. "You haven't had a vacation in over a year. With what you have been through with the divorce and the case we worked on together, you need a break."

Megan brought their food and set it down in front of them. "Thanks, Megan," smiled Mark.

"You're welcome," she smiled back.

After she left, "In answer to your question, the holidays will be here soon. I may take a week to ten days off. I'd like to take Cameron back to Michigan, to visit my parents, so he can get to know his grandparents. We live so far apart. It's hard to find time to spend together. It was nice seeing them at Mike and Jenna's wedding, but they were only able to spend a week with us."

He and Zack were just finishing up their dinner when Tammy came up to their booth.

With her heart racing, she glanced over at Detective Williams, and then at Mark. She caught his eyes. "Is this a good time, or would you like me to come back?" Her nerves were on edge with thoughts of what Detective Williams wanted to talk to her about. She felt her voice shake as she asked the question.

Mark wiped his mouth on his napkin and gestured with his hand for Tammy to have a seat. Megan came back to fill their coffee and take their plates away. Mark caught her eyes again as she sat down.

"Would you care for anything to drink, Tammy?"

She broke away from Mark's intense gaze and looked up at Megan. "Umm… I'll have a cola, if I may."

"Sure, I'll be right back."

She glanced back over to Mark. His gaze bore into her, and she wished she was anywhere but here, in this booth, with him. She tore her eyes away to glance over at Detective Williams. "Mark said you wanted to see me about the attempted kidnapping of my daughter Bethany?"

Zack had been studying the two when Tammy came up to their booth and wondered. Was something going on between them? He cleared his throat. "Yes, the man that tried to kidnap your daughter is part of a human trafficking ring here on the island. When we were interrogating him, we grilled it out of him that a man offered to sell Bethany for a large sum of money." Tammy's face drained of color as she sat there, trying to take in what Detective Williams just told her. "He said his boss told him that the man was desperate for money. Do you know of someone close to Bethany that would want to sell her?"

Tears started forming in her amber eyes as she tried to internalize what he just asked. Megan brought back her cola and set it down in front of her. She waited till she left before she could even speak. "Why would anyone, even if they were close to my daughter, sell her to a human-trafficking ring?" her voice quivering as she answered with her own question.

"Like anything else, he or she needed money and was willing to sell her for it. Do you have any enemies, or a disgruntled boyfriend or ex-husband?"

She shook her head. "No, I don't know of anyone who would do such a thing. She is very much liked at school. I don't have a boyfriend, and as far as her father is concerned, he has had no contact with her since he left when Bethany was only two. Last I heard, he was somewhere in Arizona, but he could be anywhere."

Mark, his blue eyes intense on her, listened as she answered Zack's questions. He could feel his blood start to boil at the thought of that sleazebag of an ex-husband leaving Tammy to raise her daughter all by herself. He clenched his fists, fighting the urge to go over and take her in his arms and just hold her.

Zack looked over at Mark. "Listen, the guy we arrested is just a go-between for the main trafficker, and finds vulnerable victims he can pick up and take back to the ringleader. From there they are forced into prostitution."

"But she's only six years old!" she cried.

He glanced back over to Tammy. "I'm sorry, but we've seen them even younger."

Tammy felt the color drain from her, as she thought about how her beautiful daughter could have been a victim, if it hadn't been for Mark and Zack saving her that day.

Mark watched her turn white as a sheet. He rushed over to her side and caught her just as she started to fall into the seat. Tammy felt strong arms and a hard chest press up against her cheek, as she struggled against the darkness that was about to envelop her...

"Tammy," Mark murmured. "Don't pass out on us, honey. Stay with us." Mark, with his arm around her, gently rubbed her upper arm, trying to slow down the adrenaline coursing through her as she regained consciousness. She slowly sat up and realized she was in Mark's arms. Did she just hear him call her *honey*, or did she just imagine it?

"I'm sorry," she tried to apologize. "It just hit me all at once that if you and Mark hadn't been there to save Bethany…" She shuddered.

Cautiously, Zack replied, "I didn't mean to upset you, Tammy, but I need to make sure you and Mark are aware that someone may still be after your daughter. And you need to keep an eye out for anyone suspicious at all times."

"But you caught the guy who was trying to take her!" exclaimed Tammy.

"Yes, but these perpetrators almost always get out of jail, with someone paying their bail bond. Also, the money changed hands. Chances are the ringleader will come after what he paid for. They may lay low for a while, knowing we have one of their men in jail, but as soon as he's out, they may strike at any time." He glanced over at Mark. "The guy that we arrested doesn't remember you as the one that took him down. What we don't know is if someone was watching from a distance. They usually work in groups of two or more. So you need to be cautious as well."

Mark, with his arm still around her, watching her, glanced up at Zack. "Were you able to get any information on who this ringleader is through the kidnapper?" he asked.

"No, he isn't talking. The police are well aware of this human-trafficking ring, but they work underground, and it's hard to catch these guys. At this time, we know the FBI is working undercover, and we will do our part in trying to uncover any information from this perp while we can still hold him in jail. We all need to work together to put away as many as possible that use children for prostitution," stated Zack.

"Thanks for letting us know. I'll keep an eye out. I'll let my brothers know as well, and I'll make sure Tammy and her little girl are kept safe."

Tammy broke out of Mark's arms and caught his eyes. "Mark, you don't have to. I have been on my own and taking care of Bethany for a long time now. I don't need your help." She shivered. The warmth of his body next to hers was too much for her. Even though what Zack told them scared the living daylights out of her, she wouldn't let herself get caught up in this attraction she felt for him because of it. And she definitely would not let him see it! She turned back to Zack. "I'll talk to the principal and her teacher tomorrow to keep an extra close eye on Bethany. I'll make sure my doors and windows are locked at all times. If I see anyone around that looks suspicious, I will call the police. Is there anything else you need to talk to me about?"

Surprised by the sudden take charge attitude, Zack replied, "No, Tammy, that's all for now. I will keep in touch to let you know if we find anything on the person who sold her."

"Thank you, Detective Williams. I appreciate you making me aware of the situation and I will be on my guard from now on." She turned back to Mark. "Could you please let me out? I need to check on my customers."

Mark threw his arms up in the air. "By all means," he said irritably. Mark came out of the booth and watched as she slid out and stood up next to him. She locked eyes with him briefly before she left to go back into the lanai to finish up for the night. But before she did, she made a quick call home to check with the sitter to make sure Bethany was all right. Even though her nerves were set on edge with what Zack had told her, she wouldn't let a certain someone know she was nervous or frightened. She would keep up a brave front, along with keeping her daughter safe on her own!

Mark watched her head into the lanai with her back set straight and a purpose he had never seen in a woman before. She mystified him. He sat back down in the booth. She totally put him in his place, making sure he knew she didn't want anything to do with him protecting her, or her daughter. Holding her in his arms set his heart a flame. Her soft warm body next to his made him want to do more than just hold her. When she pulled away, he felt a chill he couldn't describe. He glanced back over to the entrance of the lanai. Whether she wanted it or not, he was going to keep an eye on both of them!

CHAPTER 2

Driving home, Tammy passed the small homes in the subdivision, set just outside the city of Honolulu, where her and her daughter lived. The houses were built with the same design and were set close together. The streetlamps lit up the road as she pulled into her driveway, to the one-car garage, two-bedroom house she called home. She pushed the garage door button on her visor and drove inside. She came into her home, only to be met by her neighbor Mrs. Langley who lives a couple of doors down from her.

Mrs. Langley was in her late fifties. She was married to a wonderful man who would bend over backwards to help his fellow neighbors with anything that needed fixing. Their children were all grown, and when she offered to stay with Bethany while she worked at the restaurant, Tammy was all too willing to accept the help. She would even go the extra mile to pick up Bethany after school if she was running late from working with the social worker who was assigned to her for her internship at the university.

Tammy was studying to be a social worker herself, and she would be getting her BA in December after she finished this last term.

"Hi, Mrs. Langley. How was Bethany tonight?"

"She was good like she always is." She smiled. "She might still be awake if you want to say goodnight to her."

"I think I will. Can you stay a few more minutes? I need to talk to you about something important."

"Sure, but don't take too long, my favorite TV show is coming on soon," she sighed.

Tammy hurried into her daughter's bedroom. Coming up to her bed, she could see she was fast asleep. She peered down onto her daughter's small, precious face. She brushed away a strand of hair from her forehead and wondered why anyone would want to take her from her, then sell her to a human-trafficking ring. What horrible person could even commit such an act? She bent down and gave her daughter a kiss on the cheek, lifted the covers over her shoulders, and turned out the light. Before she closed the door, she turned back to gaze at her precious daughter. With determination she whispered, *"No one is going to take you from me. You can count on it."*

Tammy came from the bedroom and asked Mrs. Langley to have a seat on the sofa. When they were both seated, Tammy took a deep breath and looked into Mrs. Langley's eyes as she expressed her feelings on the information she received at the restaurant that night.

"I don't want to alarm you, but Detective Zack Williams came into the restaurant tonight, and gave me some information on the attempted kidnapping of Bethany. He told me that someone was trying to sell her to a human-trafficking ring. Of course, the person who tried to take her was caught, but he said the money changed hands. And because the money had changed hands, the person in charge of the trafficking ring more than likely will come after her again. We just don't know when. I wanted you and Mr. Langley to be aware, if you see anyone around that you don't know, or looks suspicious, to call the police immediately. Keep all the doors and windows locked at all times when you're here, and even at your home."

Mrs. Langley's eyes got big as she listened to what Tammy was telling her. "Do you mean someone could still be out there that would take our sweet, precious Bethany?" she asked in astonishment.

"Yes. Until the police are able to bring this human-trafficking ring down, we have to stay alert and not trust anyone."

Mrs. Langley shook her head. "I can't believe it!" She looked into Tammy's eyes with determination and took her hands in hers. "But know this: I will not let Bethany out of my sight when she is in my care! No one will get near her!"

Tammy smiled and breathed a sigh of relief. "Thank you, Mrs. Langley. I appreciate all that you and Mr. Langley do for us. I don't know what I would do without you both."

They both rose from the sofa and Tammy walked her to the door. Tammy gave her a hug and said goodnight. When she closed the door, she locked it, then proceeded to go throughout the house to make sure every door and all the windows were locked including the basement windows.

With that done, she went upstairs to get ready for bed. But before she went back to her bedroom, she went over to the front window and slightly pulled back the curtains. She looked around the front yard and into the street. She couldn't see anything out of the ordinary. She backed away and let the curtains fall. She went to get ready for bed. Once ready, she decided to make herself a cup of tea to help her relax.

She needed to work on her paper for class but didn't know if she would be able to concentrate on it after what Detective Williams told her tonight.

When she finished making her tea, she went into the living room and sat down on the comfortable sofa. With her legs curled up, she took the coverlet and placed it over her lap. She looked around the room. It was small but quaint. The walls were painted a creamy beige color, with soft, scenic pictures in vibrant colors placed on the walls in various areas of the room. The gas fireplace at the far end of the wall brought comfort to her when she was nervous or upset.

She could relax watching the flames flickering in the dim light, and the worries of the day would just fade away.

She sighed, remembering the first time she saw this home when it was for sale a few years ago. Her father had passed away and she was surprised he had left her a small inheritance. She wasn't real close to her father, but she would always make an effort to go see him during the holidays. Her mom had divorced him when she was young and remarried a man who had become her dad and influence in her life. She rarely saw her father when she was growing up, but after she graduated from high school, she wanted to find him, to find out why he never came to see her.

Along the way she met Roy Gardner. He was handsome, successful, and had a personality that quickly swept her off her feet. He was a salesman for a company here on the island and appeared to have money to burn. They fell in love and were married six months later. The first several months of their marriage had been pure bliss. They had spent every minute together until she found out she was pregnant with Bethany. Then things changed. She would have thought he would have been happy about them having a baby, but he wasn't. He started to withdraw from her. He never touched her intimately again since the day he found out about the pregnancy. When she asked him why, he told her he didn't want to hurt the baby. When she was born, she thought when he saw his precious daughter for the first time he would fall in love with her. But he didn't even want to hold her. Time passed. Roy and she grew farther apart, leaving her with the full responsibility of raising their daughter. He would be away on long business trips, till, one day, when she went to the mailbox, she found divorce papers being served on her. He didn't even have the decency to face her. He just left.

In the divorce decree, he gave her the house, but the house payments were so high, there was no way she would be able to make the payments. She put the house up for sale and used any money left over for her and Bethany. She huffed and took a sip of her tea. It sure wasn't much, enough for them to move into a small apartment and pay the bills for a few months till she got a job.

When she received the letter from her father's estate, and the modest check, she quickly went house hunting and found this little gem, just perfect for the two of them. She was able to pay cash for the home, and with her job at the Hawaiian Lanai, she was able to pay her bills along with being able to save a little for a rainy day. She met the Langleys shortly after they moved in. It was both a godsend and an answer to prayers when Mrs. Langley offered to watch Bethany. She truly felt blessed.

But now, what was she to think. She thought about tonight, when she found herself in Mark's arms. She had felt warm and protected, his strong arms pressing her to his hard chest. She remembered his voice softly murmuring words of comfort when she was coming back from the dark. But when he told Detective Williams he was going to keep an eye on her and her daughter, she quickly took offense. Not happening! She was not going to depend on any man; even if she was attracted to him!

Finishing her tea, she came up from the sofa to take her empty cup to the sink. Suddenly, she heard a noise outside her door. With her heart thudding loudly, she set her cup down on the table. She quietly walked to the door, grabbed the bat sitting by it, and waited. It was well after midnight. She never had to defend herself, but if someone was out there, she would fight tooth and nail to defend her and her daughter!

She jumped when the doorbell rang. She carefully looked in the peephole through her door. With it being dark, she could barely make out the figure standing outside her door, but it looked like

Mark. She put on the outside light, took a look out the side window, and there he stood. Mark TreVaine was on her doorstep!

What in the world was he doing here this late at night? She quickly opened the door.

"Mark! You scared me half to death! What are you doing here?" she asked out of breath.

"I'm sorry, Tammy. I didn't mean to scare you. I saw your lights still on and wanted to make sure you were all right." He glanced at the bat she was holding in her hand. He smiled, his eyes glistening. "You won't hit me with that if I come in, will you?"

She smiled and shook her head. "No." She set the bat back down by the door and let him come in. She closed the door behind him. When she came up to him, she expressed, "Please keep your voice low. Bethany is asleep."

He half smiled. "I promise."

"Come in and have a seat. Would you like a cup of coffee or a cup of tea?" she asked softly.

"Tea would be nice." He had had all the coffee he could stand at the restaurant.

He took a seat on her loveseat. His eyes took in the blue cotton shorts that showed off her long tan legs, with a matching tank top that softly showed her curves and the shape of her breasts. He watched her hips flow back and forth as she picked up her cup and headed for the kitchen to make the tea. *Okay, Mark,* he said to himself. *You are here for one reason and one reason only. Stay focused!*

While she was making the tea, he took a look around the small living room and found it very inviting. She had good taste in decorating. He noticed there was no TV in the room. The sofa and loveseat made done in a rich burgundy color, with end tables made of dark oak on each side of the sofa, and a coffee table made of the same wood in the middle. A reclining rocking chair was sitting directly across the loveseat. The glass-colored lamps on each of the end tables gave a soft glow to the room. There were some knick-knacks placed on the tables, giving the room a homey look. It gave him a feeling of warmth inside him. He could picture himself sitting here with her, in front of the fireplace on the far wall, roaring to life, sharing some wine, maybe a kiss or two.

He brought himself up when she reappeared with his tea and a cup for herself. Thank God! His mind was running away again, which seemed to be a lot lately! She handed him the mug. His fingers brushed hers and she felt the instant tingles going throughout her body. She sat down on the sofa, as far away from him as possible.

He smiled. *She definitely isn't making this easy for me.*

Tammy broke the silence, "Mark, why are you here?"

He took a sip of his tea, then set it on the table. He leaned forward with his arms on his thighs and his hands folded. "Tammy, I really did come here to check on you. And I also wanted to clear the air between us. After what Zack told us tonight, I'm concerned for you, and especially for your little girl, Bethany." Tammy tried to cut in. "No, Tammy, just wait and hear me out. We are in this together, whether you like it or not. If what Zack told us is true, and someone else was watching me take the kidnapper out, he would have also seen me bringing Bethany back to you. So the person would know what you look like, and not only that, but my son as well. So when you stood your ground and told me that you didn't need my help, I beg to differ. I think we need each other, to keep our kids safe."

Tammy sat paralyzed while she took in what he was saying. As she stared into his eyes, she asked, "So you think Cameron could be a target as well?"

"It's possible. We don't know for sure, but we have to take all precautions," he stressed. He came up off the loveseat and sat down beside her, keeping a safe distance. "Listen, I have a proposal. You and Bethany move in with me."

Shocked! "Mark, I…"

"Wait, Tammy, listen. If the perpetrator knows you are living with me, he will think twice about trying anything. But with you here all alone, anything could happen."

Shaking her head she responded, "But Mark, this would turn Bethany's life upside down, let alone mine! I have a sitter for her when I work who lives just two doors down from us. I can't just uproot her and our routines to move in with you. Even if I did agree, what would people think?"

Staring into eyes that showed her shock and uncertainty, he moved a little closer and put his hands gently on her upper arms. "Look, I don't care what people think. My main concern is your safety and that of your daughter's." He smiled. "And I don't want to lose one of the best waitresses our restaurant has ever had."

She smiled in return and let her eyes fall away. She hadn't let them know yet, but after she graduated and received her BA degree in social work in December, she had a job lined up after the first of the year. She was afraid to tell them too soon, in fear of her losing her job. And she really needed it to pay the bills.

"Tammy," Mark said softly.

Tammy lifted her eyes to his. With his warm, strong hands still holding her and his blue eyes holding her captive, she shivered. "Mark, I don't know…"

"Just think about it. Our relationship will be purely platonic. I have a guest room with twin beds you and Bethany can have. When this is all over and the police have caught everyone involved in the trafficking ring, you can move back home. No harm done," he insisted.

None but her heart, she thought ironically.

"I'll think about it."

As she stared into his eyes, she felt her heart suddenly beat faster as she leaned in and softly asked, "And our relationship will be purely platonic?"

Mark lowered his eyes and caught a glimpse of her firm breasts slightly peeking out of her tank top. He swallowed. Feeling her soft skin under his hands and the electrifying energy between them, he gazed back up into her beautiful amber eyes. "Yes, purely platonic," he whispered back.

Feeling a magnetic pull, he slowly bent his head to touch his lips to hers when he heard, "Mommy!"

They both jumped and instantly broke apart. Tammy rushed up to her little girl, who stood in the hallway, carrying her Mr. Snow Bear. "Bethany, sweetie, what is it?"

"I heard voices, and I got scared!" she answered.

Tammy picked her little girl up and brought her out into the living room and up to Mark. "Mark stopped by. You remember Mark. He took us to the ice cream shop with his son Cameron."

With her head resting on her mom's shoulder, she nodded her head yes.

Mark gave her a big smile. "Hi, Bethany. Sorry if I woke you."

"Why are you here?" she asked.

"I just wanted to check on you and your mom."

"Why?" she asked in her small voice.

Tammy answered for him. "He was just being nice, and now you need to get back to bed. We both have to get up early in the morning. You have school and I have…a meeting." She turned back to Mark. "I'll be right back."

Tammy tucked her little girl back in and gave her a kiss on the cheek. "Now go back to sleep. I love you."

"Love you too, Mommy," as she rolled over and closed her eyes.

When Tammy came back out, Mark was standing by the door. "Sorry if my coming here woke Bethany. Will she be able to get back to sleep?" he whispered.

"Yes, no worries."

"Well, I'll get going. Promise me you will consider what I suggested."

Tammy opened the door for him. When she caught his eyes, she couldn't help but see the concern he had for her and Bethany. Softly, she answered, "I promise."

When he left, she closed the door behind him. Leaning back against it, she knew there was no way they would move in with him. It would be too dangerous; just the feel of his warm, strong hands on her arms and the almost-kiss left her in a spin. She turned to lock the door and went to turn out the lights. Six o'clock would be here soon. She could only hope she would be able to sleep!

Mark, walking to his car, checked the area out to make sure all was clear. When he got into his car, he sat there for a few minutes, turning his head to stare back at her door. He wondered what got into him tonight. He was so close to kissing her. He would have to be more careful. He could easily lose his head over her. He told her he would keep their relationship purely platonic if she and her daughter moved in with him. He started the engine. As he pulled out into the street, he swore to himself he would try and keep his word!

CHAPTER 3

Tammy walked her little girl into school the next morning. She gave her daughter a kiss on the cheek and told her she would see her after school. She went into the principal's office and asked the receptionist if she could speak with Principal Maynard.

"One moment, Mrs. Gardner, and I'll check to see if he is available."

"Thank you." She took a seat and waited.

A short time later, Principal Maynard came out of his office. When he approached her, "You wanted to see me, Mrs. Gardner?" he asked.

Tammy rose from her seat. "Yes. And if I may ask, I would like to speak to Miss Crawford, Bethany's teacher, as well. It's important."

He turned to his receptionist and asked to have Miss Crawford come to his office. He opened the door and gestured with his hand to go in. "Please, step into my office and let's see what this is all about." He pulled out one of the chairs for her to take a seat. Her eyes followed him as he came around his desk and gingerly sat down across from her.

Mr. Maynard was a man of average height, in his late forties, with a full head of gray hair. With a pair of dark rimmed glasses perched on his face, he was quite good looking, if you liked the studious type. Recently divorced, she had heard through the grapevine he had an affair with one of the young teachers here at the school. His wife found out and divorced him immediately. She started to feel uncomfortable as he studied her across from his desk.

Concerned, he asked. "I hope this has nothing to do with how Miss Crawford is teaching Bethany?"

"Oh no, Mr. Maynard. Bethany loves Miss Crawford. This matter is something else entirely but needs to be addressed as it does concern her."

Miss Crawford opened the door of the principal's office. "You wanted to see me, sir?" she asked.

"Yes, have a seat. Mrs. Gardner has something she wishes to discuss with us, about her daughter Bethany."

She took a seat beside Tammy, and in a panic turned to her and asked, worry crossing her face, "Is something going on? Did I do something to offend Bethany?"

Miss Crawford was an attractive woman, in her late twenties with dark brown hair, cut short in the latest style. She had a soft voice but could be stern when she needed to be. The kids just loved her.

"Oh no, Miss Crawford!" she exclaimed. "You're doing a great job. But something happened to Bethany recently that I should have brought to your attention sooner." She went on to tell them about the attempted kidnapping, of which they caught the person trying to take her, but may be getting out on bail. She explained that someone had sold her to a human-trafficking ring, and the police informed her that he would more than likely try again, but they didn't know when. "We have no idea who that person might be, so we need to keep an extra close watch on Bethany, and no one but me or Mr. and Mrs. Langley picks her up after school unless I give my permission," explained Tammy.

Shocked, Miss Crawford cried, "Yes! Oh my, yes! I'll keep a very close eye on her from now on! And I will let my aides know as well."

Tammy went on to say, "I've had a talk with Bethany since the incident, and she has been told that she is to come to you if she sees any strangers around the playground or on the school grounds to let you or an adult know immediately."

"Thank you, Mrs. Gardner, for bringing this to our attention. I will also put out an email to the rest of the staff as well," stated Principal Maynard.

Tammy rose from her seat and shook his hand. "Thank you, Principal Maynard, for seeing me this morning. If the police have any updates on who might have done this, I will let you know."

"Good. And you're welcome, Mrs. Gardner. We want to keep all our children safe while they are attending school."

She turned and shook Miss Crawford's hand and left the office, feeling a little better. She could only pray that God would keep her little girl safe.

When she left the building, Tammy was unaware of a man sitting out in a car along the street. He watched Tammy get into her car and drive out of the parking lot. He pulled out, following her at a distance to her next destination.

Tammy was a little late for her appointment with her counselor to go over her evaluation of her first nine months with Ms. Beret, a social worker who Tammy was training under during her internship. She was a short, stout older woman. She had dark eyes, and her jet-black hair, with a splattering of gray throughout, was clipped short. She was excellent in her field of social work, and she was learning a lot studying under her. She hoped she would get a good review from her.

She knocked on Ms. Sinclair's door. "Come in." Tammy opened the door and took a seat in front of her desk.

Ms. Sinclair was a thin woman of medium height. Her long gray hair was pulled up in a bun on top of her head. Her stark green eyes were set behind wire rimmed glasses that fell down on the end of her nose, so, when she looked up, Tammy felt that those eyes could actually see right through her!

"Hello, Tammy," Ms. Sinclair greeted her.

"Hello, Ms. Sinclair. I'm sorry I'm late for our appointment. I had to speak to the principal where Bethany attends school and her teacher. I'm afraid it took longer than expected."

"Oh? I hope everything is all right with Bethany," she responded.

"Yes, she's fine, and she is doing well in her studies. We just had to clear up a matter."

Ms. Sinclair had a feeling Tammy was not telling her everything, but she wasn't going to pry. "Good. Well, let's get started. I have another meeting coming up shortly." She handed Tammy a thick book. "Here is your fourth and final book to finish your internship through mid-December. I am pleased to inform you that Ms. Beret is very happy with how your performance as an intern is progressing. She states she is impressed with your professionalism when you are present for a session with one of her patients, and that you wait to ask questions after the patient has left her office. Most of your internship has been in her office here at the university. Ms. Beret expressed she would like to take you out into the community, to show you how to deal with mental health patients living in their homes and interacting with others in their neighborhoods. I'm not going to sugarcoat this, Tammy. Some of these neighborhoods can be dangerous. Ms. Beret promised she would only take you out a few times, so you could get the feel of how to cope with someone with mental instability outside of an office experience. She thought you would be strong enough to handle it."

Tammy, listening, knew that some part of her internship would deal with going out into the field. Although she was a little apprehensive, she knew she had to put her best efforts forward to pass and get her degree. After the first of the year she would be working with special-needs children, which was truly the field where she wanted to work and excel. There were so many children out there who needed help, and her heart went out to them. She sat up taller in her chair. "If Ms. Beret thinks I'm ready, then I am confident I will be able to handle any situation as long as she is by my side to guide me," she said determinedly.

"Very well, I will let Ms. Beret know, and you are free to go. Good luck with the rest of your internship, and if you have any questions or concerns going forward, you know where to reach me."

"Thank you, Ms. Sinclair."

Tammy rose from her chair and left the office. As she closed the door, she took a deep breath and said to herself, *Just three more months, Tammy. Just three more months and your life will change for the better, for you and your daughter.*

She had some time left before she had to pick up Bethany, so instead of going home, she decided to go to the library and catch up on the paper she was writing. Then she'd take a look at the book Ms. Sinclair had given her. With that in mind, she headed out.

When she entered the library, she looked around and found a table at the far end of the open room, next to a wall of books. She took a seat, pulled her laptop out of her briefcase, and got started. She was writing about the effects of autism and what the parents go through raising these children and adults with this developmental disorder. Her sister Camille and her husband were raising their eight-year-old son, who was non-verbal and had some serious behavioral issues. It was trying at times, but she reported in her last letter to her that they were making a little progress with some of the programs at the school he was attending.

She was so engrossed in her work, she see didn't see the man walk by her table, stop, then walk on. Sometime later, Ruby, a young gal she met in her psychology class, came up to her table and asked if she could join her. "Hi, Ruby. Sure, have a seat. I'm just working on my paper."

"Thanks." Ruby took a seat across from her, slammed her book bag on the table, pulled books and notebooks from it, then proceeded to shuffle papers around.

Tammy looked up from her laptop and, with great restraint, spoke in a soft voice. "Ruby! You do know this is a library, don't you?"

Looking back at Tammy, she grinned. "Oh, sorry, I'll be quiet now."

Tammy sighed, shook her head, and went back to work. Ten minutes later, she heard a pencil banging on the table along with pages turning and lots of sighing going on! Tammy soon regretted letting Ruby join her. Well, there was no sense trying to get anymore done on her paper there. She packed everything up and quickly got out of her chair.

Ruby glanced up as Tammy was walking by. "Are you leaving?" she asked.

"Yes, sorry, I have to run. I have errands to do before I pick up my daughter from school," she lied. Better than hurt feelings.

"Oh, okay. Have a good rest of your day, then," she commented.

"You too, Ruby," she returned as she hurried out of the library.

Tammy decided to drive over to a little park on the other side of the university. There was a food truck parked along the street, so she picked up some lunch and went over to a table far away from everyone else and hoped no one would bother her. She sat down, unwrapped her sandwich, and popped the lid on her soda.

While she was eating, her eyes took in the beauty of the park.

There was a small pond with a fountain gushing out in the middle of it, with picnic tables scattered all around the pond. Colorful hibiscus plants and other tropical foliage intertwined throughout the park. There were several palm trees, with tropical flowering bushes behind her, giving her a little shade as the temperature on the island crept up into the upper seventies. She was glad she had pulled her hair up in a ponytail near the top of her head this morning. With wisps of hair falling down along the sides of her cheeks, she felt the light breeze caressing her face and arms. Suddenly, she felt her body relax. If only she could stay in this moment. No cares, no worries, just peace.

When she finished her sandwich and soda, she got up to put her trash in the waste receptacle. She looked up and noticed a man walking towards her. He stopped and sat down at a table next to hers. She caught his eye. She felt her skin begin to crawl. He was a big man, with broad shoulders, dark hair, and a full beard. His piercing grey eyes looked menacing as he stared at her. He wore faded blue jeans and a white t-shirt that stretched across his massive chest.

She quickly looked away and went back to her table. Her heart started to race, wondering what she should do. Well, she was not going to sit here and let him see that she was rattled! For all she knew, he could be harmless and she was blowing this situation all out of proportion! She got up from the table and calmly picked up her briefcase and purse. She made sure she was as far away from his table as possible when she walked to her car, which was parked in a lot across from the park. When she opened her car door, she glanced back to see if he was still sitting at the table, but he was nowhere to be seen! Was he following her? She quickly looked around the area and behind her but didn't see him. With her heart in her throat, she knew exactly where she was going to go. She got into her car and quickly pulled out of the parking lot and headed for the Hawaiian Lanai. She knew Mark would be there, and also Palani, his head cook. She only hoped someone would answer the phone as she dialed the restaurant's number.

Mark was having a hell of a time concentrating on the reports he needed to finish before tomorrow. With the weekend coming up, he knew there would be no time to work on them before the auditors came in on Monday. His mind kept wandering back to last night when Zack informed him and Tammy that their lives could be in danger from the human traffickers, along with their kids. He smiled, remembering Tammy opening her door with a bat in her hand! He didn't have any doubt that she would use it if it was an actual intruder. After she let him in, he discussed the prospects of her and her daughter moving in with him. He wondered if she had given it some thought after he left last night. Sitting close to her on the sofa, he remembered her soft skin against his hands when he held her, and the kiss they almost shared, if it hadn't been for Bethany waking up. Half of him wanted to take her in his arms to protect and possess her. The other half of him says *stay away!* He wondered which one was going to win out.

His thoughts were interrupted when the phone started ringing. He knew Palani was in the kitchen, prepping for tonight's specials with his crew coming in shortly. He would answer the phone. But when the phone kept ringing, his irritation came through as he answered it, "Hello, Mark TreVaine here!" he bellowed.

"Mark!"

When Mark heard Tammy's breathless voice on the other end, his heart kicked up, "Tammy?" he exclaimed.

"Yes, it's me," she answered nervously "Mark, I'm about five minutes from the restaurant. Can you let me in? I will explain when I get there."

Listening to her voice he knew something was up. He could hear the fear as the words tumbled out of her mouth. "Yes, I'll be waiting at the front door," he returned.

"Thanks, I'll see you in a few." Then the line went dead.

Mark left his office only to end up pacing in the foyer, with his nerves fraying as he waited for Tammy to arrive.

When she came up to the door, he quickly opened it to a frantic woman who rushed into his arms. He embraced her as she wrapped her arms around his waist and held on tight.

Tammy felt the warmth of his body close to hers. Her face snuggled into his broad chest. She didn't want to let go. But then she realized that she just threw herself at a man she hardly knew, and her boss to boot! She tried to pull away, but he held on.

In his arms, Mark could feel her body shaking. Something had definitely upset her. Even though he felt her trying to pull away, he held on to her until he felt her body relax against him.

Tammy slowly leaned back and raised her head to stare into his deep blue eyes. "I'm sorry. I didn't mean to throw myself at you," as she came out of his arms.

"Hey, I can see you are upset about something. Let's go inside and you can tell me what's going on." He held the door for her as she walked into the bar area and took a seat in one of the booths. "Can I get you something to drink?" he asked.

"A water, please."

While he was getting her water, Tammy tried to calm herself. She was probably overreacting. She kept an eye on her rearview mirror on her way over here. She didn't see anyone following her. Mark brought her water to her and set it on the table along with one for him. He caught her eyes and asked, "Tammy, can you tell me what happened?"

She took a sip of her water and began. "I was out at this park by the campus, enjoying my lunch and taking in the beauty around me, when a man came and sat down at a table right next to mine. He was big. And there was something about the way he looked at me that made me extremely nervous. I got up from the table and went to my car. When I turned back to see if he was still sitting there, he was gone. I drove straight here. I kept watch in my rearview mirror but didn't see anyone following me." She took another sip of her water. "Maybe I'm just being paranoid. Ever since Detective Williams let us know that Bethany could still be in danger, I've been jumpy."

His concern for her safety as she explained what had happened. "Can you give a full account of what he looked like to Zack?" he asked.

"Yes, but what if I'm just overreacting, Mark? The guy could be completely innocent of any wrongdoing, but when I looked back and he wasn't there, I had this strange feeling come over me that he had been following me."

"Look," stated Mark. "Whether it was by chance, and he was just enjoying his lunch, or the fact that he may be following you, you need to give this information to Zack. It may be nothing, or he could be connected to the human-trafficking ring. You need to report it." Mark pulled out his cell phone. "Let me call Zack to see if he's available to come to the restaurant." He punched in Zack's number. He glanced over and caught Tammy's eyes while he waited for Zack to answer.

"Detective Williams," he answered.

"Zack, Mark here. I have Tammy here at the restaurant with me. She had an incident happen at the university while she was there and needs to report it. It may be related to the case."

As he listened to Zack, he continued to watch her. Her hair was pulled up, with soft wisps falling down around her cheeks. She looked so young and innocent. She had diverted her eyes away from him while she waited for Zack's response.

"Tammy." She turned her eyes to him. "Zack can be here by two forty-five."

She shook her head. "I have to be at the school to pick up Bethany by three fifteen. It wouldn't give me enough time."

He relayed the message to Zack. He continued to listen. "I'll let her know and get back to you. Thanks, Zack." Mark ended the call. "Zack has another call he has to make on another case. He said he could meet you back at the restaurant or at your home later this evening."

Since it was her night off, she would prefer him to meet her at the house. "Could you ask him if he could meet me at my home by seven p.m.? That would give me enough time to fix dinner and get Bethany started on her homework. Also, could you give him my phone number, so he could verify that he will be coming tonight?"

"Sure, what's your number?" He punched it into his phone as she gave it to him. "I'll send a text off to him, so you should hear from him shortly."

She looked at her watch. "I need to get going. I like to be at the school a little early and it's already two thirty." She slid out of the booth, with Mark getting up to walk her to the door.

When they reached the door, she turned back to him, "Thanks, Mark, for your help. I'll see you tomorrow."

When she turned to leave, he caught her arm and pulled her around to face him. He searched her eyes. "Have you thought about what I proposed to you last night?" he asked.

Her eyes showed the uncertainty of moving in with him. "Mark I..." She looked away.

"Tammy," he said softly. She glanced back up, their eyes locking. "I know you are a very independent woman. You've raised your daughter single-handedly, and from what I can see, you've done an excellent job. But I am concerned about you and your daughter's safety. With the possibility of someone following you, both your lives could be at risk."

He made sense, but she was more afraid of losing her heart if they moved in with him. He said it would be purely platonic, but for how long? After the almost-kiss they shared, she didn't want to take the chance. She took a deep breath as she answered him, "Mark, I appreciate the offer, but I'm not sure it would be a good idea for us to move in with you."

"Look, if you're worried about the kiss we almost shared, I promise I won't try it again. I promised to keep our relationship platonic, and I will keep my word. Please think about it."

She didn't know what to think! Why was he so insistent? He's concerned, yes, but… She ended up nodding her head yes. "Okay," she murmured as she turned to leave, "I'll think about it, but no promises."

Mark watched her walk towards the parking lot. He wondered if he should have walked her to her car. He didn't like the fact that someone may be following her. He went back inside to his office. He sent a text off to Zack for him to meet Tammy at her home at seven o'clock and to verify he could be there via her cell number. He went back to work on his reports, hoping he could concentrate on them. Along with tonight's reservations, it was going to be a long night.

Zack was at Tammy's home promptly at seven. When she answered the door, Detective Williams stood tall and handsome in a dark blue suit, crisp white shirt, with a red-and-white-striped tie around his neck. His eyes were dark brown, and his olive skin contrasted against the white collar of his shirt. Her eyes traveled to a man directly to his left. His bald head shone in the light. His black eyes had a serious look to them as he met her eyes. He was also dressed in a dark suit.

"Good evening, Detective Williams. Please, come in," she invited.

"Thank you, Tammy."

As they entered her home, he turned to introduce the detective that was with him. "Tammy, I would like to introduce you to Detective Motts. He works in the forensic art unit. He will be able to draw a picture of the man that you saw at the park. We can see if it matches any persons stored in our intel."

Bethany chose that time to come and see who arrived. "Mommy, who's here?" she asked. When she saw the two men, she latched onto her leg and hid her face. Tammy pulled her from her leg and picked her up.

"This is Detective Williams and Detective Motts. You remember, I told you he would be coming tonight." She nodded her head.

"But not that one!" she exclaimed as she pointed her finger at Detective Motts. A man of average height, dark-skinned, and when he smiled, it left you feeling warm and happy. They all chuckled.

"I know, sweetie, but he's here with Detective Williams to help Mommy figure out something important. Can you go and finish watching your movie in the lanai while I talk to them?" She nodded yes. Tammy put her down. "Off you, go then." Bethany scurried back into the lanai.

"Sweet kid," Detective Motts commented.

"Thank you," answered Tammy. "Can I get either one of you something to drink?"

The two men looked at each other, then Zack answered, "No thank you, Tammy. I think we better get started."

Tammy ushered the two detectives into the living room. When they were all seated, Zack began. "As you know, Mark called on your behalf, to inform me that you saw a man at the park who you think may have been following you."

"Yes," Tammy answered. "But I'm not really sure, it was a feeling I had."

He smiled. "Sometimes those gut instincts almost always prove to be right. Can you describe him to us?" asked Zack. Detective Motts took his pad of paper out and a pencil, ready to draw the suspect as she described him.

"The man was tall, with a massive chest, arms, and thighs. He looked like he worked out. He was dressed in faded blue jeans and a white t-shirt." She took a moment before she continued. "His hair was dark, in a crew cut, and he had a full beard that he kept trimmed. His eyes were gray in color, and when he looked at me, I felt I was looking into the eyes of a predator. He made me extremely nervous. I calmly got up from the bench and walked back to my car, which was parked in a lot across from the park. When I opened the car door, I looked back to see if he was still sitting there, but he was gone. I looked all around but couldn't find him. That's when I got into my car and headed over to the restaurant. I kept looking in my rearview mirror, but it didn't appear that he was following me at that time."

Detective Motts finished up with his drawing and handed it to Tammy. "Does this look like the man you just described?" he asked.

Tammy looked at the picture. "The eyes could be a little closer together, and his nose looked to be hook-like. His lips were fuller." She handed him back the pad.

As she watched, Tammy was amazed at how fast Detective Motts could redraw the man she described with the changes she mentioned. He handed her back the pad. Tammy glanced down at the drawing. She looked up, shocked! "That's him! That's the man I saw!" She handed him back his drawing. "That's amazing! How do you do that?"

Detective Motts shrugged his shoulders and smiled. "I have always loved to draw ever since I was a kid. When I became a cop, I decided to use my ability to draw to good use," he answered.

"Is there anything else you would like to add before we go?" asked Zack.

Tammy turned back to Detective Williams. "No, not at this time." Zack pulled out his wallet and handed her his card.

"If you think of anything else you want to add to the case, please don't hesitate to call me. Detective Motts will take his drawing back to forensics to check and see if he can match this description to anyone on intel that has a criminal offense. We will contact you with our findings." They all rose from their seats.

As Tammy walked them to the door, she smiled. "Thank you both for coming. I hope I'm not just being paranoid. The man could have just been enjoying his lunch."

Zack turned back to Tammy. "Listen, Tammy, we need to check all the bases. If you see the man again or anyone else that might be suspicious, you call me any time, day or night. I wasn't kidding when I said you and your daughter are in danger as long as this trafficking ring is still in operation. Until we can bring them down, stay alert and watch your back. I will see if I can get someone out here to watch you and your daughter tonight, when you are working, and Bethany, when she is at school."

Tammy's heart started up. "Detective Williams, you're scaring me!"

Detective Williams took a breath. "Look, Tammy, I'm sorry. I am not here to scare you. Just be aware of your surroundings and take precautions until we can get this set up."

Tammy, with her heart beating faster in her chest, replied, "Okay. And you'll let me know if you are able to send someone out?" she asked, the fear clearly in her eyes.

"Yes, as soon as I am able to get someone here, I will call you. Lock your door."

When the two men walked out the door, she nodded. "I will, and thank you again." She closed the door behind them and locked it. She leaned back against it. Her eyes moved, and what she saw almost devastated her. Her precious daughter was standing there with a frightened look on her face, tears streaming down her cheeks. "Oh, Bethany!" she cried, coming down on her knees as her precious daughter rushed into her arms. Her little arms entwined tightly around her mom's neck as she sobbed.

"Oh, Mommy, please don't let that bad man come and get me." Tammy came up with her daughter in her arms and carried her over to the rocking recliner and placed her on her lap. Rocking her gently, she hugged her daughter tight.

"I swear to you with all my heart that I will never let anyone take you from me! I love you."

"I love you too, Mommy."

As she continued to rock and sooth her, her mind reflected on Mark's proposal. She sure didn't feel comfortable staying here alone with just the two of them now. She tried to work it out in her mind on how it could work. With her internship, her work, and Bethany's schedule, it would be chaotic. She closed her eyes and took some deep breaths. She prayed that God would send her a sign on what she should do, and to protect them both from the evils of this world.

CHAPTER 4

Mark and Jack were running around like crazy men, trying to keep up with the customers piling into the restaurant. Along with the reservations, the overflow was overwhelming. Keeping the customers happy was another stressor! They definitely needed more help. He would talk to Mike when he got back. Megan, one of his top waitresses, a tall, slender woman, with her pretty blond hair pulled back in a bun, came up to him, clearly upset.

"Sorry to bother you, boss, but there's a man sitting at the bar causing trouble. He's pretty drunk. Todd cut him off, but I'm afraid he might start a fight. He's right over there." She nodded her head over to where he was sitting.

Mark looked over to where Megan had indicated. With his back to him, he could see he was a large, stout man. He was already yelling obscenities at the bartenders. *Great, just what I need with a packed house!*

"Thanks, Megan. I'll handle it." Mark pulled his phone out and put a call into the police station to send a car out, in case he didn't have a driver to take him home. He walked up to the man who was being downright belligerent! Mark placed his hand on his shoulder. The man turned to him.

"Who the hell are you?" he slurred. Mark had to really contain himself as the pressure of the night was getting to him.

"Sir, I am the owner of this establishment. And I can see that you have had too much to drink. Do you have someone who can give you a ride home?" he asked as patiently as he could.

"I don't care who the hell you are, nobody is going to tell me I've had too much to drink!" He turned back to the bartender. "Now you give me another whiskey, or I'll damn well come back there and grab the damn bottle myself!" He pulled out his wallet and threw a fifty-dollar bill on the bar. "My money's good here!"

Mark, with fire in his eyes, took the fifty and stuffed it in his shirt pocket. "Sir, you will not be served another drink. Try going behind the bar and you will soon regret it. Now, I'm going to ask you one more time: do you have a ride home? If not, the police are on their way to escort you to wherever you need to go."

"Oh hell," the man yelled irritably. "I'll get out of here! This place sucks! I'll go someplace else that will serve me a drink!" The man tried to get up, but Mark pushed him back down.

"You are not going to drive anywhere and cause an accident," he told the man sternly. The man stood back up and tried to take a swing at Mark. He ducked, and just that fast, Mark had the guy pinned up against the bar just as he heard, "Mark, do you need some help?" asked the officer.

He turned to see Officer Jeff Morgan behind him. "Yeah." He pulled the guy out to the officer and held him while he got the cuffs on him. "Get him out of here."

As the officer hauled him out to the patrol car, you could hear him yelling obscenities, with customers staring at the man all the way out the door! Once he was settled inside the car, Officer Morgan came back in to let Mark know he was going to haul him down to the police station to dry out. "Do you want to file a formal complaint, Mark?" he asked.

"Not tonight, Jeff. I've got my hands full. Call me tomorrow afternoon and we'll talk." "Okay, Mark. Hope your night goes better."

"Me too," he replied. Then he turned and went back to work.

It was well after nine o'clock when he and Jack were able to sit down and take a break. "Man, can this place get any busier?" asked Jack.

Mark shook his head. "It was the busiest I have ever seen it on a Thursday night. We definitely need more help." He took a sip of his coffee. He needed a ton of it to keep him going the rest of the night.

"Hey, what happened in the bar? I didn't get a chance to see what was going on," asked Jack.

"Just a guy who had too much to drink," he answered. "He was getting a little out of hand. Thank God we don't have to deal with too many of them. The majority of our customers know when to stop."

Jack could see his boss looked worn out. He honestly didn't know how the man kept going with working all day in the office and working straight through the night.

"You look exhausted, Mark," he commented. "You sit and relax the rest of the night and I will close up," he offered.

"I won't argue with you, Jack. I feel I could crash right here in the booth!" Mark looked out over the bar lounge and saw Zack coming in. Zack spotted him as Mark waved him over. Even though he was dead tired, he wanted to know how it went with Tammy.

Jack got up as Zack approached the booth. He slid in. "Can I get you anything to drink?" asked Jack.

"Just a black coffee, Jack, and thanks," he replied. He turned to Mark. "You look like death warmed over," he commented.

"You don't look so good yourself," returned Mark.

Zack ran his hands down his face and chuckled. "You're right. It's been a hell of a day." Jack brought his coffee to him and set it in front of him.

When he left, "How'd it go with Tammy?" Mark wanted to know.

Zack took a sip of his coffee and set it back down on the table. With his hands still holding the mug, he answered. "It went well. She described the man to us. Then Detective Motts took the picture back to his department to check intel, to see if he could match it up with anyone with a criminal background. I haven't heard back yet. We should know something by morning."

Alarmed, "By morning?" he shot back. "What if the guy was following her, and what if he decides to do something tonight? With her and her daughter alone in the house, anything could happen to them!"

Zack was slightly taken aback. "Mark, just calm down. I have taken the necessary precautions and have a man out watching the house. Is there something going on between you two? You sound overly concerned over an employee of yours," he remarked.

Mark sat there, silently steaming. After the day he had, in which the night didn't go any better, Zack's words struck a nerve! "Of course I'm concerned! Why wouldn't I be? I would be concerned over any one of my employees in the same situation!" he practically yelled.

"Whoa… Okay! Sorry, I just thought…" After seeing Mark's expression, he thought better of expressing his opinion on the situation. "Never mind what I thought. I do have one problem, though."

"What's that?" he asked irritably.

"The officer I have out watching the house can only cover until the shift change. I've asked around, but no one else can pick up the next shift. We have two men out sick, and no one wants the overtime."

"So what you're telling me is no one will be keeping an eye on them through the night."

"Correct."

Mark thought a minute. She may not like it, but he was not going to leave them alone no matter how tired he was. "What time is the shift change?" he asked.

"Eleven o'clock," answered Zack.

Mark looked at his watch. It was just after ten. He took a look around the restaurant and saw most of his customers had already left. Tammy lived a half hour from the restaurant. If he hurried, he could be there by eleven thirty. With urgency, he turned to Zack, "Zack, could you radio your man and ask if he could stay a half hour later? I will take the night shift."

Zack, hearing the urgency in his voice, replied, "Are you sure you want to do this? You look exhausted."

"Yes, I'm not leaving those two alone, not with a possible predator at large." Mark needed to get going if he was going to make it. He came up out of the booth and turned back to Zack. "I've got your coffee, Zack. What type of vehicle is your officer driving?"

"He's in a black Ford SUV."

"I'm going to start closing up. Tell your man I will be there by eleven thirty, if not before."

Zack watched him leave. While he sat there and finished his coffee, he thought, *Mark may not admit it, but there is something going on between the two of them. The way they looked at each other last night. His sudden outburst when I asked him if something was going on. There is no doubt in my mind that he has feelings for her. I hope Mark isn't getting in over his head. He knows the rules around here. They don't date employees, or aren't supposed to.* He shook his head and came up out of the booth. As he was walking out of the restaurant to radio his officer, he thought to himself, *It will be interesting to see how all this unfolds. To see if I'm right!*

It took a little while before Tammy was able to get Bethany settled. She assured her that someone from the police department would be watching out for them, and they would let no one come near the house. It was a little after eleven when she finally crawled into bed herself. As she lay there, she wondered how she was ever going to finish her internship with all of this going on in her life.

How could she go out into the field with her instructor, without constantly looking around and checking behind her back? Would the police be able to have someone with her and Bethany throughout the day and night? It sounded too complicated for her tired brain to figure out. She closed her eyes and prayed for sleep to come.

She just started to drift off when she heard her phone go off with an incoming text. She wearily got up out of bed to pick her phone up off the dresser. *Who in the world would be texting me at this time of night?* She thought about Camille. She hoped everything was all right with her sister and her family.

When she brought up the text, much to her surprise, it was Mark!

Tammy, it's Mark. Hopefully I didn't wake you and you are still up. I am out here in your driveway. If you will let me in, I will explain.

Tammy set her phone down, grabbed her robe and slipped it on. She went and turned on the outside light. She opened the door just as Mark was getting out of his car. He walked up to her and stood for a moment, his eyes taking her in. She had on a short robe, wrapped tightly around her. She looked like she had just gotten out of bed. Her hair was disheveled, and when his eyes traveled down her body to those long tan legs, his heart kicked up. She couldn't have looked more beautiful if she tried.

He shook himself and asked, "May I come in?"

She flushed and couldn't avoid the tingles going throughout her body as his eyes roamed over her. She clutched the robe tighter around her, as she nodded and let him in. She closed the door behind her. She came up to him and asked in a whisper, "Mark, what's going on?" When she gazed into his eyes, her heart lurched; he looked utterly haggard.

"Do you mind if I sit down? I don't think I can stand up a moment longer."

"I'm sorry, of course." She led him over to the couch. When they were both seated, in a low voice, he explained why he had come.

"Zack came into the restaurant to let me know that he had spoken with you and that he had an officer watching the house. He also told me that he could only be here until eleven, when the shift changed. There wasn't an officer available to relieve him, so I volunteered. I hope you don't mind. I would have texted you sooner, but we had one hell of a busy night, and I wanted to get through the closing as soon as possible." She was amazed at this man who continued to want to protect them.

"Mark," she answered him, "I don't mind, but you look absolutely exhausted. How are you going to stay awake?"

He gave her a tired smile. "I was hoping I could bunk out on your couch. I'm a light sleeper, but I doubt anyone would try to break in with someone else being here."

They locked eyes, and it took her a few moments to answer him. She didn't want him to stay in his car for the night, and she didn't know if she wanted him to sleep on her couch. What would Bethany think when she woke in the morning and saw him there? She also knew she didn't want to be alone.

Softly, she said, "Okay, but just for the night. I don't want this to be a habit of yours, coming in the middle of the night."

He smiled. "Cross my heart."

She couldn't help but return his smile. Getting up, "I'll get you a pillow and a blanket."

He took her hand in his. His touch ignited her. "You don't have to do that. I'm perfectly fine with the pillows on the couch."

She smiled. "What kind of hostess would I be if I didn't at least bring you a decent pillow and blanket?" She pulled her hand away to go to the linen closet to get the pillow and blanket she promised him. By the time she got back, she found Mark sprawled out on the couch, sound asleep. She covered him up with the blanket and lifted his head to put the pillow under him. He hardly moved. As she studied him, she couldn't resist running her fingers over his forehead, to softly push back a lock of hair that had fallen down across his brow. "Goodnight," she whispered. She pulled herself away from him to go and make sure the door was locked.

After shutting off all the lights except the overhead light in the kitchen, she went to her room. When she finally lay her head on her pillow, she thought about how his touch always sent her into orbit. As she closed her eyes, she drifted off, imagining how it would feel, with his arms around her and his lips next to hers.

Mark woke to a little oval face, her amber eyes, so much like her mom's, staring at him. He quickly sat up. He rubbed his hands over his face to wake himself. Placing his hands on his thighs, he turned to the little girl and smiled. "Good morning, Bethany. I suppose you're wondering why I am here."

"No," she replied nonchalantly. "Mommy told me." She climbed up on the couch beside him. With her legs kicking up and down, she looked up at him with her big eyes and blurted out, "She said the officer couldn't stay, so you came to watch over us. She said she felt safe with you here." She wiggled around and got up on her knees beside him. She put her arms on his shoulder. Smiling, she whispered, "You wanna know what else?" Mark couldn't help but grin at this adorable child who was quickly capturing his heart.

"What?" he whispered back.

"I think she likes you!"

"Bethany!" her mom called from the kitchen. "Your breakfast is ready!"

"Coming!" she yelled. Bethany climbed down off the couch. She started to run for the kitchen, then turned around and grinned. "Oh, I forgot. Mom said to tell you coffee's ready!"

Mark had to laugh as she scooted off into the kitchen. He got up off the couch and went into the kitchen to join them. The smell of eggs, bacon, and fresh coffee made his stomach grumble. "Good morning!" he said as he walked up to her to see what she was cooking.

She turned and smiled. "I hope you like scrambled eggs and bacon. Your coffee is by the coffeemaker. I remembered you like cream in your coffee. I hope it's not too much." She knew she was rambling, but she hadn't had a man in the house to cook for in a long time. His hair was ruffled, and his clothes were wrinkled after his sleep, but he still looked as handsome as ever. The magnetic chemistry she felt with him standing so close to her made her heart flutter, and her body start shaking. She watched him walk over to the counter where the coffeemaker was. He picked up the mug of coffee and took a sip.

"Hmm… Perfect." He caught her eyes, and smiled. She was fully dressed in black jeans, a light-blue silk sleeveless top, and black sandals. Her soft brown hair was flowing down her shoulders and back. This morning she had put on a little makeup. The mascara enhanced her eyes, and the soft pink lipstick made her lips even more kissable. He needed to stop this train of thought before his mind led him to other things he'd like to do with her, so he asked, "May I use your bathroom, so I can wash up? Then I will be more than happy to help with breakfast."

"Oh, I'm sorry," she said in frustration. "Yes, it's down the hall, on your right. If you need a toothbrush, there's a new one along with some toothpaste in the top right-hand drawer."

"Thank you, I'll be right back." Mark set his cup down on the counter. With his eyes still on her, he walked close behind her, their bodies almost touching, as he headed to the bathroom. He could feel the energy flowing between them and wondered if she felt it, too.

Tammy, holding her breath, let it out as he walked by. How was she ever going to keep her scruples about her with him in her house, in such close proximity? She shook herself and finished cooking up the bacon. She pulled out another pan to start frying the eggs. The bread was on the counter, ready to put in the toaster.

"Mommy, is it almost ready? You said it was ready. I'm hungry, and it's almost time for school!"

"Yes, sweetie, the eggs are almost done. I just have to put the toast in the toaster, and we have plenty of time before school." Bethany placed her elbow on the table, with her head resting on her hand, and sighed.

Mark came back into the kitchen. With his hands rubbing together, he asked, "What can I do to help?"

Tammy pointed at the bread. "If you would like to toast the bread that would be a big help; the eggs are done, and the juice is on the table."

"Right." Mark got busy making the toast while Tammy dished up the eggs and bacon, putting them on each plate. She carried them to the table, where she set Bethany's down in front of her first. She went back for the coffeepot as Mark brought the toast to the table. She refilled their cups, then they both sat down and joined Bethany at the table.

"This is great," said Mark. "I rarely have time to cook a good breakfast during the week. On the weekends, I manage to fix something for Cameron and me."

"Is Cameron with you all weekend?" inquired Tammy.

"No," he returned. "Just on Sundays and my day off. Sometimes I have him during the week in the evenings when Sherry has to be somewhere. When Mike and Jenna come back from their honeymoon, I won't be working so many nights. Just on the weekends. It will be a relief to get back to my normal schedule. Working all day and then into the night has completely worn me out."

Tammy studied him while he ate his breakfast. With his hair combed back and his clothes tucked in, he seemed irresistible to her. She watched as he and Bethany bantered back and forth in the conversation they were having. She smiled. She could still feel his strong arms around her as she lay her head on his broad chest, clinging to him for all she was worth yesterday. He glanced over and caught her eye. He grinned. She was startled at the thought of being caught staring at him. She quickly looked down at her food and started eating.

Mark on the other hand saw the longing in her eyes. He was wishing he could be alone with her. He wanted to hold her again, and maybe, if she was willing, kiss those luscious lips of hers. See what she tasted like. He quickly switched his thoughts and took a breath. He knew Bethany had school, but he wondered what she did all day. Curious, he asked, "What are your plans for today, Tammy?"

She glanced up surprised that he would inquire about her day. Before she could answer, Bethany spoke up. "Mom has a class today at the university."

He looked back at Bethany. "She does?"

Bethany smiled and nodded her head yes.

Intrigued, he glanced back at Tammy and asked, "What class are you taking?" Something else he didn't know about her.

She swallowed the food she had been chewing, thinking, *Well, the cat's out of the bag, I might as well tell him.* She didn't have to let him know she would be leaving after she got her BA degree.

"I'm taking a class in sociology. I'm studying to become a social worker. I also have an internship that I am finishing up as well, to graduate in December." The way he was staring at her, she hoped he didn't ask any more questions.

Taken aback, Mark had no idea she was attending the university. He wanted to know more, but Bethany, impatient, piped up. "Mom, it's time to go!" Tammy looked at her watch.

"Oh, sorry, sweetie. It is time to go!" She hurried and picked up the breakfast dishes and put them in the sink.

"Hey, let me help with this." Mark got out of his chair, picked up the glasses and cups, and followed her to the sink.

"Thanks, Mark. Just set them on the counter. I'll get them later. We really do have to go." Impatiently, she asked him, "Could you move your car?"

"Sure, just let me grab my keys and jacket."

"I'm sorry, Mark. I hate to rush off, but…we'll be late if we don't go now." Mark placed his hands on her upper arms and smiled.

"Don't apologize. Thank you for breakfast. It was excellent. And just to be clear, you didn't have to cook breakfast for me, I could have picked something up on the way home."

Their eyes locked in a moment of time. He was tempted to kiss her but held back. As she held his gaze, she felt her insides turn to mush. She needed to stop this. He was only concerned about her and Bethany, nothing more.

"Make sure you keep an eye out. I'm not sure what Zack has set up yet," he murmured. She nodded.

"MOM!" cried Bethany.

He dropped his arms. Retrieving his keys and jacket, he followed her out through the garage to his car. When he backed down the driveway, he waited until she was out of the garage and on her way. Sitting there for a few minutes before he took off for home, he realized it was getting harder to keep the attraction he felt for her in check. He would have to keep his mind on something else while he was with her, or he would be in deep trouble.

CHAPTER 5

It wasn't long before Tammy parked her car in the school parking lot. Normally she would be in line with the other moms and dads to drop their children off, but she wasn't comfortable with that arrangement anymore. She got out and walked around the back of the car to the rear side door, to help Bethany out and take her into the school.

As they were walking up to the doors, Bethany looked up at her mom and asked, "How come you're walking me into the school and not dropping me off?"

"It's just an extra precaution. Hopefully it won't be for long, and we can get back to normal."

"It's because of the kidnapper, isn't it?"

Tammy stopped. She got down on her haunches and brushed some hair off her precious daughter's cheek and placed it behind her ear. She took a deep breath. "Bethany, I don't want to frighten you. You are one of the bravest little girls that I know. But we both need to be careful and keep a watch out for anything out of the ordinary for a while."

"Like watching for strangers at school," she mused.

"Yes." She smiled. "Like watching for strangers at school."

"Okay, Mommy, I'll make sure if I see anyone to go tell an adult."

"That's my girl!" She rose up and took her little hand in hers and went into the school.

Once Bethany was settled in her classroom, Tammy hurried off to the university. She should just make her class on time. She would need to speak with her instructor about her paper she hadn't finished. Due to the circumstances, he may show her some leniency. She could only hope.

When she went to her car, she took a quick look around but didn't see the man she saw yesterday lurking about. As she was driving over to the university, she wished she knew what type of car he drove. It would help to try and track him, or to see if he was following her. She should hear from Detective Williams soon, to see if he was in the system. She grabbed the wheel tighter and prayed for their safety and for this to be over soon.

When Mark came into his home, the first thing he did was put on a pot of coffee. After heading to his bedroom to shower and change, he came back to the kitchen to pour himself a cup. He took a seat at the counter, pulled out his phone, and checked his messages. There was one from Mike, letting him know their estimated time of arrival on Sunday. He couldn't wait. He should have hired a temp to help with the accounts payable like Mike had suggested, but he thought he could handle it. He had no idea how much more stress it would put on him. The weekend would be no exception. Thank God they had hired Jack. They had a full house both nights with reservations as well as customers coming in to see if they could get a table. Well, only two more days and he could relax a little.

He thought about Tammy. She was a mystery to him. *'How long has she been an employee of ours?* he wondered. *It must be at least four years,* he thought. He never knew she was a single mom, raising her daughter on her own, and now finding out she was attending the university, and would be getting her BA degree soon, blew his mind! There was definitely a need for social workers, with all the mentally disabled people in the world, not to mention drug abuse. It's no wonder the crime rate is so high.

Now, that made his heartbeat throb, as he thought about her working with some of these people. He hoped she would choose a department less dangerous. He didn't want to think about it. He was getting too emotionally involved. He needed to stop. He would only get hurt in the end. She doesn't even want him around. She made it clear she could handle things on her own. But when she was in his arms yesterday, he felt the fear within her. Feelings came out of him that seemed to burn deep down inside of him that he just couldn't shake. He only wanted to protect them and keep them safe. *Really, Mark,* he said to himself. He knew in his heart he wanted more.

He sighed as he looked at his watch. He needed to get going. On his way out the door, he dialed up Zack's number to see if he had gotten any information from Forensics on the guy Tammy had described to them.

As he was driving to the restaurant, Zack answered his call, "Detective Williams."

"Hi, Zack. Have you heard anything back from Forensics yet?"

"So far, Mark, they haven't come up with any match in Intel. Detective Motts came in this morning, and he is still working on it. Sorry, I wish I had better news."

"Me too, but thanks," he returned.

"How'd it go last night?" inquired Zack.

"Good. I confess I took over her couch and sacked out there. I was so tired I could have slept on a cement floor. I would have sacked out in the car, but I figured if someone was watching the house, knowing someone was with her, they wouldn't try anything."

Hmm… Okay, Mark, he thought.

"You're probably right," he surmised.

"What are your plans to keep a watch on them till this is over?" asked Mark.

"We're working on it. We are short-staffed and are looking at calling in from other departments. Too bad Jason flew back to Waco last week. He would have been a good one to put on the case."

"Any chance you could call him back?"

"No, he informed me when he arrived back in Waco he was put on another case. We have a meeting with the FBI agents working on this particular case later this afternoon. Because we have become involved through Tammy's daughter, we need to come up with a plan to stop this trafficking ring. We'll be getting more information on where they are at with the case when we meet with them."

"Is there any way I can sit in on the meeting?" asked Mark.

"At this time, no. But I will keep you updated. Do you happen to know Tammy's agenda for the day?" Zack asked in return.

"She was dropping Bethany off at school, and then she was going over to the university for a sociology class she is taking. She's studying to become a social worker," he answered.

"Wow, that's impressive!"

"I know! You would think after four years of working for us that I would have known this, but Mike always handled the background check on all our employees. I never got involved. The financial end takes up most of my time."

"You do a lot more than just the financial end, Mark. You're out there in the restaurant every weekend to help the staff and make sure everything goes smoothly along with Mike. I honestly don't know how you two do it, let alone know what your employees' lives are like. Take a look back at Tonya and Nathan. Neither of you had any idea that they were stepbrother and sister, what they were dealing with to make them steal liquor from your restaurant till it all came down. Thanks to you and your brothers, and several police departments, we were able to bring down one of the biggest loan-sharking and drug-trafficking rings here on the island. So don't sell yourself short. Even with background checks, they don't tell you how the person lives, just if they have a criminal record."

As he listened, Mark knew Zack was right. They had so many employees that it would be hard to get to know all of them on a personal level. He would make an effort from now on to get to know each one a little better. Maybe they could have an employee party, a cookout, with some good quality down time. He would speak to Mike and Jenna when they returned.

"You're right, Zack. Thanks for lifting me up. I can use some positives in my life right now."

"You're welcome," answered Zack.

"And Zack?" he said with concern.

"Yes," he returned. "Just to let you know, Tammy is on the schedule for tonight and tomorrow. She is due in at four tonight and tomorrow at three thirty. She has an older couple that watches Bethany while she works who live a couple of doors down from her. You might want to check with Tammy to get their names, to have someone watching them while she works. I'll keep watch while she is here at the restaurant."

"Right, thanks for the info. I'm on my way to a homicide that happened in the city last night. I will check back with Forensics later to see if any information has been revealed, then after the meeting with the FBI agents, I will touch base with you and Tammy and give you both an update."

"Thanks, Zack. I'll be waiting to hear from you." Mark ended the call just as he pulled into the parking lot at the side entrance of their restaurant. He parked the car and sat there for a few minutes, trying to digest everything that had happened in the last nine months, ever since he started suspecting someone was taking liquor out of their restaurant. It was mind blowing. His divorce becoming final, and now this! Life just took one turn after another, and it never seemed to end. He got out of his car and went into the restaurant. No one was in at this time, but he knew Palani would be in shortly with a couple of his kitchen crew, to get started on tonight's specials.

He unlocked his office and went in to log on to his computer. He pulled up the report he needed to finish. Staring at the screen before him, thinking about Tammy and what she was doing, hoping no one had been following her, his mind was in a whirl. There was nothing he could do till he heard from Zack. He ran his hands through his hair and down the sides of his face, trying to come to grips. *Focus, Mark*, he said to himself. *Focus!* With that, he got to work.

Coming out of her sociology class after talking to the professor, Tammy was thankful he gave her an extra week to finish her paper and turn it in. She was headed to the grocery store, to stock up over the next several weeks. She would be starting her last quarter with Ms. Beret to finish her internship next week, so this was one thing she wanted to get out of the way, and not have to worry about running to the store while she was able to get acclimated to her grueling schedule again.

She pulled into the parking lot at the Hawaiian Food Store, one of her favorite stores. They had everything she and Bethany needed, even some cute sundresses, t-shirts, and stretchy workout capris. Not that she had a lot of time to work out, but she and Bethany liked to take long walks in one of the beautiful parks on the island, or just take a walk in their neighborhood. They loved to stop and visit with their neighbors if they were out working in their yards.

She got out of her car, went into the store, and grabbed a cart. With her list in hand, she started out.

About halfway through her shopping, Tammy was at the meat

department, trying to decide on what meats she would purchase, when a cold chill came over her. Goosebumps came out on her arms, and the sensation spread throughout her body. She quickly looked around the area but didn't see anyone who would give her this feeling of someone watching her. She shook herself, trying to shake off the fear that someone may be lurking around every corner. She picked out her meats and moved on. She hurried through the rest of her shopping, looking around at every turn, but still not seeing anyone that resembled the guy she saw yesterday. When she paid for her groceries, she put them in her car and headed home.

Once there, she hurried to put them all away. Never having enough time before she had to pick up Bethany from school, she went to get ready for work. Mrs. Langley was due to come at three thirty to look after Bethany, so she always made sure she was ready before rushing to start her night. It was hectic during the week, but she always made room for downtime on her day off, and on Sundays, when the restaurant was closed. When she was ready, she hurried out the door. She would just make it on time to pick up Bethany after school.

At the restaurant, Tammy was working the bar lounge tonight, along with one of the new girls who had been in training over the last two weeks. She was busy setting up her station when Kim came up to her to let her know that she started two tables off with water and menus.

"Thank you, Kim. Do you feel confident to handle them on your own tonight?"

"I think so."

"Well, if you have any questions or you need help, Carol is our floater tonight. She will be working in between the lanai and in the bar. I will assist when I can. So don't be afraid to ask. We like to keep our patrons happy."

"Okay, thank you, Tammy. I'll go see if I can start them out with drinks."

"Good. I'll just finish setting up and we're all set to go."

When she was done, she took a look around the lounge. There were five booths all together in an upside-down L-shape. There was one booth sitting next to the corner booth, with three other booths lined up against the windows looking out over the lanai. There were six tables sitting in the middle of the lounge to accommodate customers. The wraparound bar that gleamed in the indirect lighting had bar stools positioned all around it. The rich dark mahogany wood lined the walls and brought a certain intimacy to the lounge. With the upbeat music from their state-of-the-art sound system, it left the customers feeling relaxed and happy after a long day at work. She was lucky to have found this job. The pay was good, and the tips were great. She never got tired of walking into such a fine establishment.

Tonya, one of the hostesses, seated some customers in one of her booths. That was her signal that it was time to get to work.

Mark, sitting in his office, finally finished the report he was working on. He checked his watch. It was almost five o'clock. He put a call into the kitchen. When one of the kitchen staff answered, he put in a request for a fried halibut sandwich, and could he bring it to the office? He missed lunch this afternoon, and he was starving. He needed fuel to get through the night.

He printed out the report for the auditors on Monday and placed it in a folder. He was behind in the sales reports, but with having to be out on the floor in short order, it made no sense to start one.

Bill came in with his sandwich and set it on the desk. "Will there be anything else, sir?" he asked.

"No thanks, Bill. I have soda in the fridge, so I'm all set." Bill nodded and left him to eat his sandwich.

After downing his sandwich and a soda, he came up from his desk and stretched, thinking, *Another night to get through.* He let out a breath, grabbed his suit jacket, locked his office, and headed out to the floor.

As he closed and locked the door behind him, he turned and saw there were customers already lined up at the door. He took another deep breath. After last night he prayed, *Lord, give me strength, and guide my steps tonight.* He approached the hostess stand, took a look at the list of reservations, and started in.

Tammy, scurrying around, thought the night would never end. Along with her own tables, she was helping Kim struggle with hers. While Carol tried to help, she was busy with the two tables in the bar along with her four tables in the lanai. She didn't even have a chance to call home to check on Bethany and Mrs. Langley. Zack had given her an update before she came into work to inform her that they hadn't found a match for the man she described to them on Intel yet. When she asked him whether or not someone would be keeping an eye on Bethany while she worked, he stated he was working on it and would try to have a man out there as quickly as possible. So now she was left wondering if her child was safe or not. She needed a break. Not looking where she was going, she ran smack-dab into Mark! Mark caught her with his hands on her shoulders.

"Whoa, Tammy." He could see from the expression on her face she was extremely frustrated and upset. "Are you all right?" he asked.

Glancing up into his eyes, she stepped back. "No, Mark. I'm not. I have to turn this order in, take coffee around, and deliver drinks to the corner booth. I also need to call home to see if Bethany and Mrs. Langley are okay. Zack said he wasn't sure if he could get someone out to my house right away."

Mark, taking in what she just told him, didn't like the idea of Tammy being left not knowing what was going on at her home. "Okay. You go turn your order in, then go call home. I'll deliver the drinks and take coffee around."

"But you still have a line-up at the door!"

"Don't worry! We'll handle it. Now go!"

Tammy didn't hesitate. She flew to the computer, put her order in, and went to make the call. The noise from the restaurant was overbearing, so she went outside where she could hear. She punched in the number and waited. She let it ring, but no answer. Her heart started pounding at the thought of what could have happened to them. She punched in the number again and started pacing. Again, she couldn't get an answer. She clicked the phone off. Oh, what was she going to do? Should she go home and check on them? What would Mark say with a full house and people still waiting for a table?

She stopped pacing and tried one more time. *Oh, please answer the phone*, she prayed. On the third ring, she heard a voice. "Hello?"

"Mrs. Langley! Oh, thank God! Is everything okay at home?" she asked, her voice in her throat. "I tried calling several times with no answer."

"I'm sorry, Tammy. I was reading to Bethany in her room and didn't hear the phone. Everything is fine here. There is a nice police officer out here watching over us. Now don't you worry, we will be all right until you get home tonight." Tammy breathed a sigh of relief.

"Okay, Mrs. Langley. We have been slammed tonight. I'm not sure what time I will be home. Give a kiss to Bethany for me."

"I will. Take as long as you need to. We'll be just fine," she soothed.

"Thank you, Mrs. Langley."

"You're welcome, Tammy." Tammy clicked her phone off as she

walked back into the restaurant with a cleared conscious that she could finish the night, knowing that Mrs. Langley and her daughter were safe.

With the night winding down, Mark was ready to sit down. It was well after ten thirty. The restaurant was still half full, with some of his customers just being served with their food. He knew it would be well after midnight before he would get out of here. He went to the coffee urn and poured himself a cup of coffee. He sat down in one of the empty booths and took his phone out of his pocket to check his messages. There was one from Zack, letting him know there were no further updates with Forensics, and he had an officer out at Tammy's house until eleven.

Great, he thought. He was hoping to crash in his own bed tonight. Her couch was a little small for his size. Even though he slept okay last night, he woke up a little stiff in places that he hadn't been accustomed to. He would need to let Tammy know. She wasn't going to like it, but he wasn't going to leave her alone. If only she would consider staying with him till this is over. It would make things so much easier. *For who, Mark?* a little voice inside him asked. *You or Tammy?* He sighed. He knew it wouldn't be easier for her. He might just as well quit arguing with himself and go find her.

He looked around the bar area and found her talking to Todd, one of their bartenders. A sudden bolt of jealousy shot through him. He knew Todd was single, and not bad looking, either. He shot out of the booth and came up behind her. He gave Todd *the look*. "Isn't there something you need to do to start closing up?" he asked irritably.

Surprised, looking straight into Mark's eyes, he nodded. "Yes, sir." His gaze came back to Tammy. "Sorry, Tammy, I need to get back to work," he said curtly. His gaze traveled back up to Mark's as he walked away.

Tammy, infuriated, turned around with angry eyes. "Mark, we were only talking for a brief moment! Is there something wrong with that?" she snapped.

Suddenly, Mark realized that he had been out of line. He groaned, as he closed his eyes and lifted his hand to pinch the bridge of his nose. He had no right to be jealous of Todd. He and Tammy weren't a couple and never would be. He dropped his hand and clenched his fists. He realized he owed both of them an apology. He caught her eyes with his. He took a breath. "I'm sorry, Tammy. I'm over tired, and I just want to get out of here."

"Well, Mr. TreVaine," she shot back, "we are all overworked, tired, and would like to get out of here!" Mark watched as she turned away from him and stomped back over to the waitress station.

Well, that didn't go over very well, he thought. But he knew it wasn't much of an apology, either. He stood and watched her for a few more minutes. She was getting checks ready for the last of her customers. He still needed to tell her that the officer could only stay until eleven. Hopefully she'll listen to him. He shook his head; she didn't deserve his anger. He was still hurting from the divorce. Who she talked to, or even if she wanted to date Todd, it was none of his business. He needed to make things right with Todd. He would talk to Tammy before she left. With the place finally starting to clear out, he went to finish closing up for the night.

Tammy, at the waitress station, wondered what had gotten into her! She would never think to yell at her boss. But when she heard his raised voice behind her, it not only made her jump, it just hit a nerve inside her. She needed to apologize. The stress they were both under didn't help with the short tempers.

After she gave her customers their checks, she started cleaning up. It was eleven thirty before she was able to leave for the night.

She went to look for Mark but couldn't find him. Maybe he had already left for the night. She couldn't wait any longer, so she decided to leave. She knew Mrs. Langley would want to get home. Jack let her out, and she wished him a goodnight.

Once home, she looked for the police officer who was supposed to watch the house, but he wasn't around. Her heart lurched as she wondered how long ago he had left. She hurried into the house to find Mrs. Langley watching a movie in the lanai. "Hi, Mrs. Langley, I'm home. How'd it go tonight?"

Mrs. Langley shut the TV off and came up off the chair she was sitting in. "It went well. Bethany was good as she always is, and the nice officer came to the door to let me know he had to leave as his shift was over."

"What time was that?" "Oh…, it was around eleven. I told him that we would be fine and you would be home soon. I hope that was okay. I've been checking out the windows since he left and haven't seen anyone out tonight." Tammy breathed a sigh of relief.

"Yes, Mrs. Langley, you did fine. Thank you for paying such close attention to the situation."

Mrs. Langley picked up her purse and walked towards the door. Tammy followed and opened the door for her, then walked out to the sidewalk with her. "You have a good night, and I will see you tomorrow, Mrs. Langley."

"You do the same, Tammy." Tammy watched until she was safely in her home before she came back in and locked the door. She leaned her back up against it and tried to relax. *How am I going to get through the rest of the night?* she asked herself. *Should I call Mark? No,* she told herself. She wasn't able to apologize before she left tonight. He could still be angry.

She went into the kitchen to make herself a cup of tea. When she put the tea kettle on, she went to check on Bethany. She opened the door to her bedroom and found her fast asleep. She walked up beside the bed and pulled the covers up next to her shoulders. She smiled down at her sleeping child and bent to give her a kiss on the cheek. She moved a little as she snuggled down underneath the covers. Tammy closed the door behind her and went back out to the kitchen to find the tea kettle hissing. She shut the kettle off and proceeded to fix her a cup of her favorite tea. With her cup in hand, she went to the window and slightly pulled back the curtain.

She couldn't see any movement in front of her house. There was a large, flowering hibiscus bush in the left-hand corner of her property. A car or a person could easily be hidden behind it. She wondered if she should go and check it out. After pondering it over, *No*, she thought. *Not a good idea!* She watched for a few more minutes with no activity. She let her hand fall away from the curtain. She turned and walked over to the sofa. She sat down and tried to relax her body, as she sipped on her tea. Thank goodness tomorrow was Saturday! At least she could sleep in a little. She had a feeling she was going to be up for a while.

Mark just finished up checking out the restaurant when he saw Jack getting ready to head out the door. "Hey, Jack! Wait up a minute." Jack turned back as Mark walked up to him. "Hey, do you know by chance when Tammy left for the night?" he asked.

"Yes," answered Jack, "it was around eleven thirty." Mark checked his watch. It was twelve forty-five.

"Thanks, Jack. I'll see you tomorrow."

"You're welcome," he acknowledged. "See you tomorrow."

When he left, Mark shut off all the lights and locked up the restaurant. As he walked to his car, he was cautious of his surroundings. With the crime rate at an all-time high, you never knew who could be lurking around the corner. He carried a handgun with him whenever he left the restaurant.

Unlocking his car, he saw a note on his windshield. He took it off and read the big scrawling letters under the streetlight. *Stay away from the woman and the girl or you will live to regret it!* He looked around, but didn't see anyone in the parking lot, in a car, or walking along the street. He got into his car, threw the note on the seat, and started the engine. Zack informed him that he would have an officer patrolling the area, off and on through the night. He thought he would go home, but after finding the note, he drove directly to Tammy's. Anger threatened to take over him as he made a mad dash to her home. Thoughts of who might have written the note whirled in his head, but one thing's for sure: *Nobody is going to threaten me!*

Tammy woke with a start. She must have dozed off. In her dazed state, she thought she heard a car door slam! With her heart in her throat, she ran to the window. Looking out, she couldn't see anyone in the street. Was someone hiding behind the bush? Panic started to set in as she tried to figure out what to do. Should she call the police?

Mark was sitting in Tammy's driveway, wondering what to do. He tried texting her, with no answer. Was she asleep? Her lights were still on. He decided to take a chance and knock on her door. Getting out of his car, he walked up to the front door.

Coming away from the window, as she was passing by the door to see out the other window, she heard a loud knock. She jumped and immediately grabbed the bat by the door. With her heart racing, she cautiously looked through the peephole. The knock came again, and she jumped for the second time! She turned on the outside light and took a peek out the side door window. She let out a breath.

It was Mark.

She opened the door, dropped the bat on the floor, and rushed into his arms! Surprised, Mark crushed her to him, as she buried her head in his chest. He could feel her body shaking as she cried out, "Mark, thank God it's you!" He held her till she was able to calm down. With the door still open, he pulled her from his arms, to close and lock it behind him. She wiped her eyes with her hands. "I'm sorry, Mark. I didn't mean to cry all over you. You scared me half to death! What were you thinking, coming this late at night?"

"I'm sorry, Tammy. I tried texting you but didn't get a response. I wanted to make sure you and Bethany were safe, especially after I got the note on my windshield tonight."

"Note?" she sniffed.

"Yes. Someone is threatening me to stay away from the two of you, or else!" He handed her the note. She read it over and felt a chill go through her. When her eyes met his, shock filled her at the thought of him and his son being in danger because of them.

"Oh Mark, I had no idea that this would go this far. What are we going to do? Whoever is trying to take Bethany is obviously watching us! Did you see anyone lurking around, or maybe a car parked along the side of the road on your way here?" she asked anxiously. Mark shook his head no.

"I didn't see a soul on the way here. But it doesn't mean that whoever is part of this human-trafficking ring hasn't driven by after everyone is asleep."

Just the thought of someone sneaking around outside her home made his blood boil. Tammy's thoughts were spinning in her head. *Should Bethany and I move in with Mark? We would be closer to the university, the restaurant, and the police station. Bethany's school will be a bit farther, but it would be doable. At least if we were to stay at Mark's, if anything happened, the police could be right there in short order. It would only be for a short time, just until the traffickers were caught, then everything could go back to normal. But am I willing to risk my heart? Being this close to him already has my heart reeling. But all I know right now is I don't want to be alone. I'll be careful, not to get too close.*

Mark was watching the emotions going across her face. He wished he could assure her that this would be over soon, and all who were involved with the crime would be caught. But he couldn't. As his eyes roamed over her body, he noticed she was still in her work clothes. His eyes traveled up along her long legs, over her small waist, to her firm breasts that showed in the t-shirt she wore. His gaze landed intently on her soft pink lips that he wanted so badly to kiss. When she looked up and locked eyes with him, his heart started to beat faster as his thoughts turned to what it would be like with her.

Tammy caught her breath as she looked deep into his eyes before she nervously asked, "Mark, does your offer for us to stay with you still stand?"

He smiled. Relief flooded through him. He came up to her and pulled her into his arms. "Yes. My offer still stands."

Surprised, her hands landed on his hard chest. The feel of his muscles under her hands made her shiver and her knees go weak.

Mark half groaned, as her touch made him want more. His eyes held her captive as she tentatively asked.

"And our relationship will be purely platonic?"

He didn't know if he could keep that promise, holding her in his arms, feeling her warm, tender body close to his. He bent his head and touched his lips to hers. The kiss was soft and sweet. He whispered, "I shall try," before he crushed her body to his and gave in to the passion he was feeling for her.

Tammy's response was of shock at first. They shouldn't be doing this. But hadn't she dreamed of this moment over and over again, to be held in his arms, and be kissed with a passion that set her world on fire? Her arms went up around his neck. She lost control of her senses and kissed him back, wild sensations moving throughout her body. It had been so long since she had been kissed so passionately by a man. She felt Mark's hands moving over her back and hips as his kiss went deeper. When his hand came around and brushed the side of her breast with his thumb, she broke the kiss and pulled back. With both of them breathing rapidly, she pushed her hands against his chest, trying to get him to release her, but he held on. "Mark," she pleaded, "I can't… Bethany… We can't…"

"Tammy, look at me." She slowly raised her eyes to his. As he caught her eyes he knew from the expression on her face, he had gone too far. He breathed deep before he continued, "Tammy, I'm not sorry for kissing you. But I understand. I got carried away." He released her. "It won't happen again." When he let her go, she felt the warmth of his body leaving her. She shook herself.

"It wasn't your fault. I got a little carried away myself." She half smiled. Hesitantly, she asked, "Will you be staying the night?"

"Yes, if it's okay. I won't leave you and Bethany alone." She nodded.

"I'll be right back with a pillow and blanket." When she returned, she laid them on the sofa. She glanced up and met his eyes. "Mark…"

He searched her eyes. "Yes?"

"I… I just want to say thank you for staying tonight. Also for letting us come and stay with you until this is over." He smiled.

"You're welcome, but just for the record, I just want you and Bethany kept safe."

Tammy felt like the wind had been knocked out of her. What was with the kiss they shared? He got carried away, he said. She nodded her head. "Well, goodnight, then."

"Goodnight." Mark watched her go to her bedroom. He didn't mean to be so blunt. He could see in her eyes that he hurt her. He needed to try and keep their relationship on a professional level.

But when he kissed her, he found he couldn't hold back. When she kissed him back, he got lost in the passion they both desired. He lay down on the couch and pulled the blanket over him. With Tammy just down the hall from him, he could only hope he would sleep.

Tammy crawled into bed, wondering if she had completely lost her senses. One minute he was kissing her passionately, then the next he turned it completely off. Now that she committed her and Bethany to living with him, she would have to make sure that there would be no more passionate kisses between them. It wouldn't take much for her to completely fall in love with him. She was already halfway there! She turned over on her side and tried not to think. But as she closed her eyes, the dreams took over.

CHAPTER 6

THE NEXT MORNING Tammy woke up to a bouncing Bethany, trying to wake her up from a dead sleep. "Mom!" she cried., "Wake up!" Tammy groaned.

"Just let me sleep a little longer…" she mumbled. Bethany proceeded to shake her.

"No, Mama! We have to get up! Mr. Mark is sleeping on our sofa again, and he'll want coffee soon!"

With her brain still in a fog, she wondered who Mr. Mark was. Once it set in, she quickly sat up. She glanced over at her daughter and asked, "You didn't wake him, did you?"

"No, Mama, I came to get you first. Do you want me to go wake him?"

"No, sweetie. We'll let him sleep a little while longer." Tammy pulled back the covers. "Come and get under the covers with me. I need to talk to you about something very important."

"Okay, Mama." Bethany crawled under the covers and snuggled up to her mom. Tammy put her arm around her little girl and wondered how to begin.

"Bethany."

"Yes, Mama?" she asked.

"How would you feel about living with Mr. Mark, just for a short time, until they catch the bad guys?"

Bethany quickly sat up, concern written all over her little face. "For how long?" she cried. Tammy raised her hand and brushed some of her hair behind her ear.

"I don't know for sure. Maybe a couple of weeks, maybe more, but as soon as they arrest the bad guys, we'll come right back home. What do you think?"

Bethany thought a moment. Tammy could tell she was in deep thought. "Can I bring some of my favorite toys and movies with me, along with some of my stuffed animals? I need to bring Mr. Snow Bear especially. I can't sleep without him!" Tammy smiled at her precious daughter.

"Yes, you can bring all of the above."

"Yay!" she cried. "I'll go tell Mr. Mark!" Before Tammy could stop her, she was off the bed and out the door yelling, "Mr. Mark! Mr. Mark!"

Well, she thought, *I may as well get up and make the coffee.*

Mark woke to a little girl yelling in his ear, "Mr. Mark! It's time to get up! I have some exciting news!"

Mark opened his eyes to a toothless smile. He quickly sat up and rubbed his hands down over his face, trying to get himself awake. He glanced down at the little girl who climbed up on the sofa and sat down beside him. He was a little incoherent for a moment until he got his bearings. Then he gave Bethany a big smile and asked, "Did you say you have big news?" She nodded her head yes. "Can you tell me what it is?" She nodded again.

"My mommy and me are going to come and stay with you!"

"Is that right?" He chuckled.

"Yeah." She nodded. "She said I could bring my favorite toys, movies, and stuffed animals." She looked up at him with innocent eyes. "If it's okay with you," she added shyly.

He laughed. "It is most certainly okay with me. You can bring whatever you want, if it will make you feel at home." She grinned up at him, climbing up on her knees. She wrapped her little arms around his neck and gave him a big hug. "Thank you, Mr. Mark!" She jumped off the sofa and ran into the kitchen to tell her mom. He chuckled as he watched her go into the kitchen. She was an adorable child. He took a deep breath. The smell of fresh coffee brewing brought his senses to life. He came up from the sofa and decided to freshen up a bit before seeing what he could do to help with breakfast.

A few minutes later he came into the kitchen to the smell of pancakes on the grill, fresh ham cooking in a pan on the stove, and coffee. "Good morning!"

Tammy turned and smiled. "Good morning!"

"Is there anything I can help you with?"

"No, I'm good. Help yourself to coffee, though. It just finished brewing."

He returned her smile. "Can I get you a cup?"

"Sure. I'll have it with cream." Mark went to the cupboard, pulled two cups out, and poured them each a cup. The cream was already out, so he put a little in each one and handed her a cup. Her fingers brushed his as she took the cup from him. So he couldn't see her reaction to his touch, her eyes dropped as she took a sip. "Hmm... So good, I needed this. Thank you." She turned back and flipped the pancakes.

He took a sip of his own coffee as he watched her finish making the pancakes. She looked right at home in the kitchen. His ex-wife never liked to cook. They either ate at the restaurant, or he would make something for them if he wasn't too tired to make the effort. Tammy piled the pancakes on a plate and set them on the table. "Can I help with anything?" he asked.

She caught his eye and smiled. "Could you grab some plates from the cupboard? The silverware is in the top drawer, there by the sink."

Mark went to work, and soon they were all sitting down for the second day in a row to a delicious breakfast. He could get used to this. Just as the thought left his mind, Tammy spoke up.

"Don't get too used to this. Starting next week, it's toast, juice, and cereal. With my final quarter of my internship beginning, there will be no time to make breakfast." He studied her for a moment before he answered.

"The last thing I would expect is for you to cook breakfast every morning for us. I rarely have time to cook in the mornings myself. When you are in my home, feel free to go about your normal schedule. No expectations and no obligations are expected."

With him eyeing her so intensely, she nervously replied, "Thank you. That makes me feel better. I just went to the store yesterday. Do you mind if I bring some of the groceries with us? I hate to let them go to waste."

"No, not at all, bring whatever you want. After you have moved your things in, we'll take inventory and pick up what we need from the store later. Cameron will be coming over on Sunday. Also, I will need to pick up Mike and Jenna at the airport at two."

Bethany piped in. "Cameron will be coming?" she asked excitedly. Mark grinned back.

"Yep!" he confirmed. "And when he finds out you are going to be there, get ready for some serious playtime!"

"Yippee!" She giggled. "I can't wait!"

He chuckled and glanced back over to Tammy. "Do you want to move in today, or would tomorrow be better?" Tammy knew there'd be no way she would be ready to move in today. "I think tomorrow would be better. Mrs. Langley will be coming at three. It wouldn't give us much time to get everything packed and loaded into the car. Plus, I'll need to make all the arrangements regarding Bethany and her care while I'm at work."

Mark studied her across the table. He hadn't considered all that it would take for Tammy and her daughter to move in with him.

"Listen, depending on whether or not Zack can have someone out here for the night, I can help in the morning before I pick up Cameron, and then on to the airport. I'll have an extra key made today and give it to you tonight at the restaurant. That way you will be able to get into the house, and you and Bethany can move in when you're ready."

She smiled. "Thanks, Mark. I appreciate all that you have done so far, but Mr. and Mrs. Langley will be glad to help us and get us settled in at your home. I don't want to put you out. You have so much to do with your own life, plus the restaurant."

Mark gazed into her pretty amber eyes as he professed, "You and Bethany will not be putting me out. I will always try to be there to help if needed. All you need to do is ask." He gave her a smile that just made her want to melt right under the table.

"Mr. Mark?" interrupted Bethany. He turned to the little girl.

"Yes, Bethany?" he asked, as he smiled down at this cute little child sitting next to him, still in her pajamas. "What kind of movies does Cameron like to watch?"

"Oh, he mostly likes movies with cars or trucks in them." Bethany's eyes lit up.

"I have the perfect movie to bring!"

"Oh yeah?" he laughed. "I bet I can guess."

They both said in unison, "*Cars*!" They all laughed. Tammy smiled as she continued to listen to the banter between the two.

When they finished their breakfast, Bethany went off to play in the lanai, while Mark helped Tammy with cleaning up thé kitchen and loading the dishwasher. He checked his watch. "I'm going to head out. I need to do a few things at home before you arrive. And I want to try and get ahold of Zack, to see if he has found out any information on the guy you described to him."

Tammy walked him to the door.

Opening the door, he turned back. Gazing into her eyes, he wanted so badly to kiss her again. He remembered the feel of his lips on hers, the tantalizing scent of her, and the rush from the passion that ignited them both when she kissed him back. He took a deep breath and focused his mind on something else. "Thanks again for breakfast. I'll see you tonight at work," he said. She gave him a warm smile.

"You're welcome. See you tonight." He turned and left out the door. Tammy closed the door behind her, resting her head against it as she closed her eyes. Remembering the kiss they shared had her trembling inside. She wanted more of that. The way he looked at her just now made her think that he was remembering too, but he said he wouldn't let it happen again. Soon they would be living together. Would they both be able to keep from touching each other? Living in such close proximity?

Bethany came running in from the lanai. "Mommy!" she exclaimed. "Did Mr. Mark leave?"

"Yes, he did, sweetie."

Her expression turned to sadness. "He didn't say goodbye!" Tammy bent down on her haunches and took her little hands in hers.

"Oh, honey, he needed to get some errands done before he went into work. You'll get to see him tomorrow. What do you say we start getting packed up, so we don't have so much to do in the morning?"

She looked at her mom and grinned. "Okay, Mommy. I'll start with my toys!"

As she watched her daughter scurry off to her room, Tammy was concerned about her daughter's reaction to Mark's leaving. She was afraid she was getting too attached. The last thing she wanted was for her daughter to get hurt when they moved back home. She had a feeling that if she didn't guard her own heart at all costs, there would be two hearts that would be breaking. She walked into her bedroom and started packing. She didn't want to think anymore. She would take it one day at a time.

On his way home, Mark put in a call to Zack.

"Detective Williams," he answered.

"Hey, Zack. Mark here," he returned.

"Hi, Mark. What's up?"

"Well, number one. I wanted to see if your forensics detective had made any headway on the guy Tammy described to you. And number two, I found a threatening note on my windshield last night to stay away from Tammy and her daughter."

"You found a note?" he asked anxiously.

"Yes," Mark responded.

"Do you have time to stop into the station? I'm going to be here for a couple of hours. We'll have someone in another one of our forensics departments look at it and try to match up the writing with Intel."

"I'll be right there." He pressed the *end call* button and headed over to the station. When he arrived, Zack met him at the door.

"Come back to my office. I have Detective Motts and Detective Carter waiting for us." Mark followed him back and was introduced to the two detectives. They shook hands and took a seat. Zack turned to Mark. "Do you have the note?" Mark pulled it out of his pocket and handed it to Zack. He read it and handed it over to Detective Carter. "See what you can make of this and let me know ASAP!"

Detective Carter looked over the note. He came up from his chair and glanced over at Zack. "I'll get right on this."

When he left the room, Mark turned to Detective Motts. "Were you able to match up the picture to anyone on your Intel?" he asked.

"I'm sorry, Mark, but so far I have not been able to match him to anyone in our system. If he is part of this human-trafficking ring, he could be one of their new mules, or he could be innocent of any wrongdoing. We will keep a watch out for him, just to be safe."

"Could I have a copy of the picture you have of him? I want to keep a watch out also. Mike will be back tomorrow. I will be sharing this information with him and Jenna."

"Of course," he answered. "I'll go get you a copy and be right back."

When he left, Mark looked over at Zack. "How did the meeting go with the FBI yesterday afternoon? Did you find out anything that would help catch these guys?"

"What we know is they have several undercover agents working inside the organization. They learned that these mules are working throughout the island. Once they kidnap a child or a teen, they drug them. Then they ship them over to the mainland, or out of the country. They've discovered that the person who heads up this human-trafficking ring is running it outside of the mainland."

"Do they know the name of this guy?" asked Mark.

When Zack answered him, he let out a big sigh. "You're not going to believe this, Mark, but it's Marco Manchez. The FBI has been following him for a while. We kind of blew their case out of the water, literally, when we went after him for his drug trafficking."

Shocked, Mark could hardly believe it! "Damn. Are you kidding me?" he asked.

"No, Mark. I'm not kidding you. Not only is this guy wanted for loan sharking and drug trafficking, he is now wanted for human trafficking! As you know, he slipped through our fingers. His flight plan had him and his wife heading to the Cayman Islands. We put out an APB on all three islands, with no results. We're thinking he had his pilot change course while in the air, so he could be anywhere in the Pacific. We froze all his assets, but he must have set up other accounts in another name. The guy we are holding in jail is not talking. This case has become one big headache. Now that you have been threatened, I will make sure we have someone watching you and Tammy along with her little girl twenty-four seven till we catch all persons involved!"

"Zack, I'm going to make this easy for you. Tammy and Bethany are moving in with me tomorrow. We both decided it would be easier, due to the fact that Tammy and I along with our children are targets. She and her daughter would also be closer to the restaurant and the police department. That way you could have one man from each shift to keep watch till this is over. With Mike and Jenna coming back tomorrow, maybe we can work on a plan to end this."

"Mark, that's the best news I've heard all week! We are so short on staff that I would need to pull from other departments just to make this happen."

Detective Motts came back into the office with the copy of the man Tammy described to them. He handed it to Mark. "Listen, just so you know, I haven't given up on matching him to someone on Intel. There are some other areas I need to check on."

Mark took the copy from Detective Motts. He took a look, folded it, and placed it in his sport coat pocket. "Thanks, Detective Motts. I will let my brothers know and keep a watch out for this guy. Listen, I have to get going." He glanced back over to Zack. "Keep me informed. Let me know if someone will be out at Tammy's this afternoon and this evening. She has Mrs. Langley watching Bethany, beginning at three. I will let Tammy know what we've discussed tonight." He rose up from his chair, thanked both Detective Motts and Zack for their time, and headed out the door. He had just enough time to get the room ready where Tammy and Bethany would be staying, get a shower, and have a key made before he had to be back at the restaurant by three.

CHAPTER 7

THE NIGHT STARTED OUT slow, then wham! It was non-stop right up until ten o'clock. Mark knew Tammy was working in the lanai tonight. Whenever he seated customers at one of her tables, he would glance her way, and he'd catch her eyes with his. He was so attracted to her that he could feel the chemistry in those brief moments. She'd smile, then look away. Almost as if she wanted to avoid eye contact with him. He wondered if kissing her last night put her off. He told her it wouldn't happen again, but he knew in his heart, when he was near her, he wanted her, all of her. Her pretty pink lips shaped like a bow pressed to his, her soft body held close in his arms. She aroused feelings he thought were buried deep down inside of him a long time ago. He breathed deep and went about finishing up the night. He would need to speak to her when they closed. He would also need to keep his wits about him.

For Tammy, the night started off as a typical Saturday night. But as the night wore on, she felt like she was being pulled apart in several different directions. She had several customers complain about how long the food was taking to come out. Plus, some of her drinks that she served needed to be fixed, or they changed their minds all together. It was a stressed-filled night! To top it off, when Mark seated customers at one of her tables, her eyes would meet that piercing gaze of his, and her heart would start to race each and every time he glanced her way. She tried not to gaze back into those deep blue eyes but found herself trying to seek him out throughout the night. She had no idea how she was going to deal with all these emotions going through her when she moved in with him.

It was almost closing time, and she knew Mark wanted to speak to her before she went home. She hurried to finish giving out her checks and get the cleanup done. She knew Zack was able to get a police officer to watch over Mrs. Langley and Bethany while she worked and into the next day, so she felt comfortable not rushing home. With everything done, and her tables set up for Monday, she went to see if he would have time to talk.

She walked into the bar lounge and found Mark and Jack, the new general manager, sitting in one of the booths having dinner. She stood and stared at the handsome man who made her belly flutter and her knees go weak every time he glanced her way. She took a deep breath. *Okay, Tammy*, she told herself, *stay calm*.

Her stomach started to growl, which reminded her that she hadn't eaten since lunch. She was too busy getting clothes packed and Bethany's things together to think about grabbing something before she started working. As she approached the booth, her nerves got the better of her, and she began to shake. Her heart was beating so hard, she wondered if anyone could hear it. *So much for staying calm*, she surmised. When she drew near the table, he looked up with amusement in those blue eyes of his, almost as if he knew what she was going through at this moment. She hated her voice shaking as she tentatively asked, "Is this a good time, or would you like me to come back?"

Mark smiled. He could see she was nervous. She didn't need to be. He didn't bite. Although, he wouldn't mind taking a nip on those soft lips of hers, maybe on the tip of her earlobe, down to those firm breasts protruding out underneath her Hawaiian Lanai t-shirt she was wearing. He quickly switched his thoughts. Holding her eyes, he came up out of the booth and gestured with his hand. He cast a smile down upon her when he gently murmured, "Have a seat."

Dropping her eyes from that warm gaze of his, she walked past him, close enough to feel his warm body next to hers as she slid into the booth. She shivered. She made sure she was as close to the far side of the booth as possible. "Would you care for anything to drink, Tammy?" he asked.

"I wouldn't mind a cola, but please, I don't want to interrupt your dinner."

He grinned. *So sweet,* he thought.

"I'll be right back." He came back with a cola and a glass of ice and set it down in front of her. He slid into the booth beside her. Even with her sitting at the end of the booth, his massive body took up most of it. With his shoulder almost brushing hers, she couldn't help but feel the magnetic pull of electricity going back and forth between them. *Can he feel it too?* she wondered. She met his eyes. "Thank you." She smiled faintly.

He smiled back, his eyes glittering into hers. "You're welcome," he murmured.

She blushed. "Please," she coaxed, "finish your dinner. I wouldn't want it to get cold." Her stomach chose that time to growl again, loud enough for Mark to hear.

One eyebrow shot up, curiosity beaming in his eyes, when he asked, "Are you hungry, Tammy? The kitchen is closed, but I can have one of the cooks make something simple for you, maybe a cold sandwich?"

"Oh... No. I can fix something when I get home. I wouldn't want to impose."

"You would not be imposing," he stated. "What would you like?" She eyed the salad sitting beside his dinner plate. Her stomach growled for the third time.

"Do you think they would mind fixing me a salad with the Hawaiian dressing?" she asked meekly. He laughed softly and gave her a wink.

"I think we can accommodate that request." He called Megan over, who was working the bar lounge tonight. He ordered Tammy's salad.

Megan half-smiled as she glanced over at Tammy with eyes that said, *What's this?* Tammy quickly looked away. She knew this would happen. The staff would start talking. Megan left to put the order in. She could hear them now. Would they believe her when they asked, that this was strictly a business arrangement? Especially after they find out she and her daughter have moved in with him? She started feeling uncomfortable as thoughts of how this may look were reeling in her head.

Mark, watching her with a steady gaze, felt her change in body language. He caught Megan's response to getting Tammy's salad. She more or less snubbed Tammy. He didn't like it. At one time he used to tease Megan on occasion. She was a knockout, with pretty green eyes, long blond hair, and curves that was pleasing to the eye. But he never felt anything for her, other than a comradeship between employee and employer. He didn't care what the staff would think about Tammy sitting with him, having a bite to eat. But he hadn't thought about how the staff would treat her, let alone when they find out about them moving in with him. Mark hardly noticed Jack silently getting up from the booth. He was now alone with Tammy.

Tammy glanced over at Mark, who was eyeing her in that unnerving way of his. Their eyes locked, and she wondered what he was thinking.

Megan brought out the salad, complete with silverware wrapped in a napkin. She set it down in front of her. Tammy tore her eyes away from Mark. She met Megan's eyes and could see she was clearly upset. She braved a smile and muttered, "Thank you, Megan. I appreciate you bringing this out for me."

Mark watched Megan half smile, turn to him and ask, "Do you want me to put the salad on your check?" She was a little sarcastic. Mark had never seen her act this way. The glare in his eyes spoke volumes as he responded to her question.

"Yes," he said curtly. "And when you finish adding it on, please bring it directly back to me, along with Jack's dinner check." He watched Megan's face turn a hundred shades of red before she turned and went to the waitress station. He turned back to Tammy. His eyes took in the shocked expression on her pretty face. "Tammy..." he said softly.

She stared back at him with fear clearly in her eyes, and suddenly she lost her appetite. "Mark, I was afraid this would happen. I should go," she began. She tried to get up. Mark pressed his hand on her shoulder.

"You are not going anywhere," he said firmly. "I will finish my dinner, and you will eat your salad."

Megan came up to their booth and set the cash tray on the table while his gaze was still riveted on Tammy. He waited until she left before he continued. "Listen, Tammy, don't let Megan's attitude affect you. No one here knows what is happening with our kids and the danger they are in from the human-trafficking ring. I still need to go over what I discussed with Zack and the other detectives. So let's just relax and enjoy our dinner while I fill you in. Besides"—he grinned—"I'm too big for you to move me, so you can't escape."

She grinned back. "I could crawl up and over the table!"

He laughed and leaned in. "Then I would have to pull that gorgeous body of yours right back down beside me." With a gleam in his eyes, he confirmed, "And don't think I won't! Now let's eat!"

She chuckled softly. She had no doubt in her mind that he would do exactly what he said. She started in on her salad. They made beautiful salads here. It was almost a meal in itself. It was a mixture of mixed greens, lettuce, sliced egg, tomatoes, and mandarin oranges, served with the Hawaiian dressing. When she took her first bite, she groaned and closed her eyes. It was so delicious.

Mark turned and remarked, "Good?"

She glanced back at him and nodded her head as she was chewing. "So good," she returned, with laughter in her eyes. They both finished their meal with little conversation. It would seem they were both hungry. Mark glanced over her way and saw she had finished every bit of her salad.

"Would you like anything else, Tammy?"

She turned and raised her eyes to his. "Oh no, it was perfect. Just right." She smiled.

Jack came and refilled his coffee and picked up the dirty plates. Megan must have left for the night. He pulled out his wallet, took a look at the checks, and threw some bills on the tray. When Jack came by again, he caught his attention and asked, "Hey, Jack. Could you take care of this for me? I need to discuss something with Tammy so she can go home, and then I will help get this place closed up." He handed the tray to him.

Jack nodded. "Of course!"

"Oh, and Jack."

He turned back to Mark. "Yes?" he answered.

"Put the change in Megan's tip jar." He smiled.

"Will do, Mark."

When Jack left, Mark turned back to Tammy with eyes that held concern for her. He placed his arm over the back of the booth and shifted his body toward her. When he started to give her the information that the detectives and he discussed this morning at the police station, she focused her full attention on what he was telling her. "I know you are anxious to get home, so I will quickly go over what I found out after talking with Zack and the other detectives. And to be honest, Tammy, it wasn't much. Detective Motts has not found a match on Intel. But he was going to try some other avenues, to see if he could come up with a match. Zack had a Detective Carter take the threatening note, to see if he could match the writing to anyone in their criminal file. Other than that, until we hear from them, we are at a standstill. I'm sorry."

Tammy's expression turned downcast as she listened to what he was telling her. Mark could see the disappointment written all over her face.

Sitting in the booth beside him, Tammy just wanted this nightmare to be over. She was hoping to hear that they found the man that she had described to them. Each day that went by, she grew more and more discouraged. She just wanted her life to go back to normal. *Will it ever be the way it was before all this happened?* she asked herself. Searching his eyes, she reminded herself that she and Bethany would be moving in with him tomorrow. Somehow, she didn't think it would. Once she got a taste of living with him, she was afraid she would never want to go back to the way things were before they tried to take her daughter. She had hoped they would have come up with something regarding the man who had seemed to be following her, and the threatening note Mark found on his windshield. And who was the person who sold her to this trafficking ring? So many questions needed to be answered. Could her ex have had something to do with it? He always seemed to have money. With him having no contact with either one of them since the divorce, she didn't think it would be possible. She didn't even know where he was living for sure, or if he remarried. How were the detectives going to find out who it was? Her mind was in a tailspin about who it could be!

Mark was gazing intently at all the emotions going across that soft oval face, and wondered what was going through her mind as she continued to lock eyes with him, without really seeing him. He placed his hand over hers. He would like nothing more than to pull her in his arms, to tell her that everything was going to be okay. He would keep her and her daughter safe. But knew he couldn't risk it here.

Tammy felt Mark's hand come down over hers, warm and tender, giving it a gentle squeeze. She slowly came out of the trance she was in and focused back on Mark's eyes. She could see the concern he held for her when she got lost in her own thoughts. Mark smiled softly. "There she is. I seemed to have lost you there for a minute or two." She looked down for a moment. He put his other hand under her chin and gently turned her back to him. Her eyes met his effortlessly. He asked her softly, "Tammy, can you tell me what's been going through your mind?"

She sighed. "I was just thinking that it seems to be taking so long for the detectives to find out anything about this case. I mean, have they even tried to look for the person who sold her?"

"I wish I had an answer for you, but I don't. I'm sorry."

Her shoulders slumped as she turned away. She checked her watch; it was well after midnight. She lifted her eyes back to him. "Thanks, Mark, for letting me know, and for the salad. I need to get going. I have Mr. and Mrs. Langley coming back to the house at ten in the morning."

Mark suddenly realized he needed to give her a key to his home. "Which reminds me, could you come back to the office with me? I had a key made for you. I don't know how long I will be tomorrow after picking up Mike and Jenna from the airport, so you will need it to get in." Mark slid out of the booth and waited for Tammy to join him. They walked back to his office. He went in and circled around to the front of his desk. He pulled out the top drawer, took a key out, and handed it to Tammy where she stood close beside him.

Her fingers brushed his, as she took the key from him. She felt the tingles going throughout her body as she caught the burning desire in his deep-blue eyes. Time seemed to stand still. He took a small step toward her, his hands catching her waist as he pulled her closer to his hard body. Caught in a trance, Tammy didn't have the strength to pull away.

"I know I said this wouldn't happen again"—his eyes focusing on her soft lips—"but I'm having this strong urge to kiss you. To feel your lips next to mine," his voice sounding like velvet.

Tammy, caught up in the moment, responded softly, "So kiss me." Tammy, mesmerized, watched, as he bent his head, his firm lips touching hers in a kiss that sent new sensations from the top of her head all the way down to her toes. She closed her eyes, her arms climbing up and around his neck as he pulled her closer to him. So close, she could feel how aroused he was. He groaned as he deepened the kiss, his hands moving ever so slowly over her back and down to her hips. One hand gently slid up to her breast. He teased the taunt nipple with his thumb.

Tammy, feeling his warm strong hand caressing her breast, was lost to the sensations he was creating inside her. It seemed like an eternity since she was touched so intimately. Through the haze of the passion they were creating together, Tammy thought she heard a door close.

Mark must have heard it too, as they suddenly broke apart at the same time. Mark looked over at the main door. He knew he left it open when they came in. It was now closed. He swore. Jack must have come to see him. He would have some explaining to do for Tammy's sake. His eyes drifted back to hers. He could see the fear of getting caught kissing in her pretty amber eyes. "Tammy…"

She looked down at the floor and up again to eyes so gentle. Shaking her head, she muttered, "I'm sorry. I've got to go."

Mark watched as she hurried out of the office. He wanted to go after her but thought better of it. He knew in his heart he was starting to have feelings for her. He needed to be careful from now on. Whoever saw them kissing could cause problems for Tammy. He flicked the light switch off, locked the door, and went to find Jack.

Tammy rushed out of the restaurant, slid into her car, and locked the door. She dropped her head against the steering wheel, her heart racing inside her. How could she have let this happen? Now that she has had a taste of the passion that set her very soul on fire, how was she going to keep from kissing him again? She leaned back in her seat. One thing was for sure. She would have to have the strength of a saint to keep from getting too close to him. She wondered who had seen them kissing. She groaned. She was afraid she was going to have hell to pay when she went into work on Monday. She started her car and headed for home. She couldn't worry about it now. She had too much to do to be ready to finish her last term at the university. She sent up a prayer for the Lord to see her through the next couple of days.

CHAPTER 8

THE MORNING CAME too soon for Tammy. She didn't sleep well, thinking about Mark, and the passionate kiss they shared, his powerful hands moving over her body so tenderly. She started to tingle just reliving it! She sighed and looked over at her alarm clock. It was seven fifteen. She needed to get up. She still had to pack some items before Mr. and Mrs. Langley arrived.

She threw back the covers and crawled out of bed. She went in search of Bethany and found her watching her favorite program in the lanai. "Hey, sweetie. Are you ready for some breakfast?" Bethany turned to her mom. She grinned.

"Yeah, but can I finish watching my show?" she asked. Tammy grinned back.

"Yes, you may. When it's over, breakfast should be ready."

"Okay, Mommy," she said as she turned back to the TV.

Tammy headed to the kitchen. She made a pot of coffee, then started in on making French toast and sausage. As she was lifting the toast off the griddle, Bethany walked into the kitchen and took a seat at the table. Tammy handed her plate to her and went to get hers.

When she sat down, Bethany asked, "Is Mr. Mark coming over to help us move in with him this morning?"

Surprised by her question, she answered carefully, "No, sweetie. Mr. Mark had things to do at his home this morning. Then he will be picking up Cameron and going on to the airport to pick up his brother Mike and his wife Jenna."

Tammy watched her sad little face when she responded with, "I missed waking him up this morning."

"Oh, honey, you'll see him later this afternoon. Now eat your breakfast. We have a few more things we need to gather up to put in the car, plus I need to pack up all the food I purchased at the store the other day before Mr. and Mrs. Langley get here. Did you put all your toys you want to take in the box I left for you?" She nodded.

"Yes, Mrs. Langley helped me."

"Good." She smiled at her daughter. "Don't forget your movie. Cameron will be sure to want to watch it with you. Now eat up!" She brightened and dug into her French toast.

While she finished her breakfast, Tammy again worried about how attached her daughter was getting to Mark. Was she missing a father figure in her life? Bethany never asked about her father, except one time when Roy and her were going through their divorce. When she asked if she had a father, she wasn't quite sure how to answer her. How do you tell a two-year-old that her father never wanted the responsibility of raising his precious daughter? She remembered telling her that, yes, she did have a father, but her dad left for a different life and moved far away from them, that he wasn't able to be a father to her, but the two of them would have a wonderful life together, and she would always love her and be there for her. It seemed to satisfy her curiosity, and she never asked again.

Looking back on their life so far, they were blessed with so much compared to other single moms. Her heart went out to all the moms who struggled each day trying to provide for their family. In her neighborhood, there was a single mom with two little girls. When she was able, she would watch her girls if she needed to go to the store, or just get some down time. Bethany always enjoyed them coming over. She loved to have playtime with them.

Her thoughts were interrupted when she heard, "MOM!" yelled Bethany.

She jumped! "Bethany! You startled me! What do you want?" she asked impatiently.

"Mom, I've been trying to ask you something!"

"What?"

"Do you think Mr. Mark likes music? I want to bring my xylophone. I need to practice my song."

Tammy didn't know if he liked music or not. Probably not a little girl pounding out a song loud enough to send someone into orbit! "Honey, I don't know if Mr. Mark likes that kind of music. Perhaps we should leave it at home."

Bethany crossed her arms and huffed, giving her mom that defiant look when she wanted her way. "Then I'm not going!"

Tammy took a deep breath, as her patience was running thin. "Bethany, you will leave the xylophone at home, and you will be going," she said sternly. "Now go and get dressed. Mr. and Mrs. Langley will be here soon, and we need to be ready." Bethany left the table, stomping all the way to her bedroom.

Tammy didn't like to say no, but she just couldn't see Mark tolerating the loud ping of a xylophone. She could hardly stand it herself! She got up from the table and picked up the dishes to put in the dishwasher. After cleaning up the kitchen and cleaning out the refrigerator, she bagged up the groceries she wanted to take, then rushed back to her bedroom to get dressed. As she came back out with her suitcases, the doorbell rang, and the mad rush began!

Mark heard the alarm go off and reached over to turn it off. He went back to sleep. When he finally woke up, it was well after nine o'clock! He groaned. He quickly sat up, threw back the covers, and headed for the shower. He would be lucky to get everything done before he left to pick up Cameron and then on to the airport.

Showered and dressed, he went into the kitchen and made a pot of coffee. Once he had some caffeine in him, he got to work. The place was a mess. He picked up all the dirty dishes lying around, changed the sheets in the room Tammy and Bethany were sharing, straightened up the adjoining bathroom, and made sure there were clean washcloths and towels for them. He took a look around the place. It wasn't the cleanest, but he just hadn't had the time to spend cleaning it when he spent the last two weeks practically living at the restaurant, and the last few days at Tammy's.

Tammy. He smiled remembering. She was a passionate little thing. Her warm, tender body pressed next to his, her lips moving with his in a slow, passionate rhythm. He found himself wanting her in the worst way. He needed to figure out how he was going to accomplish that without causing waves at the restaurant. He'd think on it. Right now, he needed to get going.

He grabbed his keys off the counter and headed out into the garage. When he backed out he saw an officer he had never seen before in an unmarked car. He waved to the officer as he drove by and thought he looked familiar but wasn't sure. He would be sure to ask Zack if someone new was on the force.

At the airport, Mark and his son waited outside the Hawaii International Terminal, marked *Arrivals*, for Mike and Jenna to come out. Cameron, anxiously looking for any signs of them, asked, "Have they landed yet, Dad?"

Mark looked at his watch. It was a little after two. "I'm not sure, Cameron. If the flight's on time, they should have landed. But if it's been delayed, they could still be up there in that big blue sky waiting to land. We'll just have to wait for a text or call from your Uncle Mike that they arrived."

He heard his son sigh. His son was never good at waiting. And at this point, neither was he. He was anxious to see them as well. He wanted to get them home and settled, so he could get back to his home and check on Tammy and Bethany. Making sure they had found everything they needed. He did leave a note on the counter for them explaining where things were, and to make themselves at home. He hadn't let his son know that he had house guests, that they would be staying with him and why. He didn't want to risk his son letting the cat out of the bag, as the saying goes, yet. He would tell Mike and Jenna later, when he had time to sit and talk with them about the situation. He checked his watch. Twenty minutes after two. This time he sighed. Hopefully, it wouldn't be much longer. He had to chuckle.

With that thought out of his mind, his son asked, "Are they here yet?"

A moment later he heard his cell phone ding with an incoming text.

The flight was on time, just waiting for luggage. We'll be out shortly, can't wait to see you.

Mark breathed a sigh of relief. He turned to his son, and with a grin said, "They're here!"

Cameron, looking back at his dad, said, "Finally!"

Tammy, Bethany, and the Langleys arrived at Mark's home. It took them all morning and most of the early afternoon to get everything loaded in both cars. Bethany kept going back to her room, saying she had forgotten something. Tammy was no different. She wanted to make sure she didn't forget anything, like her laptop, iPad, her homework, and anything else she needed for school. And then there were all of Bethany's books, notebooks, pencils, and paints that she needed to bring. Honestly, it felt like they were moving in permanently, with all the stuff they had to bring!

Tammy turned into the circular driveway and parked her car in front of the house with the Langleys close behind. When they all got out of their cars, Tammy took one look at Mark's home and was awestruck! "Wow, Mom! It looks like a museum!" cried Bethany.

Set on two acres was a big, sprawling ranch home. Sandstone was placed on the walls throughout the portico, from the floor to the ceiling, with long, narrow windows on each side of the door. The front door was painted a burnt orange color and had a glass window with a Hawaiian scene etched in it. The rest of the home was painted a medium beige color with white trim. Shrubbery and colorful hibiscus adorned the immaculate yard, with palm trees placed in different areas to bring out the beauty of the home.

As they walked up to the front door, the white pillars coming down from the ceiling to the sandstone floor made the home look museum-like.

Tammy unlocked the door, and they all went inside. It was just as impressive as the outside. The living area was huge, with the walls painted a cream color with a hint of yellow. A gas fireplace was centered on the far wall. The grey leather furniture and plush carpeting gave warmth to the room as well as the beautiful paintings that adorned the walls.

Mrs. Langley commented from behind, "Nice, but a little dusty."

"Mildred!" scolded Bob.

"Well, it doesn't look like it's had a good cleaning in weeks! Let's start getting everything brought in and we'll all give it a quick clean. It's the least we can do for Mr. TreVaine letting Tammy and Bethany stay with him until this ordeal is over."

Bethany ran out into the lanai and was looking out the window "Mom!" she yelled. "It has a pool back here! Can I go swimming?"

"No, sweetie. Maybe later. We have work to do. Now, come and help us bring all your stuff in."

She huffed, "Okay," as she stomped over to the door. Tammy shook her head. She'd been noticing a lot of stomping going on when she didn't get her way. She hoped this phase would be over soon.

Once all their belongings were brought in, they went to work. She didn't know how long Mark would be, but wanted to have as much done as possible before he came home. Mark left a note to inform them which room was theirs. Tammy went in search of furniture polish and window cleaner. She eventually found some in the laundry room. She and Bethany found the bedroom where they would be sleeping and started there, while the Langleys started in the kitchen.

Two hours later, they had everything cleaned and put away. Tammy put some coffee on and asked Bob and Mildred if they would like a cup. Mildred looked at her husband and back at Tammy. "No, dear. It's almost five o'clock, and we thought we would catch a bite at our favorite restaurant on the way home. But thank you anyway," answered Mildred.

"You're welcome. And thank you for all your help! We couldn't have done it without you." Tammy walked them to the door.

Mildred turned to Tammy as she was ready to leave and inquired, "When you need us to watch Bethany, you will call us, right? We will both come."

"Yes," she tentatively answered. She still didn't know how all of this was going to work. "I will need to go over my schedule with Mark and see when he would like you to be here. I will let you know later this evening. I know for sure I will need you on the weekend schedule."

She knew Mark always helped at night on the weekends but wasn't sure how his schedule went now that Mike and Jenna were back, or if he would even consider watching Bethany in the evenings. Maybe that would be asking too much of him. He lived such a busy life.

Mildred placed a gentle hand on Tammy's arm. "Just let us know, dear. Have a good rest of your evening."

Bethany ran up to the door to give Mr. and Mrs. Langley a hug. She pulled away and waved her hand. "Bye!" She grinned.

When they left, Bethany, jumping up and down, exclaimed, "Can I go swimming now?" Tammy smiled down at her daughter.

"If you will give me ten minutes to get dinner started, we can go for a swim."

"Yay!" she shouted. "I'll go put my suit on!" Good thing she packed their swimsuits! She wasn't aware Mark had a pool but thought maybe they could spend a day at the beach, since they were closer. She hurried into the kitchen to start dinner.

Mark greeted his brother and new sister-in-law with a big hug. Cameron followed suit. He and Mike loaded their luggage in the trunk while Jenna and Cameron climbed into the back seat. Once they were all settled inside the car, Mark put his BMW into drive and headed out of the airport. Traffic was heavy, but soon cleared out once they were able to get on the highway. Mark could hear Cameron asking a lot of questions about the pictures Jenna was showing him on her cell phone.

Mike wanted to know how things went at the restaurant while they were gone. Mark glanced over at his brother who was the spitting image of himself. Being identical twins, without people knowing them personally, most couldn't tell them apart. He focused his eyes back on the road.

"Mike, aside from Monday and Tuesday, which are our slow days, we were slammed the rest of the week. We really need to focus on hiring more staff. The staff is getting worn out, especially on Friday and Saturday nights. I for one should have taken your advice about hiring a temp to help with the accounting. It was all I could do to keep up with payroll, reports, and working out on the floor every night. Jack is doing a great job, but it took the two of us and our hostesses to keep up with the reservations and the overflow of customers. And just to let you know, I'm taking tomorrow off. I need to refuel as I haven't been able to get much rest this past week." He wasn't going to expound on that last sentence. He wanted to wait until he had Mike alone to explain what had been happening in his life since the day he took them to the airport for their honeymoon.

Mike, listening to his brother, sensed something was off. Watching him give the updates on the restaurant, he seemed tense, like he was holding back. The stress lines on his face showed how this past year had affected him. He looked worn out. "Listen, why don't you take Tuesday off as well, bro. Jenna and I can handle it. And hey! If you need Wednesday, take it. You deserve some down time. You haven't had a vacation in over a year."

Mark took a quick glance at his brother. "Thanks, bro. I was thinking about taking a week to ten days sometime around the holidays. And I am going to take you up on that offer. I'll plan on coming in on Thursday. I'll give Jenna a call in the morning to update her on what's been done and what she will need to do to finish up. The report is done for the auditors coming in tomorrow."

Mike, studying his brother across the seat, again felt a certain distance in his voice. "Okay, Mark, I'll let her know."

Mark was relieved. With three days off he could catch up on some work that needed to be done at his home. Mark asked his brother how their trip went, and the rest of the way was taken up with Mike expressing all the sights of Paris, along with some of the finest restaurants they enjoyed eating at.

Half-listening, he pulled into Mike's driveway, as his thoughts went back to the officer he saw outside his home earlier today. He looked so familiar, but he hadn't seen him on the force before. It bothered him. He wore sunglasses, so his face was slightly hidden.

He would be sure to get ahold of Zack and maybe do some investigating on his own while he had this time off.

He helped take in Mike and Jenna's luggage. Mike turned to him and asked if he and Cameron would like to stay and have pizza with them.

"Can we, Dad, can we?" an excited Cameron asked.

Mark, looking down at his son hated to disappoint him, but he really wanted to get home to see if Tammy and her daughter were able to get settled. "We would love to, but Cameron and I have plans. We'll take a rain check on that pizza some other time."

"Aww, Dad! Why can't we stay? I'm hungry!" he practically shouted.

Mark looked down at his son with eyes that brooked no argument. He expressed in a stern voice, "Cameron, we need to go. I'll fix something when we get home."

Cameron marched over to the door and waited for his dad. With his arms crossed, and anger written all over his little face with not getting his way, Mark was well aware of this behavior since the divorce.

Mark turned back and shook hands with his brother, then gave Jenna a hug. "Glad you're home and that you both had a good time on your trip to Paris. I'll see you later this week." Mark ushered an upset Cameron out the door.

As Mike and Jenna watched the door close, Jenna turned and eyed her husband. "Is it me or is something going on with your brother?" she asked.

Mike, full of speculation in his eyes, glanced over at his wife and wondered the same thing. "I don't know, Jenna. Something's off. I felt it in the car on the way over here. Maybe with a few days off he'll come around." Mike was sure his brother wasn't telling him everything when he asked about the business. When he could get him alone, he would confront him and find out what's going on.

Looking in his rearview mirror on their way home, Mark saw his son sitting in the back, with his arms crossed, pouting, as he looked out the window. He was not a happy camper. He decided to wait till they were home before he explained things. Then Cameron would see why they couldn't stay for pizza.

CHAPTER 9

Tammy, stepping out of the lanai onto the patio, couldn't get over the beauty of the sparkling, pristine, kidney-shaped pool, with the flowering hibiscus plants in brilliant colors placed perfectly around the outer perimeter of the pool. A hot tub, the water gently bubbling, was positioned next to the pool, with a waterfall flowing down into the water. Looking out over the manicured lawn, rich, green shrubbery outlined the perimeter of the back yard. The heavenly scent of the flowering trees and colorful birds of paradise along with anthuriums, in shades of red and pink, were planted in various areas of the property. Palm trees swayed in the gentle breeze. It made her feel she was in another world that she never wanted to come out of.

Bethany, impatiently pulling on her hand, cried, "Come on, Mom! Let's jump in!"

Tammy laid the extra towels she had brought out with her down on one of the lounge chairs. They walked up to the edge of the pool. Holding hands, they counted to three. With one big splash, they both jump into the warm water. Tammy swam a little ways away from her, turned around, and watched her daughter dogpaddle toward her. She laughed.

"You are getting really good at your swimming skills, Bethany!"

They played and splashed in the water till Tammy needed to go in and check on dinner. Bethany had paddled over to the other side of the pool when Tammy yelled out. "Hey, Bethany, I need to check on dinner. We need to go in now."

Bethany paddled back toward her mom. "Oh, Mommy, can't we stay in a little longer?" she pleaded.

Tammy knew this would happen when it was time to get out. She smiled down at her daughter with dancing eyes. "Okay, just five more minutes. Then we have to go in."

"Yay!" she shouted, splashing all around. She watched her daughter climb up the steps and out of the pool to get one of the beach balls. She threw it over to her, and the game began! She laughed; she could get used to this!

Mark and Cameron came into the house through the garage door. Cameron, who was still not talking to his dad, walked down the hall to the living room. His arms were still crossed when he looked around the room. Mark watched his son, wondering whether he was in for a temper tantrum. When Cameron's eyes grew big, he let out a loud, "Wow, Dad! Somebody cleaned our house!"

Surprised, Mark looked around his home, and sure enough, somebody had cleaned it. The wood furniture in the living area was polished to a glossy finish, and the glass table that sat off to the side of the lanai's sliding glass door gleamed in the sunlight coming in. Cameron sniffed. He went into the kitchen, with his dad following behind him. He opened the oven. "Somebody has been cooking in our kitchen, and it smells really good, Dad!"

Mark had to chuckle. This was starting to sound like the story of the "Three Bears." He wondered where Goldilocks was, when he got his answer. The sounds of laughter came in through the lanai.

"It sounds like somebody is out in our pool, Dad!" Cameron ran out into the lanai and glanced out the screen door. "And look, Dad!

There they are! What are we going to do, Dad? Are you going to call the police?"

Mark couldn't help himself. He burst out laughing. "No, son. We are not going to call the police. Do you recognize the little girl in the pool with her mom?"

Cameron took another look. Squinting, he tried to figure out who she was. Suddenly he remembered. "Is that Bethany? The girl you saved that day we went to the ice cream parlor?"

"Yes, son. What do you say we go out and say hello, and I will explain why they're here at dinner."

Cameron didn't even waste time answering his dad as he threw open the screen door and barreled out! He ran over to where Bethany was, pulled his sandals off, and jumped in!

"Cameron, you're home!" cried Bethany.

Cameron, laughing, asked, "What are you and your mom doing here?"

Laughter bubbling up inside her when she retorted, "We've come to stay with your dad!"

Mark, hearing and watching the two, knew the cat was already out of the bag so to speak. He would clarify things after they had dinner.

He turned, and what he saw made his heart stop. He watched Tammy, looking like a goddess, come out of the water. In a modest two-piece turquoise tankini, the wet suit clinging to her body showed every single curve. His eyes fastened on her firm breasts revealing in the suit. It left him imagining all the ways he wanted to touch that gorgeous body of hers, starting with her long brown hair that clung to her shoulders and back. Her tanned skin glistened in the sun as the water ran off her body. He swallowed. He couldn't take his eyes off her as she ran to the lounge chair to pick up a towel. If the kids weren't here, he'd pull her down with him and make love to her right here on the patio floor! He continued to gaze at her intently as she nervously wrapped the towel around her, covering up that perfect body of hers.

Walking toward him, Tammy saw the hunger in his deep-blue eyes that left her trembling as she came up next to him. He looked devastating in a yellow knit shirt and khaki shorts. Brown sandals adorned his feet. It was the first time she had ever seen him in casual wear. He was always in a suit or sport coat. Her body tingled under his watchful gaze. She held onto her towel a little tighter as her words tumbled out.

"Mark, I hope you don't mind. Bethany wanted a swim after we put away our things and started dinner." She was so nervous whenever she was around him, especially after he'd seen her in her swimsuit, that her voice slightly shook. She needed to distance herself from him. "Speaking of which, I need to go check on it!" She yelled back to her daughter, "Bethany, it's time to get out. Dinner will be ready soon."

"Aww, Mom!" she pleaded. "Can't we stay in a little longer?"

"No, Bethany. Your five minutes was up five minutes ago! Now, get out of the pool! You need to dry off and get into some dry clothes," she said sternly.

"You too, Cameron, it's time to come out," he confirmed.

They watched the kids come out of the pool, complaining all the way into the lanai. She had set two towels on the table for them to dry off when they came in. Mark took one and Tammy the other. When they were as dry as possible, Tammy led Bethany back to their room. They both took a quick shower and changed into dry clothes. She combed out Bethany's hair, then her own. Once their wet suits were hung in the bathroom to dry, they headed out to check on dinner.

Bethany went to find Cameron, while Tammy went into the

kitchen. She opened the oven door to check on the chicken casserole she had put in, seeing it was just about done. The only thing left was to make the salads and put the potato rolls in to warm.

Mark came up behind her as she closed the oven door. "It smells delicious. What are you cooking?" he asked in anticipation.

Startled, she turned around only to find him so close their bodies almost touched. Her heart started to pound. She leaned back against the stove, trying to put a little distance between them. "Uh… I made a chicken casserole. I hope you and Cameron are hungry. There's plenty for all of us."

He caught her pretty amber eyes with his. His urge to kiss her and feel the passion again between them was overpowering. His eyes moved to her long brown hair caressing along her back and shoulders. It was still wet from her shower, and the scent of coconuts made him want to reach up and run his fingers through the long strands. His eyes roamed slowly down her body, stopping at her breasts slightly peeking out from the loose-fitting top she was wearing. When his eyes continued his perusal, he admired her flat stomach, her long smooth legs, all the way down to her bare feet. His eyes traveled back up to her eyes with a purpose. He started to lean down to her soft lips as he whispered, "Starving."

With her heart beating wildly, she watched those deep-blue eyes move inch by inch closer to her. She knew it wouldn't be long before his lips met hers. She wanted more than anything to be caught up in the passion they shared last night. But not with the kids in the next room, who could walk in on them any minute. When he bent his head to touch his lips to hers, she slipped out and away from him. "Mark, the kids," she pleaded.

Mark, with the hunger still blazing in his eyes, filled with arousal, tried to calm the stirrings deep inside his body. When he glanced her way, he saw the apprehension in her facial expression and knew she was right. He seemed to lose his head when he was close to her. He placed his hands in his pockets and took a deep breath. He gave her a slight smile. "What can I do to help with dinner?"

She relaxed a little. "Could you put on a pot of coffee? And maybe get the rolls ready for the oven?" she asked tentatively. "I'll make the salads and set the table, and we should be ready to eat."

He felt the tension leaving him from the pent-up emotions he was feeling. This time he gave her a real smile and said, "Sure."

They got to work, and it wasn't long before they called Cameron and Bethany to the table. When they were halfway through dinner, Cameron turned to his dad. "Dad, Bethany said that her and her mom are going to be staying with you until they catch the bad guy."

"Yes, Cameron. It's true. They will be staying with me. When your mom gets here, I will be sitting down with all of you and explain all that has happened since the day we went to the ice cream parlor. But for now, let's enjoy this delicious meal that Bethany's mom put together for us."

Listening, Tammy had forgotten that she would be meeting his ex-wife sometime in the future. Suddenly she felt apprehensive. What was this woman going to think about them staying with her ex-husband? Did Mark still have feelings for her? She knew through the grapevine that he was shocked and terribly hurt when he found out she was having an affair. It's been a little over a year since it happened.

She was brought out of her thoughts when her daughter nudged her and asked, "Mommy, did you bring the cherry cobbler from home?"

"I did!" she said, smiling down at her daughter. She looked around the table. "Is everyone ready for dessert?"

With a resounding yes from everybody, Tammy got up from the

table to serve up the cobbler. Mark followed suit and started to pick up the supper dishes.

"Come on, you two. Let's give Tammy a hand and get these dishes put in the sink."

With that done, Mark asked if she would like a cup of coffee. When she said yes, he poured them each a cup and added a little cream to both. Tammy took the plates of cobbler to the table, while Mark followed with the coffee.

When they were all seated again, Cameron raved, "Boy, it's been a long time since we've had a meal like this, and dessert too!"

"Hey!" Mark retorted. "I'm not that bad of a cook!" he said with amusement in his eyes.

Cameron laughed. "Let's face it, Dad. You like to cook hamburgers and hotdogs!" They all laughed.

"Someday I'm going to surprise you and cook something exotic!"

Cameron, continuing to laugh, said, "Right, Dad!"

"You just wait and see!" He chuckled. He looked over at Tammy and winked.

Tammy, blushing, couldn't resist. "I think I would like to see that myself!"

Surprised, Mark never backed down from a challenge. With determination set in his eyes, he looked around the table at each one of them. "All right, I accept the challenge. A week from today, you will have one of the best meals you will ever eat!" His eyes narrowed in on Tammy. She chuckled.

With twinkling eyes, she responded, "I can't wait!"

When they finished their dessert, the kids went off to watch their movie in the other room while Mark and Tammy cleaned up the kitchen. While she was rinsing the dishes, Mark put them in the dishwasher. He needed to go over some things with her, so, casually, he announced, "I'm taking the next three days off from work. I need some down time after the two weeks I put in. Also, there was a cop out here, in an unmarked car, watching the house when I left to go pick up Cameron. I hadn't seen him before, and I want to get with Zack to see if they had hired a new man on the force, or if it is someone in another department on the island."

Tammy stopped what she was doing. She turned to him to inquire, "I hear some doubt in your voice. Do you think it could be someone tied to the human-trafficking ring?"

"I don't know, Tammy, but I got a bad vibe when I drove by his car. I'm going to do some investigating on my own while I'm off. When you are at work, please don't mention anything about what's going on to your co-workers until I've had a chance to talk to Mike."

She didn't know what was ahead of her when she went into work tomorrow, so she tentatively asked, "Which reminds me. Did you find out who saw us kissing last night? After Megan gave me the look, I need to prepare myself for the worst tomorrow night."

"It was Jack. He was bringing in one of the register trays to put away when he saw us. I had a talk with him. Our secret will be kept safe."

Tammy breathed a sigh of relief. At least she wouldn't have to worry about the kiss, but what about Megan? She was clearly upset, seeing her sitting with the boss. She would have to come up with something to defuse the situation should Megan approach her. "That's good to know." She turned away from him to finish rinsing the dishes.

Mark noticed the downcast expression running across her pretty face. "Tammy," he said softly. He grazed his fingers along her chin. "Look at me." She turned toward him, and effortlessly met his eyes. "I want you to know that I don't regret the times we kissed. In fact, I don't care if people know it. But I realized last night, because of the rules we set, it could be very hard on you at work. And I don't want that for you. I will be more discreet when I'm working out on the floor with you." Standing so close to her, and feeling her soft skin beneath his fingers, it was hard for him to resist. "Tammy, I feel something for you that I haven't felt for a woman in a long time. So I hope you won't mind…if I kiss you again," he whispered.

Tammy, with her eyes locked with his, couldn't move. She felt his arms go around her and pull her close. When his firm lips pressed against hers, she was lost, lost to the feel of his lips moving in a slow, sensual rhythm. Her arms traveled up around his neck as she pulled him closer to her, the passion building until she thought she might explode.

Mark groaned as he felt her response to his kisses. He crushed her to him as he deepened the kiss. The passion he felt for this woman surpassed anything he had ever experienced before. He wanted her in his bed, to feel her soft skin next to his, their bodies moving to the rhythm of their own heart's desire.

Suddenly, he heard bells ringing far off in the distance of his mind. He was so caught up in the moment he dismissed it completely until the bells didn't stop. When he heard little feet running to the door, he painfully broke the kiss.

Dazed, Tammy peered into eyes filled with raw desire that matched her own. "Did I just hear bells ringing?"

He half smiled as he dropped his arms from around her. "That would be my ex-wife. Sorry, I need to go see her."

When he walked around her, she felt like she had been hit with a cold bucket of water! It took her a few moments to get ahold of herself. She turned to finish cleaning up the kitchen. When she was done, she splashed cold water over her swollen lips, straightened up her hair with her fingers, and hoped when she met his ex-wife, she didn't look like she had been making out with her ex.

Tammy stepped into the living room. She saw Mark sitting across from an attractive woman with jet-black hair and sparkling green eyes. Dressed in jeans and a t-shirt, she looked very much at home here.

Cameron, sitting next to his dad, remarked, "Bethany and her mom are going to stay here."

The expressions crossing her face were ones of mild shock and surprise as she stared at Mark. Sherry wasn't sure how to process this information. There was an instant surge of jealousy that struck her. She always knew he was devastatingly attractive, and the thought of him with another woman jolted her, which was ridiculous. She was in her own relationship with Al. But it seemed to be out of place for him to invite a woman and her child into his home whom he hardly knew. Her eyes traveled behind him to the woman in question. "Is this the woman who is staying with you?"

Both Mark and Cameron turned around to see Tammy standing directly behind them. Cameron turned to his mom and said, "Yep!"

"Cameron, why don't you go and finish watching your movie with Bethany while we three adults have a talk." Cameron sighed as he got up off the sofa to go into the entertainment room.

Mark watched till his son was in the room, before he turned to Tammy and gestured for her to come and sit down. Tammy came around the sofa and up to the woman. "Tammy, this is my ex-wife, Sherry. Sherry, this is Tammy."

Tammy held out her hand. "It's very nice to meet you." She smiled.

Sherry didn't return the favor and just nodded, eyes glaring into her.

Tammy's smile faded as she dropped her hand and took a seat on the loveseat, clearly snubbed by her. Mark was watching his ex's behavior. He didn't like Sherry's rudeness towards her. His eyes traveled over to Tammy's and locked. He gave her a reassuring smile. He would make sure to let her know not to let his ex-wife get to her. He glanced back over to his ex and started in.

"Tammy and her little girl are staying with me because of an incident which involved a human-trafficking ring several weeks ago. I'm not sure if Cameron had mentioned it to you. If he did, it was a short version and not the full scope of what has happened since then."

"Well, he did mention some girl being captured by a bad man and that you and an officer helped save her. I didn't think much about it after that," Sherry confessed.

Typical, he thought dryly.

"Listen, Sherry," he spoke with conviction, "I'm going to explain the situation to you, and I want you to pay close attention to what I'm about to tell you, because it involves our son as well."

That statement made her sit up and take notice. "What do you mean?" she asked, concern written all over her face.

Mark glanced back over at Tammy to see how she was doing. Sitting there like a wooden statue, his first inclination was to get up and bring her back to sit beside him. He didn't like the fact that she was so far away from him. After the way Sherry snubbed her, he knew Sherry could be vicious at times when it suited her. He locked eyes with her again in a meaningful gesture, to let her know everything would be okay. He turned his eyes back to his ex.

Mark started explaining what had happened since the day of the incident outside the ice cream parlor. When he finished, Sherry sat up and practically yelled at him at the top of her lungs. "Do you mean to tell me that my son is in danger from a human trafficker all because of that woman and her little girl?" pointing her finger at Tammy. "Why couldn't you have walked away? Then this would never have been an issue with my son!"

Mark's blood began to boil as he tried to control the anger inside of him. How in the world did he think he was ever in love with this woman! How could she be so selfish! Did she ever really know him? Mark leaned forward with eyes that showed the anger he was feeling. He took a deep breath, trying to control his anger before he spoke. "First of all, Sherry, he is our son, and do you really believe I would walk away from someone in distress?" he asked impatiently. "What if the situation was reversed? Would you not want someone to go after the guy who was trying to take our son?"

Flustered, she answered him. "Well, of course I would want him to go after him! But it's not the same thing!"

Mark rose from the sofa, and just as he was about to say something he was sure he would regret, Tammy came up to him.

"Listen," she said softly, "I'm going to go and check on the kids. You two need to be alone to talk this through, for both our kids' sakes." As she walked away, she gave a slight smile to Sherry as she left the room.

He felt some of the anger leave him as his eyes followed her. Just her voice had a calming effect on him. He sighed as sat back down on the couch. With eyes full of determination, he focused on his ex-wife. "Look, Sherry, it happened, all right? I can't turn the clock back. We all need to work together to keep both Cameron and Bethany safe. The first thing I want you to do is talk to the principal and his teacher tomorrow morning, to make them aware of the situation. The police already have the details and they're working on it. You as well need to keep a close watch on him. You should also inform Al, so that all who are with him stay alert."

Al was the man Sherry was living with. He didn't know much about the relationship, nor did he care.

Sherry, sitting across from him, listening to what he said, knew he was right. She stood up from the chair, regaining her composure as she started walking toward the door. She turned back as she reached it. She looked him square in the eyes and said with confidence, "I'll make sure everyone is notified as to what is going on. Please give my apologies to Tammy. I didn't mean to upset anyone. Telling me our son is in danger was such a shock. If you could go and get Cameron for me, we'll go."

Gladly, he thought.

When he went into the room, the movie they were watching had just ended. "Cameron." His son turned toward him. "Your mom's waiting for you, it's time to go."

"Aww, Dad. Do I have to?"

"Yes, son," he answered. "You'll be back on Thursday, so remember what I told you about keeping an eye out for strangers."

"I will, Dad."

"Good. Now say goodbye to Ms. Gardner and Bethany."

"Goodbye, Ms. Gardner. Goodbye, Bethany," he said sadly as he went out to his mom.

"Goodbye, Cameron! I'll see you Thursday!" shouted Bethany.

Mark followed them out to make sure they were safely in their car. After they left, he looked around. It seemed all was clear. He didn't know if Zack would have a car out tonight. He would be sure to set the alarm system when he went in. When he came in through the door, Tammy and Bethany were just coming out of the kitchen. He smiled and asked, "Do you have a moment? I'd like to show you the alarm system, so you can set it when I'm not here."

"I was just about to put Bethany to bed, so if it can wait, I'll be out in just a bit."

His eyes glimmered as he shot back. "It can wait."

It took a few minutes to get Bethany settled. She wanted a story, so she read one from one of her favorite story books they brought from home. When she was finally able to leave her, she came out of the bedroom, only to find Mark was nowhere to be found. She searched the rooms, and finally, looking out through the lanai, she saw him sitting in a lounge chair, watching the roaring fire in the outside fireplace. She strolled out onto the patio and placed a gentle hand on his shoulder. He jumped. Turning to catch her pretty amber eyes, his blue eyes smiled into hers. He took her hand and guided her down to sit beside him. She returned his smile while she studied his handsome face.

"You wanted to show me the alarm system?"

Staring into her eyes, he wanted to do a lot more than show her the alarm system. He wanted this woman with his entire being. He'd thought of nothing else since he watched her come out of his pool earlier. He reached up with his hand and placed his fingers through her long tresses and moved them back behind her ear.

Tammy saw the hot desire in his eyes as he ran his fingers through her hair. She had been waiting a long time for him to notice her, never dreaming that she would be sitting here, so close, that all she had to do was lean in, touch her lips to his, and feel the passion explode inside her again. She needed to put a stop to these feelings before she couldn't. His eyes continued to hold her in place. She felt his finger slide down her cheek, to her neck, and ever so gently to the middle of her chest. His hand slid in to capture her breast.

"Mark, I…" She groaned and closed her eyes, as his hand worked like magic to bring out new sensations throughout her body. With his other arm, he pulled her up against his chest, lowered his head, and took possession of her lips. Mark felt the passion ignite deep inside him as he moved his hand over her firm breast. He pulled his hand away long enough to reach under her tank top to lift it above her breasts. He unclasped the front of her lacy bra and brushed it away, leaving her breasts exposed to his hand, exploring every inch of those perfect mounds. Her response to his hand made him want more. His lips traveled down to capture one firm breast and then the other, teasing her with his tongue and teeth while his hand traveled down till he found her navel. He circled his thumb around her sensitive area before he explored further. When his hand found her center through her clothes, he heard her cry out. He eased her body around, so she was lying next to him on the lounge. His lips found hers again in a gentle kiss. He lifted his head and gazed deep into her eyes.

"Tammy," he breathed, "I want you. I want you here and now. Are you on birth control?"

Tammy came out of her dazed state to see his eyes burning with hunger for her. Oh, how could she have let this happen! She needed to stop this now! "Mark… I can't." She tried to get up, but he held her there.

"Hey," he whispered, "if you're not on the pill, I can go get something. I won't let you get pregnant."

She stared into eyes that were guarded as she answered him. Her eyes pleading, she whispered, "I'm sorry, can you please let me up? I'm not ready for this."

His eyes narrowed. "You were ready a few minutes ago," he taunted. He tried to kiss her again. She placed her hands on his chest to stop him from going any further.

"Please," she insisted. He saw the anguish in her eyes and let her go. "Mark, please understand. To answer your question, I'm not on any birth control. I haven't been in a relationship since before my ex-husband left me, so I didn't feel the need. I'm scared, Mark. I need to be sure before I enter into a relationship with you or any man. I've been hurt. I don't want to go through that again."

He understood more than she knew. He'd been hurt to the point he couldn't function. He knew he needed to slow down with her. He wanted her, but as hard as it would be, he would wait. He smiled and gently placed his hand on her cheek. He gave her a gentle kiss. Bringing her back up across his lap, he gently fastened her bra back in place, then pulled her tank top down over her waist. "I understand," he whispered. "Now go to bed, before I'm tempted to kiss you again."

She reached up and placed her hand along the side of his face, feeling the roughness of his shadow beard against her fingers. With tears starting to form in her eyes, she searched his, and whispered, "Thank you."

Within seconds, she was up and gone, leaving Mark to wonder how he was going to keep his heart in check. He was falling for her. He was ready, but she wasn't. He sat and watched the fire for a long time before he finally decided to go to bed. He needed to be up early to co-ordinate schedules and get with Zack on the cop that was out here earlier. He turned the fireplace off, made sure all the doors were locked, but before he set the alarm, he pulled the curtain aside by the front door to have a look out front.

All was clear so far. He didn't see a car sitting out on the street. He would text Zack, to set up a meeting with him to go over any new information on the case. He let the curtain drop, set the alarm, and headed to his room. As he walked by the guest room where Tammy and her daughter were staying, he stopped. There were no sounds coming from the room. She must have fallen asleep. He sighed and headed towards his room at the end of the hall. When he fell into bed, he prayed that sleep would come.

Tammy, wide awake in the twin bed next to her daughter's, tried to stay quiet, so she wouldn't wake her. Her emotions were in turmoil. She wanted so badly to give in to these feelings she had for him, but what happens when the moment ends? Then what? Would he still want her after she gave him what he wanted? She couldn't risk it. She'd been there, done that. Hearing steps coming down the hall, they stopped. She held her breath, her heart beating rapidly. When she heard him move on, she let it out. She closed her eyes and told herself not to think. Morning would come way too soon!

CHAPTER 10

THE NEXT MORNING, Mark got a look at the most fast-paced, hectic morning he had ever seen since his marriage to his ex-wife. He had forgotten what it was like to rush around to get Cameron off to school and himself to work on time. Coming into the kitchen, Bethany was sitting at the counter, eating a bowl of cereal, while Tammy was running around gathering up their things to take with them. She stopped when she saw Mark pouring himself a cup of coffee.

"Mark." He turned towards her. "I forgot to go over our schedule with you last night. It can get pretty hectic in the mornings." When she caught his gaze, he seemed distant to her. She nervously went on. "I have Mrs. Langley coming at three thirty today to watch Bethany. I thought it was best to keep the same schedule. I hope you don't mind." His eyes narrowed in on her.

"No, I told you when you moved into my home to feel free to do whatever you need to do." He was a little irritable, and it showed through his words.

Tammy didn't like the abruptness in his voice. Well, if he was going to be like that, she could too!

Before she could get any words out, Bethany asked, "Mr. Mark?" His eyes shifted to the little girl. "Are you grumpy this morning?" That shocked him! Kids could always pick up on adult behavior. He needed to keep his emotions in check. He smiled.

"I'm sorry Bethany. I am a little grumpy. I didn't sleep well last night," he confessed.

Her little face scrunched up as she asked, "Why not?"

He chuckled. "Let's just say I've had a lot on my mind." His eyes drifted back to Tammy's. She blushed, as he watched her in that unnerving way of his. She dropped her eyes and focused on her daughter.

"Bethany, are you ready to go? We need to leave a little early to get you to school on time."

"Yes, Mama. I'll go get my bookbag." She jumped off the chair, running to the bedroom.

Tammy stood there, not knowing what to say. *This is ridiculous*, she thought to herself. She was in his arms twice yesterday, in heated passion, and she couldn't find the words to express how she was feeling at this moment. She glanced over to watchful eyes. He set his cup down and strolled over to her. As she opened her mouth to say something, he stopped her.

Placing his finger across her lips, "You don't need to say anything. You need to get Bethany to school and start your internship. We'll talk later." His intense gaze left her reeling, along with his touch sending tingles down her spine.

Bethany came running out to let her know that she was ready. "Okay, Mama, we need to go or we'll be late!"

She tore her eyes away from his to glance at her watch. "Oh, you're right!" She hurried to gather the rest of her things. As she was walking out the door, she turned and caught his eye. When they were able to talk again, she would tell him about her marriage to Roy, how it closed her off to getting involved in a relationship with anyone. She heard her daughter yelling to hurry up. She pulled her eyes away and closed the door.

Mark, his eyes locked with hers, watched as she turned and walked out the door. He felt the silence. They'd only been with him one day and he was already contemplating what it would be like when they went back home after this was over. He didn't like it. After the passion they shared, he knew in his heart he wouldn't want to let her go. He let out a breath.

He took a sweet roll out of the fridge and warmed it up in the microwave. He refilled his coffee cup and took a seat at the counter. As he was sitting there, he wondered what her marriage had been like. She said she hadn't been in a relationship since before Bethany was born. He must have hurt her pretty bad for her to keep erecting these walls every time he wanted to take another step to making love with her. One day he would find out what happened between them, and then he would work on breaking those walls down. He smiled as he thought about how he would accomplish this goal. He finished his roll and coffee and placed the dishes in the sink. He needed to get ahold of Zack this morning to see if he had any more information on the case, and to see if the guy sitting out in front of his house yesterday morning worked for the police department. It gave him an uneasy feeling. If Zack had nothing to give him, he'd look into it himself.

After Tammy dropped Bethany off at school, she drove over to the university to attend one of Ms. Beret's sessions with one of her patients. When she entered her office, Ms. Beret was seated behind her desk. She looked up as Tammy took her usual seat to observe her patient's session for today. "Good morning, Tammy."

"Good morning Ms. Beret," she replied.

"Before my patient comes in, I wanted to go over a field day with you. Ms. Sinclair said you had no objections on visiting patients on their own turf?" she inquired.

Her heart started to beat a little faster when she answered, "No, Ms. Beret, I have no objections on going out, but I need to inform you of an incident involving my daughter that leaves me apprehensive about it." She started to explain what had transpired over the last several weeks, but was interrupted when Ms. Beret's patient entered her office.

"We'll discuss this later," she said in a hushed voice. She turned to her patient as Abby took a seat on the sofa. "Hello, Abby." She smiled. "You know my intern, Tammy."

"Yes, hello," she answered shyly. Tammy nodded and smiled at the young girl. Ms. Beret came out from around her desk with her pad and pen in hand. She took a seat in the plush chair next to the sofa where Abby was sitting, and the session began.

Tammy ended up sitting in on several of Ms. Beret's patients that day. Taking notes throughout each session and asking questions when the patient left kept her on her toes. She was learning so much about each patient, and how mental illness affected each one differently. It was two o'clock when her last session finished. Tammy's head was in a whirl as she tried to process all the information she took in.

Ms. Beret looked at her watch. "I'm sorry, Tammy. I have an appointment at two thirty and I must leave."

"Oh, but I wanted to discuss the incident involving my daughter with you."

"We'll discuss it on Wednesday, before we go out into the field. Can you be here at nine thirty?" she asked. It would be a stretch, but she could make it if she dropped Bethany off at school a little early.

"Yes, I will be here."

"Good, I'll see you then."

Tammy sat and watched her leave her office. She needed a few minutes to gather her thoughts. She didn't think she would be going out into the field this soon. She was hoping she could have stalled going out until this whole thing with the human traffickers was over.

She would need to talk to Zack, to see if he could have someone keep watch that day, or she would never be able to relax enough to be in a home with someone with mental illness.

Mark came into Zack's office and took a seat in front of his desk. "Hey, Zack," said Mark. "Thanks for fitting me into your schedule."

"No problem. When you called, you mentioned something about someone sitting out in front of your house yesterday morning?"

"Yes. He was someone that I'd never seen before and wondered if you had any new hires, or if he was from a different department?" he inquired.

"Well, we haven't had any new hires lately. Let me check the schedule to see if the lieutenant might have pulled an officer from another department to cover both you and Tammy yesterday." He logged into his computer and pulled up the schedule. Looking through it, he saw where they had a man watching over Tammy and her little girl right up until they moved into Mark's home. Then another officer took the next shift until seven o'clock, then he was called away on an emergency. They were so shorthanded in all departments, and with the crime rate skyrocketing, it was hard to keep up. It didn't appear that they had an officer out at Mark's during the time he specified.

"Sorry, Mark, but it doesn't look like we had anyone at your house yesterday morning. Can you describe the driver and the car he was in?"

Surprised, he answered, "Yes, he was in a black sedan. He was clean shaven, his hair was dark and cut short, looked to be a big man. He wore dark sunglasses, so I can't give you a full description of him. But he looked kind of familiar to me. Like I've seen him somewhere before."

"Well, it's not much to go on. Do you know the make and model of the car?"

"I'm pretty sure it was a 2020 Ford Taurus."

"Did you happen to get the license plate number?" asked Zack.

He shook his head. "No. Sorry, Zack. I was on my way to pick up Cameron and then on to the airport. I assumed at the time it was one of the police department's officers. It didn't hit me until later to question who he was."

"Let me do some checking, and I'll let you know what I can find out." He hesitated. He wasn't sure if he should ask… "So, how'd it go with Tammy and her daughter moving in?"

Mark stared back at Zack and wondered if he was fishing for something. He shrugged his shoulders. "Fine. They were all moved in when I came home after dropping Mike and Jenna off at their home. I noticed there was one of your officers at the house when I drove in, but when I looked out the window before I set the alarm, there was no one out there."

"Yes, the officer got a call and had to leave. According to the report, they did have an officer drive by several times last night. We are having a rough time covering all the calls that come in every night. It's going to be hard to keep your home covered. We have a man on Tammy and her daughter, but it may be hit and miss at your home."

Mark, digesting the information Zack had given him, wondered if he shouldn't talk to his brothers to help out. He wasn't sure if Peyton would be available, since he just started his new job several months ago. Mike, just getting back from his honeymoon, may not want to get involved in another case. He made a decision.

"Listen, Zack, can we keep this under wraps? I have a few days off, and with your permission, I would like to do some investigating on my own into the case."

"What do you have in mind?"

"Maybe I can scout around. Maybe check out some of those bars in the downtown area where no one in their right mind would go. I might pick up some information leading to the traffickers."

Zack looked at him like he needed his head examined. "Look, Mark. Most of our calls come from that area. It's dangerous. There are a lot of drug users, drug pushers, homicides… You could get hit with a stray bullet if you don't know what you're doing. My advice to you is to stay away from that area. I don't want to be called to a homicide and find out it was you. Let the police and the FBI that is working on the case handle it."

"So, tell me, have they put anything together on the man Tammy described, or the note I found on my car window?"

"As far as I know, no. But we're working on it." He watched Mark turn away from him, frustration printed all over his face.

He turned back. "Look, I can't stand on the sidelines, waiting and wondering when this guy might strike. It's my son and Tammy's daughter we are talking about. What about the guy you have in custody? Have you gotten any more information from him?" he asked with urgency.

"No, he's still not talking. I know you don't want to hear this, but he's due to make bail in a couple of days. His bail was set at a hundred thousand dollars. Some anonymous person is coughing it up."

Mark stood up from the chair and started pacing. He ran a hand through his hair and down his neck. He turned back to Zack. "So, what you're telling me is he's going to be back out on the streets!"

"I'm sorry, Mark. It happens all the time. It seems nowadays it's the person committing the crime that has the advantage over the victims."

Mark sat back down in the chair. Looking straight in Zack's eyes, determined, he stated, "Look, Zack. We have to do something. I can't just sit here and wait for something to happen. By then it might be too late."

"I understand what you're saying, but technically it's the FBI's case. We only became involved because of Bethany's near kidnapping. We can do our best to keep you and all others involved safe. Other than that, it's up to the FBI to bring down this trafficking ring." Watching Mark, Zack realized that what he told him only brought out the anger inside of him.

Mark stood up. He was beside himself with the thought that this guy getting out could have another attempt at taking another child. He glanced back at Zack. "Zack," Mark said with determination, "I'm not guaranteeing you that I won't go out and try to get information on this trafficking ring."

"Listen, Mark," returned Zack. "The guy who's being released, his name is Ned Morris. The FBI is going to have surveillance on him. So don't do anything stupid. Now this is off the record. If you get the itch to go out, call me. I'll go with you. We'll both go undercover. The last thing I need is for you to lose your life over this."

With fire in his eyes, Mark shot back, "You don't think I know how to use a gun?"

"Oh, I know you know how to use it, but I don't want you to land in prison for it, or dead!" This last remark seemed to calm Mark down a bit.

"Okay, Zack. I'll let you know. Keep me informed of any new updates."

Zack sat there and watched as Mark left his office. He prayed Mark would call him. Otherwise, he would be stepping into a war zone he might never get out.

Mark left the building feeling like he wanted to hit something. The thoughts of that jerk getting out and back on the streets in a matter of a few days made his blood boil! He decided he'd take a trip downtown during daylight hours to get a feel for the area. As he started out, he'd make a few stops along the way.

Mark was heading through downtown Honolulu, driving an old Chevy Nova. He stopped at a dealership, one that his buddy owned, to drop his BMW off for safekeeping. He wasn't going to drive it downtown where it could be hijacked. He parked in front of an old building with graffiti painted on the walls. Getting out of the car, Mark was wearing an old denim cap and dark sunglasses. Looking around the area, the streets were littered with paper, the alleyways were strewed with garbage bags along the walls, and the homeless people were going through bags of garbage to see if they could find something of worth or food to eat. It was a sad state. Across the street was a bar.

Well, he thought, *I might as well try that one first.* He walked in and took a seat at the bar, facing the window, where he could watch if someone came near his car. Not that it was worth anything, but he promised Nick he would pay retail price if anything happened to it. He sat down on one of the barstools, when the bartender came up to him.

An older man, wearing a short-sleeve stripped shirt that had seen better days, the buttons gapping as it stretched across his large stomach. He wore an old pair of black trousers that hung down below his waist. His white hair was spiked at the top of his head, and his face looked worn, showing the hard life that he lived. His faded blue eyes gave Mark the once over as he asked, "What can I get you to drink?"

Mark stared back at the man. He noticed he was missing a few of his front teeth. Probably from the bar fights he had been in, he assumed. "Give me a whiskey on the rocks." Mark pulled his wallet out and threw some bills on the counter. "And pour it in front of me."

The bartender looked back and huffed. He brought the whiskey over, put some ice in a glass, and poured the whiskey. Mark lifted it to his lips, took a sip, and grimaced. *Cheap whiskey*, he thought. *Just what I expected in a dump like this.*

"That'll be ten bucks."

Mark cocked his eyebrow and replied, "A lot of money for a shot of whiskey."

The bartender leaned up against the bar, grabbed his shirt, and growled into his face, "It's called inflation. Is there anything wrong with that?" He let go of Mark and shoved him back against his chair. For an old man, he showed a lot of strength.

Mark, who was shocked by the fact that he would try such a move, had a hard time holding back from flying over the counter and putting his lights out. It's no wonder that most of his teeth were gone. "I'll give you twenty more if you can tell me if this man has been in this bar before, or if you have seen him around town." Mark pulled the picture out of his back pocket and placed it on the counter. The bartender stared at the picture. He looked up with greedy eyes.

"Who wants to know?"

"I want to know!" he answered sternly.

"It's going to cost you," he drawled.

"How much?" he asked.

"Two hundred!" he taunted.

Mark turned around and swore under his breath, but not before he took a look to see if anyone was listening. He pulled out his wallet and slapped two one-hundred-dollar bills on the counter. The man went to grab the bills. Mark stopped him. "Not so fast! Tell me who he is, and where I can find him!"

Clearly upset he didn't get the cash before he had to answer, he spit it out. "His name is Jed Rawlings. He comes in here on occasion. But his usual hang out is over on Hyde Street at the Outback Bar."

Mark stood up, leaned over the bar, and by the same token, took ahold of the bartender's shirt. "Are you shooting me straight?" he demanded menacingly. "Because if you aren't, I'll be back, and you will regret you ever crossed me."

"I'm shooting you straight," he mumbled, the fear clearly in his eyes.

Mark let him go. He folded the picture, placed it back in his pocket, and walked out the door. The bartender saw that he didn't finish his drink. He picked it up and chugged it down while he watched the stranger get into his car. He would be sure to let Jed know someone was looking for him.

When Mark got into his car, he couldn't believe his luck! They just might have a lead on the case!

He took a drive over to Hyde Street to check out this bar and where it was located. When he pulled up in front of it, he noticed there were steps leading down to the entrance. He watched as men and women walked in and out of the bar. *Some rough-looking characters,* he thought. He waited for an hour to see if the man called Jed Rawlings showed up. With no sign of him, he decided to head back and have Zack check Intel before he came back.

Coming back into the dealership, Mark parked the car near his BMW. He went up to Nick and thanked him for the use of one of his cars. "Listen, Nick. I may have to borrow that car again. Can you keep from selling it for a few weeks? I'm working on a case with the police department."

A little white lie, he chided.

"Tell you what, Mark. Keep the keys, and I will mark it as sold. You can pick it up any time you need it. Just remember, you crash it—"

Mark interrupted, "I know, I know, I own it." Mark grinned and lifted his hand to shake Nick's. "Thanks, Nick. I owe you one. Don't hesitate to come into the restaurant and I will buy you and your family dinner."

"Thanks, Mark. I'll do that."

On his way back to the police station, he put in a call to Zack.

"Detective Williams," he answered.

"Zack, are you still at your office?"

"No, I'm out on an investigation concerning a previous homicide in the city. What's up?" he asked.

"I have the name of the guy in the picture that Tammy described to you and Detective Motts. I want to see if you could run it through your Intel."

"How did you come across that information?" he demanded.

"Never mind how I came across it. We need to see if he has a criminal background."

Listening, Zack had a feeling. "I'll be done here in an hour. I'll meet you back in my office then."

"Good. I'll go grab something to eat and meet you back there." He ended the call.

When he arrived back at Zack's office, both Detective Motts and Zack were waiting for him. As he sat down, Mark pulled out the picture. Looking from one to the other, he informed them, "His name is Jed Rawlings. He spends his time at the Outback Bar, downtown."

Zack didn't hesitate to grill him on how he got the information. "How did you come across this?" Mark could tell Zack was visibly upset.

"I took a drive downtown. The first bar I went into, I hit the jackpot!"

Zack turned to Detective Motts. "Go see what you can find out about this Jed Rawlings and get back with me ASAP!" He nodded as he left the office, closing the door behind him.

Zack turned back to Mark. He was silent, trying to decide how he was going to handle this. Mark and Mike have been good friends. They helped the police department in one of the biggest cases on the island, and he didn't want to jeopardize his relationship with them. "Listen, Mark. I appreciate you getting the name of this guy, but I clearly asked you not to go to the downtown area without someone with you. You could have been killed!"

"Look, Zack. I'm a big boy. I can take care of myself. You know this. Besides, I went during the day. Nothing happened."

Zack took a breath as he stared into the eyes of the man sitting across from him. He had no idea what he could have been up against. "Okay, tell me what you did to get the information, and don't leave anything out. Depending on who this guy is, you may have just set yourself up for disaster."

Mark explained how he changed cars and went into the downtown area, walked into the first bar he saw, and asked the bartender if he ever saw the guy in the picture. When he told him that yes, he knew him and where he could find him, he went to check out this bar on Hyde Street. "It's a real dive," expressed Mark.

"Most all of them are," returned Zack. "So, what now?" he asked.

"Well, we're going to wait and see what comes back on this guy. Then we'll go from there."

Detective Motts chose that moment to come back into the office. He placed his hands on the desk, and with a confused expression, he glanced at Zack. His voice slightly above a roar, he stated, "I can't find anything on this guy! Nothing is showing up on Intel! It's like he never existed!" He turned to Mark. "Are you sure that was the name he gave you?"

"Yes," Mark practically yelled. "Jed Rawlings is the name he gave me!"

Detective Motts through his hands in the air. "I wish I had something to tell you, but there just isn't anything there. I tried matching his name to the picture I drew, and nothing. Without more information on the guy, I'm afraid we're getting nowhere."

Zack's expression was grim. "Thanks, Frank. Keep me informed if you come up with anything else."

Detective Motts left the office, upset he wasn't able to give them anything on this guy. He would try again.

Zack turned to Mark. He looked like he would explode any minute. "I know what you're thinking. You are not going down there without me with you," he informed him. Mark stared into Zack's eyes with a piercing gaze.

"So," he asked, "when can you go? I want to check this bar out and see if we can find out for sure if that is his actual name, preferably tonight."

Zack could see that he wasn't going to change his mind about this. He knew if he said he couldn't go, he'd go on his own. "Tell you what. Meet me back here at eight o'clock. Make sure you are in some kind of disguise. We have a beat-up old van we'll take for just this type of undercover work. We'll check out this bar, and if he doesn't show, promise me you will let the FBI handle it." Mark wasn't sure he could promise his request.

"Let's hope we find him tonight. I'll be here at eight." With that, Mark left his office and headed out. He had to make another stop on his way home.

CHAPTER 11

Mark walked into his home and introduced himself to Mr. and Mrs. Langley. "I hope you don't mind, but I brought my husband with me since it takes twenty minutes to drive here. I didn't want to drive home alone so late at night," Mrs. Langley apologized.

"No, I don't mind at all." He smiled as he shook hands with them both. "It makes me feel better that you are both here."

"Bethany is watching a movie, and dinner is almost ready. Would you like to join us?" she asked.

"Thanks, but I picked up a sandwich just before I came home, so I'm all set."

Bethany came running into the living room when she heard voices. "Mr. Mark! You're home!"

Mark picked up the little girl when she flew into his arms. She wrapped her little arms around him and gave him a big hug. Mark hugged her back and asked how her day went. She prattled on about what happened at school and what she and her friends did at recess time.

"I didn't see any strangers around."

He smiled and put her down beside him. He came down on his haunches. He searched her little face. "And if you see any strangers, you will tell an adult, right?" She nodded her head yes. He stood up and ruffled her hair. "Good girl. Now, go finish your movie. I have to go out in a little while, and I need to check my emails." He watched Bethany run back into the entertainment room.

He turned back to the Langleys. In a low voice, he mentioned to them that he was going out with a detective to see about finding the guy Tammy saw a few days ago. "Could you keep Bethany busy? I don't want her to see me in a disguise. I wouldn't want to scare her, and I'm not up to answering twenty questions." He chuckled. "You know how they are at that age."

Mr. and Mrs. Langley laughed.

"Oh yes, we know," cried Mrs. Langley.

"Don't you worry, we'll keep her busy," said Mr. Langley.

"Good." He turned to head back to his study. When he turned on his computer, he checked his emails and saw he had a couple from Jenna. He answered the ones he needed to and deleted the rest. Once that was done, he headed to his bedroom to get ready for tonight.

Mike was sitting in the bar lounge after the small rush of customers came into the restaurant. Mondays were usually slow. Jack, their general manager, had Mondays off, so he would be closing the restaurant tonight. He was still feeling the jetlag from his honeymoon and felt like he was dragging all night long. Jenna had long gone home. He was eager for the night to end. He checked his watch. Two more hours to go.

Megan came by to refill his cup. After she filled it, she set the coffee pot down on the table. He glanced up to meet her eyes to say thank you when she burst out, "Mike, can I ask you something?"

He cocked an eyebrow up and smiled. "Ask away."

Megan sat down in the booth across from him and met his eyes. "Have you heard anything about Mark and Tammy having an affair?"

Mike looked dumbfounded. "No, I haven't. With me being gone

for two weeks, Mark and I haven't really talked since Jenna and I got back." Mike leaned forward. "What makes you think they are having an affair?" he asked sardonically.

Megan started to feel uncomfortable and thought she shouldn't have said anything. "I'm sorry, Mike. It's just that some of the employees are talking. They've been seen sitting together at times and look to be pretty chummy."

Mike, listening, did not like gossip. He had had enough of it when Kalea worked for them. "Look, Megan. I don't know what's going on, but sitting in a booth together doesn't mean that they are having an affair. I would appreciate you and the rest of the employees not discussing this further without knowing the facts. Understood?" he asked abruptly.

"Yes, sir," she mumbled. Megan got up from the booth a little shaken. Mike had never spoken in that tone of voice to her. She should have kept her mouth shut. She hoped she didn't lose her job over this.

After she left, Mike was trying to internalize what Megan had asked of him. He wondered now if that was why his brother's mind seemed to be somewhere else on the way home from the airport yesterday. He also appeared to be nervous about something. Could Mark and Tammy be having an affair? He hoped not. He knew the rules about dating employees. His eyes caught Tammy coming from the Hawaiian room. He wondered. He noticed she didn't seem to be her usual joyful self when he would seat customers in her section. She'd smile, then turn away, as if it was effort to be pleasant to her customers. As he observed her taking a cash tray to the hostess on duty to be cashed out, she appeared to be somewhat downcast. Whether his brother and Tammy were involved, she had a little girl to take care of. He would talk to his brother to get to the bottom of it.

Mark and Zack entered the Outback Bar. Mark was dressed in faded ripped jeans, a white t-shirt, paired with a blue plaid shirt opened in the front, and worn-out boots. He had dyed his hair black and put on a black mustache, along with a baseball cap on top of his head.

Zack was wearing black faded jeans, a black t-shirt, with a black vest opened in the front, and black boots. He also had on a pair of dark rimmed glasses perched on his face. He had spiked his hair and sprayed it with a red color right down the middle from front to back. Both had a small revolver tucked in an ankle holster inside their boots. As they looked around the room, they saw two open areas at the stand-up bar. They strolled over and leaned up against the railing. It wasn't long before one of the bartenders came up and asked what they wanted to drink.

He was a rough-looking character, built like a wrestler. His black hair was shaved close to his head. He wore a t-shirt that stretched across his massive chest, letting his bulging muscles show in his arms. He had on a white apron over his black pants, tied around the waist. His dark eyes peered into the eyes of the men standing at the bar when he yelled over the noise of the crowds, "What can I get you two fellas?"

"Give me a scotch, straight up," answered Mark.

"Give me your best draft beer on tap," said Zack.

When the bartender went to get their drinks, Zack turned to Mark. "Let me handle this. I've been in this bar and know there is a gaming room in the back. Do you know how to play poker?"

Mark nodded his head. "I'm familiar with it."

"Good. Looking around the room when we first came in, I didn't see a man fitting this Jed Rawlings' description. Let's see if the bartender knows of him and if he might by chance be in the back."

Mark nodded as the bartender set the drinks down on the

counter in front of them. "That will be four fifty for the scotch, and three fifty for the beer," he stated.

Zack pulled out his wallet and handed him a twenty. He made sure he saw the wad of bills in his wallet. "Keep the change. Listen, do you know a man by the name of Jed Rawlings? We heard he is a patron of this bar."

"Yeah, I know him. What's your business with him?"

"My friend and I heard he has a poker table in the back." Zack leaned in a little closer to the bartender's ear. "We were wondering if he could get us in. We know it's by invitation only, but we're looking to play some cards." He cocked his eyebrow up and shrugged his shoulders. "Maybe win a little money. Is he here tonight?" inquired Zack.

The bartender eyed the two, sizing them up. "Give me a minute," he responded.

Zack turned to Mark, "So far so good. Let's see if he can get us in."

They each sipped on their drinks while they waited. Mark glanced around the bar. It was a real dive. The carpet was frayed, and the tile floor was worn. The tables and chairs were marred and looked like they could use a good overhaul. The clientele was a mix of drug pushers, users, prostitutes, and men and women out to have a good time.

His eyes caught on a woman standing over on the side wall along with some others. Nice-looking woman, wearing a red tight-fitting sleeveless V-neck sweater, which showed off her large breasts. Her tight-fitting black leather skirt hung down to her mid-thigh. Black tights covered her long legs and she wore red stilettos to match her sweater. His eyes traveled back up to her platinum blond hair, pulled back into a twist with soft curls coming down along the sides of her cheeks. Her eyes were heavily made up, and her lips were covered in a bright-red lipstick. He watched as she turned to another woman standing with her. She said something to her, turned around, and locked eyes with him. She slowly waltzed up to him, swinging her hips in a provocative way. She nudged up against him and smiled demurely.

"Hi, honey," she purred. "You look lonely tonight," as she softly ran her finger down his neck, to his muscled chest, traveling down to his waist. "I can make your loneliness disappear and show you a real good time," she taunted. "How about it, handsome?" She smiled as she rubbed her large breasts up against him.

Mark moved slightly away. He grabbed her hand and placed it away from him. "Sorry, but I already have someone." He nodded his head toward Zack.

Zack, listening and watching the charade that was before him, decided he'd play along. "Yeah, lady, back off my man!"

Embarrassed, her stark blue eyes wide, the woman backed away. With her arms up, palms out, she stuttered, "Hey, I'm…s-sorry." Glancing back and forth between the two, she blurted out, "I never would have guessed that you two were *together*-together."

They both watched as she turned and went back to her place against the wall, where she turned to the other woman and expressed what happened to her.

Zack and Mark turned to each other and burst out laughing. Mark placed his hand on Zack's shoulder. "Thanks, man. I owe you one."

As they turned back toward the front of the bar, Zack replied, "No problem. Just don't get any ideas," he chided. Mark chuckled and sipped on his scotch.

While they were finishing up their drinks, the bartender came back and leaned over the bar. "Are you two still interested in a game?" Both nodded. "Come this way." He instructed them to come around the bar, and he led them to a back room down the hall. He opened the door and took them down several stairs into the room.

As they entered, four men were sitting around a gaming table. Mark's eyes perused the men, recognizing the man seated at the head of the table. Jed sized up the two men with his steel gray eyes.

"I hear you're looking to play some cards," he drawled.

Zack nodded. "You got it!" he affirmed.

"Take a seat." He gestured with his hand. Both men sat in the empty chairs, with Zack sitting across from Mark. Each of the men had a drink beside them. "Either of you care for a drink before we get started?" asked Jed.

Zack knew better than to order a drink. It could be laced with drugs. "No thanks," they each replied.

"That will be all, Gil."

When the bartender left, Jed turned to the newcomers. "Either one of you know how to play poker?" eyeing Zack as he spoke.

"I've played a few hands, but I have to admit, I'm not very good at it. One day, I hope to win big!" He gave a sly smile as his eyes traveled over to Mark.

Mark shrugged. "Deal the cards."

The man sitting next to Jed cut the deck and the game began. After three rounds of poker, with Mark winning all three rounds, he could feel the tension building all around him. Maybe he should have let one of them win. He glanced over at Zack who had a grim look, as he too felt the tension.

"I thought you said you weren't a good poker player?" Jed growled, glaring at the man who just won a lot of their money.

Mark, staring back, shrugged his shoulders. "I never said that," glancing over at Zack. "He did." Mark started gathering up his winnings when he heard the hammer of a gun click. He turned to see a gun pointed straight at him.

"I don't like to be cheated out of my money," Jed expressed in a low and menacing voice.

Mark took a breath. He needed to stay calm if he was going to live through this. He glanced over at Zack who he knew was set to act if needed. Mark took his hands away from the money and raised them. "Hey, I didn't cheat you out of your money or anyone else's here. I won the money fair and square. Now, I thought when we were asked to sit in on a few rounds of poker, I was playing with mature adult men. Now my friend and I are not here to cause any trouble. If you want the money, you can have it. Just let me leave with the money I came in with."

While Jed and Mark continued to have a stare down, Zack was waiting to see if a bullet would fly. He formulated a plan in his mind if Mark couldn't talk his way out of it. He watched as Jed released the hammer and put his gun back in his shoulder holster. He noticed that the gun was a nine-millimeter Glock. The same gun he had when the police department issued it to him. He wondered…

Mark breathed a sigh of relief when Jed placed his gun back into his holster. "Take the money." As he lowered his hands to gather up the money, the man on his left pulled out his gun and pointed it directly in Mark's side. He glared at Jed.

Angrily, he cried, "Hey, Jed, the man said he would give it back. I say he do it!"

Jed quickly pulled his gun and aimed it at the man holding the gun to Mark's side. "I say he take it!" he roared! Again, he pulled the hammer back. "Put the gun away, Hank, or you will be dead along with him." You could cut the tension with a knife, as they all sat still, waiting to see who was going to win this battle. You could see the sweat on his brow when the man called Hank pulled his gun away and placed it in his holster. Jed, with his gun still in his hand, pointed it at Mark. "Get your money and get out!" he growled. Waving his gun between the two, he stated, "If I ever see either one of you here again, you'll will wish you had never set foot in the place. Do I make myself clear?"

Mark glared back. "Very clear. Come on, Mac, let's get out of here. Maybe the patrons in the bar up the street will be more friendly!" Mark picked up his winnings and stuffed them in the pockets of his jeans. Both men left the way they came in.

The men at the table turned back to Jed. "Are you really going to let them get away with all our money?" asked Hank.

Jed stared back at the man who was ready to kill for it. "Go and follow them. And when you finish the job, bring the money back here. I'll be waiting." The three men got up from the table and left. Jed watched them leave. He had a woman waiting for him. He'd kill some time while he waited for them to come back.

Zack and Mark exited the bar and got into their van. Both men sat and watch the three men fly out the door of the bar. When the three men spotted them, Zack slammed his foot on the accelerator and took off. The three men raced to jump into one of their cars. With the squeal of their tires, they followed the van down the street. Zack, looking in his rearview, mirror saw the car coming up fast! Mark, turning around and looking back, saw the car creeping up on their tail. He turned to Zack. "I hope you have a plan to get us out of this," he shouted as he hung on for dear life when Zack took a corner too fast.

Zack, turning onto First Street, almost lost control of the vehicle, but was able to right it and push down hard on the accelerator. With the three men hot on his tail, he weaved in and out of traffic. "I just need to get to the next street."

The street he was talking about was coming up on their right. Mark, sitting in the passenger seat, prayed they wouldn't crash as Zack slammed on his brakes turning down Third Street, running a red light. Thank God there was little traffic this late at night. He watched behind him as the men chasing them did the same thing. Zack again sped up. When the three men were just about on their bumper, two patrol cars pulled out with their lights flashing and sirens blaring.

Zack kept going. Looking in his rearview mirror, the car was still on his tail. Looking ahead, he saw a vacant lot to the right. This could be risky, but he was going to chance it.

"Hang on!" he shouted. He took a quick right turn, hit the curb, and flew into the vacant lot. He slammed on his brakes. In his rearview mirror he watched as the car continued to drive on past him, with the police cars hot on their trail. They both watched until the police cars were out of sight.

Mark turned to Zack. "That was close! Now I know what Craig meant riding in the passenger seat with you! Are you for real? We could have been killed!"

Zack chuckled. He pulled the van around and headed back down the street. "Well, you better get used to it if you're still determined to work on this case. It was all part of the plan. And by the way, you are going to have to turn in your winnings for the state's evidence."

"What? I won that money fair and square!"

Zack glanced across at Mark. "I had no idea that you were a seasoned poker player. If I had known, I would have warned you not to win. It cost us the time we needed to find out if this Jed guy is part of the human-trafficking ring."

Mark sighed. "Sorry, Zack. It just irks me that this guy was following Tammy, and yet there is nothing in your Intel system on him. It felt good to be one up on this creep."

"Well, unfortunately, we lost our chance to get information on him."

They were silent for most of the way back to the police department. Both lost in their thoughts. Zack, breaking the silence, asked, "You like her, don't you?"

Mark took a breath. He didn't want to have this conversation. Yes, he liked her. He was possibly falling in love with her. But he wasn't going to let anyone know. "Hey, I only want to protect her and her daughter. That's all, nothing else."

Zack glanced back over to see Mark looking out the window. He knew he wasn't telling the truth. He had feelings for her. Just the way he reacted to the sound of her name spoke volumes. He was only kidding himself by denying it.

CHAPTER 12

Tammy, pacing the living room floor, was worried sick that something had happened to Mark after Mrs. Langley had informed her that he and a detective had gone out to find the guy that she thought had been following her. It was getting late. She tried to tell herself that he was fine. He was with a detective, most likely Detective Williams. As she continued to pace, her thoughts started to run away with her. Were they lying in the streets after being shot, or had they been abducted? Oh, this was no good! She needed to stop! He was fine! They were both fine! She checked her phone.

Oh why didn't he at least text me to let me know he's okay? Checking the time, she knew if she didn't try to get some sleep, she would never get through the day tomorrow. Creeping into her room, she lay down on the bed, only to toss and turn until she finally gave up. She looked at the clock. It was well after two o'clock in the morning.

She quietly got out of bed, careful not to wake Bethany, and came out into the kitchen. Maybe a cup of hot cocoa would help her to relax. She poured some milk into a pan and added the sugar and cocoa. While she was slowly stirring, lost in thought, she didn't hear the door to the garage open.

Mark came down the hall into the kitchen to see Tammy at the stove. Damn, if she wasn't the most beautiful woman he had ever laid eyes on. Her tanned skin and long slender legs showed in the cotton shorts and tank top she was wearing. His eyes softened as he watched her stirring something on the stove that heightened his senses. The aroma of hot chocolate filled the room as he silently came up beside her.

Tammy suddenly felt the presence of someone near her. In the dim light she turned to see a man with black hair and a black mustache. Her heart began to pound. She tried to run, but the man quickly caught her. She tried to break free, but he held on, turning her around to face him. "Tammy, it's me," he murmured softly.

When she heard his voice, she stopped and stood still. Staring into the deep blue eyes she was so familiar with, and feeling his warm hands on her arms, she knew it was him. With her heart still pounding, she threw her arms around him and gave him a fierce hug. She whispered, "Thank God you're all right!" And just that quick she pulled away, slapped her hand across his chest and in a hushed and angry voice she cried, "Is this going to be a habit of yours? Scaring the living daylights out of me?"

With his arms still around her, "I'm sorry, Tammy. I didn't think anyone would be up. Can you forgive me?"

"Yes, but you could have texted me, to let me know you and Detective Williams were safe! I've been worried sick!"

Looking down into her pretty face, his eyes twinkling, "You were worried?" he mused.

"Yes!" He bent to give her a kiss when she remembered. "My cocoa!" She broke free from his arms to rush over to the stove. She turned the burner off and pulled it to the other side. When she picked up the spoon she left in the pan, she quickly dropped it, burning her fingers. "Ouch!" she cried.

Mark rushed to her side. He pulled her over to the sink to run cold water over them. Enveloped in his arms, Tammy closed her eyes as strong hands held her fingers under the cool water. She felt his mouth close to hers as he whispered, "Does this make it feel better?"

She turned her head towards him and nodded, their lips almost touching, wanting his kiss. He turned the water off and went to the cupboard where he kept the first aid supplies and pulled out the antibiotic cream. With a soft cloth, he gently dried her fingers. He then applied a little of the antibiotic cream to the two she had burned. When he was finished, she lifted her eyes to his. The tenderness she saw touched her heart. With Tammy being so close to him, Mark couldn't help but bend down and touch her lips with his, in a heated kiss that left them both breathless.

Tammy felt the heat of his kiss. She wrapped her arms around him and relished the heady taste of him that sent ripples down her spine.

Mark, feeling the passion build within them, pulled her closer and felt the contours of her body, so soft and supple, rubbing up against his, leaving him wanting. As much as he wanted to learn every inch of her, he knew in his mind this wasn't the time or place to start their relationship. Slowly pulling his lips from hers, he raised his hand to softly run his fingers through her pretty hair.

Tammy, dazed by his kiss, opened her eyes and couldn't help but raise her fingers to her lips and giggle.

Mark, a little put out, "Does my kissing make you laugh?"

"I'm sorry. On the contrary, I love kissing you. It's just that… Your mustache is drooping." She giggled again, amusement clearly in her amber eyes.

He reached up and pulled it off, not without some pain. He grimaced. He let her go to go throw it in the trash.

Tammy, eyeing him, hoped she hadn't hurt him with her comment. She went over to the stove to see if the hot cocoa was salvageable. Stirring, softly, she asked, "It looks like the hot chocolate is drinkable. Would you like a cup?"

Turning back to her, he answered, "Sure." He ambled over to the cupboard and pulled two cups out and set them down on the counter next to her. She felt the tension as she poured the hot chocolate in the cups and placed the pan in the sink. She shouldn't have laughed. He must think she didn't care at all for his kisses when it was totally the opposite. She would like nothing more than to be in his arms all day, with his lips pressed to hers, lost in the passion that would be theirs to cherish. She handed him his cocoa. They both took a seat at the counter. She took a sip. She turned toward him. Hesitantly, she asked, "Mrs. Langley told me you and a detective went to find the guy who might have been following me. Did you and Zack have any luck?"

He smiled as he sipped his hot cocoa. "As a matter of fact, we did. We found him in a bar in downtown Honolulu. His name is Jed Rawlings. Unfortunately, we didn't get a lot of information. We sat in on a poker game, in which I won too many hands." He went on to explain what transpired between him and the guy named Jed and how they escaped with their lives.

"Oh, Mark! What were you thinking? You both could have been killed!" With wide eyes, she asked with urgency, "What if those men come after you and Zack?"

"Tammy," keeping his voice low. "You need to relax. That's why we went in disguise. So we wouldn't be recognized."

She looked at his hair. "Did you use a permanent color on your hair?"

He shrugged. "I don't know. I just picked up a color at the store and left."

"Well," she chided, "if it was permanent, you're going to wear it a while." She chuckled, her eyes twinkling. "Or you could shave it all off!"

He didn't think this was funny at all. He should have thought about whether or not it was permanent. He thought it would just wash out. Those men could very well come after him. Well, he couldn't worry about it now. He'd deal with it later. He looked at the time.

"It's late. It will be morning soon."

She gazed into his eyes and down to those firm lips of his. She found herself wanting to kiss him again but thought better of it. "You're right," she agreed. She came up from her chair and put her cup in the sink. She turned back to him and smiled, "Goodnight, Mark."

"Goodnight." He sat there a while, mulling over how the night went while he finished his cocoa. Tammy's comment on his hair made him think, *Damn, I just might have to shave it off!*

The next morning, Mark overslept. When he came into the kitchen, he found Tammy and Bethany had already left for the day. They must have left in a hurry. Some of Bethany's toys were strewn all over the living room. He glanced over at the coffee pot and saw there was still half of a pot left. He poured himself a cup. He took a drink and immediately threw it out. He hated old coffee. He poured it out and started a fresh pot. When it finished brewing, he pulled a sweet roll from the fridge. After warming it up in the microwave, he took his coffee and sweet roll over to the counter and sat down. He was just about to take a bite when the doorbell rang.

Who could that be? he wondered. When he opened the door, he stood and stared into the eyes of his twin brother.

Shocked, Mike stood and stared back at his brother. *What the hell?* He composed himself and asked, "May I come in?"

Mark stepped back. "Sorry, Mike. Come in."

As Mike was walking past him, he commented, "Nice hair."

Mark didn't comment back. He closed the door and went back into the kitchen.

Mike followed, his eyes catching the toys strung all over the place. It wasn't like his brother to let Cameron leave toys around.

He saw a doll on the couch and wondered when his nephew started playing with dolls. Something was definitely going on.

"I just made a fresh pot of coffee. Would you like a cup?"

Mike noticed the sweet roll on the counter. "Sure. And I'll have one of those sweet rolls, too."

Mark poured his brother a cup, grabbed another sweet roll from the fridge, and warmed it up. He placed them in front of Mike, then took a seat beside him. They drank their coffee and ate the rolls in silence.

Finally, Mike couldn't stand it anymore and asked, "You want to tell me what's going on with you?"

Mark took a breath. He knew he needed to inform his brother but didn't know where to begin. "This is going to take a while. You want a warm-up?"

"Sure."

Mark got up and poured them each another cup of coffee. When he set the coffee pot down, he slowly started to pace. He stopped and faced his brother. "A lot has happened since you and Jenna left for Paris." He paused a moment before continuing. "Mike, when Cameron and I dropped you and Jenna off at the airport, Cameron wanted to go to the new ice cream place on the outskirts of Honolulu. When we got there, Tammy, one of our waitresses, and Zack, came running out of a clothing store. Tammy was in a panic and crying that her little girl was gone. We heard screaming across the street. Zack and I flew over to a parking lot, where we heard the sounds, and saw a man trying to get Bethany into a van. Bethany kicked the man in the shins and was able to get away from him. Zack went after Bethany, while I took care of the guy trying to take her. Zack was able to arrest him and haul him off to jail. I took a frightened little girl back to Tammy and ended up taking them to the ice cream parlor, to help get their minds off what just happened, so to speak." He wasn't about to share his feelings that he was starting to have for Tammy, at least not yet. Mark went on to explain Zack coming into the restaurant to inform them that Bethany, along with Cameron, could be in danger with this human-trafficking ring and to be on the alert, with Tammy being followed, and Zack and he going out last night to find this guy.

Mike, listening, wanted to know, "And did you find him?"

"Yes."

"And…?" expressed Mike.

Mark took another breath. His brother wasn't going to like what he was about to tell him. "We found him at a bar in downtown Honolulu called the Outback."

"The Outback!" he exclaimed. "Mark, that bar is always on the news about shootings and knifings being committed there! You could have been killed!"

Mark thought if he heard that phrase one more time he would explode! "Mike, you don't think I know that?" his voice escalating. "I was well aware of the danger, but I had to find this guy. The police's intel had nothing on him. We were wondering if this guy even existed until I went down there to investigate myself and found out that this bar was his regular hangout. We were able to join in on a few rounds of poker, with him and a few of his cohorts."

"You didn't win, did you?"

Frustrated, Mark burst out, "Yes, Mike, I won all three hands! It wasn't the smartest thing I ever did, but I wanted to get back at this guy. I wanted to know why he was following Tammy and if he was connected to this trafficking ring. But I blew it and found myself with a gun pointing at me. I was able to talk myself out of it, and we left with the money, only to wind up with Zack and I being chased through the downtown area. Just so you know, Craig was right, you never want to be in the passenger seat when Zack is driving. I thought for sure I had seen my last days!"

Mike, stunned at what his brother revealed to him, was thankful he and Zack weren't shot or killed in a car crash. Concerned, he asked, "So what now?"

Mark sighed. "I don't know, Mike. I need to go down to the police station and turn my winnings in for the state's evidence. I'll find out if the men chasing us were caught and thrown in jail. And just so you know, because I'm not going to be able to hide it, Tammy and her daughter are staying with me."

Mike hadn't expected this news, but it now made sense seeing the toys all over and the doll on the couch. Once it sunk in, he smiled. "Well, I'm a little relieved. When I saw the doll on the couch, I wondered when Cameron got into playing with dolls." They both chuckled. Turning serious, Mike came out with it. "Mark, the employees are talking. Megan came up to me and outright asked if you and Tammy are having an affair. Just to let you know, I was shocked at first, but after watching Tammy last night, I began to wonder if it was a possibility. Are you two having an affair?" he asked carefully.

Mark picked up his coffee and took a drink. He needed a few moments before he answered. "How did Tammy look?" he asked in return.

"She seemed to be a little down, not herself. She didn't engage with the customers like she usually does. Her mind seemed to be on something else."

Or the employees are giving her the cold shoulder, Mark thought. It made him angry at what she must be going through and not being able to talk about it. He would clear the air when he went back to work. Mark turned to look directly into his brother's eyes and stated, "At this time, Tammy and I are not having an affair. But if we do decide to have a relationship, it's not any of our employees' business."

"You know the rules, Mark!"

"At this point I don't care about the rules! I only want to keep Tammy and her daughter safe. You need to know that someone sold her daughter. Also, the guy that tried to take her is getting out of jail in the next day or two. Someone in his organization paid his bail! Hell, he could have already been released! We all need to stay on alert in and around the restaurant when Tammy is working. The police have someone watching her daughter when Bethany is at school, and when the Langleys are here watching her while Tammy is at work. No one at the restaurant knows this. I will inform them when I return."

Mike didn't like the thought of waiting on this. A lot could happen between now and Thursday. "Knowing what you have told me," he said with concern, "this can't wait until you return to work. They need to be informed now."

Mark blew out a breath. He knew Mike was right. "Okay. Call an emergency meeting a half hour before we open the doors. Hopefully all the staff can be there; if not, we will inform each one personally."

"What about Cameron? Is anyone able to watch him, since he is also at risk?"

"Not at this time. I let Sherry know what was going on. She was to let the school know to keep an extra watch on him. Sherry and her live-in will keep a close eye as well when he is with them. Listen, I hate to cut this short, but I need to get showered and head down to the police station. I'll see you back at the restaurant before the meeting. You know the way out."

Mike watched his brother head down the hallway to the master bedroom. Clearly, his brother was dealing with a lot right now, but he had never dismissed him so abruptly. He slid off the chair and walked over to the door. When he opened it, he turned and glanced back. Right then, he vowed he would help his brother find and put these human traffickers away. Too many kids are being exploited and sold for sex. With that thought in his mind, he walked out and closed the door behind him. He got on his phone to set up the meeting for this afternoon, then he would find more answers on his own.

Down at the police station, Mark asked to see Zack. The sergeant on duty excused himself, only to come back and inform him Detective Williams was in a meeting and would be out shortly. Mark, sitting in the lobby, was anxious to find out if the officers were able to apprehend the men who were sitting in on the poker game, and if they were able to get any information out of them regarding the human-trafficking ring. He didn't have to wait long before Zack came out and asked him to come back. Mark followed him back to the conference room where, surprise surprise, his brother Mike was sitting next to Lieutenant Fillmore. His eyes turned to a gentleman he had never seen before.

"Mark, I want to introduce you to Agent Flynn Carmichael. He is working on the case along with the other FBI agents. Agent Carmichael, Mark TreVaine."

Mark shook hands with him, an older man, but could see he kept himself in shape. He took a seat across from his brother and cocked an eyebrow up at him. Mike got the meaning.

"Did you really think I would let you go it alone after our talk this morning?" Mark shrugged his shoulders and turned to Zack who was sitting next to him. Zack sensed some tension between the two brothers and hoped they would work through it. He may need them later down the road if they were able to work up a sting operation with the FBI agents.

"Were the officers able to apprehend the men in the poker game who came after us last night?" Mark inquired.

"Yes, but we will more than likely have to let them go, unless we can find something substantial that we can hold them on."

"Have they been interrogated?"

"To a point. I wanted to stall until we met today. Did you bring your winnings with you?"

"Yes." Mark pulled an envelope from his back pocket and handed it to Zack.

"Sorry. When this is over, it will be returned to you," informed Zack.

Mark nodded and asked, "So what have you discovered?"

"I'm going to turn this meeting over to Agent Carmichael. Hopefully it will clear some things up that took place during the poker game. Agent Carmichael, would you care to let us in on what has been happening with the case?"

Agent Carmichael leaned forward with his hands folded on the table. Looking directly at Mark, "Mark, I just want to say you took a hell of a chance yesterday when you went downtown to find out information on Jed." Glancing over at Zack and back at Mark, he continued. "And then when you two sat in on a poker game, you're only sitting here today because of Jed Rawlings. He is one of our undercover agents. I know you are all wondering if the three men sitting in jail are part of the human-trafficking ring we've been working on. The answer is yes."

Mark sat forward. "If these men are part of the trafficking ring, and you know this, why would you let them out of jail? Why don't you just charge them?"

"Because, Mark, this ring stems beyond this island. It travels through Seattle on down through LA," explained Agent Carmichael. "We have agents working undercover in all three states. We need these men back out on the streets to lead us to all the main ringleaders. Also so they don't find out that we have special agents working inside the organization watching them. We're finding some of them are working online and luring vulnerable young girls and boys to meet with them. Then they are taken and drugged. When they are dependent on the drugs, they use that addiction to exploit the victims and use them for sex. We were very close to catching the head guy that set up this trafficking ring when several police departments, and from what I understand, all three of you TreVaine brothers, scared him off."

"Now just a minute, Agent Carmichael," stormed Lieutenant Fillmore. "We took down the largest drug deal to ever hit this island. We had no idea that Marco Manchez was head of a human-trafficking ring as well as his drug smuggling and loan shark business. We had our suspicions, but we had no idea that it was Ben Gillard and Gwen Sacks of the sheriff's department, who ended up being part of the drug heist. When we were able to interrogate them, that's when we learned that Ben tipped Manchez off to get him off the island. So don't sit there and blame us or the TreVaine brothers for scaring him off! Now, Agent Carmichael, I think you should take into consideration that Detective Williams and Mark here took down one of the mules who tried to kidnap a little girl in broad daylight. We are still holding him in jail, but he will be released tomorrow, thanks to someone in the organization who paid his bail. If I had my way, the guy would never be out on the streets again!"

Taken aback, Agent Carmichael apologized, "I'm sorry. I didn't mean to offend anyone of you here. You did a damn good job putting away his drug-smuggling organization. It's just that we are so close to breaking this human-trafficking case wide open and arresting the perpetrators involved that we don't want any more interference."

"Look, Agent Carmichael, my son and Tammy's daughter are at risk here. I went to find this guy because we couldn't find a thing on him. We needed to know if this guy even existed. If he is one of your agents, why was he following Tammy?" asked Mark, concern and frustration came out of his voice.

"He was following her that day to get an idea of her daily routine. She was checked out to make sure she wasn't the one who sold her daughter."

Mark did all he could do to contain himself.

Agent Carmichael sensed he needed to explain further. "Mark, when we received the report on the near kidnapping, we check out all possibilities. Tammy is in the clear."

Mark calmed himself and asked, "So, have you been able to find out who sold her daughter?"

"I'm sorry. We're still working on it."

How many times have I been told that line over the last few days? Mark thought sarcastically.

Mike, sitting at the conference table, hearing everything that was said, could clearly see what his brother had been up against. No wonder Mark had seemed so distant to him. He would surely help him resolve this case even if they had to interfere on their own. There was no way he would let his brother go it alone now that he knew the risks that were involved. He would be sure to let his brother Peyton know what's going on, in case they needed him down the road.

Detective Williams spoke up. "Listen, I know you want us to stay out of it. But the fact is, our police department has become involved. Perhaps if you're willing, we could help you out in this sting you are about to set up. We would like nothing more than to get Manchez and this human-trafficking ring he set up. We've been after him for a long time. We would all like to see him behind bars."

Zack stared into the eyes of the man sitting across from him. He meant what he said. He had a personal vendetta against Manchez. The number of men and women he killed through his drug deals, let alone his own men he hired, and now exploiting children? He had had enough. He would put this man away or die trying. Everyone at the table waited for Agent Carmichael's answer.

Agent Carmichael glanced at each one around the table. He wasn't sure what they could do, but… "I will discuss this with the other agents." He turned back to Lieutenant Fillmore. "I will be back here when you release Morris. Keep the others in jail until I meet with you tomorrow. Maybe there is something you can do to help out. And now, I need to get going."

They all rose from the table. He reached over and shook hands with each one before he left the room.

They all watched Agent Carmichael exit the conference room. Mark turned to Lieutenant Fillmore. "What do you think?"

Lieutenant Fillmore took a breath. "I don't know, Mark. We'll have to wait and see tomorrow. In the meantime, Zack and I need to go and interrogate our new prisoners. We'll see what we can get out of them." He got up from the table and headed out the door of the conference room.

Zack glanced over at the two brothers and honed in on Mark. "Hey, I know you are anxious Mark for this to be over but try not to stress. We're watching both Tammy and her little girl." He glanced over at Mike. "Mike. Thanks for coming in. Sitting here, I felt some tension between the two of you. I hope you work it out. We may need you both." With that he left to join the lieutenant.

The two brothers sat at the table, not speaking until Mark felt he needed to apologize. "Mike, I'm sorry. I didn't mean to be short with you this morning. But… can you see what I have been up against? Until last night, we were getting nowhere. And they still don't have a lead on who sold Tammy's daughter. I feel trapped in something that is out of my control."

Mike leaned across the table. "Mark, let me say this. I will do everything in my power to help you keep your son and Tammy's daughter safe, along with you. I've got your back."

Mark smiled. "Thanks, bro."

Mike checked his watch. "What do you say we head over to the restaurant? Palani can fix us a sandwich before we start the meeting. I'm hungry."

"Sounds good. Let's go," answered Mark.

As they were leaving the building, Mike commented, "What are you going to do about your hair?"

Mark chuckled. "I don't know. I might have to shave it off. But for now, I'll wear a cap!"

A man sitting in a black sedan was on the phone as he watched Mike and Mark leave the building and get into their cars. As he pulled out to follow Mark, he was getting a little perturbed as he listened to the abrupt voice on the other end. Impatiently, he answered the man. "I told you I would get you the girl."

"You had better," returned the man. "I don't like people who screw up, especially those who work for me. It won't go well with you."

"I *said* I would get the *girl*!" he growled into the phone.

"You do that." The line went dead.

He threw his phone across the seat. He would be glad to be done with this. *Then,* he swore, *I'm out!*

CHAPTER 13

Tammy, rushing into the restaurant, received the message too late to make the meeting. It was always such a rush just to make it on time when the doors opened at four o'clock when she had to be at the university. She walked pass the hostess station and back to the locker room, where she put her purse in and pulled out a clean apron for the night.

As she was walking out into the bar lounge, Megan, one of her co-workers, came up and gave her a hug. Shocked, after last night's cold shoulder treatment from everyone, she wasn't sure how to react. Megan pulled away to burst out, "Tammy, I'm so sorry. I had no idea what you must be going through, and Mark's son being in danger as well as your daughter! Just know we will all be on the lookout for anyone suspicious lurking around the restaurant."

Surprised that everyone knew, hesitantly, she responded, "Thank you, Megan. That means a lot to me. And about Mark and I… There's nothing going on between us."

Megan flipped her hand. "Oh, I'm sorry I jumped to the wrong conclusion. I mean, the bosses made the rules, right? Mark would never date you, or me for that matter." While walking to their waitress stations, Megan leaned over. "I'll let you in on a little secret. I used to dream about being with Mark, but since I met Eddie, who is the love of my life, I've forgotten all about him." She smiled. "So don't get caught up in the way he looks or smiles at you. It's just a façade."

As she watched Megan go out into the lanai to start her shift, Tammy's heart dropped. *Is it all a façade on his part?* she asked herself. *It certainly isn't on mine. Is he only interested in getting one thing from me? Then move on, leaving my heart shattered and broken*? This only proved that she needed to guard her heart at all costs.

She turned to set up her station for the evening. She glanced up to see Mark and his brother Mike in conversation at the far end of the lounge. Mark, his eyes shifting, locked with hers. His intense gaze bore into hers until goosebumps came out on her skin and her heart began to beat faster. She stood, frozen in time. Remembering being in his arms, his kisses so passionate, she didn't want to believe it wasn't real.

Tonya came up to her to tell her she had sat customers at two of her tables. She pulled her eyes away. She turned to begin her shift wondering how she was ever going to fight these feelings she had for him.

Mark, barely listening to what Mike was asking him, was lost in the amber eyes staring back at him. He hadn't seen her all day, and his eyes were drinking her in. He had seen Megan talking to her when he and his brother came out of the office. He wondered what she had said to Tammy. Observing her facial features, he could see she looked downcast when Megan walked away. He hoped she wasn't giving her a hard time. He made it clear at the meeting what was going on in their lives.

Mike nudged his brother. "Mark, are you listening?"

Mark, coming out of his trance, narrowed his eyes back on his brother. "I'm sorry, Mike, what were you saying?"

"I asked if you wanted to have to have dinner with Jenna and I. She should be out shortly."

Mark shrugged. "Yeah, I can stay and have dinner."

"Good, let's go grab that corner booth that's open."

Mark followed his brother over and slid into the booth. Mark knew Tammy was working the bar area. His eyes fastened on her as she waited on each of her tables.

Tammy could feel Mark's eyes following her as she went about taking orders and placing them on the computer back at her waitress station. She tried to ignore the flutters in her stomach at the thought of waiting on them. She made a decision. She went over to Carol and asked, "Hey, Carol. Do you think you could wait on Mark and his brother for me? I'm not feeling well, and it would really help me out."

"Oh my goodness, Tammy! Of course I will. What you must be going through. I'm surprised you can even function. Now don't you worry, I will be glad to wait on them, just give me a few minutes to get my customers orders in."

Tammy breathed a sigh of relief. "Thank you, Carol, I really appreciate this."

"You're welcome."

Mike, sitting across from his brother, knew his mind was somewhere else. He said there is nothing going on between him and Tammy, but as he observed his brother, his eyes never left her as she waited on her customers. "Mark," asked Mike, "do you know what you want to eat?"

Mark tore his eyes away and glanced back at his brother. He shrugged. "Just my usual." He focused back on Tammy, wondering if she was ever going to come over and wait on them. He got his answer when Carol walked over to the booth and asked if they wanted anything to drink.

"Hi, Carol. Just bring me a coffee with cream and a cola for Jenna. She should be out soon. Mark?"

"Just bring me a coffee with cream as well," he answered.

"Sure thing." She smiled. "I'll bring your drinks right out."

"Thanks, Carol," replied Mark.

To keep his brother's attention, Mike spoke up. "Mark, I'm going to go ahead and run an ad for more help starting tomorrow. I really should have done it weeks ago, knowing how busy we were getting, but with the wedding and the honeymoon, there just didn't seem to be enough time. And I like your idea of having an employee day. Give them something to look forward to, instead of the day-to-day grind of their daily life."

Mark leaned forward. "I think it would boost their morale. The extra help would enable them to take more breaks, more than not; some don't even get one. It's been non-stop these past two weeks. I know tempers were flaring this past weekend with the stress of handling it all." *I know mine was*, he mused.

Jenna came and slid into the booth beside Mike. She was an attractive woman, petite, with long dark brown hair and brown eyes, and a personality that left you smiling. "Hi, guys! Have you ordered yet?"

Mike, smiling down at his wife, answered, "Just drinks. Do you know what you want?"

"I think so. What are you having?"

"I'm going to have the swordfish," returned Mike.

Jenna turned to Mark to ask what he was having. Clearly, he was somewhere else. She followed his eyes and found them on Tammy, who was taking an order in the next booth. She knew that look. He was definitely attracted to her.

Mark watched Tammy go back to the waitress station.

Carol had come back with their drinks and was just about to take their order when Mark got up out of the booth. "Excuse me a moment. Carol, I'll have my usual, cheeseburger with the works, and a salad with the Hawaiian dressing. I'll be right back." Mark hurried over to where Tammy was putting in an order. "Hey, is everything okay?"

She looked up to find Mark right in front of her. With Megan's words still ringing in her ears, her nerves were on edge.

"Why did you give your booth to Carol?"

Staring into his blue eyes, shocked that he would confront her on this, she tried to answer him. "Mark, I just… I just… Could we talk when I get to your home tonight? This isn't the time, and I really have to get this order in and check on my customers."

Mark, holding back, but wanting to know what went on with her and Megan, relented. "Okay, I'll hold you to that. I'll see you when you get home."

When you get home. The words stuck in her mind as she watched him slide back into the booth where Mike and Jenna were siting. If only they were real. She was so confused. She would clear the air tonight. She had to know what this was between them, a game or something more.

Mark slid back into the booth with Mike and Jenna in deep conversation. They both turned toward him. "Is everything okay?" asked Jenna.

"It's fine. Just needed to check on something," he replied. He really wasn't in the mood to make conversation. He now wished he hadn't agreed to have dinner with them. He just wanted to be alone to think. His eyes continued to watch Tammy as she waited on her tables. She didn't return his gaze.

"Mark," determined, Mike yelled, "Mark!"

Mark glanced back at his brother, irritated by the interruption. "What?" he asked.

"Jenna and I were discussing a time we could have an employee day. Halloween is coming up in a few weeks, and we thought that maybe we could have a costume party. We could give out prizes for best costume and such. What do you think?"

Mark shrugged his shoulders. "I don't know, Mike. I'm not really into Halloween. I was thinking more like a casual holiday where we could take them to a luau or have a picnic at one of the parks on the island, so we could get to know our employees better."

"I think that's a wonderful idea! If we have it at a park, everyone could bring a passing dish. We could have it at one of those parks near the beach," suggested Jenna.

Mike jumped in. "Why not the beach behind the restaurant? We could have it catered and eat in the lanai!"

"Or everyone could bring a passing dish, which would bring the employees together more as they work to figure out a menu," insisted Jenna.

Mike stared down at his wife and then turned to Mark. He smiled and shook his head. "She loves to argue."

"I do not!"

Mark chuckled. Their food came, and it would seem everyone was hungry as the conversation was limited. When the food was gone Mark excused himself. "Listen, I'm going to head out. Whatever you decide about the employee day will be fine with me. But first I need to get through this case." Mark pulled out his wallet and threw some bills on the table. He slid out of the booth. "I'll see you two later."

Mike and Jenna watched him leave. "Do you want to fill me in on what's going on with him besides being totaling into Tammy?" asked Jenna.

He turned to his beautiful wife. "Jenna, a lot happened while we were on our honeymoon, and I just found out this morning what has been going on with him." Mike told her about the near kidnapping of Tammy's daughter, how Mark got involved, the police involvement,

Zack and Mark going out last night to find the man who was following Tammy, only to find out he's an undercover agent.

"Well no wonder he's been distant!" she exclaimed. "How can we help them?"

"Well, after sitting in on the meeting this afternoon with Mark at the police station, there's not a whole lot we can do. It's the FBI's case. We need to sit tight and keep a look out for anyone suspicious in and around the restaurant. Although Agent Carmichael indicated that he may be able to use us in the sting operation that they're in the process of setting up," he explained.

"Really?" she asked with enthusiasm. "It would be so exciting to work on another case. Have you gotten ahold of your brother Peyton? He needs to be updated as to what's going on."

"No, I haven't. But I plan on it tomorrow."

"Good. Listen, I need to get going myself. Cuddles has been alone all day. I need to get home to see how she's doing, and if she has eaten anything. It's going to take some time to get familiar with her new surroundings." Cuddles was Jenna's black-and-white tuxedo cat. "If she hasn't come out, I want to see if I can coax her out from underneath the bed."

"I'll walk you out. I want to make sure you are safely in your car."

"Thanks, but I can manage."

"Jenna, did I not just inform you of what Mark is dealing with? I'll walk you out," he insisted.

When they left, Zack came in and took a seat at the bar. Todd came up and asked what he would like to drink. "Give me a draft beer, Todd, and thanks." Todd came back with his beer and set it on the counter. Zack pulled out his wallet and threw some bills on the bar top. "Keep the change."

"Thanks!"

While he was enjoying his beer, Mike came up behind him and took the seat beside him. "Hey, Zack. We need to talk."

Mark arrived home to Mr. and Mrs. Langley playing a game with Bethany. "Hi, what game are you playing?" he asked.

"We're playing Fish!" Bethany answered excitedly.

"Fish, huh? Can anybody play this game?"

"Yes, but after we finish this one. I'm winning!" They all chuckled.

"Okay. You finish your game and I'll go make coffee." He turned his attention to the Langleys. "Would either of you like a cup?"

"Yes, please," they both replied.

Mark came back with three cups of coffee just as the game ended with Bethany winning. She hooped and hollered when she won. Mark sat down at the table. "Just want to warn you all that I am an expert at playing Fish! Deal the cards!"

Bethany laughed. "You're so funny, Mr. Mark!" He chuckled. "We'll see who's funny when I win this game!"

Mr. and Mrs. Langley laughed along with them, listening to the banter between the two. During the game, Mark learned a lot about the Langleys, how they met Tammy and her daughter. How they offered to watch Bethany while she worked and sometimes when she attended the university. They were a nice couple and devoted to caring for Tammy and Bethany. The game finished out with Bethany winning again!

"Can we play again?" she asked.

"Tell you what," Mark encouraged. "It's almost bedtime. You go with Mrs. Langley and get ready, and you and I will watch a movie before you go to bed. How does that sound?"

Bethany jumped from her chair. "Yay!" impatiently she hollered. "Come on, Mrs. Langley!"

Chuckling, Mrs. Langley rose from her chair and followed Bethany back to her room.

"Shall we finish our coffee in the family room, Mr. Langley?" he asked.

"Sure, but call me Bob, and my wife's name is Mildred."

"All right, Bob, I'll bring the coffee pot in for a warm-up."

Once they were settled, it wasn't long before Bethany stormed in and jumped up on the sofa next to Mark. "What are we watching?" asked Bethany.

"What would you like to watch?"

"Hmm, let's see," she pondered. "I'll surprise you." She went over to the cabinet and picked out a movie he had watched with Cameron a hundred times. "How about this one?" she asked. He smiled.

"Okay." He turned to the Langleys. "Bob and Mildred, if you want to head out, I can take it from here."

"Are you sure?" asked Mildred.

"Yes, it won't be long before Tammy's home, and I can put her to bed."

"That's fine with us," answered Bob. Mark started to get up when Bob stopped him. "No need to get up. Mildred and I know the way out. You two have a good night and enjoy the movie."

When they left, Mark put the movie in the DVD player. Bethany snuggled up against him. He put his arm gently around her in a fatherly embrace, and the movie began. He was so bored with the movie his eyes started to close.

Tammy walked into a quiet house. The lights were still on as she walked around to the living room. There was a bright light coming from the family room, so she went to investigate. There she saw Mark and her little girl snuggled up together fast asleep. Her heart melted as she watched the two. She went over and turned off the

TV. She came up and touched Mark's shoulder. He jumped and opened his eyes at the same time.

"Hey, you're home." He yawned and looked down to a sleeping girl still in his arms. He smiled. He glanced back up to gentle eyes. "I'll put her to bed for you," he whispered.

"Okay," she whispered back. He turned and picked her up off the couch and carried her back to their room. Tammy followed. After Mark laid her on the bed, Tammy tucked her under the covers and gave her a kiss on the cheek. She placed her hand on her forehead, brushing some of her hair away that had fallen over her brow. "Goodnight," she whispered.

They both left the room and closed the door. Can I interest you in a glass of wine before bed?" he asked. They needed to talk.

"Sure," she said, "just let me get out of my work clothes, and I will be right with you." She turned to go back into the room. She changed into a pair of lightweight dark-blue cotton capris and a matching soft tee. She left her feet bare of shoes.

When she came out, Mark was in the kitchen. He had poured them each a glass of wine. He turned when she walked in. He smiled, taking in the outfit she had changed into. *Nice*, he surmised as he handed the glass of wine to her. "It's a nice night. Would you like to go out by the pool? I can light the fireplace and we can relax while we enjoy our wine."

"Sounds nice," she murmured. She followed him out to the patio and took a seat in one of the lounge chairs in front of the fireplace. She watched as he brought the fire roaring to life. Those blue eyes caught hers as he strolled over and sat in the lounge chair next to hers.

He had also changed into a pair of white shorts with a pale-blue knit shirt, opened at the collar. The outfit showed off those strong, tanned muscles of his. Her hands wanted to reach out, to touch and feel his skin under her fingertips. She remembered being in his arms a few nights ago, pressed up to that gorgeous body, their lips locked in a passionate kiss that brought goosebumps out on her delicate skin. She turned her eyes away before he could see the want in her eyes and took a sip of her wine. She felt her body relax a little as she focused her eyes on the flames licking in the fireplace.

Mark saw for a brief moment the desire in her pretty eyes. He was having a time holding back from picking her up and sitting her back down on his lap, holding her in his arms, kissing those soft pink lips of hers. But he needed to know what happened between Megan and her tonight.

They sat there in silence, the silence so deafening, until Mark couldn't stand it any longer. "Tell me what Megan said to you when you started your shift."

Shocked, Tammy turned and asked, "What?"

"I saw you and Megan talking. When Megan left to go into the lanai, your facial features gave you away. What did she say?"

She sighed. She had no idea he had been watching them. She needed to clear the air about Megan's comments so… "Megan told me she had a crush on you, but when she met Eddie, she forgot all about you. She told me not to take you seriously when you smile or look at me a certain way. That it was all a façade." She turned to see him, watching her with a steady, narrow gaze.

"And you believed her?"

As she stared back at him, she answered. "Mark, I don't know what I believe. I know the rules you and Mike set when you opened your restaurant. And I feel even if I want to get close to you, you won't be able to. I don't want to get hurt in the process." She looked away and took another sip of her wine.

Mark knew she was hurting just from the words Megan had said to her. He also knew she had scars from her previous marriage. He needed to know. "Tammy?"

"Yes," she answered.

Gently he asked, "Can you tell me about your marriage?"

She took another sip of her wine. She sighed. She's wanted to tell him about her marriage to Roy for a while now, why she had a hard time trusting. *I guess this was as good a time as any.* She leaned her head back against the lounge and began.

"His name was Roy Gardner. I met him when I was looking for my natural father."

As he listened, he reflected, *Roy Gardner… Why does that name sound so familiar?*

She continued. "My father left when I was young. My mother remarried, and don't get me wrong, the man she married was a wonderful father to me and a great influence in my life. When I found my natural father, he was living on the island of Maui. I visited him several times, and we were able to form a bond. When I was taking a flight over to see him for the holidays, Roy was on the same flight. He was handsome and debonair and said all the right words. We instantly fell in love with each other and spent every minute we could together. We were married six months later, and life was great until I got pregnant with Bethany."

As he listened, he tried not to let the jealousy over their relationship get to him.

"Then what happened?" he asked softly.

"As soon as I told him, he lost interest in me. He never touched me intimately again. When Bethany was born, I had hoped he would fall in love with her." She turned to him, tears forming in her eyes. "He didn't even want to hold her, Mark! How could you not want to hold your own daughter? Anyway, we grew farther and farther apart. He had been gone on a three-week business trip when, one day, I went to the mailbox and found divorce papers served on me." Tears slid down her cheeks as she remembered the hurt inside her from the two years of loneliness as she raised their daughter singlehandedly.

Mark came up out of the lounge, took her wine glass, and set it on the table. He pulled her up and into his arms and let her cry. Anger surged inside him as he thought about what she must have gone through. No wonder she had walls erected around her. Then Megan's words just infused the hurt. He held her close. When the tears stopped, he pulled slightly away. Placing his hands gently along the side of her cheeks, he wiped the tears away with his thumbs. He looked deep into her eyes. "I am so sorry for what you must have gone through. But know this. You are an amazing woman. You're raising your daughter, and she is just as amazing as you. And as far as Megan is concerned, don't listen to her. I am very attracted to you, and if we decide to start a relationship together, it is our business and no one else's. Do I make myself clear?"

She nodded her head yes, as he bent to place his firm lips down on her trembling ones. The kiss started out soft and slow until the passion built. They clung to each other as the fire inside consumed them.

Tammy, feeling the heat, knew she had fallen in love with him. She let her feelings go as she kissed him, tasting the wine intermingled with his. She wanted more.

Mark couldn't get enough of this strong, determined woman who took a bad marriage and turned her life around, to become someone who was a hard worker, a student, and a loving mother. Her passionate kisses had him wanting her, to feel her next to him, under him, his hands roaming her tender body until he exploded inside her. He suddenly pulled away from her before he lost control. It was too early.

"Tammy," he groaned. "I want you, god how I want you, but you're not ready."

Breathless, she pulled him back against her. "But I am ready," she whispered. "I want you too."

He took her arms from around his neck and placed her hands in his. "Trust me on this. If we make love now, you will regret it. And I want no regrets. When we make love, I don't want any walls between us. Not my ex or yours. We'll take our time and get to know each other. And when the time is right, we will be free to love again."

She gazed into blue eyes that showed his compassion for her and felt he was right. She dropped her eyes for a few seconds, then lifted them effortlessly back to him. She took a breath, "You're right, Mark. It's late. If it's all right, I'll say goodnight."

He let go of her hands. Softly, he murmured, "Goodnight." He watched her go back into the house. When she was inside, he went and turned off the fire in the fireplace. He took a look around the perimeter of his back yard.

There were hedges lined around the property line, with a rod iron fence partitioned around the pool and Jacuzzi to keep the animals out. As his eyes returned to the hedges, the hair on the back of his neck came up, with goosebumps coming out on his skin, as he realized someone could easily be hiding behind them. A person would be able to see and hear every word that was said, let alone seeing them making out. He decided to do a walk around, just to be safe.

When he started walking toward the hedges near the house, he heard some rustling. His heart started to pound. He ran toward the sound. When he approached the area, he thought he saw a figure running to the road out front, but he couldn't be sure. It was too dark. It could have been an animal. He went through the house and out the front door, to check out in front of the house. He walked down the driveway. He didn't see anyone walking or a car parked in the street. *I think my imagination is getting the better of me*, he thought as he walked back into the house. He made sure all the doors were locked and set the alarm. He took one more look out the window. All seemed clear. He shut the lights off and went to bed.

Eyes looking out from the shrubbery that surrounded him, his heart pounding, he watched until the lights went off in the home. *That was close!* Going to his car parked down the street, *I'll be more careful next time,* he said to himself.

CHAPTER 14

TODAY WAS THE DAY Tammy was to go out into the field to learn how to deal with mental patients in their own environment. After getting to bed late last night, then lying in bed wide awake for an hour before she finally dosed off, she barely made it on time to meet with Ms. Beret at nine thirty. Her breathing was irregular when she reached her office. She tried to stifle the pain from the anxiety starting to spread throughout her chest, so she stopped to take some deep breaths before she entered her office. It took a few minutes but when she had calmed herself and the pain subsided, she knocked.

"Come in!"

Tammy opened the door to Ms. Beret's office and walked in. Taking in the files on her desk, and the books placed on the shelves positioned on the wall behind her massive walnut desk, her office reminded her of a den in a historic home. The oil paintings on the walls and soft lighting gave the room a relaxing atmosphere, while the furnishings where she held her sessions looked like a comfortable living room, warm and inviting. She took another deep breath and told herself to relax her body so she could focus on the day.

"Good morning, Tammy!"

"Good morning, Ms. Beret."

"Are you ready to meet our first patient?" she asked.

"As ready as I'll ever be. But just so you know, I am quite nervous."

"Oh, there is nothing to be nervous about. We will be perfectly safe. Now, let's go over his chart and then we'll head over to his home."

She nodded and took the seat next to her desk. It took several minutes for Ms. Beret to explain the person's mental stability and what to expect when they arrived at his home. "Do you have any questions, Tammy?"

"Not at this time, but I'm sure I will once the session is complete."

"All right, then let's get going. It doesn't do to be late for the appointment. We don't need to deal with a negative reaction to our tardiness."

"No, Ms. Beret."

Walking out of the office, she wondered what that meant. She was never in a session where there was a possibility of violence. She wondered if Zack had secured one of his men to follow them. Zack had left last night before she could ask him. She was in too big of a hurry this morning to even think about checking her phone for any messages. She would check it when she was in the car, to see if he had texted her. Of course, she had no idea where they were going, so unless there was an officer at the university ready to follow them, she was on her own. Once in the car, she pulled up her messages; none from Zack.

As Ms. Beret pulled out into traffic, Tammy could feel the anxiety starting to build inside her. She never suffered from anxiety until she found herself alone with a newborn baby to care for. Roy provided for them financially until the divorce, but wanted nothing to do with helping her, or being around the baby when he was home, which was not much. It was a sad time in her life. A wonderful counselor, along with the support of her sister and husband, helped her through it. She tried not to show what she was feeling to Ms. Beret, but when she took a few deep breaths to calm herself, Ms. Beret inquired, "Tammy, are you all right?"

She turned to glance over at Ms. Beret and decided to tell her what was going on in her life, since she hadn't had a chance to inform her. "I'm sorry, Ms. Beret. I'm feeling a little anxious. I need to tell you something, and I hope it won't affect my evaluation on my last semester with you."

"What is it, Tammy? I know you were going to tell me something this past Monday, and I'm sorry I had to rush out. We have some time before we get to the patient's home. Tell me what's going on."

Tammy took another deep breath. "A few weeks ago, my daughter was almost a victim of a human-trafficking gang. If it hadn't been for my boss Mark TreVaine, and a detective, Zack Williams, who just happened to be in the area to stop the man, she would have been taken. Ms. Beret, someone sold her. The police have been investigating, but they still have no clue as to who would have done this. My daughter and I have been under surveillance since the incident, but I have no clue if one of the officers was able to follow us out here for the session."

Tammy watched as Ms. Beret pulled into a subdivision just outside of the city of Honolulu. It wasn't the best of areas, but Ms. Beret said it was safe. She stopped the car across from the house where they were to go into. She shut the engine off, turned, and smiled. "Tammy, I'm sorry. I wish we would have had time to discuss your situation, but we are here now, and we can't cancel the session without upsetting the patient. Even if an officer was not able to be here with us, know you are perfectly safe with me."

Tammy nodded her head and took another deep breath. They both exited the car and as they were walking up the sidewalk to the front door, Tammy sent up this prayer: *Lord, give me wisdom and strength to see this through. Protect and keep us safe from danger. Thank you. Amen.* With that said, Ms. Beret knocked on the door.

Detective Zack Williams was in a meeting with the lieutenant when his phone vibrated with an incoming call. He pulled his phone out to check who was calling him. "Excuse me, Lieutenant. I need to take this."

He left the conference room and pressed the call icon on his phone. "Detective Williams," he answered.

"Hey, Detective Williams, Officer Riggs here," he returned. "I'm out here at the university and just saw Tammy leave with another woman. Was I supposed to follow them? Normally Tammy doesn't leave the university this early."

Zack swore under his breath. He forgot Tammy had a field day with her social worker today. "Can you still see the car en route?"

"No, sir. They've been in route for about five minutes."

Zack swore again. He thought a moment. He still had her phone number. "Listen, I have her phone number; hopefully she has her GPS on. Give me a minute and I'll get right back to you."

"Clear," he returned.

Zack pushed end, then brought up Tammy's number. He checked to see if her GPS app was working. *Damn, it's off!* He called Officer Riggs back. When he picked up, "Hey, Cam, her GPS is turned off. Go into the building where they came from and see if you can get the social worker's name and phone number. Then call me right back."

"I'm on it."

Zack headed back into the conference room.

"Is everything all right?" asked Lieutenant Fillmore.

"I'm a little embarrassed to say this, but I forgot all about Tammy going out with her social worker to see a patient of hers today. Officer Riggs has lost track of them, and Tammy doesn't have her GPS on."

"Does the social worker have her GPS on?" he asked.

"Officer Riggs is checking on it. We should know shortly. When will Craig be back on duty?"

Detective Craig Jenson had been on a four-week leave after the major case they worked on together.

"He's due back next week. I'll be glad to have him back. We are so short staffed."

"Any chance he would come back early?" asked Zack.

"What are you thinking?"

"I'd like to put him on to follow Tammy. These new officers have a tendency to hesitate, call for permission to do something that they should have known to do. Now, he's lost sight of where they are going when they left the building."

"I see what you are saying. I'll give him a call. He may be ready to come back." Lieutenant Fillmore checked his watch. "I need to head down to the jail. They're letting out Morris in an hour, and I want to be there. See what the feds' plans are for tracking him. I'll keep you briefed on what transpires and what they want to do with the other prisoners."

"Thanks, Lieutenant."

Lieutenant Fillmore came up out of his chair and headed for the door. He stopped and turned back. "Zack?"

"Yes," he answered as he was checking his phone.

"Let me know if you are able to track Tammy. We don't want anything to happen to her if someone is following her besides us."

He looked up as the lieutenant was getting ready to walk out the door. "Will do, Lieutenant."

When he left, Zack pressed Officer Riggs' number on his phone. He didn't like how long it was taking for him to get back to him.

"Officer Riggs," he answered.

"Hey, Cam. Zack here. Did you find out anything?"

"I was just about to call you. Yes, I was able to get the social worker's name and number and where they are going. They're headed to a subdivision ten minutes from downtown Honolulu. Not a good part of town. There has been several domestic violence calls in several of the homes there."

Zack was very aware of that part of Honolulu. He had to investigate a homicide there once. "Let me know when you arrive and text me the address. I'm going to pick up someone and I will be right there for backup. If you need someone before I get there, don't hesitate to call into the department," instructed Zack.

"Right, I'm on my way."

Zack pulled up another number, pressed the call icon, and waited. As he listened to it ring, he was just about to give up when he heard a voice on the other end.

"Mark TreVaine," he answered.

Mark managed to get dressed, put on a pot of coffee, pour one to go, and threw a cap on his head, all in a matter of minutes. He really needed to do something with his hair. He hated to wear a hat. He ran out the door just as Zack was pulling up in his drive. He opened the door and slid in.

"What's going on?" he asked, wondering what the emergency was about.

"Did you know Tammy was going out with her social worker today?"

Mark's heart began to pound. "No, she didn't mention it." Their conversations didn't stem around her schedule at the university. "Why?"

"She had mentioned it to me on Monday, and I completely forgot about it until I got a call from the officer who was put on to keep an eye on her."

Turning in his seat toward Zack, he asked, "And…?"

"At first, when Tammy and her social worker came out of the building at the university, the officer wasn't sure he was supposed to follow them. He's new, and by the time he called to see what he should do, their car was out of sight," explained Zack.

Mark, in a panic, asked, "Did you find out where they were going?"

"Yes, but they are not in one of the best areas. It's just on the outskirts of Honolulu, and I thought between you and I, and Officer Riggs, we could keep an eye out for anyone who might want to harm them."

Mark, sitting in the passenger seat, trying to digest what Zack just told him, thought if anything happened to her... "Can you get this thing to go any faster?"

"Sorry, the traffic is thick. I'm doing the best I can. Just try to stay calm."

Just try to stay calm, he says. In such a short time, this woman had come to mean more to him than he realized. With his heart pounding in his chest, he wasn't sure he'd make it through the drive there!

Thirty minutes later when they arrived at the address Officer Riggs had texted him, Zack pulled up next to his car. "What have you got, Cam?"

"Well, the red Camaro parked just up ahead of me belongs to Ms. Beret, the social worker. I've been here for about twenty minutes and there's been no activity in that run-down ranch home to your right, directly across from where her car is parked."

Both men looked over to the home that had seen better days. The paint was peeling off the siding, and the roof looked like it was sagging on one side of the house. Mark noticed that most of the homes in the area were in the same shape, some more than others.

"Okay, Cam. I'll pull around and sit a little a ways behind you. Keep your eyes open to anyone suspicious."

Cam nodded. "Right," he answered.

Zack pulled the car around and parked along the road. Mark turned towards Zack and asked, "Now what?"

"We wait," returned Zack.

Inside the home, Tammy sat ridged and tried to listen to Ms. Beret ask questions to the man named Charlie. He was a short, stocky man in his mid-forties. He had a bald head, with gray hair growing out along the back and sides of his head and down to his shoulders. His clothes were a little worn and somewhat dirty. His stark blue eyes kept wandering over to her as he answered and discussed what was troubling him. He was a little put out when he opened the door and saw her standing with Ms. Beret. "Who's she?" he had asked abruptly. His eyes zeroed in on Tammy as Ms. Beret calmly apologized.

"Charlie, this is Ms. Gardner. She is an intern of mine and studying to be a social worker like me. My week has been so busy I failed to let you know she would be coming with me. I hope you don't mind." She smiled.

He had stared at her for a minute longer before he shook his head no, then stood aside to let them in.

Tammy, sitting on a chair that was torn and ragged, with her pad of paper on her lap and pencil in hand, took notes while Ms. Beret continued to engage Charlie in the session. At one point he turned his head toward her and asked, "What are you doing here and why are you writing on that pad of paper?" angry eyes staring straight at her.

Tammy looked over at Ms. Beret to get a sign if she should answer him. Ms. Beret took control and answered for her. "Charlie"—his eyes glancing back to her—"I told you when we arrived—"

He sat forward and interrupted. "I asked her!" he yelled. His angry eyes shifting back to Tammy. "Now tell me why you need to be here and why you are writing down what I say to Ms. Beret?"

Tammy swallowed. With her heart pounding in her chest, her voice shook as she tried to explain why she was here, but not before she got a nod from Ms. Beret to do so. "Charlie, as Ms. Beret stated when we arrived, I am here to observe and take notes, so I can learn to be a good social worker like Ms. Beret. If it bothers you, I will stop. I don't want to upset you. I will sit quietly as you continue on with your session with Ms. Beret."

He seemed to calm down as his eyes traveled back to Ms. Beret. "I don't want her to take notes!" Ms. Beret calmly took control and expressed to him, "Charlie, if it is okay with you, we will continue our session and Ms. Gardner will no longer be taking notes. We have about fifteen minutes left, and I need to know what else you would like to discuss or help you with before we leave. But if you want to stop, we will, and I can reschedule you for another time early next week."

Charlie sat back in his chair. "No, Ms. Beret. Let's finish our session. As long as you promise she won't be taking notes. I have a couple of issues I need to discuss."

Ms. Beret nodded her head. "Okay, Charlie, let's proceed, then."

Charlie began again, letting Ms. Beret know of his concerns since he had seen her last. Tammy could sense he still wasn't comfortable with her being there, as he would glance her way off and on throughout the rest of the session. As she listened, he expressed how he thought the neighbors had it in for him. That he had words with the neighbor next door. The neighbor accused him of selling drugs and if he ever saw him selling to a minor, he would have him thrown out of his home.

"Ain't nobody, gunna throw me out of my home! And I ain't selling drugs! I haven't used or sold drugs in a long time! Why would he accuse me of it?"

Ms. Beret helped him get through the problem he was facing, and he seemed to internalize the information that was given by her.

When the session ended, Tammy couldn't wait to get out of there. Her nerves were shot. Sitting there and trying not to show how nervous and afraid she was of him was a stressor! Ms. Beret set the next appointment. They all got up from their chairs. Ms. Beret and Tammy headed for the door, with Charlie following behind. He opened the door for them.

As the women were walking out and away from the door, he stopped them. Looking across the road, he saw a police officer in a patrol car. His eyes then took in a black sedan sitting a ways from the officer's car, with two men sitting inside it.

"Hey," he yelled. "What's going on? Why is a police officer here?"

The two women stepped further away from the door as Charlie started to pace, showing his distress at seeing the vehicles parked along the road. He stopped, his voice escalating to a roar. "And why are there two men sitting in that black car over there? I've done nothing wrong! I've been clean for five years!"

"Now, Charlie," answered Ms. Beret. "Just calm down. I'm sure they are not here for you."

Ignoring her, his angry eyes glaring at Tammy, he stepped toward her, raised his arm, and pointed his finger right in her face. "You!" he snarled. "You are the one who sent them! I never should have let you into my home!" Ms. Beret stepped in front of him to try and calm him, but he shoved her out of the way.

Tammy, trying to keep from having a full-blown anxiety attack with him in her face, took a step backwards. Tears started to form in her eyes, as she tried to talk some sense into him. When she opened her mouth, someone grabbed her from behind as Detective Williams stepped in front of her. Charlie tried to fight him off, but

Zack was too fast. Within seconds Zack had him pinned to the ground with his hands behind his back.

Ms. Beret cried, "Stop! Please, Charlie is harmless. What are you doing? Let him go!"

Zack lifted him up off the ground still holding onto his hands.

"Please, officer, he's upset. He means no harm. I'll take full responsibility," she pleaded. Zack let him go. Charlie jerked away from him, shaking out his arms and hands. With Officer Riggs on one side and Zack on the other, he seemed to calm down a little. Tammy, enfolded in Mark's arms, was shaking uncontrollably. Tears were streaming down her face, as she watched the scene unfold.

"Tammy," he murmured, "you're all right. He can't hurt you." Running a hand through her hair and placing her head on his broad chest, he whispered, "My God, you scared me." He kissed the top of her head and squeezed her close to him. Tammy felt safe with Mark's arms around her as she let the tears fall. When she was able to bring herself under some semblance of control, she raised her head to glance over at Charlie. Detective Williams and Officer Riggs were talking to him, keeping him a safe distance from her. "Charlie," she cried. His eyes moved toward her. "It isn't you that they are here for, it's me. I'm so sorry to have caused you any stress or harm. It wasn't intentional." He nodded.

Ms. Beret turned toward Tammy. "Tammy, I will need to stay with Charlie while one of the officers explains what is going on and to ease his mind on what happened."

With tears still in her eyes, she nodded. "I'm sorry, Ms. Beret, I didn't mean for this to happen."

She smiled. "I know, Tammy. Do you have time to stay at the university until I get back? We'll talk then. I will have my secretary clear my schedule till one o'clock."

She nodded. "Yes, I'll see you back there."

"Officer Riggs," ordered Zack, "take Mark and Tammy back to the university. Then go back to the department to file a report. I can handle it from here." He glanced over at Mark. "Mark, can you stay with Tammy? I'll meet you back there when we are finished."

He looked lovingly down at her, and answered, "I won't leave her side."

After Officer Riggs dropped them off at the university, Mark took Tammy to a bistro inside the building where she would meet Ms. Beret when she returned. He left a message at the desk to where they would be. He purchased two cups of coffee and took them to the table where Tammy had taken a seat, to wait for him to return. He set one down in front of her, as he slid in the chair across from her.

"How are you doing?" he asked her gently.

She took a sip of her coffee. "I'm better. Thank you for the coffee."

"You're welcome." They sat for a few minutes without talking, until Mark had to know.

"Tammy, can you tell me what went on inside the home?"

Her eyes glanced up to his, so full of concern for her that it took her a moment before she could answer him. She had never had anyone care so much for her in her life, not even her ex-husband. Her eyes fell away, not sure where to begin. "Well"—her eyes meeting his—"when we arrived at the home, Ms. Beret forgot to let him know that I was coming. I could tell it upset him, but he let us in. During the session, he became agitated and asked why I was there and taking notes. Ms. Beret again tried to explain why I was there, but he insisted I tell him. I'm afraid I was pretty shaken up during the whole session. I had been fighting an anxiety attack since I first arrived at her office." She took another sip of her coffee. "When the session ended, he walked us to the door. When he saw the officer, and you and Zack, sitting along the road he became more agitated and accused me of sending them out to get him. He was an ex-drug user and drug pusher, you see, and you know the rest. Mark, I'm not sure I'm cut out to be a social worker. I wasn't able to handle the situation under the circumstances surrounding my life."

Tears started forming in her eyes as she thought, *What if I'm not able to handle dealing with autism patients? The field I want so badly to work in?*

Mark took her hands in his and said with conviction. "Tammy, don't let this one situation scare you from finishing what you set out to do. You are going to make a great social worker. Once this case involving your daughter is wrapped up, you will be able to handle things better. I honestly don't know how you are holding up so well now." She smiled.

"Thank you, Mark. I appreciate your encouragement." She took a breath and realized that his strength and knowing that he would do everything in his power to keep her and her daughter safe was what kept her going. "Mark, I need to tell you something…" Zack and Ms. Beret choose that moment to come and join them at the table.

Ms. Beret was the first to inquire about how Tammy was doing. "I'm fine, Ms. Beret. I'm sorry about all this and upsetting Charlie."

"You have nothing to be sorry for. It was my fault for not informing him I was bringing someone with me. Between Detective Williams and I, we were able to calm him once we explained why the police officer was there, along with both of you men." Her eyes went back and forth between the two. She turned toward Tammy. "Something did come out when we talked with him, and I'm going to let Detective Williams let you both in on the discussion we had with him."

Zack took over. He glanced toward Tammy. "Tammy, when I explained why we were there and the near kidnapping of your daughter, he mentioned that he noticed several kids had come up missing in the area who used to play in the streets. Their parents still live in the neighborhood. One of those parents is his next door neighbor. When Charlie asked where his daughter was, since he hadn't seen her playing with the other kids, he got real mad and told him to mind his own business."

Tammy leaned forward. "Do you think Charlie's neighbor could be part of the human-trafficking ring?"

"It's a possibility. But he could have sold her. It's a run-down neighborhood, and if the man needed money, well…" He shrugged.

Tammy's heart dropped. *How in the world can this be happening, to sell your own children?* Tammy had heard about human trafficking, but never really paid attention until it involved her daughter. When this was over, she would make sure more people were made aware.

"Are you going to investigate this neighbor?" asked Mark.

Zack's eyes shifted to Mark. "Yes, and I'm sorry, Ms. Beret." His eyes turned to her. "I will also need to further investigate Charlie."

Ms. Beret was silent for most of the conversation. "I understand, Detective Williams. Charlie has been investigated before, when he was using and selling drugs, but I can assure you he has been clean for the past five years."

"I understand, but if Charlie can remember anything regarding the children missing, it could possibly help us in the case the FBI and our department are working on. It could help save another child's life," stated Zack.

"Do you think he knows more than what he is telling you?" asked Mark.

"Watching his body language, I think he could be holding back. His neighbor accused him of selling drugs. He could be trying to get rid of Charlie if indeed he did sell his daughter. I'm going to give Charlie a couple of days to settle and relax after today. Then I'll try and see if I can get more information out of him. In the meantime, we'll go and talk with the neighbor." He checked his watch. "Listen, I need to head back to the department." He rose from his chair and held out his hand to Ms. Beret. "It was a pleasure meeting you. I may need to come back and ask you a few more questions."

She took his hand to shake. "Just so you know, Detective, I cannot discuss the patient's mental state or what he deals with on a day-to-day basis, due to confidentiality."

Zack nodded. "I understand. Mark, Tammy, I'll see you later."

When he left, Ms. Beret put her hand on Tammy's arm. "I want you to know that this first time out will not affect your evaluation considering your circumstances. We will wait to go out until the police put this human-trafficking ring away and your daughter is safe."

"Thank you, Ms. Beret. I'm sorry if I didn't handle the situation more professionally."

"You did fine." She patted her arm and turned to Mark. "I'm sorry, I hadn't properly met you."

Mark held out his hand. "Mark TreVaine." They shook hands.

"Are you and Tammy together?" she asked.

Tammy jumped in, shaking her head, not giving Mark a chance to speak. "Oh no, Ms. Beret. Mark and I are only friends. My daughter and I are staying with him until this is over. Mark's son is also in danger, and sometime, when we have time, I will explain everything that has happened."

"Okay, Tammy, I will hold you to that." She had a feeling that Mark saw her as more than a friend. She didn't miss the love he expressed when he was holding her earlier today. "Now, I need to get back to my office." She rose from her chair. "It was very nice meeting you, Mark." Her eyes returned to Tammy's. "And I will see you on Monday."

"Yes, I'll see you Monday," she answered as Ms. Beret turned to leave the room. Tammy's eyes returned to Mark's. The expression that she saw was not one who was happy with her as she locked eyes with him. She was afraid she had hurt his feelings again. Their relationship seemed to be heading into something she had only dreamed about with him, but she couldn't let anyone know. Especially Ms. Beret! It was just too soon. If she only knew for sure what Mark was feeling. Was it friendship, or was it more?

Mark, gazing into her amber eyes, knew he felt more for her than just friendship. How can she not know? His heart went ballistic when he thought she was in danger this morning. But if friendship was all she wanted, he would try to hold the line with her. He didn't want to go through having his heart crushed again. "You are my ride home. Are you ready to go?"

She could hear the coolness in his voice. Her heart dropped. She did hurt him. Her eyes slipped away from his when she bent to retrieve her purse. "Yes, I'm ready. Mark…" she murmured, glancing back to eyes that told her nothing. "I'm sorry."

He rose from his chair. "Nothing to be sorry about, we're just friends, remember?"

CHAPTER 15

IF TAMMY THOUGHT her nerves were shot earlier today, riding in the car with Mark, so close to her, in complete silence, topped it. She wondered how she could break the ice that surrounded them when they got home. When Tammy pulled up in front of Mark's home, they both went in, Mark going to his study, while Tammy went into the kitchen. Setting her things down on the counter, she wondered what she should do. Her mind went around in circles until she thought, *Maybe an apology lunch?* She went to the refrigerator and found some leftover fried chicken. She pulled it out along with some lettuce and greens to make salads. Once the salads were together, she made her homemade salad dressing. She pulled some rolls from the cupboard and warmed them up.

While she was preparing their lunch she wondered, *What if he doesn't want to have lunch? What then?* She would soon find out. She set everything out on the glass table next to the lanai, complete with place settings and silverware. All she needed were drinks. She grabbed some sodas from the fridge and placed them with the salads. *Well,* she thought, *it's now or never!*

She took a deep breath and headed down the hallway to his study. With her heart beating rapidly, she gently knocked on the door. She waited a moment and wondered if he had heard her knock. She raised her hand again, when suddenly it opened. "Is there something you want?" he asked, blue eyes glaring down at her.

Throwing her off guard with his abrupt question, she stammered, "Umm… I made us some lunch and I…I wondered if you would…would join me?" Her eyes dropped away from his.

Mark felt the anger and hurt wash out of him as he caught the fear in her eyes before she looked away. This was not what he wanted, for her to be afraid of him. He needed to let go of the anger and hurt that his first wife left in him. She didn't deserve his bad attitude just because she said they were just friends, even when he knew he wanted more from her. Wasn't it him that was holding the line on their lovemaking? Making sure she was ready? Maybe it was time to forge ahead. His eyes softened, and a slight smile came out as he answered her. "I'm sorry, Tammy. Yes, lunch sounds good. Just give me a minute and I will be right out."

Raising sad eyes to his, she nodded, turned, and walked back down the hall. He felt all kinds of a heel as he watched her walk away. He would make it up to her. He finished the email he was working on, closed his computer, then left to join her.

Sitting at the table, waiting for Mark, she pondered what she would say to him. She didn't mean to hurt him with her words. She had a lot of baggage with her first husband, which made her say things to protect her from getting hurt again. She knew he was still hurting from his first marriage. She wanted to know what his marriage was like before the divorce, but should she ask? Would he talk about it? She would soon find out as Mark came from his study and took a seat across from her. He smiled.

"This looks great, Tammy. I left in such a hurry this morning I wasn't able to grab some breakfast."

"Same here," she answered. "I guess we need to give up those late nights!" she taunted. As his piercing gaze met hers, she thought, *Oh, why did I say that? Will I never stop saying things I shouldn't?*

A grin broke out on his handsome face. "Not on your life! One of these days, we are going to be in it all night. That's when I will teach you all the things that lovers do to please each other."

She was sure she turned ten shades of red when she responded, "Does this mean we are going from friendship to lovers?"

Fascinated at her response to his words, his blue eyes turned to an even deeper blue, imagining what it would be like with her. He couldn't help but murmur, "Is it what you want?"

Goosebumps broke out all over her skin, catching the fire in his eyes as his gaze bore into her. She returned her answer with the same question. "Is it what you want?" she asked softly.

He smiled, amusement showing in his eyes. "Let's eat this wonderful lunch you prepared for us, then we'll talk."

While they were eating their lunch, Mark let her know he would be going back to work tomorrow. She had the day off and was looking forward to it. She planned on catching up on her homework and relaxing most of the day. When they finished eating, they took their dishes to the sink. Mark put on a pot of coffee. When it was ready, he poured them each a cup.

"Would you like to have our coffee in the lanai?" he asked.

She smiled. "I would love that." She followed him out to the lanai, bringing the creamer and some spoons and napkins with her. Mark set the cups down on the table. Tammy fixed their coffee while he opened up the sliding glass door and a couple of windows. With the breeze coming in, it gently blew across her face and arms. Tammy closed her eyes. She felt her body relax, letting the events of the day go. She opened her eyes when Mark came and sat down next to her, taking a sip of his coffee.

"Hmm, good," he sighed. She agreed.

"You make good coffee." She smiled, as she took a drink of her own. Sitting next to him, Tammy could feel the electricity that was generated between them. She tried to ignore it, but it was impossible with him sitting so close to her. She decided she needed a diversion, so bravely she asked, "Mark, would you mind if I asked about your marriage to Sherry?"

Mark, surprised by the question, knew this time would come. She was open with him about her ex-husband when he asked, so he needed to do the same, even if it opened old wounds. He took her hand and placed it in his. He gazed out the window into the distance, his thumb moving back and forth over her hand.

"Sherry and I met when I was in the service. Mike and I had gone into a bar one night, and there sat a beautiful woman with dark hair and green eyes at one of the tables. She was with some friends that night. I was drawn to her, so I waltzed right up and introduced myself. We hit it off and started dating. We fell in love and were married six months before I was discharged from the Air Force."

Listening, Tammy had to tamp down the jealousy she was feeling inside.

"Sherry got pregnant with Cameron three months after we were married. I was excited about the pregnancy, but I was also worried about how I was going to provide for my family after I got out of the service. Shortly after Mike and I were discharged, Mike came to me and asked if I wanted to invest in a restaurant with him. We took a look at this restaurant that was for sale along Waikiki Boulevard. Both Mike and I came up with a small investment, and we were able to put a down payment on it. The rest we took out in a bank loan. That's when the Hawaiian Lanai was born." He smiled. "It took a lot of work the first few years, but it paid off. In the meantime, Cameron was born, and I split my time with my family, the restaurant, and I did online courses to get my BA degree in marketing with a minor in accounting." Still holding her hand, he turned toward her and caught her eyes with his. "Life was good between us, but then the arguments started when my life got so occupied with the restaurant. Then trying to keep up with Cameron and school activities, I didn't see it coming. I thought even though we argued, we still had a good marriage; until one day she came home and informed me she was leaving. That she was in love with someone else. All the plans that I made for us were shattered, along with my heart. You need to know, Tammy, that it hit me so hard I wasn't able to function for weeks. If it wasn't for my friends and Mike, I don't know if I would have made it through."

Tammy placed her other hand over his, squeezing it tenderly as she gazed into his eyes. "Mark, I am so sorry. It seems we both have had our hearts shattered, which is why we both need to be careful going into a relationship. We both need to be sure."

Mark released her hand and put his arm around her. "Tammy," he murmured, "You are so different from her. You are warm and caring." He grinned. "You know how to cook. When I look back at the last few years of our marriage, I wasn't able to spend the time that was needed to keep our marriage together. It was as much my fault as it was hers. She's a good mother to Cameron, and I am grateful for that, but I have no feelings for her anymore."

She felt relieved knowing he no longer cared for his ex-wife. "Thank you, Mark, for sharing." She smiled tentatively. "I understand all that you went through. Divorce is never easy, especially when kids are involved. I know you are still hurting. I wish there was something I could do to erase all the pain inside you."

"You know, just talking about it has lifted some of the weight from keeping it inside me. I never talk about my past marriage to anyone except Mike. Being identical, we can sense when something is wrong or feel each other's pain. We've always been able to confide our troubles to each other." His eyes narrowed in on her as he inquired, "Enough about me. Are you feeling better since this morning's outing with Ms. Beret?"

"Yes." She smiled. "It was pretty harrowing." Her eyes softened as she expressed how she was feeling at this moment. "Thank you for rescuing me. And I'm sorry for jumping in and telling Ms. Beret we are just friends. Quite frankly, Mark, I don't know what we are. I feel like we are in a yo-yo type relationship. One minute we are nothing to each other, so my co-workers don't get upset, the next we are friends." She hesitated, gazing deep into his eyes. "Next, when I'm in your arms, I feel so safe. When we kiss, I've never felt such passion with anyone else. Which is it?"

He brushed his hand gently across her cheek into her hair, running his fingers through the soft tendrils, placing a few strands behind her ear. He leaned in and touched his lips to hers ever so gently. He lifted slightly. "I want to be friends, and I want to make love with you. Shouldn't we have both?" he whispered. He touched her lips again, this time in a kiss that sparked a passion that consumed them both. Mark tried to pull her closer to him, but the chairs seemed to be a barrier between them. He lifted his head. "These chairs are a problem," he breathed.

She smiled and came up from her chair. She sat down across his lap, her arms entwined around his neck.

"Hmm, that's better," he murmured softly, his arms going around her, pulling her close. He blew into her ear and gently tugged on her earlobe with his teeth. It sent tingles all the way down to her toes. He captured her lips again, and she was lost, lost in his kiss that never seemed to end. She felt his hand gently massaging her stomach, slowly moving up to her firm breast through her knit shirt. His hands felt so good on her, but she wanted more. She wanted his hands on her skin. She broke away just long enough to pull her shirt up over her head. She watched his hungry eyes roam over her breasts, covered by the lacy bra she wore, again bringing goosebumps out on her skin. Gazing at the lacy bra, hiding her firm breasts from him, he wanted his hands on them. He undid the front clasp, brushing it away, exposing both of her lovely breasts to him. She arched her head back as he took one of her breasts in his mouth, his tongue circling around her hard nipple. He suckled hard and then moved to the other, giving her the same pleasure. She groaned, as his lips followed up along her chest, to her neck, tugging on her ear. Then crushed his lips to hers in a kiss that left her weak and wanting.

When he finally lifted his head, "Tammy," he moaned, "I want you. God, how I want you." The burning desire showed as his eyes moved attentively from her eyes to her breasts, his hand cupping them, then moving slowly down to her hips and around to her center.

She wanted him too, but she knew time was short. She needed to pick up Bethany from school soon. "Mark," she breathed, "I want you, too. So much, but I have to get ready for work and pick up Bethany in an hour." She leaned her head down on his shoulder, kissing his neck. "I'm sorry, but I'm going to need to get up."

He didn't want to let her go. He kissed the top of her head down to her soft lips in a kiss that left them both breathless. When they broke apart, he traced his finger along her swollen lips. He sighed. "We seem to choose the most inappropriate times to start our lovemaking." He clasped her bra back together and sighed. "Okay, you go get ready and I'll go clean up the kitchen."

She came up off his lap and retrieved the shirt she had thrown on the floor. When he came out of the chair, she ran her arms up around his neck and kissed him with a passion she didn't know she possessed. When their lips slowly broke apart, she whispered, "I wish we had more time."

"Me too," he breathed. "Now go, before I decide to take you right here."

She gave him one last quick kiss and left the room.

Mark, trying to calm the heady emotions he was feeling whenever she was in his arms, told himself, *Next time, I'll make sure we both have plenty of time to explore these feelings we have for one another.*

CHAPTER 16

Jenna was struggling with this report that needed to be done by tomorrow afternoon. She knew Mark would be in tomorrow morning, but would there be enough time to finish it before the auditor came in? The auditor was supposed to have come in on Monday, but she stalled him until tomorrow. She was glad she did. Mark had worked on it and said it was ready, but after she went over the report, she found several mistakes. This report was too big to handle through emails. Would he be willing to come in this evening and work on it with her? She hated to ask, knowing the events that happened while her and Mike were away on their honeymoon. She would go ask Mike what she should do. She walked over to his office and softly knocked on his door. She waited a minute, then, opened the door to see if he was in his office. She peeked in and saw he was on the phone. He waved her in when he saw who had knocked. She took a seat in one of the leather chairs in front of his desk. When he finished his phone call, he turned to her and winked.

"Hi, sweetheart!" He grinned.

"Hi, handsome!" She grinned back.

"What brings you into my office?" He leaned in. "Did you come to seduce me?" he asked in that seductive drawl, wiggling his eyebrows at her. "We could lock the door and spend the rest of the afternoon on that couch over there," nodding in that direction.

She blushed. No matter how hard she tried not to, he always managed it. "Mike, be serious!" she chided.

Watching the blush come out on her pretty face, he grinned. He never got tired of it. "I am being serious!" His eyes took her in. "I will never get tired of wanting you, and loving you, Mrs. TreVaine."

She blushed again. "Later, Mr. TreVaine," she admonished. "I have something important to discuss with you."

Mike knew when he lost the battle. He sighed. "Okay, what's up?"

"I'm having trouble with this report that I need to have ready for the auditor coming in tomorrow afternoon. I know Mark has been dealing with a lot over the past several weeks, but there were several mistakes made, and I can't figure them out so the report balances. Do you think I should ask if he would come in for a short time tonight to help me? He would know where to look to correct the problem, since he handled everything while we were away."

"Jenna, he's coming in tomorrow morning. Won't that give you enough time?"

"Honestly, Mike, I'm not sure. Mark didn't have time to do the daily and weekly reports over the last couple of weeks. Catching up with those has left me with no time to work on this."

"Well, you can always call him and see if he would come in," he suggested.

"Okay," she said as she rose from her chair. "I'll go give him a call."

When she turned to go, he called out, "Hey, aren't you forgetting something?"

She turned back. Gazing into those blue eyes of his, she knew what he wanted. She walked around his desk, leaned down, and placed her lips next to his. He grabbed her waist and pulled her down on his lap, kissing her with a passion that was theirs alone. When they broke apart, he murmured, "Are you sure you don't want to lock the door and spend a little time on the couch?"

She smiled and gave him a hug before she sprang up off his lap. "Later, babe," she mused. "I've got work to do."

He watched her leave the office with a gleam in his eyes, thinking, *Yes, Mrs. TreVaine, later.*

It was a little after four when Jenna heard a knock on her door. She looked up to see Mark standing in the doorway. "Hi, Mark! Thank you for coming in. I'm sorry to have interrupted your time off, but there were some areas in your report that didn't make sense."

"No worries, Jenna. I was having trouble finishing it last week. I'm not surprised that there were some mistakes. I'm glad you caught them."

"Do you want me to come to your office to work or would here be okay?" she asked.

"Do you have a copy of the report?"

"Yes."

"Bring it to my office along with the daily and weekly reports you were able to finish, and we will compare them on my computer."

Jenna gathered all the reports and headed over to his office. When she went in, Mark, seated at his desk, was pulling up the reports on his computer. She pulled a chair up beside him, pulled the reports from the folder, and spread them out on his desk for his review. Good thing he kept his desk free of clutter. Mark, looking over the report he had filed, could see it didn't balance. He was so tired last week that he completely overlooked it. With him not having time to do the daily and weekly reports, he could see where he messed up. At the time, he was just glad he finished it. He didn't bother to double check it.

He picked up the phone and made a call out to the hostess station. Tonya was on duty. He asked her to bring in a carafe of coffee with some cream and sugar to his office. "Okay, Jenna. This may take a while. Let's go over these reports you were able to do for the last two weeks, to see if we can find the problems and correct this report in time for the auditor tomorrow."

They got to work, and three hours and two carafes of coffee later, they were able to bring the report current, with a balanced sheet.

"Whew!" cried Jenna. "I'm glad we were able to finish this tonight! You know Arthur, he can spot a mistake in a second!"

"Yes," he commented, "I know him well. What do you say we get these reports put away, and we'll see what's happening out on the floor. If it's anything like the last two weeks, they may need some extra hands."

Jenna agreed. She gathered up all the reports and put them back in the file folders. Mark went out ahead of her.

He wanted to see Tammy. He had left before she came back with Bethany after picking her up at school. He got a glimpse of her when she rushed past him to deliver drinks in the Hawaiian Room. His eyes traveled over to the hostess station, and he could see that they were slammed again. There were customers standing in line waiting for a table, while the waitstaff and hostesses were running around serving the customers that were already seated. He wasn't dressed to seat people, but he could bus tables and help wherever he could.

Jenna came up behind him after she put the reports away and locked the office. "Well, Mark." She sighed. "It looks like we have our work cut out for us."

"Yes. it does," he commented. "Let's go see where we can help."

"Are you going to wear that hat on your head?"

He had completely forgotten he was wearing a hat. He must be getting used to it. He needed to do something with his hair by tomorrow. Their regular customers would wonder what had gotten into him. He grinned down at her and stated, "Yep!"

The night was a rush of activity, with Jenna helping Mike seat customers, running coffee around, and he helping the busboys clear tables for the next round of customers. By the time the night ended, they were all exhausted and ready to go home.

As the three of them headed over to an empty booth, Jenna glanced up to her husband and sighed. "Next time I'm going to bring an extra pair of comfortable shoes! My feet are killing me!"

When they seated themselves in the booth, Carol came over and asked them if they wanted anything. The kitchen was about to close. Mike and Jenna ordered a light sandwich and coffee, while Mark just wanted a cola.

"I see what you meant when you said Wednesdays were getting just as bad as the rest of the week! Good thing I started running the ad for help yesterday! Even with the two of you helping, it was hard to keep up," said Mike.

Mark nodded. "It's been crazy lately. You need to speak with Palani, to see if he needs more help as well. The orders have been coming out slower than usual."

"I noticed. I'll check with him tomorrow. How did the report come out?" he asked.

"Between Jenna and I, we were able to correct and get it to balance. Should be good for the auditor tomorrow."

Carol brought out their drinks. She set them down on the table in front of them. "Your sandwiches will be coming right out." She smiled.

"Thanks, Carol," replied Mike.

When Carol left, Mark noticed a late customer coming into the lounge. He took a seat at the bar. Bill was the bartender on duty tonight. He watched as Bill served him a beer, took his money, and went over to the register. As he studied the man, there seemed to be something very familiar about him, but he couldn't place him. He had on a gray business suit, with a black felt tip hat perched on top of his head. He didn't get a good look at his facial features, so he couldn't be sure…but he resembled the guy who was sitting out in his car that morning in front of his home when he went to pick up Mike and Jenna at the airport. He leaned forward onto the table and commented to Mike, "Hey, Mike, take a look at the gentleman seated at the bar in the gray suit. He looks very familiar, but I can't seem to place him. Have you any idea who he is?"

Both Mike and Jenna turned around to get a look at the man Mark was referring to. Mike turned back. "He came in last night, about this same time. I'm not sure who he is, but I had the same thought. He looked familiar to me, too."

Mark continued to study him as he drank the beer, thanked the bartender, and left. He got a better look at his face this time. He did resemble the guy in the car outside his home, but again, he couldn't be sure. He had on a pair of dark sunglasses that day. He would get with Zack in the morning and see if they could come up with any information on him. He finished his cola, and since everything was set for the auditor coming in, he turned back to Mike and Jenna. "Listen, I'm going to get going." He glanced over at Jenna. "Jenna, I won't be coming in until noon tomorrow. Do you think you can handle things until I get here?" he asked.

Surprised, she answered, "Sure, no worries, I'll be fine. I'll get started on the daily report and get the cash drawers ready for a deposit."

"Great, I'll see you two tomorrow." Mark came out of the booth and headed for the door. He wanted to see if he could catch the man sitting at the bar. Outside, he looked around but didn't see him. He started walking toward his car when darkness enveloped him, and he fell to the ground.

Mark woke up to flashing lights and two medics ready to put him on a stretcher. He moaned, reaching back and touching the lump on the back of his head. He could feel blood from the open wound. His eyes searching around, he saw his brother Mike bending down to ask, "Mark, you gave us the scare of our lives! What happened?"

Mark groaned as he tried to sit up. He winced. "Someone hit me from behind." The emergency medic, who had placed a pillow behind his head, gently pushed him back down, pressing a cool compress on the back of his head and insisted he lie still.

"Mr. TreVaine, we need to take you to the hospital, to make sure you have no internal bleeding. I'm pretty sure you have a concussion."

Panic gripped him as he thought about Tammy. He tried to sit up again. "I can't go to the hospital. Where's Tammy? I need to get to her."

This time Mike gently pushed him back on the pillow. "Listen, bro, you need to go to the hospital. Tammy left a while ago. I'm sure she is at your home safe and sound."

"You don't understand." He gripped Mike's arm. "I got a note on my car to stay away from her and her daughter. I need to go to her. Make sure she's safe." He groaned again, the pain shooting inside his head. "Call Zack." He winced. "See if he had one of his detectives follow her home."

Mark, with his heart racing, was desperate to make sure nothing happened to Tammy and her daughter. *What if this guy sitting at the bar had something to do with the attempted kidnapping?* "Mike," he insisted, his face showing the pain he was enduring. "After you talk to Zack, will you go check on them? Otherwise, I'll…go…" He tried again to sit up, but the throbbing in his head made him lie back down again.

Mike hated to see his brother in such pain. He would find out who did this! He didn't want to leave him. He looked over at his beautiful wife with pain in his own eyes, torn between getting in the ambulance with his brother or doing what Mark asked him to do.

Jenna met his eyes and knew what she needed to do. "I'll go with Mark to the hospital. You go check on Tammy and her daughter. I'll keep you posted."

He turned back to his brother just before he closed his eyes from the pain. "Jenna's going with you. I'll get a hold of Zack to meet me at your house. I will let Jenna know as soon as I arrive at your home. Try not to worry." He nodded his head as the medics lifted him onto the stretcher and into the ambulance.

As soon as the ambulance left, Mike walked Jenna to her car. He opened the door for her and gave her a quick hug. "I'll see you back at the hospital."

She got into her car, but before she closed the door, she pleaded, "Mike." He turned back. "Be careful."

"Always. I love you," determination in his steps as he walked away.

"Love you too," she murmured softly as she closed the door and started the engine. As she left for the hospital, she prayed for her husband, that he would find Tammy and her daughter safe.

Mike went over to his Corvette, to find all four tires slashed. Shocked, he immediately called Zack. "Detective Williams," he answered.

"Hey, Zack, Mike here," he returned, panic clearly in his voice.

Zack was just getting ready to get some rest. He had been working night and day on homicide cases, along with the case involving Tammy and her daughter. He could hear the fear in Mike's voice as he asked, "What's going on?"

"You're not going to believe this, Zack, but Mark was hit from behind just outside the restaurant. A couple leaving the restaurant found him lying on the ground, out cold. They called the police and an ambulance. When we saw the flashing lights from the windows, we rushed out and found Mark coming to, with the medics getting ready to put him on the stretcher."

"Did anybody in the area see what happened?"

"The police are still investigating. I need to know, Zack, were you able to have someone in your department follow Tammy home. Mark was in a panic to make sure she and her daughter were safe."

"Hang on a minute, Mike." He put Mike on hold and checked the schedule. He did have someone on at nine p.m. He never knew when she was going to leave from work, so he made sure someone was there early. He tapped the hold button. "Mike?"

"Yes."

"As far as I know, one of the officers was there to follow her to Mark's."

"Okay, one other thing. When I went to get into my car, all four tires on my Corvette were slashed. I need to get over to Mark's to check on Tammy and her daughter. When they lifted him into the ambulance, I promised him I would let him know as soon as possible."

"Are any of the officers still there?"

Mike took a look around and found two officers getting ready to go back to their patrol cars. "Two are still here but look to be getting ready to leave."

"Get ahold of one of them to file a report on your car. I'm on my way!"

Zack pulled up in the side parking lot of the restaurant. He rushed out of his car to find Mike filing a report with the officer on duty. "Hey, Officer Stone. Are you about finished here?" asked Zack.

"Yes, I think I have all that I need, Detective Williams." He turned to Mike. "I'll get back to you in the morning. In the meantime, I'll call a tow truck. Where would you like it to be delivered?"

"Have them take it to the Chevy dealer on 12th Street. I'll call them in the morning."

The officer nodded, wrote down the address, closed up his pad, and held out his hand to shake Mike's. "Try to have a good rest of your night. We'll get to the bottom of who did this to your car."

"Thanks, officer," returning his handshake. When he left, Mike turned back to Zack.

"All set?" asked Zack.

"Let's go!"

Tammy felt on edge all night. She had been aware Mark had come into the restaurant when she clocked in. He was working in his office with Jenna, she was told. Her nerves always got the better of her when he was here, but by the time she saw him coming from his office, the night had turned into a non-stop hectic nightmare. She did all she could do to keep up with the flow of customers coming into the Hawaiian Room that were seated in her section. Even though they were busy, their eyes would meet. Devastating in blue jeans that fit his narrow hips to a tee, along with a white t-shirt that showed off every muscle in his chest and arms, she would catch him out of the corner of her eye, busing tables and pouring coffee. When he would glance her way with that sexy smile of his, she'd blush and turn away, embarrassed by the fact she was caught watching him. Fortunately, the Hawaiian Room was the first to clear out just before nine o'clock. She hurried to help with clean up and headed to Mark's around nine thirty.

She was so tired she couldn't wait to put her feet up. Hopefully, the Langleys had put Bethany to bed. She came in through the front door and found Mr. and Mrs. Langley in the entertainment room watching a movie. "Hi, how did your night go?" she inquired.

"Oh, you're home!" Mrs. Langley said as she got up out of her chair. Mr. Langley shut the TV off and joined his wife. "It went well, as always. Bethany is sound asleep. But there is one thing that disturbed us tonight," she expressed.

"Oh?" Tammy's heart beat a little faster in anticipation of what Mrs. Langley was about to tell her. "What is it?"

"After the officer came to tell us he had to leave, there was a black Ford Taurus that pulled up in front of the house along the road after the officer drove off. We thought it was another officer or detective to take his place, but he got out of the car and started walking up and down the road. We've never seen any of the officers do that. They always stay in their cars."

"What time did this happen?"

"It was around eight o'clock. Bob kept watch to make sure he didn't come near the house. He looked suspicious even though he was dressed in a nice dark suit."

Tammy's eyes went to Mr. Langley. "Can you give me more information on what he looked like Mr. Langley?"

"Well, as Mildred said, he was dressed in a nice dark suit. I couldn't tell if it was dark gray or black. He wore dark sunglasses and one of those fancy felt-tip hats. I couldn't tell what color his hair was. After about an hour, he got back into his car and left. Do you think we should report it to the police?"

Tammy thought a moment. "You know, it may be nothing, but if it's someone checking out Mark's home, it might be a good idea to let the police know. I'm going to call 911 to see if they can send an officer here. Can you stay to talk to them?" Mr. and Mrs. Langley looked at each other and nodded.

"Yes, Tammy, we'll stay," answered Mildred.

An officer came within a few minutes after she made the call. The Langleys told the officer what they saw and gave a description of the man. He said he would file the report and wished them a good night. Mr. and Mrs. Langley left shortly after, and Tammy was left alone in the house, aside from Bethany sleeping in their room down the hall. She decided to peek in. She went down the hall and quietly opened the door. Her little girl was all curled up with her Mr. Snow Bear sound asleep. She closed the door.

She decided before she went to bed, she would make herself a cup of tea. It always calmed her when her nerves were on edge. In the kitchen, she filled the tea kettle with water and placed it on the stove. She turned the burner on and waited. When the water began to boil, she poured some in a cup with one of her favorite chamomile tea bags. She took her tea into the living room and sat down on the sofa, curling her legs up underneath her. It was quiet. *Too quiet,* she thought.

Chills started to spread throughout her body. Did she lock the door when the Langleys left? She came up off the couch to check. Yes, the door was locked. She breathed a sigh of relief. As she walked away from the door, she thought she heard a rustling noise. She couldn't quite place where the noise came from. Then it hit her! Did Mark remember to lock the sliding glass door in the lanai and close the windows before he went to work? She ran out and found them all opened! She locked the door and quickly closed and locked the windows! She backed out of the room and wondered when Mark was going to be home.

Mark had always been here since they moved in. Should she call the police? She calmed down and told herself she was being ridiculous. She went and took a peek out the front window. She didn't see anyone out there. She let the curtain fall and went back to her tea, just as a black Ford Taurus pulled up in front of the house.

Sitting back a ways from Mark's home, he had watched the patrol car leave. It was a few more minutes before he saw the old couple leave the house. *It's about time!* he thought. He had been sitting there a good half hour, waiting for them to leave. He waited until the cars were out of sight, then slowly pulled up in front of Mark's home. *This should be clear sailing now that the TreVaine brothers are out of the way*, he mused. *I'll soon have the little girl, drop her off at the warehouse, and get the hell out!* There was only one problem. *The mother.*

He thought a moment, the glint in his eyes shimmering in the night as a plan formulated in his mind. He could knock her out, throw her body into the trunk, grab the little girl, and take the girl to the warehouse. Then he would get rid of the mother's body, by dropping her off a cliff into the ocean. *Piece of cake.* His eyes gleamed as an evil smile broke out on his face.

He took a pair of black gloves out of the glove compartment along with his forty-four-magnum pistol. After he put his gloves on, he took a look around through the windows of his car and checked in his rearview mirror. Off in the distance he saw headlights. They looked to be coming up fast for a subdivision. *Shit!* he swore. He pulled away from the home and turned down a side street with his lights off. He turned the car around, so he could keep watch, and waited.

Zack and Mike pulled into Mark's driveway. They both rushed out of the car and up to the door. Inside, sitting on the couch enjoying her tea, Tammy heard a pounding on the door. She practically jumped out of her skin! Her heart was racing as she wondered what she should do. Should she answer it, or lay low and let whoever it was think that no one was here? Lots of people left their homes with the lights on, she surmised. The pounding came again, this time with voices! Was one of them Mike's voice she heard? She jumped up off the couch and ran to the door. She looked in the peephole and saw both Mike and Zack standing outside the door. She quickly opened it. Both men rushed in.

"Tammy, are you all right?" asked Mike.

From the tone in Mike's voice, she instantly knew something was wrong. "Yes, I'm fine. What's going on?" Her heart started racing. "Did something happen to Mark?" she asked frantically.

"Let's go into the living room. I'll explain everything." All three took a seat. "Tammy," Zack said calmly, "Mark is in the hospital."

Mike, noticing the fear in her eyes, took her hand in his. "He's going to be okay. They want to make sure there was no internal bleeding," Mike tried to explain.

No internal bleeding? she repeated in her head. Mike was not doing the best job of explaining this to her as the look of fear went completely into shock! "Wha… What happened?" she stammered, feeling her whole body start to shake.

"Let me explain, Mike," said Zack. He knew Mike was still too shook up about what happened to his brother to make a lot of sense to her. "Tammy, when Mark came out of the restaurant tonight, someone came up behind him and knocked him out. Mike didn't even know that anything had happened to his brother until he saw the flashing lights outside the restaurant. When he went to see what was going on, he saw paramedics kneeling down over Mark. Mark came to and wanted to know where you were. He was going to try and check on you, but the medics insisted he go to the hospital to be checked out. According to the medics, he took a blow to the back of the head. They were concerned he may have a concussion and possible internal bleeding. Before they put him in the ambulance, he was in a state to know if you and Bethany were safe."

Tammy, stunned, never thought it would come to this. Yes, they had threats, but they were so careful. Always checking, making sure no one suspicious was around. "He's going to be okay?" Her voice was shaking.

"Yes, as far as we know. Mike needs to get back to the hospital.

I will go with him as well. If Mark is up to it, I will need to ask him a few more questions."

Tammy needed to see him. She made a decision. "I'm going with you."

"Tammy, I'm not sure they will let you see him," answered Mike.

"I don't care. I need to be with him, even if it's sitting out in the waiting room, waiting to hear how he is doing. Just let me gather up a few things and Bethany." She came up from the couch to go down the hall, only to be encountered by her little girl holding Mr. Snow Bear. She looked up at her mom with sorrowful eyes and asked, "Is Mr. Mark, okay?"

"Oh, Bethany, I didn't hear you come out of our room." She picked her up and hugged her little body to her. She carried her over to the two men sitting on the couch. Both men stood up as Tammy introduced them. "Bethany, you remember, Zack, the detective who came to our house last week." She nodded her head, staring back and forth between the two men. "And this is Mike, Mr. Mark's twin brother." A smile broke out over her delicate face.

"You look just like Mr. Mark!" she exclaimed. "Only... Mr. Mark has black hair. How come, Mommy?" she asked with a puzzling look on her face.

"Another time, Bethany. Right now we need to get ready to go to the hospital." She glanced at the two men. "Give me a few minutes to get Bethany dressed and I will follow you to the hospital."

When she left the room, Mike turned to Zack. "Cute kid. I can see how my brother has become attached to them both."

"Attached? Do you really think that this is all it is between the two?"

"Well, they got thrown into this situation together. Of course they would care about each other. But Zack, it would create a big problem at the restaurant if they started to have a relationship together. Are you forgetting about Kalea? How she interfered with some of my relationships?"

Zack just shook his head. *Yeah.* He remembered.

Tammy came from the bedroom with a duffle bag in her hand and Bethany in the other. "Are you ready?" Mike asked.

"Yes," she answered him. "Just let me grab my keys and purse. We will follow you there."

"Better yet, Tammy," Zack stated, "Mike and I will follow you there." With that, they all left the house, making sure the lights were off and the door was locked on the way out.

He watched as the car belonging to the mother pulled out of the driveway, with a blue Sedan following behind. When the taillights were out of sight, he pulled slowly up in front of the house. The lights were turned off, and he was sure the house was locked up. He knew the house had an alarm system. He didn't know if it was set, but he wasn't going to chance it. *Damn it!* He was hoping this night would be over so he could go back to the way he was living before he got involved in this whole kidnapping thing. After they had given him the money for selling her, he was supposed to be done. It was an easy exchange. He got the money and gave them the location of the girl. Then Morris got caught and thrown in the slammer when he tried to take her! Then, the main trafficker called him and demanded he get the kid or pay him back. He had so many debts to pay from his gambling online that there was no way he'd give the money back! What a mess! He never should have gambled. He made a good living, but he couldn't stop. He slammed his fist on the steering wheel! *I've got to find a way to get that kid!* He pulled out onto the road and tried to figure out his next move.

At the hospital, they all rushed in through the emergency room doors, to find Jenna sitting in the waiting room. She stood up as Mike ran up to her and wrapped his arms around her for a fierce hug. He let her go long enough to ask, "Have you heard anything yet?"

"I'm sorry, the doctor hasn't come out. I'm assuming they are still examining him. They wouldn't let me go back there with him."

"How long has he been back there?" he asked.

"Over an hour," she responded.

"Let me go check at the desk and see if I can get an update on his condition."

Before he left, Jenna touched his arm. "Listen, I hope you don't mind, but I called Peyton. He said he would get here as soon as he could."

He drew a sigh of relief. "No, that's fine. I've wanted to call him, but I kept putting it off, waiting to see how this case was going to go. He gave her another kiss on the cheek. "I'll be right back."

When Mike left to go check on his brother, Jenna spotted Zack, then Tammy, with her little girl in her arms, standing in the background of the waiting room. She came up to them to give them a report on Mark. "Hi, Zack. Hi, Tammy." She smiled. Jenna's eyes shifted to the little girl. "And who's this?" she asked.

"Hi, Jenna. This is Bethany. I hope we are not imposing, but I had to make sure Mark was going to be okay. Plus, I didn't want to stay by myself, with Mark being in the hospital."

Jenna smiled. "Why don't you come over and sit down. Bethany must be heavy in your arms. There's a loveseat off to the side where you can lay Bethany down if she wants to go to sleep."

"She does get heavy. Thank you, Jenna." Zack brought over the duffle bag he carried in for her and set it beside the loveseat. "I'm going over to see if Mike has found out anything yet."

"Okay, Zack," replied Jenna. Jenna sat down in the chair next to the loveseat. She watched as Tammy pulled out a blanket and a cute little bear dressed up in a winter sweater, with a knit hat on top of its head. Bethany took the snow bear in her arms, while

Tammy wrapped her up in a blanket. She swayed back and forth, hoping Bethany would fall back to sleep. Jenna smiled as she watched Tammy with her daughter. She wasn't quite ready for a child in her life, but when the time was right, she wanted to have at least four children with Mike.

Wait a minute! She and Mike had never discussed how many children they would like. Would he want that many? They both said they wanted children. She guessed that was something they better be on the same page with. She would mention it to him, after they got through this case.

Bethany started to close her eyes. Within minutes she was sound asleep. "Hey, Jenna, could you please get the small pillow in the duffle bag?" she whispered.

"Sure." She reached in and pulled out the small pillow and placed it at the end of the loveseat.

Tammy laid her down and made sure she was fully covered, to be sure she didn't get a chill. Hospitals can get drafty, especially with the doors opening and closing throughout the night. She came over and took a seat beside Jenna. "Can you tell me any more about what happened tonight at the restaurant?"

"Well, Tammy, we don't know much. When he left the restaurant around ten, we assumed he was going home. We didn't know anything had happened to him until we saw the flashing lights outside the restaurant. When we went outside to investigate, we found the paramedics hovering over Mark. He didn't come to for ten minutes while the medics worked on him. When he was able to answer some questions, he said he was hit from behind by someone. As far as we know, no one saw what happened. A couple stumbled upon him, who called the police and the ambulance. We'll have to wait and see if the police were able to gather any more information."

She nodded. "That's what Zack had told me. I was hoping you would know a little bit more being right there."

"I'm sorry, Tammy, but there's not much more I can tell you. Now, we just have to wait to see how he is doing. Hopefully, the doctor will be out soon."

Tears started forming in her eyes as Tammy visualized what must have happened. "Oh Jenna, I had no idea that this would happen. We are always careful to make sure no one was following us."

Jenna took her hand. "From what Mark told us, he was taken by surprise. He has no idea who hit him."

Tammy took a breath and leaned back in her chair. She said a prayer for Mark, and for the doctor who was treating him. Hopefully they would hear from him soon.

Mike and Zack came back and took a seat. There were no updates on his condition, but the nurse thought the doctor would be out shortly. Quietly they waited. It seemed like hours before the doctor on duty came out to give them a briefing on Mark's condition. All of them rose from their chairs to listen to what he had to say.

"Hi, I'm Dr. Hawthorne. I was the doctor on call to treat Mr. TreVaine when he came into the emergency room." He turned to Mike and smiled. "I can tell you must be his twin brother. He's been asking for you."

"Can we go back and see him?"

"Yes, but only two at a time. Your brother suffered a blow to the back of the head which required stitches. He has a slight concussion, but there was no internal bleeding. I'm going to keep him overnight for observation, but he should be able to go home tomorrow afternoon. I will be prescribing a pain medication for the headaches for five days and then he should be able to take an over-the-counter pain reliever. He will need to lay low for at least a week." His eyes traveled around to each one and asked, "Do you have any questions?" They all shook their heads no. "Okay. Mike, if you could come with me, I will take you back. The rest of you will have to wait until we have him in a room. It shouldn't take very long."

Mike turned to Jenna. "I'll be right back. I need to see him."

"I know. You go ahead, I'll be right here waiting." Mike kissed her cheek and followed the doctor back through the emergency room doors.

Mike was led back to a large room with curtains separating the patients. When they reached Mark's bed, the doctor informed him that he gave Mark a light sedative, to help him relax. "He was in a state when they brought him in, something about a woman and her daughter? It will most likely make him sleepy, so I don't know how long he will be able to stay awake."

Mike nodded and held out his hand. As he shook hands with the doctor, he expressed, "Thanks, Dr. Hawthorne, for taking good care of my brother."

"You're welcome. I will be here the rest of the night. If you need anything, just have the nurse on duty give me a call." He walked away, on to the next patient.

Mike slightly pulled the curtain aside and stepped up to the bed. Seeing his brother, his face slightly ashen from the trauma he went through tonight, made his heart sick. He touched his shoulder. Mark instantly opened his eyes.

"Mike," he asked groggily. "Are Tammy and Bethany all right?"

"Yes, they are both fine. They are both out in the waiting room."

He breathed a sigh of relief. He closed his eyes and opened them again. He was so sleepy. He could hardly stay awake. Before he drifted off, he whispered, "Watch over them for me…."

As Mike watched him drift off, he made a promise. "No worries, bro," he said softly. "I'll make sure they are kept safe."

Two nurses came in. "I'm sorry, sir. You will have to leave. We are going to take Mr. TreVaine up to his room now. If you can give us twenty minutes, you will be able to see him at that time. He'll be on the third floor, Room 302."

Mike nodded. "Thank you."

When Mike returned to the waiting room, he was surprised to see his older brother Peyton already sitting with Jenna and the others. Zack was over by the door on his phone. Peyton rose when Mike came up to him and extended his hand. "How's he doing?" asked Peyton.

"He's doing okay. The doctor gave him a sedative, so I wasn't able to talk with him much. But what I did get out of him was to watch over Tammy and her little girl." He glanced over at Tammy, and back to Peyton. "And that is exactly what I am going to do."

Peyton glanced over at Tammy and smiled. She returned the smile. Turning back to his brother, he asked, "Zack filled me in when I came in. Is there anything I can do to help? I was able to get a few days off, so whatever you need, I'm here."

Zack came over as he was putting his phone back into his pocket. "I have an officer coming over and standing guard outside Mark's room tonight. Do you know what room he will be in?"

"Yes," said Mike. "They're taking him up to the third floor, Room 302. They said to wait twenty minutes, then we can see him."

"Let's all go up to the third floor. They have a waiting room up there. They can call us in when they have him settled," suggested Zack.

They all turned to head over to the elevator, but Mike held back. He walked up to Tammy and smiled. "Can I carry Bethany for you?"

She gave him a smile back. "Thanks, Mike. I wasn't sure they would let me see him, since I'm not family."

His eyes softened as he stared down at her little girl. Such a sweet child; someday he would like a few of his own. His eyes traveled back to Tammy. "Mark knows you're here. He'll want to see you and Bethany when he wakes."

She swallowed and nodded, trying to hold back the tears. "Okay, if you could carry Bethany for me, I'll get the duffle bag. She does get heavy if I have to hold her too long."

He went over to the loveseat and lifted the little girl in his arms. Tammy followed him to the elevator and up to the third floor. They entered the waiting room, where Mike took and laid Bethany down on one of the sofas. They all took a seat, waiting for the nurse to come in, to let them know he was ready for visitors.

Tammy was the last one to see him. Jenna said she would stay with Bethany. When she walked into the room, she stopped at the door, trying to pull herself together before she came up to his bed. She glanced over to see Mike was still in the room. Tammy slowly went up and stood beside him. She took hold of his hand and gave it a gentle squeeze. Even though she tried not to, the tears started flowing down her cheeks, as she placed her other hand on his forehead, brushing some of his hair that had fallen down over his brow.

Mike, watching Tammy, saw the love she had for his brother. Even though he didn't want to admit it, he was pretty sure his brother felt the same. Somehow, they would get through this. Mike got up from his chair and left the room, to give them more privacy.

Tammy bent down and kissed his cheek. Even though he was sleeping, she whispered softly to him, "I'm so sorry, Mark. I never meant for this to happen to you." Her tears streaming down her soft cheeks landed on his rugged, handsome face.

Mark, in a fog, thought he could hear Tammy's voice. He felt her squeezing his hand. He squeezed back. Tammy felt his fingers closing over her hand. She softly pressed her lips on his.

Tenderly she asked, "Mark, can you hear me?"

Mark, fighting to come out of the darkness, barely lifted his eyes.

He couldn't see her very well but could feel her hand in his and the gentle kiss she gave him. He tried to smile as he whispered, "Stay… Please stay," as he drifted off into a deep sleep.

CHAPTER 17

MARK WOKE TO a sleeping Bethany snuggled up beside him, with her Mr. Snow Bear between them. He shifted to try and get a little more comfortable. He winced and groaned at the same time. His head was throbbing, and his whole body ached. He turned his head to see Tammy sleeping in a recliner chair, covered up with one of the hospital blankets. As he watched her sleeping, his only thought was how beautiful she was. Her amber hair was spread out along the back of the head rest, and with her eyes closed, she looked like a porcelain doll, with her peaches-and-cream complexion. He gazed down at the little girl sleeping on his chest with his arm around her. He smiled. He knew his heart had been taken by them both. He would do anything to protect them. As soon as he got out of the hospital, he was going to find out who tried to take him out. Something inside him told him it was the guy sitting at the bar. He was sure he knew him from somewhere, but where? He needed to get with his brothers and Zack, to see if they could help him find out anything on this guy.

His thoughts were interrupted when the nurse came in. She was smiling as she approached his bed. "I see you have a bed partner! How are you feeling?" she asked softly, as not to disturb the little sleeping girl.

"I'm a little sore, and my head is throbbing," he answered in a cracked raspy voice, his throat so dry from not having anything to drink since last night.

"That's understandable. You've got quite a lump on the back of your head. I'm going to take your vitals. Then I will bring you something for the pain."

He glanced at her name tag as she was taking his blood pressure. "Nurse Briggs, is there any way I could get some coffee? Enough for Tammy and I, and juice for Bethany?" he asked.

"Sure, just let me check your stitches and I'll get right on it."

When she left, Tammy was waking up. She thought she heard voices as she came out of her slumber. She pulled the blanket off of her and discovered her daughter wasn't in the chair with her. Frantically she looked around. Her amber eyes met Mark's. He was awake! She rushed up to his bed, to find Bethany sound asleep beside him. He smiled.

"Are you looking for someone?"

She breathed a sigh of relief seeing her daughter lying next to him. "Oh Mark, I'm so sorry! Last I knew she was sleeping in the chair with me. How are you feeling?" keeping her voice low.

"It's okay, and to answer your question, my head is throbbing, and I feel like a truck ran over me. The nurse was just here. She's bringing me in some pain medication." He gasped as he tried to shift his body again. He gave up. She could see that he was uncomfortable.

"Here, let me get Bethany so you can at least get yourself in a more comfortable position." She hurried around the bed to pick Bethany up and place her in the chair. Once she was settled, she went back to see if she could get him anything. "Can I get you some water or coffee?"

"The nurse is bringing us some coffee, and juice for Bethany, but I need to get up."

"Do you think you can get up on your own, or do you need help?"

"I think I can make it," he grunted as he sat up and swung his legs over to the side of the bed. He stood up, and sat back down again, feeling a little off-kilter.

"Are you sure you don't need a hand?"

He winced. "Maybe I do."

She came up beside him and helped him get to the restroom. Once he finished, she guided him back to bed.

The nurse came back with his pain medication and some water. "Here you go, Mr. TreVaine. Coffee and juice are on their way." Mark took the pills and downed them with the water. "Would you like some breakfast, Mr. TreVaine? There's a menu over on the table you can order from. Just call down to the kitchen and they'll get it right up to you. Your wife and daughter can order something as well."

Tammy, surprised that he didn't clarify her remark, "Oh, we're not—"

Mark interrupted. "I am hungry. We'll take a look," he returned. The thoughts of Tammy being his wife and Bethany his daughter suddenly had a pleasant ring to it.

"Okay. Let me know if you need anything else. The doctor is doing his rounds; he should be in shortly."

When she left, Bethany was waking up. She sat up in the chair, yawning and rubbing her eyes. When she saw that everyone was awake, she jumped off the chair to run and climb back up in the bed with him. "Are you feeling better, Mr. Mark?" she asked in her small voice, snuggling up against his side. He smiled as he put his arm around her. "I am feeling a little better, Bethany." *As soon as the pain medication kicks in, I'll feel a lot better.*

"When will you get to come home?"

"I don't know. We'll have to wait until the doctor comes in. Are you hungry?"

She grinned and nodded her head.

Tammy, gazing at the two of them, felt her heart melt. She could see that Bethany was growing more attached to him with each passing day. He glanced her way and held out his hand to her. Tammy placed her hand in his. Staring into those deep-blue eyes of his, she knew her heart was taken, and she would do anything for him. Did he feel the same? She knew they had chemistry, that he wanted her. Was it love, or just an attraction on his part?

Watching the expressions crossing over her soft features, he asked, "What's going on in that pretty little head of yours?"

She smiled. "Nothing. Bethany and I need to get going. She's going to be late for school as it is."

Listening, Bethany cut in. "But Mom! I'm hungry! I want to eat breakfast with Mr. Mark!"

Mark squeezed her hand. "Let's order breakfast and then if you want to get going, I won't stop you."

She shook her head and smiled down at his handsome face, his shadow beard enhancing his features. "You know, TreVaine, you always have a way of convincing me to do things I shouldn't."

He grinned. "Not everything…yet," his blue eyes gleaming into hers.

Mike stood in the doorway, taking in the scene before him. He walked up to the other side of the bed. "Sorry to interrupt, how are you feeling, Mark?" he asked.

Mark turned his head, to see his brother standing beside him. "Hey, bro. I'm a little sore, but doing okay."

An aide came in with their coffee and juice and set it on the table. Tammy moved away from the bed to retrieve the table and wheel it up to the side of the bed. Tammy poured a cup for Mark and one for her, adding a little cream to both. "Mike, would you like a cup?"

"Is there enough?" he answered.

"I think so." She poured another cup with some cream and handed it to him.

"Thanks."

"You're welcome. Bethany, come with me to get washed up while Mr. Mark and Mike talk. Then you can have some of your juice."

"Okay, Mommy. I do have to go." Tammy picked her up and took her to the restroom. Thank goodness there were towels and washcloths on the shelf.

When they were alone, Mark pushed the button to bring him up in a sitting position, so he could drink his coffee. "Has the doctor been in yet, this morning?" asked Mike.

"Not yet. Hopefully soon. I need to know when I can get out of here."

"The doctor that treated you last night thought you could go home this afternoon, but things can change, so don't get your hopes up."

"Mike, I need to find out who that guy was sitting at the bar. He looks similar to the man I saw sitting out in front of my house the morning I came to pick you and Jenna up at the airport. I can't be sure…but can you get ahold of Zack this morning? I need to talk to him, give him a description, to see if he can match him up on their intel."

"I've already talked to Zack. He said he would be coming to see you this morning. He needed to ask you a few questions. You can give him a description then. By the way, Peyton came in last night."

"Peyton is here?"

"Yes, you were out of it when he came in to see you. He'll be staying for a few days."

"Good. Maybe we can formulate a plan if Zack is unable to find anything out about this guy. Also, ask the employees if he has been in the restaurant before the last two nights. I know I have seen him before," he said as his thoughts contemplated the situation.

"I had that same feeling. It's been a while, but I'm pretty sure he was a regular customer several years ago. Then he just disappeared. I'm not sure any of the employees would remember him, but I will ask."

"Thanks, Mike."

The doctor chose that moment to come in and examine him. "Good morning, Mr. TreVaine. I'm Dr. Holden," he stated as he looked over his chart. He set it down at the end of the bed. "I see Nurse Briggs has been in. All your vitals look good. Let's take a look at the stitches on the back of your head."

Mike excused himself while the doctor checked him over. Tammy and Bethany came out of the restroom, to see the doctor had come in. She took Bethany's hand and led her out of the room, to see Mike standing outside the door and an officer standing across the hall. She knew the officer had been placed to keep watch, if the person who hit Mark decided to come into the hospital. A precautionary measure, they assured her. She turned her focus on Mike, not knowing quite what to say to him. Here she was, an employee of theirs, spending the night in a hospital room with his brother. What must he think! When Mark asked her to stay with him, she felt impelled to do so. Mike had come back in, only to find his brother was out from the sedation. She told him she would be staying with him. He nodded and left the room.

Nervously, she greeted him, "Hi, Mike. How are you?"

He smiled. "I'm fine. I want to thank you for staying with Mark last night. I was going to stay, but I could see this morning he was in better hands."

She blushed, feeling a little embarrassed when she answered. "You're welcome. I just want you to know that I never expected this would happen. We were both so careful to make sure no one suspicious was around."

"You don't have to apologize, Tammy. It wasn't your fault. But you can bet we are going to find out who did this and put him behind bars."

Bethany pulled on her hand. She glanced down at her daughter. "Mommy, I want some juice."

"If you can wait just a bit, we can go in and get your juice."

"But I want it now," she whined.

Tammy, holding her patience, explained, "The doctor is with Mr. Mark right now. As soon as he is finished, I promise you we will go back into the room, then you can have your juice."

"What's he doing?" she asked impatiently in her small voice.

Mike chuckled and answered Bethany's question for Tammy. He came down on his haunches and smiled. "Hey, Bethany." Her eyes turned to his as he tried to explain. "Mr. Mark has a big bump on the back of his head. So the doctor needs to check him to make sure it is healing, and to let him know when he will be able to go home. So it shouldn't be long. Do you think you can wait?" She nodded her head yes. He grinned, ruffling her hair as he stood up.

"Thanks, Mike," she said, smiling up at him. "She can be a child of twenty questions."

"No problem. My nephew Cameron is the same way."

The doctor came out. He turned to Tammy. "Mark would like to see you. Something about breakfast?" he asked.

She grinned and took Bethany's hand. "Okay, let's go get your juice and see about breakfast."

When they went into the room, he turned to Mike. "Everything looks good. The stitches are going to need to be taken out in a week. I see the doctor on duty last night prescribed some pain medication to take for five days. If he finds he doesn't need it after three days, he can take an over-the-counter pain reliever. Make sure he gets rest for the next few days. I am going to go ahead and discharge him, so he can go home this afternoon. I've explained all this to your brother. Do you have any questions?"

Mike shook his head, "No, Dr. Holden. I'll make sure he follows your orders."

"Good." He held out his hand to shake. Mike took his hand.

"Thank you, Dr. Holden, and the hospital, for taking care of my brother."

"You're welcome. Have a good day."

After he left to check other patients, Mike re-entered the room.

Mark watched him come up alongside his bed. "I take it the doctor filled you in?"

"Yes, and I told him that I would make sure you followed his orders. Between Tammy and I, we should be able to accomplish it."

"Don't forget about me!" cried Bethany. They all laughed.

"I don't think we could ever forget about you," chuckled Mark.

"Listen, I'm going to take off. I want to stop in at the house and see Peyton. I left him sleeping, then I need to check on my car."

Surprised, "What happened to your car?" asked Mark.

"Well, after I sent Jenna off to the hospital last night, I went to my car, only to find that all four tires on my Corvette were slashed. I had the officer on duty tow it over to the Chevy dealer."

"You're kidding!"

"No, it was a shock to me. I have a feeling that whoever did it wanted us both out of the way."

Mark thought a moment. "I think you're right, Mike," he agreed.

"When you get home, give me a call and I will try to swing by," Mike said as he turned to leave.

"Will do," said Mark.

He called out, "Hey, Mike." He turned back. "Don't forget what I asked of you."

"No worries, bro. I won't forget."

It was after four o'clock before Mark walked into his home, with Tammy and Bethany following behind. He was surprised Peyton greeted them at the door. He let his brother help him to the couch in the living room. "How are you doing, Mark?" he asked.

"Better, now that I'm home." Puzzled, he asked, "How did you get in?"

He chuckled. "I have a key and the code to the alarm system, remember?"

"Oh yeah, I forgot you had a key." His head was starting to throb again. He was overdue for his pain medication. After they left the hospital, they waited at the pharmacy for a half an hour before it was filled.

Peyton glanced over to Tammy and her little girl. "Hi, Tammy. Hi Bethany!" he greeted. Bethany ran up to him.

"I know you! I saw you at the coffee shop!"

"Yes, you did! I can see you are just as cute as ever!"

She giggled. "Are you going to stay with us?"

His eyes shifted to Tammy's, then back to Bethany. "No, I'm staying with Mike and Jenna. But if you don't mind, I would like to stay and visit for a while."

"No, I don't mind," she answered excitedly.

"Bethany," her mom interrupted, "can you take the duffle bag to our room?"

"Do I have to?" she whined.

"Yes, Bethany," she returned sternly.

"Okay..." she muttered as she picked up the duffle bag and stomped back to her room. She turned back to the men.

"Sorry. Mark, here are your meds. Can I get both of you a cup of tea before I start dinner?"

"Tea would be nice, and a glass of water? And you are not making dinner!" he said determinedly. "We will order out!"

She grinned. "Yes. sir!" she shot back as she went to the kitchen. Tammy hurried to make the tea. She pulled some pastries out of the fridge and warmed them up. Placing everything on the tray, she took it out into the living room and set it on the coffee table. She turned to leave when Mark grabbed her hand.

"You aren't joining us?"

"Oh, I'm sure you and Peyton have a lot to catch up on. I need to get Bethany started on her homework. What would you like for dinner? I can get it ordered for you when you're ready."

He turned to his brother. "Are you staying for dinner, Peyton?" he asked.

"Sure. Let's order a pizza from that pizzeria not too far from here."

"Sounds good," he agreed. "They make the best pizza!"

"Then pizza it is!" She grinned. "Don't forget to take your pain medication. You're overdue," she reminded him as she walked away.

She didn't have to tell him twice; his head was killing him! He took one from the bottle and down it with some water. He set the glass down and grabbed a pastry and a cup of tea. "Help yourself, bro."

Peyton reached over and picked up a pastry and the other cup of tea. "Don't mind if I do." He leaned back against the back of the couch, savoring the rich taste of the blueberry pastry. "This is so good. Thanks, Mark."

"Don't thank me, thank Tammy."

Peyton set his tea down on the coffee table and leaned in. "And what about Tammy. I was surprised to hear she and her little girl were living with you. Is there something more going on than just protecting them?"

Mark took his time answering him. He wiped his fingers off with a napkin, took a sip of his tea, then set his cup on the end table. He was a little irritated when he asked in return, "How much information did Mike give you?"

"He filled me in on Bethany's near kidnapping, how she and her mother are still in danger, due to the fact she was sold by someone. I'm surprised the police haven't put them in a police protection program to keep them safe until they capture who's responsible. Why would you take it upon yourself to protect them?"

"Did he tell you that it was Zack and I who stopped the kidnapper?"

"He mentioned something about it, but didn't go into detail," he answered.

"Look, Peyton. Zack came into the restaurant one night after the incident and informed both Tammy and me that these human traffickers usually work in teams. So when I took the guy out who was trying to take Bethany, Zack said the guy didn't remember who had knocked him out. What he did say is that someone else involved could have seen me, and Cameron, who was with me at the time, along with seeing the kidnapper getting caught and taken to jail. Yes, Tammy and her daughter could have gone to a safe house, but I felt it was best for them to stay here with me. So they can go about their normal life. The police department has someone watching Tammy and Bethany whenever they go out and when the Langleys are here watching Bethany when Tammy works. The police department is so short-staffed they can't always be here when we are together. We haven't had any problems, until last night, when I got hit on the head and Mike's tires were slashed. Now, to answer your first question, Tammy and I are not involved at this time, but I do have feelings for her. Like I told Mike, if and when we decide to have a relationship, it is nobody's business but ours. And before you say anything, I don't give a damn about the rules we set in the beginning when we opened the restaurant!"

Peyton, listening, could see his brother's passion for Tammy and her daughter and the need to protect them at all costs. Hadn't he felt the same about Stacy when they first met, and still did? He was right. It was nobody's business but theirs, and if love was involved, the better. He met his brother's eyes. With determination, he asked, "What can I do to help?"

Mark let out a breath. "I was hoping you'd ask that question. Here's what I need…"

Tammy helped Bethany get her homework out of the way. Then they both showered and put on a fresh set of clothes. After sleeping in the same clothes all night at the hospital, it felt good to freshen up. "Hey, Bethany, let's go out and see if the guys are ready to eat. They both mentioned they wanted pizza, so let's go order one!" she exclaimed.

"Yay!" she cried, jumping up and down. "I love pizza! Mommy?"

"Yes?"

"Is Peyton eating with us?" she asked.

"Yes, he is. Now let's go, I'm starving!"

Bethany rushed from the room, with Tammy following behind. She heard her daughter exclaim with glee, "Cameron! You're here!"

"Hi, Bethany! You wanna go watch a movie with me?" he asked with enthusiasm.

"Yeah!" she cried. Both kids rushed from the living room into the entertainment room. You could hear them arguing about which movie they wanted to watch.

Tammy, seeing that black-haired beauty sitting next to Mark, with her hand resting on his shoulder, felt a sharp surge of jealousy hit her. She had forgotten Cameron was coming tonight. She calmly took a seat on the loveseat, hoping her feelings wouldn't show in front of his ex-wife. She watched as Mark removed his ex's hand from his shoulder and commented, "Shouldn't you be going?"

Frustrated, Sherry rose from the couch, but not before she shot daggers at Tammy. "You know, Mark is Cameron's father. I should have been told about this!"

Mark, sitting there, stewing at the fact that his ex, didn't have the decency to give Tammy a proper greeting, but plunged right in with an accusation, made him react with anger in his voice. "Sherry." She turned her head towards him. "If I had wanted you to know, I would have had someone call you. It was late when it happened. I'm fine. There was no need to disturb you at that time of night. Now, you need to go. I will expect you back here at eight thirty to pick up Cameron."

Angry eyes shot back at him. "Well, excuse me for caring!" she shouted as she walked out and slammed the door behind her.

Mark glanced over to see Tammy's reaction to his ex-wife's rudeness. Shock and dismay were clearly etched in her face. Peyton had removed himself from the room, to go see what movie the kids had chosen to watch, when things started to get a little sticky between the two. Mark rose from the couch and sat back down next to Tammy. "Tammy," he murmured softly, "I'm sorry you had to hear that. You do not deserve to listen to our anger or put up with her rudeness toward you."

Gazing into his eyes, she wondered how they would ever make a relationship work between them. "Mark," she whispered back, "I have caused so much trouble in your life since we moved in with you. Maybe we should go to a place where they will keep us safe until this is over. I don't want anything else to happen to you or your brothers because of us."

Mark's heart started to pound at the thought of her and her daughter leaving him. He took her hands in his. "Look, there is no way I am going to let you leave to go to a safe house. If you don't know already, I care deeply for you, and I love your daughter. Don't let my ex-wife's words upset you. I care nothing for her."

"She seems to still care a lot about you," she muttered.

"Only because I have another woman in my life," he responded tentatively. "She's jealous. Why, I don't know. She has Al. From what I've heard, they're suited for each other. Promise me you won't leave me."

Gazing into those blue eyes of his, she nodded. "I promise," she whispered. He leaned in and gave her a kiss that showed just how much she meant to him. The kiss was sweet and tender.

She kissed him back, not caring who saw them. She loved him. She wanted to spend the rest of her life with him. Who cares what his ex-wife thought of her. She heard giggling near her, and the kiss was broken. Tammy looked down to see her daughter and Cameron in front of them, grinning from ear to ear! Cameron spoke first.

"Uncle Peyton wanted to know when we can order pizza!"

"Yeah," cried Bethany. "We're hungry!"

Both Mark and Tammy looked up to see Peyton standing in the doorway of the entertainment room, with a grin on his face. Mark would have a word with him later!

Tammy beamed down at the two invaders. "Hungry, huh?" She grinned. "Okay, let's order pizza!"

After the pizza was gone, Mark was feeling it. He wanted nothing more than to go to bed and sleep. Tammy started picking up the plates and taking them into the kitchen. He checked his watch. Sherry should be here in a half hour to pick up Cameron. He sighed, wondering if he would be able to stay awake that long.

Peyton, observing his brother, thought he should go lie down. The doctor told him he needed to rest. He knew he was worried about his ex-wife picking up Cameron. He never knew what he saw in that woman. He never really knew her, since he spent the last twelve years in the service. But when he was home, they always seemed to clash. He noticed that she always had to be the main attraction at family functions. And when Mark had any down time, she ran him ragged with her to-do list. It was just as well that it was over between them.

"Hey, Mark, you look like you need to go lie down," stated Peyton.

"I do, but I want to wait until Sherry picks up Cameron. You saw how she was earlier. Tammy doesn't deserve to be treated like that."

"Listen, bro, you go get some rest and I'll stay until Sherry gets here."

He grunted. "How is that going to work? You and Sherry never got along when you were home on leave. I'll stay up."

Tammy came in from the kitchen after cleaning up. She took one look at Mark's ashen face and knew he needed to go to bed. "Hey, the doctor said you should be resting. Let's go."

"I'll go when Sherry picks up Cameron."

"No, Peyton and I can handle it. You need to get some rest. I'll go and get Cameron to say goodnight, and then you will go to bed." She left to get his son.

When he came and gave his dad a hug and said goodnight, he ran back to finish the movie he was watching.

"Okay, time to go," Tammy insisted.

"You're awfully bossy all of a sudden!" he remarked.

"Only because I don't want to see you pass out right here at the table!" she declared.

Mark slowly rose from the table, a little unsteady at first. Peyton stood up, ready to catch him should he sway his way. Tammy took ahold of his arm to help him keep his balance. "Ready?"

He nodded. Peyton followed them back to Mark's bedroom to make sure he didn't fall. Once he was seated on the bed, "Do you need any help?" asked Peyton.

"No, thanks, I'll manage with Tammy's help."

Peyton saw the look he gave her, which spoke volumes. "Then I'll leave you to it."

When he left, Tammy helped him get out of his t-shirt. While he stood up to get out of his jeans, Tammy pulled back the covers, so he could climb into bed. Tammy tried not to look at his masculine body as she helped him with his shoes, so he could get his jeans off, but when she stood before him, her breath caught at the sight of him.

He smiled. Suddenly, his body started to wake up. He was enjoying her eyes moving over his body. He pulled her next to him. He bent down to nibble on her ear. "Do you like what you see?" he whispered, showering kisses down her neck, back up to her tantalizing lips just waiting to be kissed.

Tammy swallowed as the tingles came out all over her body. "Yes, you're magnificent…" She barely got out the words before his lips closed over hers. Tammy placed her soft hands on his chest, moving around his back, then sliding them up and around his neck, enjoying the feel of his skin on her hands as the passion took over them both. She wanted to explore every part of him, to taste every inch of him.

With her hands moving over him, Mark started to lose control. He pulled her down on the bed with him, laying her on her back while he did some exploring of his own. His hand cupped her firm breast, teasing her nipple with his thumb.

Tammy groaned, she didn't want to stop him, but he should be resting. "Mark…" she whispered.

"Tammy," he moaned, "let me love you."

She wanted it as much as he did, but her conscience wouldn't let her. She took a breath and pushed him back. She caught his eyes. "Mark, as much as I want to make love to you, I won't be responsible for you having a setback. You need to rest."

He collapsed down on the pillow. "Okay," he breathed; he was feeling it. "I'll let you go this time, but after I've rested, don't plan on leaving this bed…." he whispered as his eyes closed. Within minutes, he was fast asleep.

Tammy got out of the bed and covered him up with his sheet and brown satin comforter. She gave him a soft kiss on the cheek and left the room.

When she came down the hall, she heard voices. She stopped when she recognized the voice.

"Did Mark go to bed?" she asked in an intrusive way.

"Yes, he was given strict orders to rest. I hope you are not intending to disturb him," irritation clearly in his voice.

"Of course not," she chided. Her eyes traveled around the room. "Is that woman with him?" Sherry hadn't been here more than five minutes, and Peyton was already getting fed up with her questions and remarks!

"That's not your business," he fired back.

"Look, ever since that woman—"

"Her name is Tammy!" he interrupted.

"Tammy," she corrected, and rephrased what she was about to say. "Ever since Mark saved her little girl from being kidnapped, Tammy has brought on nothing but trouble for him. Moving in with him when they should have gone to a safe house! What was she thinking?"

Peyton had had enough. "I think you had better leave, before I say something that I will regret."

Sherry could feel the anger radiating off him and knew she had gone too far. They never did get along while she was married to Mark. She calmed herself enough to ask, "If you would go get Cameron for me, we'll go."

"With pleasure!" he said, relieved.

Tammy watched him go to the entertainment room. Soon, both kids followed him out.

When they were just approaching Sherry, Tammy ran her fingers through her hair, took a breath, and walked out. She came up beside Bethany, her eyes glaring into Sherry's. She had the decency to look away. Sherry took her son's hand, said goodnight, and left.

Peyton turned around and saw Tammy standing with Bethany. The expression on her pretty face told him she was upset. "How much did you hear?" he asked.

Tammy looked down at her daughter. "Bethany, can you go run and get your pajamas on? I'll be in to tuck you in in just a few minutes."

"Okay, Mommy," she pouted as she stomped back to their bedroom.

Tammy shifted her eyes back to Peyton. "Can we go sit down?"

He nodded and followed her back to the couch. He took a seat across from her.

"To answer your question, I heard her tell you what a bad person I was."

"Tammy, that's not what she said," he tried to console her.

"It's what she meant. The woman clearly doesn't like me. I don't know, Peyton. Maybe we should go to a safe house till this is over. I don't want anything to happen to either one of you. Look what's happened already. It scares me, Peyton."

"Look, Tammy. Mark wants you and Bethany here. As far as Sherry is concerned, don't let what she says bother you. I never liked her from the beginning. Our personalities clashed every time I came home from leave. Unless the police recommend it, you should stay with Mark."

She nodded. "Okay." She came up off the couch, to go tuck her daughter in. She stopped and turned around. She caught Peyton's eyes and asked, "Could you stay the night with us? I'm a little apprehensive about being here, with Mark being laid up."

He could see the fear in her eyes when she asked. He was actually going to suggest it, but he didn't want to impose on their privacy. He smiled. "Sure. I think I would feel better too. Just in case the police are not able to cover for the night. Zack is supposed to let me know if that is going to happen. Go tuck your little girl in, and don't worry."

She smiled back. "Thanks, Peyton."

"You bet."

After tucking Bethany in and reading her a story, she decided to get ready for bed herself. After she put on a pair of light-blue cotton shorts with a matching tank top, she brushed her teeth and threw on a matching floral robe. When she came out of the bathroom, Bethany was asleep.

Not wanting to go to bed yet, she headed out into the kitchen. After putting some water in the kettle, she set it on the burner to heat up to make some tea. She checked the time and realized it was almost time for Mark's medication. She pulled two cups from the cupboard and put a teabag in each one. When the tea was ready, she set the cups on a tray along with a glass of water and one of his pain pills. She headed down the hall to the master suite.

Peyton came out of Cameron's room just as she came to Mark's door. "Need some help?" he whispered.

"Oh." She smiled. "Yes, please," she whispered back, as not to wake Bethany in the next room over.

He opened the door and waited until she was able to set the tray down on the nightstand. Hearing the door close behind her, she made her way into the master bath in the dim light to turn on a light, so she would be able to see. Coming back to his side of the bed, his back to her, she stood, watching him sleep. She hated to wake him, but if he didn't take his pain medication, he would wake up in terrible pain. She quietly sat down on the edge of the bed and touched his shoulder.

"Mark," she spoke softly. "You need to wake up for a minute, to take your pill." He groaned. "Mark." This time she shook him.

He turned around, half sitting up, his eyes half opened, ready to throw the person out who interrupted his sleep. His blue eyes came alive when he realized Tammy was sitting beside him. He sat up a little too fast, feeling a splitting headache. He pressed his hands against the sides of his head to release some of the pain he felt. The comforter and sheet slid down to his waist, exposing that gorgeous chest of his. Tammy turned her eyes away as he groaned. "Damn, it hurts."

"Here." Tammy handed him the pill and the glass of water. "Take this."

He took the pill from her and downed it with some water. Giving the glass back to her, in a cracked voice, he murmured, "Thanks."

"Would you like some tea?"

He half smiled. "That'd be great." When he sat up a little straighter, she handed him a cup. He leaned back against the headboard and took a sip. While drinking his tea, his eyes started a perusal of her exquisite delicate body sitting beside him. She was wrapped in a short floral robe, her long slender legs showing out beneath it. She had beautiful legs. Desire started to surge through him as his gaze moved to her amber eyes.

Tenderly he asked in a soft voice, "Is Bethany asleep?" Even though his head still hurt, he had her in his bed. He wasn't going to let her leave now.

"Yes," she whispered. Tammy, sitting on the bed next to him, could see the hot flame of desire in those deep blue eyes. Mesmerized, she couldn't move. A voice in her head said *run, before it's too late*. She watched as he set his cup down on the nightstand. Then took hers and did the same. He pulled the drawer open and took out a condom and placed it on the tray. His eyes traveled to hers and locked. Her heart started beating hard and fast, contemplating what it would be like with him. He pulled on the sash that tied her robe. When it opened, he slid the robe off her shoulders, exposing the lacy tank top she was wearing, conforming to her high, firm breasts. He wanted to see more. He raised the top up over her head and threw it to the other side of the bed. His eyes devoured her. He pulled back the covers.

With a soft, velvety voice, he murmured, "Come lay with me, Tammy. I want to explore every contour and taste every inch of your exquisite body."

Desire riveting through her, she did as he asked. Feeling his skin next to hers, tentatively, she moved her hands, caressing his chest, down to his waist. Lower, she could feel how aroused he was. He started kissing her neck, traveling down to her breasts, when suddenly she stopped him. Mark, raising himself up, burning desire in his eyes, "Tammy," he breathed. "Don't tell me you want to stop, because I don't know if I can."

Searching his eyes, she expressed her concern for him. "I just want to make sure you're up for this. How's your headache?"

He smiled down into her amber eyes, reassuring her he was fine. It touched his heart to know how much she cared for him. "Let's find out," he whispered tenderly. "And to assure you, my head is much, much better," bringing his lips down to touch hers in a hot, demanding kiss.

She returned his kiss in a desire that matched his own. They kissed. They touched, until finally he was inside her, moving in a slow, sensual motion. Tammy could feel herself spiraling out of control. Her body tingling with the rapture he was creating.

"Mark..." she gasped, "Please, I don't know if I can hold out much longer."

He kissed her swollen lips, murmuring, "Just a little longer, sweetheart." He moaned. "You feel so good."

He kept up the torture until her nails dug into his shoulders, crying out, "Now, Mark! Please!" He shot off like a rocket, exploding inside her until they both cried out in a climax that neither one had ever experienced. He came down to rest, shuttering on her trembling body in the aftermath of their lovemaking.

When they were able to catch their breath, and their heartbeats slowed, Mark raised himself up to gaze into her eyes. "Tammy," he whispered softly, "I have never felt such joy in loving a woman as much as I have you. You were incredible."

Tammy placed both hands on each side of his ruggedly handsome face. "I feel the same way. I have never felt so loved by anyone in my entire life."

He placed his lips on hers in a kiss that showed all he was feeling for her. He moved his hand down and under her hip, bringing it up to him. Gently, he started moving again, loving the feel of her wrapped in his arms. Just when Tammy thought she didn't have enough energy to move, she found herself rising up to the challenge, exploding in ecstasy once again. When they were both sated, Mark excused himself.

When he came back to bed, Tammy thought she should go check on Bethany. Mark wrapped his arm around her and snuggled up close. "Is Peyton staying the night?"

"Yes," she whispered.

"He'll handle it if she wakes. Now that I've had a taste of you, I'm not letting you out of this bed until morning. Now go to sleep, I'm exhausted."

She smiled. "Now who's being bossy!"

CHAPTER *18*

Tammy woke up to an empty bed. She sprang up, wondering what time it was. Looking at the clock on the nightstand she had an hour and fifteen minutes to get ready, get Bethany off to school, and on to her class at the university. She leaped out of bed and gathered up all her night clothes, which were scattered all over the bedroom. Hurrying into the bathroom, she dressed and splashed some warm water over her face. She found one of Mark's combs in a drawer and ran it through her long tresses. Just as she was about to leave the room, Mark came in with two cups of coffee. Dressed in a pair of sweats and a t-shirt, he caught her eyes and smiled. He handed her a cup.

"Thank you, I wasn't expecting this." She smiled.

"You're welcome."

After their night together, Tammy was feeling a little shy around him. "How are you feeling?" she asked him tentatively.

She noticed his eyes held a certain mischief in them as he answered her. "Surprisingly, when I woke up, I hardly felt any pain in my head." He grinned. "Must have been all that love-making we did last night."

She blushed, remembering all the ways they made love together. She took a sip of her coffee, trying to focus on all she had to do today.

Mark saw the blush come out on her pretty face and couldn't help teasing her a little, knowing she had a busy day ahead of her.

He took a step closer, close enough to take her into his arms. "You know, we could continue from where we left off last night," he beckoned her. "How about it? I'd love to take you back to bed. Press your warm tender body next to mine, kiss you all over, and love you until you scream," he murmured.

Goosebumps broke out all over Tammy's skin. Oh, how she would love to take him up on that. But her responsibilities beckoned her. Seeing the amusement in his eyes, she gave him a sweet smile. "Sorry, TreVaine, as much as I would like to indulge, duty calls. I've got to get Bethany to school, and I have a class this morning." She gave him a quick kiss and left the room before she had second thoughts. Mark watched her leave, a grin breaking out across his handsome face. He had a feeling that life with her would never be dull.

After getting cleaned up, Mark came out to find Peyton sitting at the counter, having a cup of coffee and reading the *Hawaiian Blaze*. Tammy and Bethany had already left for the day. He went and refilled his cup, then joined him at the counter.

"Is there anything interesting going on?"

"Just the same old stuff, crime in the city, drug busts, homicides…" answered Peyton. "There is one article about you, though."

"You're kidding!"

"No." He handed him the paper. "Read it for yourself."

When Mark took a look, the caption read,

Restaurant Owner Attacked Outside His Own Restaurant.

Mark Trevaine, co-owner of the Hawaiian Lanai, was taken to the hospital by ambulance, after being attacked outside his restaurant on Wednesday night.

It went on to say that no one saw the incident, and that no suspects have been apprehended. The case was still under investigation.

"Great, just what I need, to have this all over the news," he remarked.

"From what Stacy told me last night, it's been on the cable news channels," commented Peyton.

"This could hurt our business. People may not want to come to our restaurant knowing there is some idiot out there attacking people!" he declared.

"I wouldn't worry about it too much, Mark. When Mike called last night, he said the restaurant was slammed again, that he was going home, and that he would stop by this morning to see how you were doing. I told him you were resting." A shit-ass grin broke out on his masculine face. "Of course, I couldn't be sure with all the noise coming from your room. Good thing Bethany slept through it. I'm not sure how I would have handled the situation."

Mark sat there, not knowing how to respond. They tried to be quiet, but when the emotions run high... They didn't think about being overheard. Hesitantly he asked, "You heard that, huh?"

Peyton raised his cup and took another sip of his coffee. "Yep!" Still grinning, "It's been what you've wanted since you and Tammy came home yesterday."

Shocked, "Am I that transparent?" he asked.

"It was written all over your face, bro."

Mark shook his head and smiled. "I've wanted her since the day Zack and I saved her daughter and took her and Bethany to the ice cream parlor. She's an incredible woman, raising her daughter on her own, working to get her BA degree in social work, while that sleazebag of an ex-husband did nothing to help her. I've fallen in love with her and her daughter. I can't imagine life without them." He turned to his brother. "Can you keep this under wraps? I don't want it to get out to the employees that Tammy and I are in a relationship, at least not just yet. When we catch whoever is trying to take Bethany and this human-trafficking ring, we will decide when to tell them."

"Your secret is safe with me, but have you told her how you feel? That you're in love with her?" asked Peyton.

"I'm sure she knows. After last night, how could she not?"

"Just so you know, Mark, women like to hear the words. It might have saved Stacy and I a lot of anguish in our relationship, if I had told her how I felt before we left the hospital that night." Thinking back to that night, he had fallen in love with a sassy, blond-haired, hazel-eyed beauty, a detective out of LA, working on a case here on the island involving his twin brothers. A bullet had grazed her upper arm in the sting operation they were involved in, to bring the drug smugglers down. His heart lurched at seeing her hurt, and he knew he was desperately in love with her. They were interrupted so many times at the hospital he didn't have a chance to tell her how he felt. At the time, when she left to go back to L.A., he thought it was a good thing he didn't tell her, but in the end, he wished he had. After being separated for six weeks, he found out she had taken a job at the police department on the big island of Kona, to be closer to him, at Mike and Jenna's wedding. He had gotten the job as helicopter pilot at the hospital there. He was now working on fixing up a home on forty acres, just outside of the city, for them to move into. He was going to surprise her with a ring this Christmas. He smiled; he couldn't wait.

His thoughts were interrupted when his brother commented, "I remember. You were a mess. Spent a lot of late nights with you."

"Yes, and I want you to know that I appreciated it. So don't wait too long to tell her you love her."

"I won't. I'll know when the time is right." He checked his watch. Zack was due in an hour and a half. He wasn't able to make it over to the hospital yesterday morning, so he was anxious to find out if he was able to find out anything about the guy who was sitting at the bar the night he was hit from behind. "Did you say Mike was coming this morning?" Mark asked his brother.

"Yes, but I have no idea what time he will be stopping by."

"Zack will be here in a bit. I'll give Mike a call to see if he can be here at the same time. In the meantime, how about some eggs and bacon?" He needed to get some food in his stomach so he could take his pain medicine. That stuff ripped his gut up. He would take over-the-counter after this if the pain comes back when he needed it.

Peyton, surprised, answered, "You cook?"

Mark grinned. "Don't look so shocked! I can handle eggs and bacon!"

Peyton laughed. "Okay, I'm in."

Mark had another thought. "How are you at handling clippers?"

Peyton shrugged. "When I was in the service, I clipped my hair all the time."

"Good, 'cause I want you to shave my head. After they shaved part of my head to put the stitches in, I might as well get rid of the rest of it."

Peyton chuckled. "I think that's a good idea; that color doesn't suit you."

"No? I thought I looked pretty good in it, especially when I wore the black mustache!"

Peyton raised an eyebrow when he inquired, "You wore a black mustache?"

Mark chuckled. "Yes, when Zack and I went out to find this guy who was following Tammy. But another time, bro. We haven't much time before Mike and Zack get here," he replied as he got up and went to prepare breakfast for them.

Mark had just put on another pot of coffee when he heard the doorbell chime. Peyton went and let Zack in. He saw Mike pulling up in the driveway, so he waited until Mike got out of his car and walked up to the door. "Hi, Peyton!" Mike greeted him. "I see Zack is already here."

"Just got here, so you're just in time," relayed Peyton. Mike walked into the kitchen, with Peyton following. Zack and Mark were already seated at the table in front of the lanai. Mark rose from his chair to shake his brother's hand.

Mike, taking in his brother's appearance, told him, "You look a hell of a lot better than you did yesterday, Mark."

"Thanks, I feel a hell of a lot better."

Mike started to laugh; he couldn't resist. "No, I mean since you got rid of the black hair!"

Mark rolled his eyes. "Now you're sounding like Peyton!" They all had a good laugh. "Come and have a seat. Do you want some coffee?"

"I'd love a cup. I haven't had my quota yet this morning."

When everyone had a cup, Mark rejoined the table. He was anxious to hear if Zack was able to get any information, so he asked, "What did you find out about the guy who was sitting at the bar the other night?"

"Actually, Mark, I went into the restaurant last night. Mike indicated he had come in and was sitting at the bar. So I decided to join him. When I introduced myself, he in return told me his name was Roy Gardner."

"You're kidding!" exclaimed Mark. "Roy Gardner," he repeated.

"Do you know him?" asked Zack.

"Not really, but I'm beginning to connect the dots." He turned to his brother. "Mike, do you remember about five years ago, we had a salesman come into the restaurant every weekend. Then all of a sudden, he just disappeared, never to be seen into the restaurant again."

Mike thought a moment. "Come to think of it, I do remember him. It's been a long time, but I'm pretty sure he said his name was Roy Gardner. He worked for some company on the island," he concurred.

"He's also Tammy's ex," Mark informed them.

"Are you sure about this?" asked Zack.

"I'm damn sure!" he shot back. "Tammy told me all about him one night. How he never wanted Bethany when she was born. The sleazebag left Tammy to raise her by herself, until he made it official when Bethany was only two and divorced her." Mark's anger was starting to get the better of him. He took a deep breath and calmed himself.

Peyton, listening, asked, "Were you able to get anything out of him? Why he's here?"

Zack looked across at Peyton, "After we introduce ourselves, I casually mentioned a guy getting hit from behind in front of the restaurant. I asked if he was anywhere near the restaurant at the time or had heard or seen anything. He seemed a little nervous when he answered me."

"What did he say?" Mark wanted to know.

Shifting his body toward Mark, he leaned back in his chair. "He said he hadn't heard of anything happening, and he certainly didn't see anything, since he wasn't there when it happened. He got a little angry when he asked if I was through interrogating him, threw some bills on the bar counter, and left."

"Did he know you're a cop?"

"I didn't introduce myself as such, but I have a feeling he knew I was."

"Do you think he may be the one who sold Bethany?" inquired Mike.

He turned to Mike, "I think it's a strong possibility. I did some investigating this morning and found out he lives in Arizona, like Tammy thought. He still works as a salesman with a medical supply company. He makes good money, but he built up a lot of debt through online gambling. My guess is if he did sell her, he did it to help pay off the debt. At this point, it's just a theory. We can't prove anything, but we all have to ask, why is he here?"

Mark, internalizing what Zack just said, asked, "Okay, how do we go about proving it?"

Zack leaned forward, hands folded on the table. "I have some ideas, but it's going to take all of you, especially Peyton."

"I'm all ears," said Peyton.

Tammy was sitting at a table in the library, trying to work on her homework for her sociology class. She was deep in her book and taking notes when a shadow fell over her. She looked up. What she saw in front of her turned her features into complete and utter shock!

"Hello, Tammy. May I have a seat?" a deep voice asked.

She couldn't believe it! Her ex! Standing in front of her! The jerk who left her and her daughter, wants to know if he could sit down with her! She hadn't seen the man in over four years! What was he doing here, and in the library? She couldn't speak, so she nodded. When he sat down, he smiled. "I guess you're surprised to see me?"

When she found her voice, "Shocked to be exact!" she exclaimed. He looked exactly the same as she remembered him. Handsome, with jet-black hair, although it now had a splattering of gray mixed in. Brown eyes, that used to turn her to mush when he would gaze at her a certain way. His chiseled lips, used to kiss her so tenderly before she got pregnant with Bethany. Now all she saw was a hollow man who deserted her and her daughter.

Anger bubbled up inside her when she asked, "What are you doing here?" trying to keep her voice down.

"You don't seem too happy to see me."

"I'm not! Now, I'm asking you again, what are you doing here?"

He smiled. She tried not to let that smile get to her as he answered, "My job brought me over to the island and I thought I would look you up. I'm going to be here for a few days and wanted to see if we could have coffee or dinner at a nice restaurant somewhere. Maybe catch up?" he asked tentatively.

She huffed. She knew his work took him all over the States. He must have been here many times without looking her up. "How did you find me?" she asked impatiently.

Boy, he thought, *she isn't the same woman I remember. I need to think fast to make it believable.* "I found out through a friend that still lives on the island where you are living. I've stopped in several times, but you've never been home. He also told me that you attended the university, so I checked with Admissions. They told me you were in a sociology class today. By the time I came to the building you were in, the class was over. I remembered how much you liked to go to the library when we were first married, so I thought I would check here first. And here you are! Studying for your class, I presume."

Staring across at him, Tammy wasn't sure she believed him. She wasn't sure Admissions would give out information on a student. Arms crossed, "What do you want?" she demanded.

"Can't a man come and see his ex? Make amends for what I did to you and Bethany?" His eyes were questioning at first, then changed to appraisal. Her skin crawled as his eyes perused her. "You're still so beautiful," he drawled. "I remember all the times we were together. We had a lot of good times, didn't we?" He smiled.

That alluring smile that always pulled her in. Not this time. She wasn't falling for the lie that spilled out of his compelling lips. Maybe before Bethany came they had good times, but after, she rarely saw him. Anger seethed inside her, remembering all the pain she endured because of him. "Sorry, Roy, unfortunately for you, I've forgotten all about our relationship and the hurt you inflicted on Bethany and I. I've moved on with my life, and for your FYI, we are doing just fine, not that you would care," she returned sarcastically. She packed up her books, came up from her chair, and with an air of defiance, shot him a piercing gaze. "You have a good life, Roy," she said, before she stomped out.

She was literally shaking as she left the library as fast as she could. She hoped after this, he would leave the island so she would never have to see him again!

Roy watched as she flung open the door and walked out of the building. *Well, that didn't go well*, he surmised. Well, what did he expect? He had to admit, he was all kinds of a heel for treating her the way he did. But, in his defense, he didn't want any kids to interrupt their life together. She ruined it when she became pregnant! They had been intimate just before they were married. He thought she was on the pill! So much for trying to get back in with her; he would have to figure out another way.

He left the library and got into his car. He got on his cell phone and made a call. "What do you want, Gardner?" Morris asked in an exasperated voice.

"That's a nice greeting, you son of a bitch!"

"You think you deserve a nice greeting? You're not the one who landed your ass in jail!"

"How was I supposed to know someone would just happen to be there to rescue the girl. And a detective no less! The mother and the girl are under surveillance by the police, so I need to handle this delicately. I knew the mother several years ago. I just need to lure her in. I have a plan to do just that!"

"Well, the plan had better be good. The boss is getting impatient. And when the boss gets impatient, heads are going to roll, and I don't want it to be mine!" he shot back.

Frustrated, "I said I have a plan!" he stormed. "When she is in my possession, I will call you to meet me at the warehouse."

"See that you do. I'll be waiting."

He ended the call and threw his phone on the seat. He slammed his fist against the steering wheel! Damn it! How was he going to lure her in when she didn't want to see him! He would have to figure out a way to make it happen. He bought a little bit of time lying to Morris. He slid his sunglasses on and drove out of the parking lot, contemplating his next move.

Tammy walked into Mark's home to find him, Peyton, Mike, and Zack sitting at the table in front of the lanai, deep in discussion. She headed into the kitchen, set her purse on the end of the counter, then stood and latched on to the edges, her hands pressing down until the whites of her knuckles showed, still reeling from the encounter with her ex. He had some nerve! Coming here and thinking he could reconnect with her after what he'd done! He never asked how Bethany was or about her life, what school she attended. Of course, she hadn't given him a chance. She just wanted to get away from him as fast as she could. Now that she's had a little bit of time to calm her nerves, was he being sincere? If she decided to meet him, would he want to meet his daughter? If he did, it would give him a chance to see what an incredible daughter he had. Unfortunately, Bethany didn't take after him in looks. She was totally her, right down to the amber eyes and light brown hair. Should she call? She stood there for a few minutes, thinking about what to do. She made a quick decision. She didn't know if he had the same cell phone number but decided to try.

She took a peek around the corner of the kitchen. The guys were still talking. She took her cell phone and walked down the hall to her bedroom. She punched in Roy's cell phone number and waited. Her heart started to pound when she heard his deep voice answer, "Hello?"

"Hello, Roy?" her voice cracked as she asked nervously.

"Yes," smiling on the other end, "Is this Tammy?"

"Yes. Ah, I've been thinking… Do you still want to meet somewhere?"

"Yes, I would like that," his voice purred.

"There's a little bistro on Honolulu Boulevard, near the shopping mall. Can you meet me there tomorrow morning at ten thirty?"

"I'll see you there," he returned. Then the line went dead. *Well, well, well,* he murmured to himself. *This may prove easier than I thought.*

Tammy looked at her phone. He didn't say good-bye. She was starting to have second thoughts. Maybe she made a mistake by asking if he would meet her. Well, it was too late now. She would go and see exactly what he was up to.

Mark went into the kitchen to find that Tammy must have come in. Her purse was on the counter. He headed down the hallway to see where she went. When he neared her room, he stopped when he heard her say the name Roy. As he listened, he overheard her ask him to meet her at a bistro near the mall. He knew exactly what bistro she was talking about and where it was located. His mind started racing, as jealously hit him straight in the heart. How did she know her ex was here? Has she known it all along? Had she been lying to him, telling him she didn't know where her ex-husband was? Anger stirred inside, as the old wounds from his previous marriage started to surface. He turned around and headed back to the men sitting at the table, waiting for him to bring them some more coffee. He sat back down at the table.

"Did you forget the coffee?" asked Mike.

"Sorry, I'll get it in a minute."

Mike could see his brother was clearly upset about something. "Is something wrong?" he asked him.

Keeping his voice low, he looked across at Mike. "When I went into the kitchen, I saw Tammy was home. I went to look for her and found her on the phone in her room. Now just so you know, I'm not one to eavesdrop on anyone's conversation, but I heard her say the name Roy. She set up a meeting with him for ten thirty tomorrow morning at the bistro near the mall." He turned to Zack, anger coming out in his voice as he hissed, "She lied to us, Zack. I think she's known all along that he's been on the island!"

"Mark," Zack spoke calmly, "I don't believe Tammy lied to us. She's not the type. I can read body language. I would have known a long time ago if she was lying."

"Maybe," he huffed.

"Mark." Mark's eyes shifted to his brother. "You're letting your past marriage control your emotions. Don't jump to conclusions until you talk to her."

Mike could see the anger in his brother's eyes as he shot back, "How am I supposed to talk to her when I was eavesdropping on her conversation? No, I'll see if she brings it up first."

Peyton, listening, piped in. "Look, Mark, I know you're upset, but maybe we could use this to our advantage."

"What do you mean?" asked Mike.

Peyton looked over at Mike as he responded, "This could be the opening we've been looking for. One of us can be at the bistro a little early, disguised, and see just what this Roy guy is up to. It could help us figure out if he's the guy who sold her."

"Just what I was thinking," returned Zack.

"I'll go!" declared Mark.

"No, Mark, you won't," Zack insisted, turning his gaze towards him.

Anger flashed in Mark's eyes when he asked, "Why not? I'll make sure nobody recognizes me!"

Zack knew Mark would not be able to handle the situation. "Mark," Zack spoke firmly, "you are too emotionally involved with

Tammy, plus you are recovering from a head injury. And I know you would not be able to sit quietly and listen without wanting to break the guy's neck. The one that should go is Peyton. This Roy guy has seen each and every one of us except Peyton."

Mark knew Zack made a good point. He wanted to break the guy's neck now. If he even touches her… Suppressing his anger, "You're right," he succumbed. "Peyton should be the one to go." He had no idea how he was going to sit back and let that happen. He would think on it.

Zack, watching the emotions crossing his face, knew he could have a problem on his hands. After going out with him to find Jed Rawlings, Mark's anger could easily blow it for them. He would have to make sure he stayed put. Zack leaned forward on the table, "Okay, men, let's see how we can play this out."

Tammy came from the bedroom into the kitchen to prepare something to eat before she needed to get ready for work tonight. She pulled some deli meat out of the fridge along with all the fixings to make a sandwich. While she was making it, she wondered if the men had eaten. She decided to go check. She could easily make more sandwiches. She came around the kitchen and up to the men seated around the table. Deep in conversation, she didn't know if she should interrupt.

When Mark saw her standing there, he motioned with his eyes to the others, and the conversation stopped. With heads turning toward her, Tammy felt like she wanted to sink down into the floor and disappear as all eyes were on her. "Um… Sorry to interrupt your meeting, but I was fixing a sandwich and wanted to know if anyone…" She swallowed, starting to feel nervous for asking. "Would like one…?" Tammy's eyes turned to Mark. What she saw in his eyes as he returned her gaze left her feeling uneasy. Something was very wrong, and she had a feeling it concerned her. She didn't know what it could be. After their time together last night, then seeing… Was it accusation in his eyes? Suddenly she felt she was back on the on-and-off-again relationship with him. She had that with Roy in their marriage together. She wasn't about to go through that again.

Finally, Peyton spoke up, "Thanks, Tammy, but we're fine."

She tore her eyes away from Mark to Peyton. "Okay, then." She half smiled and murmured, "I'll leave you to your meeting." She turned and walked back into the kitchen, her heart going into panic mode as she remembered the look in Mark's eyes. She took some deep breaths to calm herself, trying to figure out what she had done to upset him. Staring at the deli meat, suddenly she wasn't hungry anymore. She put everything away and headed back to her bedroom. She would get ready for work and pick up Bethany a little early from school. She hadn't been able to spend a lot of time with her lately. A trip to the ice cream shop might do them both some good. All she knew at the moment was she didn't want to be here!

All heads turned toward Mark. Staring back at them, he asked, "What?"

Peyton, answering his question, retorted, "Brother." He spoke in a low tone. "The expression on your sordid face, when you were in a hammerlock with her, tells me you've tried and found her guilty before you know the facts! Tammy doesn't deserve that, least of all from you!"

"Are we done here?" Mark fired back.

"Yeah, we're done." Peyton got up from the table, looking down at Mark. "For what it's worth, my advice to you is to take a look back over the last several weeks, then calmly go and talk to her. Don't let the anger fester inside you. She's not Sherry."

"He's right, Mark," Mike agreed. "From what I've seen, Tammy is a good person. I don't think she would lie about her ex being here, especially with her daughter in danger."

Mark could feel the tension inside release as he listened to his brothers. He knew in his heart they were right. She wasn't Sherry. It just that listening to her on the phone brought up all the hurt he endured because of his ex-wife. He needed to curtail his anger if he wanted to have a lasting relationship with a woman. He wanted that woman to be Tammy. He closed his eyes and took a deep breath. He would talk to her, even if it meant her being angry at him for eavesdropping. He opened his eyes and spoke in a calm voice. "Okay, I will talk to her, and I'll try not to jump to any conclusions until I hear what she has to say."

"Good," he returned. "I'm going to head out. Mike, I'm going to need to shower and get into some clean clothes if I'm going to be here for the night. Are you ready to go?"

"Hey, Peyton," said Mark. "You don't need to be here with me tonight. Bob and Mildred will be here tonight to watch Bethany until Tammy gets home. I'll be fine. The pain is starting to come back, and I'm feeling it, so I plan on resting."

"Okay, bro." He looked over at Zack. "Are you available to come over to Mike's? We can finish setting up for tomorrow."

"I have some things to wrap up this afternoon, but I can be there around seven. Will that work?"

"Yeah, that'll work," he answered. "We'll order dinner when you get there."

"Sounds good," confirmed Zack.

Mark walked them all to the door. As Zack and Peyton walked out the door, Mike held back. He turned to his brother. "Look, Mark. I know you. Don't do anything stupid. Let Zack and Peyton handle it in the morning. I will make sure you are kept abreast of the situation."

Mark stood eye to eye with his brother; he wasn't sure he would be able to stay away. Mike felt the hesitation in his brother, his eyes boring into him. "Mark, promise me you will wait until after they meet."

Mark, returning his glare, said, "Mike, I can't make any promises. But what I will promise is I will talk to Tammy, and then I will decide what to do."

Frustrated, Mike responded. "Just so you know, if you interfere, and you blow this, we may never know if he's the one that sold Bethany. So think about that before you act!" Mike let out a breath before he continued. "Listen, I know in your heart you want to do all you can protect them. It was the same for me and Jenna, but this is different. You've already been attacked by someone. The next one may be a bullet. I don't want to lose you because you tried to do it alone."

"No worries, Mike. Listen, my head is starting to throb. I need to go take my pain medicine."

Looking at his brother, Mark appeared to have a grim look about him. He nodded. "Okay, I'll see you later. Try and get some rest." Mike walked out the door, not sure he convinced his brother to stay out of it for now. He would be here in the morning to make sure he stayed put!

After Mark closed the door, he grabbed his head. He wasn't kidding when he said his head hurt. He went into the kitchen and took one of his pills. He stood for a few moments, hoping the pain medicine would take effect soon. Tammy's purse was still on the counter. He debated whether to go talk to her now or wait until she came home from work tonight. He knew it would drive him nuts if he waited. He walked down the hall and knocked on her door.

"Tammy?"

No response.

He opened the door. He could hear a blow dryer on, in the adjoining bathroom. He quietly walked up to the door. What he saw hit him in the heart. There before him, Tammy in a short robe was bent over, her buttocks barely showing, as she dried her hair. She came up, with her long tresses flipping back down her back. Looking in the mirror, he saw a soft breast peeking out from the robe she was wearing. He remembered having that breast in his hand last night, caressing her, loving her. He shook himself. He needed to focus and not let his feelings for her get in the way of finding out if she deceived him about her ex.

Out of the corner of her eye, Tammy saw a figure standing in the doorway. She turned and found Mark staring at her in the mirror. She turned the blow dryer off and hurried to close the robe tighter around her. When she turned to face him, his eyes caught hers, and they locked. She had no idea how long he had been standing there. Goosebumps broke out on her skin as his eyes left hers to travel over her body. She remembered last night with him. Loving her in a way she had never been loved before. Then when she seen the look in his eyes earlier, it felt like he hated her. The emotions he set off inside her were overwhelming. *Oh, why did I let myself fall in love with him?* she asked herself.

She found her voice as she asked softly, "Mark, what are you doing in here?"

He smiled. "I knocked, but you didn't hear me over the blow dryer."

She gave him a slight smile. "What do you want?"

I want you, he wanted to say as he worked to keep his hands off her. He cleared his throat. "I need to talk to you, before you go in to work."

Her heart started to pound. *This is where he tells me it's over between us,* she thought. *Tammy, you're getting way ahead of yourself. It may be nothing, but what she saw in his eyes when she asked if anyone wanted a sandwich led her to believe it was definitely something. "If you would be so kind as to give me a few minutes, I'll be right out." He nodded and left the room.

Tammy came out to smell fresh coffee brewing in the kitchen. She found Mark sitting at the counter with two cups of coffee in front of him. When she sat down beside him, he slid a cup over to her. "I wasn't sure but I thought you might like a cup."

"Thank you." Her voice was trembling as she answered him. Mark noticed right away that she was nervous. He took a sip of his coffee, wondering how to start. They didn't have much time before she needed to go pick up Bethany, so he just blurted it out. "Tammy, I came into the kitchen to get the guys some coffee earlier when I noticed your purse on the counter. When I went to find you, I overheard you talking to a man named Roy." Tammy's eyes got big as she was just about to say something to him, appalled he was listening in, when Mark continued. "Now, don't get upset with me. I'm not in the habit of listening in on people's conversations. Before you came home, I had called a meeting with Zack and my two brothers. Wednesday night, before I got hit over the head, a man came into the restaurant and took a seat at the bar. You had already left. I thought he looked familiar to me. I asked Mike if he knew who he was. He didn't, but said he looked familiar to him too, said he had come in the night before around the same time. It bothered me, because he looked similar to the man who was sitting out in front of my house when I went to pick up Mike and Jenna at the airport. I gave a description of the man to Zack. He did a search and informed me today that his name was Roy Gardner. He's your ex, isn't he?"

Stunned, Tammy couldn't believe it! His next question stunned her even more!

"Have you known he has been on the island for the last three weeks?"

Shocked, she stumbled over her words. "Mark, I... No!" her voice escalating. "I had no idea he was on the island until today!" She could see from his expression that he didn't trust her. "Mark, you have got to believe me! I'm telling you the truth! This morning after my class, I went to the library to work on my homework. He waltzed right in and asked if he could have a seat. I was shocked to see him. Mark, I haven't seen him in over four years!"

Mark was quiet until he asked, "What did he want?"

"He said he was sorry for the way he treated me and Bethany, and wanted to know if we could go and have coffee or dinner somewhere to catch up. I told him no. That I didn't want to have anything to do with him and that Bethany and I are doing just fine without him. I walked out and left him sitting there."

"But then you came home and made a date to meet with him." His voice, hardened by sarcasm, could not hide his resentment.

The tone in his voice made her lash out. "You don't believe me, do you? You think I've known all along that he's been here! Well, I don't have to sit here and listen to you accuse me of lying! I need to go pick up Bethany." She got up off the stool when he grabbed her arm.

"Wait!" She turned to him, their eyes locking. "We'll talk when you get home." She pulled her arm out of his grasp.

With fire in her eyes, she shot back, "Don't count on it!" and left.

Mark sat there and rubbed his hands down his face. He didn't handle that well. The pain in the back of his head was still throbbing. He decided to go and get some rest. He wasn't much good to anybody with the way he was feeling. He would apologize when she came home and clear the air between them. At this point there wasn't much else he could do.

Tammy burst into tears as soon as she got into her car. *How could he believe that I knew he was here? After all the time we have spent together, does he really think I am lying?* She wiped her tears with her hands. She started her car. She never should have moved in with him. But the thoughts of leaving him tore at her heart. She pulled out of the driveway onto the road. She needed to get a grip. She didn't want Bethany to see her upset. The last thing she needed was to answer questions she wasn't prepared to give.

CHAPTER 19

AFTER GETTING BETHANY settled before the Langleys were to arrive, she went to find Mark. She didn't see him when they came in, and he didn't grace them with his presence. She quietly opened the door to his bedroom and found him sleeping. She closed the door and breathed a sigh of relief. She had no idea what she would say to him. Better that they had some distance until she figured out what to do. When she heard the doorbell, she rushed to the door to let the Langleys in. Once inside, she gave them instructions and informed them Mark was sleeping and not to disturb him. She went and gave her daughter a kiss and left for the night.

At the restaurant, Tammy readied her station. She was feeling a little uneasy when Mike sat some customers at one of her tables. He gave her a brief look, turned, and left to serve more customers coming in. She wondered if he knew what was going on. If he did, did he think she was lying too! With her thoughts in a whirl, she hoped she would be able to get through the night. As it turned out, the night was a rush of customers coming in and out of the restaurant. Tammy hardly had time to think, let alone handle her section. She was glad when the restaurant slowed down. She was ready to leave for the night after the day she had. She needed to think about whether or not to meet with Roy in the morning. It left her uneasy finding out that he had been on the island for three weeks instead of a few days. She was getting some of the cleanup done when Mike approached her.

"Hey, Tammy," his tone indicating it was important. "Zack is here. He would like to ask you some questions. Can you come with me?"

"I was just getting some cleanup done so I could go home," she returned.

"It can wait." Looking into the same blue eyes as Mark's, she could see he meant business. She put her cloth down and followed him into his office. She took a seat beside Zack, while Mike went and sat behind his desk.

With her heart beating rapidly, Zack turned to her. He could see she was nervous. He needed to handle this carefully. "Tammy," he began, "Mark informed us that you have a meeting in the morning with your ex-husband, Roy Gardner. Now, just so you know, Mark didn't mean to eavesdrop on your phone conversation. When he came back to the table earlier today, he was clearly upset. I need to know, have you had a chance to talk with him?" he asked gently.

Tammy knew what everyone at the meeting must be thinking. Tears formed in her eyes when she nodded, answering him, "Yes, he approached me about it. He let me know he had overheard me talking to Roy." Anticipating his next question, "But I swear to you, I did not know he was on the island until this morning when he walked into the library where I was studying!" she exclaimed. She felt her heart beating out of her chest with fear, at thought of not being able to convince him that she wasn't lying!

Calmly, he asked, "Can you tell me what transpired when he came to see you?"

Tammy took a few breaths, trying to calm herself, so she didn't go into a full-blown anxiety attack. She focused her eyes on Zack's as she answered him. "I was literally shocked when I looked up and saw Roy standing there. At first I couldn't speak. He asked if he could sit down. I nodded. I asked him what he was doing here. He said he was here for a few days on business and wondered if we could go have coffee or dinner somewhere to catch up. He said he felt bad about what he did to Bethany and I. Well, of course I didn't believe him! I packed up my books and told him no, then left."

"So, what made you turn around and make a date to see him?"

She slumped back in her chair. "I had a little time to think about what he said on the way home, even though I was still reeling from seeing him. I thought maybe he was being sincere, about catching up and wanting to connect with Bethany after all this time. So I made a time to meet, at a bistro by the mall." She sat forward, recalling something else Roy had said to her. "But there is one thing that bothers me and makes me wish I hadn't set a time to meet him."

Zack raised his eyebrows, meeting her eyes. "Oh? And what was that?" he asked.

"When I asked him how he found me, he said he had a friend on the island who told him where I lived, and also that I took classes at the university. He said he went to Admissions to find out what class I was taking, but when he got to the building, the class was over. He knew from our marriage in the beginning that I loved to come to the library, and that is where he found me."

Zack took notes throughout the questioning. That statement also bothered him. He was quiet for a few moments.

Tammy, not knowing what he was thinking, panicked. She looked from Zack to Mike. "You believe me, don't you?"

Zack looked up from his notes. "Did Mark mention he has been on the island for three weeks?" he asked.

Tammy nodded. "Yes, he did say that, but I'm afraid I got upset with him when I felt he didn't believe me, when I told him what had happened this morning. That it was the first time I had seen him. I left the house, and I haven't talked to him since."

Mike, knowing his brother, more than likely didn't handle it well.

Zack continued. "Tammy, the fact that he has been here leads me to believe that he could have had something to do with the kidnapping."

"Oh please, you don't really believe that do you?" she asserted. "He never really participated in raising her, but I'm sure he would never hurt her."

"Tammy," he answered her with reluctance, "someone sold your daughter. Now I can't prove it, but the timeline that he's been here lines up with when the attempted kidnapping took place. We also found out he's in debt from some online gambling. He could very well be the one who sold her."

Stunned, Tammy sat back in her chair. Never in her life would she have ever thought her ex-husband could do such a thing! She wouldn't believe it! Frustrated, she asked, "Do you need anything else from me?"

"No, but I do want to let you know that Peyton will be at the bistro, in disguise, when you meet with Roy. I will be at Mark's in the morning to put a wire on you as well. That way, we will be able to hear whatever is said between you and Roy."

"Is this really necessary?" she asked. Zack could see she didn't want to believe that Roy could be involved.

"Listen, Tammy. Roy may or may not be involved, but we have to make sure."

Searching his eyes, Tammy knew he needed to cover all the bases in his investigation. She rose from her chair and nodded. "Okay, I'll see you in the morning. Goodnight, Zack. Goodnight, Mike." She left the office feeling depressed and prayed it wasn't Roy who was behind all this.

Mike watched her leave before turning to Zack. "What do you think?" he asked.

Zack sat back in his chair. "Well, I feel she is telling the truth about not knowing her ex has been here. But she's having trouble believing he'd do something like this. We'll know more in the morning. By the way, can you make sure someone gets Tammy to her car and follows her home? I have someone staked out at Mark's home all night, but we are so shorthanded, no one was able to cover here."

"No problem, Zack. I'll make sure she gets to my brother's."

"Good." Zack rose from his chair and shook Mike's hand. "I'll see you in the morning," he said as he left the office.

Mike decided that while he was here, he might as well check his emails. Glancing through, there was nothing important he needed to take care of. He logged out and went to see what was left to do before he closed the restaurant.

Tammy came out to the lanai where she had been working, to finish up, only to discover Carol had everything done. She went up to Carol to apologize. "Sorry, Carol. I didn't mean for you to handle all the work."

"Hey, don't worry about it. Mike let me know he needed to talk with you. You go on home. I'm getting ready to head out myself."

"Okay, thanks, Carol." Tammy went to get her purse out of the locker room. She waved at Jack as she opened the door to head out. Walking to her car, she pulled her keys out of her purse. She slid the key in and turned the lock. When she tried to open the door, a hand came firmly over her mouth. She froze, feeling a gun pointing in her back. Panic rose up inside her, wondering where the officer was that was supposed to be watching out for her.

"Don't say one word, and if you scream, I'll shoot you where you stand," a deep voice demanded. She knew that voice. Roy! She tried to move, but he pulled her head back against his chest and shoved the gun further into her back. "Don't turn around," he grated. "Put your purse in the car and lock it!" He lowered his hand as she did what he wanted. "Now, let's take a walk." He moved her along till they came to a black sedan sitting not too far from her car. He opened the door. "Get in!" When she slid into the seat, he slammed the door. Rushing around the front of the car, he got behind the wheel. Pulling out of the parking lot, he headed toward the highway.

Tammy, sitting in the passenger seat, shaking, wondered what was going on with her ex and where on earth he was taking her!

Mike came from his office to find that most of the customers had left. He went to find Jack, to see if he would finish closing up for the night. He wanted to make sure Tammy got to Mark's. It took him a few minutes, but eventually He found him in the kitchen with Palani, going over the specials for tomorrow. Jack looked up just as Mike came up to him.

"Hey, Mike. Is there something I can do for you?" he asked.

"Yes. Can you close up for the night? I need to make sure Tammy gets home."

"Tammy?" he questioned. "Mike, she left fifteen minutes ago."

Damn! She must have left shortly after she left his office! He looked at his watch. Mark's house was twenty minutes from here. He would call Mark to see if she made it.

Watching the expression cross Mike's face led Jack to ask, "Is everything all right?"

"I hope so. Thanks for closing, I've got to go." He hurried out of the kitchen and out the door of the restaurant, only to find his left front tire slashed when he got to his SUV. He slammed his fist on the hood of his vehicle. He was supposed to make sure she got to Mark's! He pulled his cell phone out of his pocket and punched in Mark's number. Then he'd call Zack.

CHAPTER 20

MARK WOKE TO the sound of his cell phone ringing. With his eyes half opened, he picked up his phone. It was his brother. Yawning, "Hey Mike, what's up?" he asked.

"I'm still at the restaurant." He looked over at the clock. It was after midnight. That wasn't uncommon on a Friday night. "Is there a reason why you're calling me?"

Mike checked his watch. Tammy should have pulled into the driveway by now. "Can you check to see if Tammy has arrived at your house?"

Mark sprang out of bed. He detected something in Mike's voice that put him into panic mode. "What's going on?" he demanded.

"Mark, I don't want you to get upset with me, but I was to make sure Tammy arrived at your house. Zack wasn't able to have an officer here at the restaurant tonight. She must have left shortly after Zack talked to her. When I came from my office, she was gone. She should be there by now."

"I'll go check," his heart thundering in his chest as he flew from his bedroom to look out the front window. He saw a police officer sitting out front, but Tammy's car wasn't in the drive.

"She's not here, Mike!"

"Okay, let's not panic. Let's give her a few more minutes."

"You better tell me exactly what is going on."

Mike gave him the update while he kept watch out the window. As the seconds ticked by, he was getting more gripped by fear when she didn't pull into the driveway. When Mike was through, Mark wondered if, somehow, she got delayed and Mike didn't know it. "Can you check to see if her car is still in the parking lot? She drives a red Honda Civic. You can't miss it."

"Hold on, I'll check." Stepping away from his SUV, he searched for her car. About midway back, he located it. *Damn it!* He ran up to the car to find it locked. Looking inside, her purse was sitting in the front seat of her car. He looked around and saw a note on her windshield. He took it off and read it.

Tell your brother if he wants to see Tammy alive again, he's to bring the girl to a warehouse on the island. He is to come alone with the girl. No cops! I will contact him tomorrow at noon with directions to the place and the time for him to deliver her.

He could hear his brother's voice yelling into his phone, "Mike! Mike! Is it there?"

He put the phone to his ear. His heart dropped, knowing this was his fault. He thought she would have had more to do before she went home.

"Mike!"

He took a breath, "Yes, Mark, her car is here, along with a note."

His heart accelerated as panic ripped through him. "Call Zack," he yelled into the phone. "I'll be right there!" Mark ended the call. He rushed into the entertainment room, to find Bob and Mildred watching a movie. He was surprised they didn't hear him yelling into the phone. He hoped he hadn't woken up Bethany.

When Mildred found Mark standing in the doorway, she could see in his eyes that something was drastically wrong. She got up off the chair and ran up to him. "Mark!" she exclaimed. "I can tell by looking at you that something has happened. What is it?"

"I got a call from my brother. An emergency has come up and I need to get over to the restaurant. Can you stay longer with Bethany? I'm not sure how long I will be gone."

"Yes, no worries. We can stay until Tammy gets home."

He hated to tell them Tammy wasn't coming home. "Listen, we think Tammy's been kidnapped. Please don't say anything to Bethany if she should wake. Not until I get the details. I'll be back as quick as I can."

Shocked, Bob replied. "Go! Don't worry about a thing here. And keep us updated!"

"Will do," he said as he rushed out the door to his car.

When Mark drove into the parking lot of the restaurant, he found police officers around his brother's SUV and Tammy's car. Mike was off to the side, talking to Peyton and Jenna. He ran up to them and asked, "What have you found out?"

"Nothing at this point, Mark," returned Mike. "They're dusting for fingerprints on both vehicles, but I doubt they will find anything. They didn't on my Corvette."

"Do you have the note?"

Mike handed it to him. It was the same handwriting as the note he found on his windshield. His heart escalated as he read the bold scrawl. He looked up, to glance over at Mike. "Has Zack seen this?"

"Zack hasn't arrived yet. He should be here shortly. After he left here, he got called out to a homicide on the outskirts of Honolulu," answered Mike.

"The person who wrote this note is the same one who left a note on my windshield to stay away from Tammy and her daughter. And as far as I know, they still haven't matched the writing to anyone on Intel yet. What are we going to do? We can't just sit here and wait." Mark felt helpless as he tried to figure out where he could have taken her. If anything happened to her, he would never forgive himself. He was supposed to keep her and her daughter safe! He didn't have a clue as to what warehouse he was referring to. There were many warehouses scattered all over the island. He wasn't sure he could wait until the bastard called to give him directions. He turned to Peyton. "How is Justice at tracking where he might have taken her?" he asked impatiently.

"I'm already way ahead of you, Mark. I just called Stacy to bring Justice over here. She said she would get here as quick as she can. All flights over here won't be leaving until morning, and of course the ferry isn't running this late at night. She's checking to see if the lieutenant would have one of the pilots for the KPD bring them over."

Mark blew out a breath.

Mike came up and put a hand on his shoulder. "Mark, I'm sorry, this is my fault. But know this. We are going to do everything we can to find her." He could see his brother was beside himself with fear of not knowing where she is. If it was Jenna, he'd be the same way, if not worse.

With his hands on his hips, Mark nodded, glancing around. "I see one of your tires got slashed again."

"Yes, and thank God it was only one. The cost to replace my tires on the Corvette was astronomical. Whoever this guy is, he wanted us both out of the way. He had to be watching the restaurant tonight, knowing there was not an officer here to follow Tammy to your home."

"I agree. And my gut is telling me it's her ex who has her. He wasn't about to meet her in the morning, knowing she had someone from the police department following her every move."

Peyton's phone went off. He stepped away to answer it.

Jenna, in the meantime, came up to Mark and gave him a hug. "I'm so sorry this has happened." She pulled away. "If there's anything I can do, just let me know. If you want, I can go and relieve the Langleys. I would be happy to watch Bethany until this is over."

"Actually, Jenna," responded Mark, "that would be a big help. As soon as Zack gets here we can figure out our next steps."

Peyton came back up to them. "That was Stacy. She said she can be here in an hour. The lieutenant gave the pilot bringing them over orders to help track where the suspect took her."

Relief flooded throughout Mark, knowing they were on their way.

Zack, getting out of his car, came running up to Mark, embracing him in a big bear hug. He pulled back and asked with empathy, "How are you doing, Mark?"

Mark was not a crying man, but he felt tears swell up in his eyes as he responded, "I was supposed to keep them safe, Zack. If anything happens to her..." His voice trailed off with the pent-up emotion he was feeling inside him. He was also feeling guilty about the way things were left between them this afternoon. He pulled himself together. He couldn't think about that now. He needed to focus.

Zack put his hands on his shoulders. He felt all kinds of guilt for not being able to have an officer here tonight. "Listen, Mark," he said with conviction, "I swear to you, we are going to find her!"

Mark nodded. "Here's a note that Mike found on her car. It's written in the same handwriting as the other one I found on my windshield."

Zack took the note and read it over. He glanced up. "This doesn't give us much to go on, since there are warehouses all over the island. But we do have some time. I'll call Forensics to get them over here, stat. Then I'm calling Craig. He's been on leave, but I know he'll come on board when I tell him what's happened. He's really good at putting the pieces of the puzzle together." He looked over at Peyton. "Is there any way we can get your dog here?" he asked.

"They're already on the way, Zack."

"Good! You men go inside and wait for everyone to get here, then we'll put a plan together. In the meantime, I need to go check with the officers, to see if they have come up with anything."

As the three brothers headed into the restaurant, Jenna held back and grabbed Mark's arm. "Mark, I'm going to go over to your house. If the Langleys want to go home, I will stay with Bethany."

"Thank you, Jenna. I can see why Mike fell in love with you. You are always there in any situation to lend a hand." He gave her a hug and let her know there was a police officer there to keep watch.

"Okay. Can you let Mike know that's where I'll be if he needs to get ahold of me?"

"No problem, I'll let him know." He thought a moment. "Hey, if Bethany wakes, she's going to wonder where her mother is. For now, tell her she's with me and will be home as soon as we can." She nodded and turned to leave. "And Jenna?" he asked. She turned back. "Could you say a prayer for us to find her, and that she will be unharmed?" She ran up to him and gave him another hug.

"Mark, you can count on it. I will be praying for all of you that He will keep all of you safe, especially Tammy." She released him and hurried to go to her car.

He watched until she was safely in her car and pulling away. As he turned to go into the restaurant, he sent up his own prayer before he joined the others.

Inside, his brothers were sitting in the corner booth. Mark joined them, only to discover there was no coffee on the table. He was definitely in need of a cup. "I'm going to put some coffee on. Would anyone like a cup?"

"Yes," they all agreed.

"I'll be right back." After he put the coffee on, he went into the kitchen to put a sandwich together. After sleeping the afternoon and evening away, he needed some fuel to get through the night. When he walked in, he discovered Palani was still working on inventory. "Hey, Palani. Still working?" he asked.

Palani looked up from the chart he was working on. "Yes. Just seeing what we will need for tomorrow's specials."

Palani was their head chef who helped get their restaurant going in the early days. A big Polynesian man, with long black hair tied behind his thick neck. He was an asset who would be hard to replace. He walked up to Mark. "I heard Tammy was kidnapped. Is it true?" he asked.

"I'm afraid so. There was a note on her car. I don't know what all you've heard, but he wants Tammy's daughter. He wants an even trade, Tammy for the girl."

Palani sighed. "What can I do to help?"

Mark half smiled, with a slight gleam in his eyes. "You wouldn't make a platter of sandwiches for us, would you? We have several detectives and officers coming in that may be hungry. I have a feeling it's going to be a long night."

Palani put his chart down on the counter. "Consider it done. What would you like?"

"Whatever you want to make, Palani. Everything you make is always good."

"I'll bring it right out as soon as I have it prepared," he said with a smile.

"Thanks, Palani. I don't know what we would do without you."

Palani laughed. "You wouldn't survive!"

Mark chuckled with him. "You are so right!"

Back out by the coffee urn, Mark filled two carafes with coffee, grabbed a bowl of cream, and headed back to the booth. When he came out behind the bar, he saw Mike had already set up a table close to the booth with cups, spoons, and napkins. He set everything down on the table.

Zack had come back in, along with a couple of officers who were also seated in the booth. They were looking through a purse sitting on the table. He realized it was Tammy's. He walked up to them and asked, "I see you have Tammy's purse. Did you find anything that will help?"

"Not much. Her cell phone was in her purse, so we can't track her," answered one of the officers.

"Just to let you know, she rarely has her GPS on, so it probably wouldn't have been any use. There's coffee on the table, let's go grab a cup. I'm in dire need of one," motioned Mark.

After everyone had a cup, Zack started in. "I've called in Lieutenant Fillmore along with Forensics. They should be here shortly. Craig is also on his way. I thought it best to include Lieutenant Carmichael of the FBI as well, as it is their case." He glanced over at Peyton. "How long before Stacy and Justice arrive?" he asked.

Checking his watch, "They should be here in a half hour."

"Good. Once everyone arrives, we'll put a game plan together. In the meantime, let's go over everything we have so far, along with what we have uncovered about this Roy Gardner, who is now the main suspect in the kidnapping. Roy Gardner," Zack went on to explain, "is Tammy's ex-husband. He's had no contact with her until this morning, in the library, at the university. They were to meet at a bistro near the mall tomorrow morning. The guy had to know that we've had surveillance on both Tammy and her daughter. It was sure bad luck we weren't able to have someone here at the restaurant tonight. Two threatening notes have been written. One against Mark, and this second one, Tammy's life, if the girl is not delivered to him by tomorrow. In his note, he will call Mark with directions to a warehouse on the Island and the time they will meet. We hope we don't have to wait for the phone call, and we will have this perpetrator in custody and Tammy freed."

Zack was interrupted when he saw Palani coming out with a large platter of sandwiches and placed them on the table. It reminded him he hadn't had time to eat yet this evening with setting up the meeting with Peyton in the morning, interviewing Tammy, and then the homicide he was called out to. Now this!

Mark spoke up. "What do you say we have something to eat while we wait for everyone else to arrive? I know some of us didn't get a chance to eat, so dig in!"

"You don't have to tell me twice," commented Zack; he was starving!

While everyone started in, Mark went up to Palani. "Hey, thanks again for doing this."

"You're welcome. Is there anything else I can get for you?"

"I think we're set. We'll take care of the mess. You go on home."

He nodded, but before he left, he spoke sincerely. "I will say a prayer that all goes well tonight, and Tammy will be rescued unharmed."

For the second time tonight, tears started forming in his eyes as he thanked him again, before turning away to get a sandwich before they were gone.

While they were eating, one by one the rest of the officers and lieutenants came into the restaurant, followed up by Detective Craig Jenson, a savvy man who was spot on in the ability to make good judgments and figuring out how a criminal's mind works. A tall man, with blond hair and vivid blue eyes that could pierce the man or woman he was interrogating. He greeted each one with enthusiasm, excited to be back to work.

While eating a sandwich, Peyton heard a familiar whine. He glanced over to see Stacy come in with Justice. Behind her was a tall man in flight gear. He went to greet them. Justice, pulling on his lead, couldn't wait to be by his master's side again.

"Whew!" greeted Stacy. "Justice can sure pull! He practically dragged me down the street to get here!"

Peyton gave her a kiss, then went down on his haunches to pet his dog. "Hey, Justice. Are you ready to go to work, boy? Huh, boy?" he murmured.

Justice could hardly contain himself, as he barked three times to let his master know he was ready!

He smiled as he came up and took the lead from Stacy. He turned to shake the officer's hand that brought them over here. "Hey," he introduced himself, "Peyton TreVaine."

"Sergeant Matt Higgins," he returned. "That's some dog you have there. His eyes never left the window of the chopper all the way here. As soon as the island came into view, he went nuts, almost as if he knew exactly where you were at!"

Peyton chuckled. He reached down and petted Justice's head. "We've been together for a while now. He was my right hand over in Afghanistan working in search-and-rescue."

"I served over in Iran for two years. I hear you are a helicopter pilot as well."

Peyton nodded. "Flew the UH-60 transport my last year there. Now, I work for the hospital over on Kona transporting patients."

"Before we get into war stories," Stacy interrupted, "I think we had better get over to the meeting," nodding her head in that direction.

"You're right." He smiled.

Coming up to the men, Peyton overheard Lieutenant Carmichael telling the police detectives and officers to stay out of it. He and his team would handle it. An uproar broke out as each detective and officer stood their ground.

"Like hell we're going to stay out of it! This has become our case as much as it is yours! I say we join forces and work together on this. Tammy and her daughter have been under our surveillance since the attempted kidnapping!" stated Lieutenant Fillmore.

"Well, we've seen how that went," Lieutenant Carmichael shot back.

Lieutenant Fillmore pushed back the rage that was slowing burning inside him. The staff shortage put them in a precarious situation all the way around. He wanted to lash out but thought better of it. Instead, he responded, "You, of all officers, Lieutenant, should know, the shortage of cops is prevalent all over the United States and especially here on the island. Now, I'm not going to argue with you any further. We have information on the suspect who we think kidnapped Tammy. If you want to discuss it, we'll be glad to. If not, we are taking over this part of the case!"

There seemed to be a standoff between the two lieutenants, each one not backing down on their stance. Finally, Lieutenant Carmichael relented. Looking around at the men, he stated, "Okay, let's hear what you got. Then we'll put a plan together. It might just lead us to some other kids that have been recently taken by this trafficking ring."

Mark, listening, didn't want to wait around for a plan. He wanted to get out there and find her. He didn't want to go home and try to explain to Bethany that her mom was taken. He couldn't bear it. He walked over to his brothers and Stacy. Glancing over at Peyton, he asked, "What do you think? Can Justice track where he's taken her?"

"Not without some help. We would need a piece of her clothing, plus some FLIR cameras" (forward-looking infrared cameras).

"We have all the equipment needed on my chopper, and we've used this particular chopper on many missions when in pursuit of criminal suspects," stated Sergeant Higgins.

"Where do we start?" asked Mike.

"Since the suspect referred to a warehouse, we should probably search abandoned warehouses in remote areas as well as in the city," suggested Peyton.

"The chopper would be faster. It would cover more ground," answered Sergeant Higgins.

"We could have a few men on the ground, along with men in the chopper," related Peyton. "We can let each other know by radio if either of us find where she's been taken. Also, Sergeant Higgins, do you by chance have a smaller camera I can rig up on Justice's collar? We used to use vests with cameras when we were working together in Afghanistan. I know the island doesn't have a K-9 unit, but I'm pretty sure I can attach one to his collar," inquired Peyton.

"I do have several different size cameras. I'm sure we can find one that will fit."

"Excellent," replied Peyton. This would give them a better chance of finding Tammy, once they located the warehouse she had been taken to.

Zack and Craig came up behind the men. "Hey, you men need to be over here." He motioned with his hand.

"Zack," replied Mark, "we've been talking. We want to go out on our own to find Tammy." He turned to Matt. "This is Sergeant Matt Higgins, from KPD. He brought Stacy and Justice over. He has permission from Lieutenant Carlson to help in the search. Matt, this is Detective Zack Williams, who has been working on the case, and Detective Craig Jenson, who just returned on a leave."

Both Zack and Craig shook hands with the officer. "I've actually heard about some of your missions," commented Zack.

"Glad to have you aboard."

"Glad I can help," he returned. He turned to Mark, "Listen, I know how anxious you are to get out there, but I think its best we stick together on this, so we're not crossing paths. Let's go see what the lieutenants have come up with and we'll go from there."

CHAPTER 21

Tammy was watching out the window as the car ate up the miles. Fear enveloped her as to what Roy was going to do with her once they reached his destination. *What happened to the man I thought I once knew?* she wondered.

It wasn't that long ago she had been so in love with him. She would have done anything to make him happy. Now looking back, she never should have called him, or set up a time to meet with him. How could she have been so stupid as to think he would want to get to know his daughter? *His daughter.* She huffed. He never wanted to be a father to Bethany. In fact, he signed off all rights to parenthood in the divorce. At the time it broke her heart, but she came through it, and was raising her daughter the best that she could. Now this idiot of an ex-husband was taking her somewhere. Where, she had no idea. Fear and anxiety rose up in her chest at the thought of never seeing her precious daughter again. She wondered if anybody had discovered she was missing yet. With each passing mile she prayed that the Lord would see her through this, and Roy would come to his senses.

Gripping the wheel, Roy had one mission and one mission only! To get the girl! Even if it means using his ex-wife to do it! If he didn't deliver, he knew he was a dead man! His fear and anger took control of him. It made him do things he would never think to do otherwise.

But when he realized he was in too deep, it was too late. *If it hadn't been for that detective and Mark TreVaine, I wouldn't be in this mess!* he thought. He hated himself for becoming someone who would kill to protect his own life. He had gotten himself so far in debt with his online gambling that he thought this was his only way out. He was the girl's father after all, even if he wanted to have nothing to do with her. He got a good price for her, too, enough to pay most of the debt. He found her on one of the social media sites. There was a picture of her and Tammy. She was a pretty little thing, just like her mom. It wasn't hard to sell her. These online predators were always looking for young girls. He would see this through, then he would slip away.

Roy exited off the highway and drove a short distance on a road Tammy was not familiar with. When he turned down a dirt road leading into a dense forest, she found her voice. "Where are you taking me?" she demanded.

"All in due time," he chided.

Fear and anger rose up inside her as she confronted him. "That's not an answer, Roy! I want to know where you are taking me and why you are doing this! What's in it for you?"

Roy, gripping the wheel even tighter, bristled, "What's in it for me, you ask? You, Tammy, in exchange for your daughter."

Shocked, she realized Mark and Detective Williams were right in accusing Roy of selling her daughter! Anger that he would even do such a thing made her want to lash out. "So," she demanded of him, "you are the one that sold her! How could you do this? What possessed you to do such a horrid thing? Did you give a thought about how it was going to affect me?"

"You ask a lot of questions, Tammy, in which I will sum it up in one answer. I needed the money."

Staring at him, she was at a loss for words. She could now see how greed and evil come together. For him to kidnap her in exchange for her daughter, all in the name of money, was the worst thing imaginable. Detective Williams was right. He must be in hock up to his ears in online gambling. She wanted to hit him! How was she going to get out of this? Maybe if she reasoned with him, he would see this is futile. As calmly as she could, "Look, Roy, I have some savings. I could give it to you to help pay off your debt. If it's not enough, I will take out a loan to pay off the rest," she pleaded.

He hit a bump in the road which jostled them both. He straightened himself in the seat as he answered her, "That's a nice gesture, Tammy. But it's too late. It's already been done. I can't go back."

She sat back in her seat, making her say things she probably shouldn't. "You're never going to get away with this, Roy. As soon as they find out I'm missing, they'll come after you, and anybody that is part of this human-trafficking ring. They will never bring Bethany to you, even if you kill me first. Then where will you be?"

Her words set him off. "Shut up!" he roared. She jumped. "Not another word! We've got a ways to go and I don't want to hear any more from you!"

Grinding his teeth, Tammy's words hit home. What if she was right? He didn't really think this thing through. He was a desperate man trying to save his own life. He had to count on Mark's love for her. Watching them at a distance, making out on the lounge chair by the pool, told him everything. He was in love with her, and he knew without a doubt he would do anything to protect her. If he ever found out he was the one that tried to take him out, him and his brothers would be out for blood. He knew them when he was a regular patron of their restaurant. They were successful businessmen. They made that restaurant what it is today. Nothing would stop them. Whatever happens, he would make it clear to him: if he didn't deliver the girl at the time specified tomorrow when he called, Tammy would die!

As tears starting to form in her eyes, Tammy tried to stay calm. She worried about Bethany waking up and finding her gone. What would they tell her? Her chest was starting to hurt, with the fear and anxiety creeping up on her. While starting with some deep breaths, she glanced over at the man she thought she once loved, never even thinking he would hurt someone, let alone kill her to get to her daughter. She had to think of a way out of this. She found reasoning with him wasn't the answer. One thing for sure, she would never let him take her daughter. She would die first. She had taken a self-defense course when she first started at the university. She thought it would be a good idea, since they lived alone, with the crime rate and all. Ideas started to formulate in her mind about how she could escape. Maybe she could sidetrack him, make a run for it when he had reached wherever he was taking her.

Forget it, Tammy, she thought. *He's got a gun.*

Oh, what was she to do? She thought of Mark. Did he know she was missing? She was sorry for the way she had responded toward him this afternoon. What she wouldn't give to be in his arms right now. Would she live to see him again? As she continued to take deep breaths to calm herself, she could only think of one thing she could do: pray!

Up in the police helicopter, Sergeant Higgins was circling the island. Detective Jenson was watching the radar screen along with Mike. They all had their earphones on, equipped with microphones, to stay in contact with each other.

Something came up on the screen. A small light was flickering down in some rough terrain down on the ground. "Sergeant Higgins," asked Craig, "can you zoom in on that light down on the ground?"

"No problem, sir." They watched as the infrared camera was able to pick up fresh tire tracks from the heat of the tires. Sergeant Higgins positioned the camera, and they were able to follow the tracks to a car, heading south through a dense forest towards the ocean. They continued to watch the screen as the car slowed down and parked in front of a building. As they looked on, two people exited the car. First one out was a female on the passenger side, next a male figure on the driver's side. Sergeant Higgins was able to zoom in even further. They watched as the man held a gun to the woman's back, pushing her along to the building's entrance.

"He's got a gun!" yelled Craig. Turning toward Mike, he ordered, "Get ahold of Zack and your brothers on the radio. Let Zack know it's at that old, abandoned warehouse on the south side of the island. He knows where it is. We've been out here on numerous occasions over the years looking for drug pushers. Let them know he is armed and dangerous. I'll contact the lieutenant to let him know we've located them." Glancing back over at Sergeant Higgins, he asked, "Is there a safe place we can land this thing? Preferably where they won't suspect we are trailing them?" he asked.

Sergeant Higgins, turning the chopper around, looked out into the distance. He saw a small area off to the right, near the water. It would be risky, but he thought he could land it. "It's a ways from the warehouse. We would have to do the distance on foot. It could take a while."

"Let's do it!"

Meanwhile, down on the ground, Mike was giving Zack the information. At the same time, he was punching in the location on his computer. Once the location came up on the GPS, they started out. "According to what Mike has told me, they are about an hour and forty-five minutes ahead of us. We'll be able to make up time on the highway until we get to the road leading back to the warehouse. Craig and I have been on this road looking for drug smugglers. It's not in the best shape. Plus, we'll be traveling through some pretty thick tropical forest."

Mark, impatient to get there, upset that they had to wait so long to find out where the bastard had taken her, practically yelled, "I don't care what it is like. Just get us there!" Mark was beside himself with fear, not knowing what this creep of an ex-husband could have already done to her! If he so much as harmed one hair on her head, he swore Roy would pay! He wasn't much of a praying man, but he prayed with his heart and soul that God would keep her safe till they got there.

With his lights flashing, Zack drove at a high rate of speed to get to their destination. Zack knew of an area, once they were on the dirt road, where he could pull off and back in. He just needed to remember where it was. Once there, they would have to walk the rest of the way in.

Stacy, sitting in the back, with Peyton and Justice in between them, remembered a similar situation she was involved in. Unfortunately for the victim, it proved to be fatal. She prayed it wouldn't be the case. She could see Mark was very much in love with her.

All of them sat in silence as the car ate up the miles. Each one formulating a plan as to how they would free Tammy, with no one getting killed!

Roy pulled up to a building that Tammy could barely make out in the dim light. Pulling out his gun, he waved it at her. "It's time to get out." She swallowed. Opening up the door, she slowly exited the car. "Don't try anything funny, like making a run for it. Or I'll shoot you where you stand."

She walked toward the building, with Roy right behind her. She could hear the ocean and knew the building must be close to the water. There was another car parked next to the building. With her heart thudding in her chest, she did as Roy instructed.

Once they came up to the door, he reached over, pulled the door open, and shoved her inside. There was a dim light coming from a kerosene lantern. A man sitting on an old crate was on his phone. He appeared to be playing some game on it. He looked up as they walked up to him.

"Well, well, well… What do we have here?" he sneered.

Tammy felt her skin crawl, as his dark eyes gleamed as they traveled up and down her slender body, zeroing in on her long legs and back up to her firm breasts, showing in the snug-fitting t-shirt she was wearing. She thought she was going to be sick, looking at the man with long brown hair hanging down to his shoulders, who hadn't seen a shower in several weeks.

He came up off the crate to slowly walk up to her. She backed away when he tried to place his dirty hand on her soft cheek. "I thought you were bringing the girl, but this one will do."

"Hands off, Morris!" he relayed with malice. "She's the bait. The girl will be here tomorrow. Grab that rope over there and tie her up. Then put her in the room with the others."

An evil grin broke out on his slimy face. "Gladly," he retorted, as he strode over to grab the rope lying on the ground next to the stack of crates up against the wall. Once he had her hands tied behind her back, he turned on his flashlight and led her toward the back of the building. He opened the door to what appeared to be a small room with wood flooring. The stench in there was horrendous. When she stepped into the room, what she saw made her heart sick.

Children, who appeared to be from the ages of five to twelve years old, she couldn't be sure in the dim light, were huddled in a corner of the room. They didn't make a sound as he pushed her over toward them. She didn't know if they were dead or alive, as none of them moved. "Wha… What have you done to these children?" shocked to the core as she asked the question.

"Don't worry, they're not dead. I gave them something to make them sleep when I fed them."

"How long have they been here?" she asked, as tears started to form in her eyes for what these kids have been through.

"That's not your business, lady. So keep your mouth shut…" He pulled something out of his pocket and held it to her face. She threw her head back as he pushed a button, the switchblade coming out, barely missing her chin. "If you want to live. Now sit down!"

She slid down the wall beside one of the kids. He came down on his haunches and tied her ankles together. When he was done, he glanced up into her eyes as his hand came up her leg. His eyes held an evil lust to them as he slowly came up over her. "You're a pretty little thing," his voice husky. "If Gardner doesn't come through with your daughter, you will do nicely."

As his hand continued its climb up her leg, she held her breath, her heart pounding in her chest, fear overcoming her as she knew it was only a matter of time before he would rape her. He stroked her cheek with his hand and murmured, "You and I could have quite a time here on the floor. I could teach you some things that I bet no man has ever taught you before." When his hand reached her panties, she felt sickened and wanted to throw up. He leaned in to kiss her. She turned her head before his grimy lips touched hers. That set him off.

He grabbed her chin with his hand and slammed her head against the wall, while his other hand tried to get inside her. Just as he was about to grind his lips to hers, the door opened.

"Morris! What the hell are you doing? A car just pulled up. You need to get out here!"

With his hand still holding her chin, his eyes held an evil glint to them. With a menacing tone to his voice, he hissed, "I'll be back. If you try and fight me, you'll wish you hadn't!" Again he shoved her head against the wall. He got up and walked over to the door.

When the door closed behind him, she closed her eyes as relief flooded through her. She tried not to cry, but the tears came. After a few minutes, she pulled herself together. She needed to think. From the moonlight coming in from the gaps in the wood siding, she could see the children lying next to each other. One of them, she thought, might be a boy. Her heart broke, knowing what they must have endured at the hands of these men. She wished she could gather all of them in her arms, giving them comfort, quietly whispering everything would be all right.

As the minutes ticked by, it seemed like hours to her. It was only a matter of time before he would be back. She searched the walls around her, looking for anything that might help them to get out of here. At the bottom of this one wall, there was a board missing. Peering out, she could see the moon shining down on the water. The gap wasn't big enough for a person to get through, but if she could get over there, she might be able to move another board out of the way, and they could all escape. But how was she to get over there? She tried to untie her hands, with no luck. She rested her head against the wall, feeling the pain from the lump that started to come out on her head.

All of a sudden she heard a noise outside where the board was missing. She tried to peer down at the bottom of the floor, to see if see could see any movement, her mind racing at what it could be. What if it was a rat! It was definitely wide enough for a rat to get in. She was scared to death of rats! With her breathing labored, she sat rock still. Listening, in the quiet of the night, the noise sounded like there was an animal digging outside. Could it be a wild boar? Oh, she hoped not! Those things scared her even more than the rats!

She tried harder to get her hands out of the ropes. If she could just stretch the rope, she just might be able to get her hands free. She worked until… Yes! One of her hands came out of the rope and then the other. She hurried and untied the rope around her ankles.

She rose up from where she was sitting and crept over to the area. As she neared the gap she found a board, probably the one missing from the wall. It wasn't her bat, but it was solid enough that it could do some real harm if she needed to. Along with the digging, she heard some whining. Could it be a dog trying to get in?

As she bent down on her knees, she peered out to see a black dog staring right back at her! Was it a wild dog? She didn't know, but she was going to chance it. She held out her hand for the dog to sniff. The dog came up to her, first sniffing, then licking her hand. Tammy petted its head. The dog seemed friendly enough. Her hand traveled down and felt a collar around its neck. He was someone's dog! Hope began to rise up in her as she spoke to the dog. "Go! Go get some help!" The dog's ears perked up. "Go!" she commanded. The dog took off! Whether it understood what she wanted, she had no idea. She tried to pull a board out from either side of the wall to no avail. She didn't dare try to bash it out for fear of them hearing her. She sat back down in dismay. Her only hope was the dog. Again she found herself praying for someone to find them.

Peyton and Stacy were on a tablet Sergeant Higgins had given them. They watched as Justice walked around to a gap in the building. With the camera on his collar, he could see everything. "Hey, guys, come over here."

Zack and Mark, who were watching the building, came up to them. As they watched the screen, Justice was slowly coming up to an arm protruding out of a gap in the wall. As Justice moved closer, they could tell by the shape of the arm it was a woman. A face came into view. As they all continued to watch, her mouth formed the word, "*Go!*"

"Justice should be coming back any minute," said Peyton.

"That's Tammy," exclaimed Mark in a hushed voice. "I need to go to her!" He turned to go, when Zack grabbed his arm.

"Hold up there, Mark! We have no idea how many men are inside the building. As soon as Justice comes back, we will need to meet up with your brother, Craig, and Sergeant Higgins on the other side of the road. We have the lieutenant and other officers coming in. We are all going to have to work together on a strategy to get her out, and to make sure no one gets killed."

Mark, impatient, knew he was right. He didn't want to risk her life if he jumped too soon.

Justice came up to his master. His body shaking as his tail wagged back and forth in excitement. Peyton, down on his haunches, put his hands on each side of his head, going down his neck, letting him know he did a good job.

Zack was on a radio call with Craig. As soon as he ended the call, he informed them, "The men are coming up through the forest and are nearing the building. He said it looked like they had a clear vision of the front of the building from there. Let's head back. We can join them to see what the next step will be."

Peyton wanted to go around to the back of the building. In a hushed voice, he said, "Listen, Stacy and I will take Justice and go around to the back. The woods curve around that way. We can remain hidden, to still see if any of the men in the building come out the back."

"I'm going with you," declared Mark.

Zack couldn't argue with them. They would have coverage for the back and the front of the building. "Okay, I'll go alert Craig and the others. Let me know when you are in position."

"Clear," confirmed Peyton.

Inside, Morris greeted the four men who joined them, with Roy coming up behind. Morris was well aware that these men were the boss's henchmen. If you screwed up, there were consequences.

"Do you have the girl?" the head guy asked, who went by the name of Jasper.

Roy, staring at the big, rugged men carrying M-16 riffles, knew he was in trouble. Standing next to one, then looking into the eyes of the man who asked the question, left him with a bad feeling inside when he answered, "No, I wasn't able to get the girl. I have her mother. The girl will be coming tomorrow."

"Oh? And how's that going to happen?" he demanded.

"Look, the mother and the daughter have been under police surveillance since Morris's kid's knapping attempt was botched. I've tried several times to get her, to no avail. I even tried to take the TreVaine brothers out, but people were coming out of the restaurant, so I had to get out of there. There was no cop around at the restaurant tonight, so I have the mother, who we will trade for her daughter tomorrow."

The man stood there and shook his head. Glancing at Roy and then Morris, he bluntly stated. "Do you know how much you two have compromised this operation?" he asked as he pointed his rifle at each one. "You, Morris, who landed yourself in jail, and you, Gardner, with a plan that could put us all out of commission."

Both Morris and Roy stood like stone statues. Not moving one inch, hearts pounding in their chests, their fate in the hands of these four men.

He turned to one of his men. "Go get the woman. We'll take all three of them out and burn the building."

"But what about the kids?" the man asked. "Won't the boss be upset if we have no kids to deliver?"

"He'll be more upset if we all get caught!" yelled Jasper. "Now go!"

Tammy saw one of the kids waking up. She went over to her. "How are you doing?" asked Tammy.

The little girl raised herself up and stared into Tammy's eyes. "Who are you?" she asked meekly.

"I'm Tammy," she said softly. "Can you tell me your name?"

"It's Alice. Are you here to save us?"

Tammy didn't know what to say. She smiled. "I'm sure going to try. Do you know of another way out besides the gap in the wall over there?"

She shook her head no. "Some of the older girls have tried to get another board off. They got caught. That man who was watching us beat them. We haven't tried since." She started crying. "I'm scared, and I want to go home!"

Tammy gathered her in her arms and assured her they would find a way. She let her go and went back over to the wall. It was now or never. She didn't know how long she had until Morris came back, but she felt this could be their only chance. She came down to the floor, lying on her back, and gave the board a hard kick. It gave a little. She did it again, only this time much harder. The board protruded out. Enough that she thought she could get out. She suddenly heard footsteps outside along the wall! *Oh, please, Lord, don't let it be Morris!* She held her breath. Suddenly she heard a familiar voice.

"Tammy?" he said in a hushed voice.

"Mark!" she exclaimed. "Thank God it's you!" He pulled the board out even further and she was able to climb out. She fell into his arms.

"I was so scared," he whispered, kissing the top of her head. "Thank God you're safe." She pulled slightly away. Panic drove her.

"Mark, I don't know how long we have until the guy named Morris comes back to check on us. There are at least six kids inside that need our help. One of them is awake. Her name is Alice. The others are still under the effects of the drug he gave them."

Mark, with his adrenaline still flowing inside him, made a decision. "Peyton, Stacy, and Justice are over at the edge of the woods over there." Her eyes followed where he was pointing. "I'll get the kids." Before she left, she told him about the board just inside the opening. "Got it. Now go!" She raced over to the woods just as Mark went inside. He whispered Alice's name.

From the small amount of light coming in from the opening, he saw a little girl sitting with the other kids who appeared to be asleep. He quietly walked up to her. "Hi, Alice," he whispered. "I'm here to help you and the others."

Just as he was about to help the little girl up, he heard a key turn in the door. He quickly got up and went behind a large crate. He raised his finger to his lips. "Shh… Lay back down," he whispered, waving his hand to indicate what he wanted her to do. She quickly lay back down.

Damn! He forgot to grab the board when he came in. He looked around for anything to grab as the sound of footsteps started to walk towards him. He ducked as the light from his flashlight beamed over to where he was hiding. The man stopped, realizing that the woman he was looking for was gone. He headed back out to the men waiting for him.

Mark blew out a breath, knowing he only had moments before they would be out looking for her. He took ahold of Alice's hand and brought her out of the building. He picked her up and ran as fast as he could into the woods where Tammy, Stacy, and Peyton were waiting. He set her down.

Tammy quickly came to her side, taking her into her arms. Alice snuggled into her, relieved she was out of that awful place. She lifted her head and asked, "What about the others?" she cried.

Tammy placed her hand on her little head, feeling her soft hair. "Don't worry, we'll get the others. We just have to wait to make sure it's safe to go back in."

Justice came up to them to check out the little girl, sniffing and wagging his tail. Alice giggled as she lay her head back on Tammy's chest. Justice lay down beside them, offering protection as she rocked her, cooing soothing words, while Stacy and the men came up with a plan. Mark went right to Peyton and Stacy and explained the situation.

"There are at least five more kids inside the building. They know Tammy is gone. It will only be a matter of minutes before they come looking for her."

Peyton, taking in the area, knew they had to rescue those kids. He radioed Zack, to let him know that children were in the back of the building, and Tammy and one other child were free. He informed them that the men inside would more than likely come out and start looking for Tammy. In the meantime, they would work to get the kids out.

Zack, turning off his radio, informed the men and instructed them to get into position with their rifles pointing at the building. With their adrenaline surging, they waited patiently for the men to come out.

Peyton motioned Stacy to go over to the end of the woods. From there she could see anyone coming around either side of the building and be there for backup. Mark went into the building, with Peyton waiting outside. With only moments to spare, one by one, Mark brought out a child and gave them to Peyton to take back to Tammy.

Inside, the man came back to inform them that the woman escaped. Shocked, Morris bellowed, "How could she have escaped? I tied her up so she couldn't move!"

Jasper walked up to Morris, rage written all over his face, rifle shoved into his chest. "Obviously, not tight enough!" he yelled. He pulled the trigger twice. Morris fell to the floor. He pointed his rifle at Roy. Roy raised his hands, never thinking he would wind up facing his last damn day on earth! He tried to talk his way out of it.

"Look, Jasper, I'm her ex…."

Two shots were fired. Roy's eyes bulged out, as he fell face down on the floor.

Waving his rifle at one of his men, he commanded, "Go get that container of kerosene and pour it over there where those crates are stacked. Then light it."

Outside, the men heard gunshots. Within minutes, smoke started billowing out from the broken windows. They braced themselves behind the vehicles as four men with rifles came running out of the building.

"Stop!" yelled Zack. "Drop your weapons!"

Jasper, looking around, seeing the officers with their guns pulled, knew they were sunk. He dropped his gun and raised his hands. The rest followed suit. The men came out from behind the cars and proceeded to handcuff each one and pulled them away from the building just as the lieutenant and several other police cars pulled up with their lights flashing.

Lieutenant Fillmore ran up to Craig. "Is there anyone else in the building?" he asked, his breath coming fast.

"Roy Gardner hasn't come out yet. We heard shots fired inside the building. Chances are he's dead. Peyton, Mark, and Stacy are getting the kids out of the back of the building," answered Craig.

The lieutenant was about to enter the building when Craig grabbed his arm. "You can't go in there. It's an old building. It's only a matter of minutes before the building will be engulfed in flames!" he exclaimed. "You stay here and help the officers haul these men down to the jail. I'll go see what I can do to help," motioned the lieutenant.

When Mark heard gunshots, his heart began to race as he lifted another child into his arms and headed out. He handed her off to Peyton. Tammy, watching as Peyton brought another child to her, saw the smoke coming from the building.

"Peyton!" yelled Tammy. "The building's on fire!"

Peyton handed off another girl to her. He rushed back just as Lieutenant Fillmore and Stacy came up to see what they could do to help. "What can I do?" he asked.

"Two more kids are in the building. Mark just went in to get another one." They watched as Mark held out another one for Peyton to take. He came out coughing and gagging.

"Mark, I'll go in and get the last one!" yelled Peyton over the noise of the fire. Mark pulled his shirt off and wrapped it around his face.

"I'll get her! I know where she's at!" He re-entered the building. Through the smoke, he saw flames licking up the far side of the wall. He hadn't a moment to lose. Getting down on his hands and knees, he crawled to where the little girl was lying. He literally had to drag her to keep from inhaling too much smoke. With his eyes burning, he could barely see the opening in the wall. *Just a little farther*, he told himself as he crawled for all he was worth.

Coughing, he heard someone call to him before he collapsed on the floor. Peyton pulled the little girl out while Lieutenant Fillmore dragged Mark from the building.

Tammy was in a panic as she watched the lieutenant pull an unconscious Mark far away from the building. Stacy took the little girl over to Tammy, so Peyton could stay by his brother's side. Tammy, Stacy, and the children watched as the building exploded in a gulf of flames, crumbling to the ground.

Zack and Mike came around the building to see Mark lying on the ground, with Peyton by his side. Mike's heart lurched as he ran up to him.

Craig, with the prisoners secured, went and checked on the kids. He looked around and saw most of the children were awake except for one small little girl. She was still unconscious. "The ambulances will be here shortly. How's the little girl?" Craig asked with concern.

Tammy was checking her pulse. "She's still alive, but I don't know how much smoke she took in. She never woke up from the drugs they gave her."

Looking down at the small face, his heart went out to her. He prayed she would make it. He bent down by her side and glanced over at Tammy. "I'll stay with her; you go over to Mark," said Craig. He could tell she was anxious to see him. She nodded and swiftly went over to his side. Stacy stayed back to watch over the other children with him.

Tammy hurried over to find Mike and Peyton lifting him in a sitting position, to help him cough up the phlegm and smoke out of his lungs, while Zack and the lieutenant looked on. Tammy bent down in front of him, her heart going out to him as he went into another fit of coughing. She took his hand in hers, holding on tight until he stopped coughing and was able to take some breaths. When he was finally able to speak, he asked, "How's the little girl?"

"She's still alive, but her pulse was weak. I'm praying she'll make it through." They all heard the sirens from the ambulances and firetrucks coming up to the scene. Zack went around the burning building to let them know where they were needed. Several of the medics started checking the children. One came up to Mark, putting a facemask on him to get oxygen into his lungs. After he breathed in the life-giving air, he pulled it off, going into another fit of coughing. Continuing to hold his hand, Tammy waited for the coughing to subside. His eyes, red from the smoke, gazed into hers. He thanked God that no harm had come to her and the kids were alive and safe.

Placing the mask back onto Mark's face, the medic asked, "Do you think you can stand up, Mr. TreVaine?" He glanced over toward him and nodded. Mike and Peyton on each side of him helped him to get on his feet. "Keep the mask on as long as you can," instructed the medic as he handed him the small oxygen tank to carry. They all walked around what was left of the burning building. The children were getting loaded into the ambulances ready to take them to the hospital. Mark refused to go in the ambulance. Mike assured them he would be taken to the hospital to be checked out, even though he kept insisting he was fine. One of the medics handed him a t-shirt to put on. He handed the oxygen tank and mask back to the medic. He took the shirt and pulled it over his head as they walked back to Zack's car.

Walking back, Tammy wondered if they arrested Roy and Morris. She had no idea how many other men had come in. She heard gunshots just before she saw the smoke coming from the building. She didn't know if the gunshots were from the police or from the gunmen. Holding on to Mark's hand, she stopped.

"What is it?" his voice raspy.

She gazed up into his blue eyes, still red from the smoke. "Do you know what happened to Roy, if he made it out?"

Mark didn't know for sure, but he didn't have a good feeling about it. Not wanting to upset her, "Honey, I don't know. We'll have to wait to hear from Zack and the other detectives."

Still holding her hand, they both turned around to view what was left of the burning building. The red-hot embers that would soon be nothing more than ashes glowed in the dark.

When they turned back to go to the car, a sense of dread came over Tammy. She would ask Detective Williams when the time was right. Right now she needed to focus on getting Mark to the hospital and home to Bethany. She needed to feel those little arms around her, holding her tight, knowing this nightmare was over.

CHAPTER 22

It was morning before Mark, Tammy, and Mike walked into Mark's home. Peyton had already taken Justice back to Mike's. Stacy went back to the big island with Sergeant Higgins. She was wrapping up a homicide report, plus she wanted to get some work done on Peyton's home he recently purchased. Peyton decided to stay a few more days with his brothers. It had been a while since they had seen each other, even if it wasn't in the best of circumstances.

Tammy heard Bethany talking to someone in the kitchen as they walked in. She went around the corner to find Jenna serving up some sausage and pancakes to Bethany and herself. Jenna looked up just as Tammy came up to her daughter. She bent down. Softly, she asked, "Hey, sweetie. How's my girl?"

Bethany quickly turned to her mother with a look of surprise, threw her arms around her neck, and exclaimed, "Mommy, you're home!"

"Yes, sweetie, I'm home," hugging her tight. She held onto her daughter until she pulled away.

Giving her mom a puzzling look, she asked in her sweet voice, "Mommy, what have you been doing? You're dirty, and you smell funny. I thought you were out with Mr. Mark?"

Tammy chuckled. She was sure she looked and smelled pretty bad. She was in dire need of a shower. Standing behind the two, looking on, Mike and Mark smiled as Tammy tried to explain to her daughter, "Well, I was out with Mr. Mark, but we ran into some trouble along the way."

Looking confused, Bethany glanced up to see Mr. Mark and his brother standing next to him. Her facial features went from confused to excited, as she broke away from her mom to run into his arms. He held them out for her, picking her up and giving her a big hug. She leaned back and eyed him. "Gee, Mr. Mark, you look bad, too!"

He laughed. Kids, they never held anything back. Always saying what's on their mind. She waved her hand in front of her face. "Whew! You don't smell good, either!"

"Bethany!" her mother scolded. Mark put her down, chuckling.

"Sorry, Mom," she said as she plugged her nose walking back to her chair. "I think I'll eat my pancakes while you and Mr. Mark take a shower!" Everybody roared!

Jenna was the first to comment. "She's not afraid to say what she feels!" Still chuckling, Jenna glanced over at the grimy group. Smiling, she encouraged, "Why don't all of you go and get cleaned up." Her eyes zeroed in on her husband. "Mike, I brought an extra pair of clothes for you. I set them on the bed in Cameron's room. I'll put on a fresh pot of coffee and make another batch of pancakes and sausage."

"Thanks, Jenna. I appreciate you staying with Bethany last night and making breakfast. I'll hurry and be back to help you."

"Hey, take your time. When I lived at home, it was nothing to help cook for a brood of siblings, in-laws, nieces and nephews!"

Tammy grinned. "Okay!" She headed down the hall.

Jenna turned her eyes toward Mark. "Go!" smiling as she waved her hand at him, and then at her husband. "All of you really do smell."

Tammy heard Bethany giggle.

Mark practically ran down the hall. He caught up with Tammy as she opened the door to her room. He took her arm, guiding her inside the room and closing the door. His arms went around her as he pulled her close. He groaned, burying his head in her neck. "I needed this," he whispered. "We haven't been alone since the other night." His lips brushed her neck and made their way to her soft lips.

Tammy raised her arms up around his neck, pulling him closer to her. She needed this too. After what she endured throughout the night, she felt safe in his arms, holding her so tight.

He lifted his head, his eyes caressing her. "Tammy, I owe you an apology for the way I handled things yesterday afternoon. Can you forgive me?"

Her eyes softened when she smiled. "Of course I forgive you. And I'm sorry for the way I reacted." She placed her head on his chest, reveling in the feel of him. As much as she wanted to stay in this moment, Bethany could come in at any moment. She pulled away from him. "I think we better get showered and dressed. They'll wonder what happened to us."

He grinned. "We could shower together"—wiggling his eyebrows—"Save water?" She chuckled and went to pull the door open.

"Nice thought, TreVaine, but not with the possibility of a little one coming to find me."

He sighed. "Okay, I'll meet you in the kitchen." He gave her a light kiss and headed for his room. Tammy closed the door.

Going into her bathroom, she turned on the shower. She smiled as she visualized the two of them taking a shower together. It sent tingles down her spine as she undressed and stepped under the warm, pulsating water.

Tammy felt better after her shower, even though she was bone tired after being up all night. When she entered the kitchen to join the others, Mark was getting cups out of the cupboard for the coffee. Mike was bringing the pancakes and sausage to the table, while Jenna followed with the syrup and cream.

She came up beside Mark and asked what she could do to help. He turned and smiled. He dropped a kiss on her luscious lips. "Can you bring the coffee pot?"

"Of course!" she answered, returning his smile. She picked up the pot, getting the juice out of the fridge on her way to the table. She went back for some glasses for the juice. When everything was on the table, they all sat down and enjoyed the wonderful breakfast Jenna prepared.

When Tammy asked where Bethany was, Jenna informed her she was in the entertainment room, watching one of her favorite Saturday morning TV shows.

It was nice to finally relax and spend some adult time with Mark's family. While they were eating, Jenna wanted to know everything that had happened last night. Mike started filling her in. Tammy grew quiet, remembering the events of the night. She shivered, reliving Morris touching her. *Are both Morris and Roy in jail?* she wondered. She didn't know. Trapped on the other side of the building, she didn't know how many were hauled off to jail or killed. Again, she remembered hearing gunshots just before she saw the smoke coming from the building. Pain started to shoot down the back of her head where Morris slammed her head into the wall. She closed her eyes, trying to fight off the pain and fatigue she was feeling. She wondered how she was going to make it through the day.

Mark, watching the emotions crossing over her pretty face, and seeing her eyes close, knew she needed to go to bed. Peyton had offered to take her home, but she refused. She was by his side until they released him from the hospital. He tried to get her to talk about what had happened between the time she was kidnapped and the time they rescued all who was involved, but she closed up. He noticed some bruising on each side of her chin when they were back in the patient room. Her wrists had rope burns where they had tied her up, but she wouldn't talk about it. She even refused to let the doctor take a look at her wrists. They seemed more pronounced since her shower. He knew what he had to do.

He came up from the table. "Mike, can I see you for a moment." Mike put his cup down on the table and joined him at the counter. "Would you get ahold of Jack to see if he can get someone to come in for Tammy tonight?" he asked in a low voice. "There's no way she should be going in to work. We all need to get some rest."

He nodded. "I'll give him a call."

"Do you think Jenna would be willing to watch Bethany for a bit longer, just until the Langleys get here?"

He glanced over to see Jenna gathering up the dishes to take to the sink. He turned back to his brother. "I'm sure Jenna will be fine with it, just let me check with her first." Mike strode over to the table. "Hey, sweetheart. Would you be willing to watch Bethany while we all crash for a bit?"

Tammy opened her eyes when she overheard Mike and Jenna talking. "Oh no, I'll keep an eye on Bethany. She's my responsibility. You've already done too much. You both need to go home and get some rest." Mark couldn't help but admire this woman who felt she needed to do everything on her own.

Jenna stepped in. "Hey, Tammy, I had already planned on staying. All of you have been up all night. You, and Mark, especially need to go get some sleep. You both have been through a lot these last few days. I already asked the Langleys if they could come at two o'clock. So you don't need to worry."

"Are you sure?" she asked.

"I'm sure. Go get some rest."

"Thank you, Jenna, I am feeling it." She rose up from the table, feeling a little dizzy. Mark caught her when she swayed, almost collapsing onto the floor. He picked her up and carried her back to his bedroom. Even in her state she tried to tell him she could walk. Mark refused to listen. With the comforter already pulled back, he gently laid her down on the bed. She felt him snuggling up to her warm soft body.

"Mark," she whispered. "What about Bethany?"

"Bethany will be fine," he murmured. "Now, go to sleep." With his arm wrapped around her, he pulled her close. She really needed to discuss the issue of them sleeping together. She closed her eyes, too exhausted to worry about how her daughter would react to her mom sleeping with Mr. Mark!

Tammy woke to darkness. She looked over at the clock on the nightstand. It was pushing nine o'clock! How in the world did she sleep so long? She sat up too fast and moaned, lying right back down again. Her whole body ached, along with the throbbing pain in the back of her head. She should have taken a pain reliever before Mark carried her to bed. She wondered what time he got up and left the bedroom. She missed him. Snuggling up to his massive body, she felt safe and secure as she fell into a heavy sleep. She thought of Bethany. Was she asleep already? Did she come looking for her? She needed to check on her.

Groaning, she pulled herself out of bed and walked into the bathroom. Peering into the mirror, she saw the bruising on both sides of her delicate face. Glancing down at her hands, the rope burns from struggling out of the ropes left them red and bruised. The injuries she sustained were minor compared to the thought of getting raped by that awful man. She thought of the children trapped inside that little room. What they must have endured at the hands of those men. She was thankful the Lord had given Mark the strength to bring all the children out of the burning building. She admired his bravery, risking his life to save another. When she saw the lieutenant drag his body out of the building before it collapsed to the ground, her heart lurched, praying he hadn't died from smoke inhalation. When she ran up to him, seeing his skin blackened from the smoke, coughing and choking, it was all she could do not to throw her arms around him, relief flooding her that he was alive. The doctor said he had suffered minor injuries to his lungs and would recover quickly.

Looking around his master bathroom, she saw the massive sunken Jacuzzi tub, big enough for two. It looked so inviting, just the thing to ease the soreness out of her muscles. *Should I?*

She closed the door and filled the tub. Looking through his linen closet, she found some plush towels and washcloths that matched the warm colors of the décor. On the top shelf was some bubble bath. Adding a little into the water, the sweet smell of lavender filled up her senses. She left her clothes on a chair and stepped in. Turning on the jets, she felt her body relax as she submerged her whole body under the water, the bubbles caressing her skin. She closed her eyes, letting go of the past several days, feeling the jets working out the soreness in her muscles. If this wasn't heaven, she didn't know what was. Over the sound of the jets, she didn't hear the bathroom door open.

Mark, staring at the woman who was floating in his tub, watched as the bubbles floated across her beautiful body. He couldn't resist the temptation to feel her silky skin next to his as he quickly undressed and stepped down into the tub to join her.

Tammy suddenly felt a body come up next to her. She came up quickly, her eyes settling on the rock-solid man who was now sitting beside her. "Mark! What are you doing?"

His eyes gleamed as he watched the soap bubbles sliding down her firm breasts. "I came in with a tray of tea and sandwiches and found an empty bed. I heard the jets and found a beautiful woman floating in my tub," he murmured in a smooth and velvety tone, his eyes devouring her. Bringing his arm around her, he pulled her down next to him. "Ah…" he sighed. "This feels great, doesn't it?" He closed his eyes, letting his body relax, as he felt the jets massage his aching muscles. Feeling her exquisite body next to his was pure pleasure in itself.

Tammy, feeling his skin next to hers, rested her head on his chest, wrapping her arm around his waist. If only they could stay in this moment. But thoughts of her daughter still being awake had her wondering if she would come looking for her, leaving her on edge. What would she think, seeing her mom bathing with him? Other thoughts swirled in her head, like what was she doing in a Jacuzzi tub, with a man who she had no idea if he had the same feelings she had for him. She wanted more than just an affair with him. She brought herself up from him.

Mark, feeling her soft body leaving him, sat up. Still holding her with his one arm, their eyes locked. He sensed something was wrong. He placed his other hand through her long, wet tresses, gently moving around to the back of her head. She winced. "Tammy, what is it?" When he found the lump, she tried to brush it off.

"It's nothing," she tried to assure him.

"Tammy, you don't have to be brave all the time. You need to let go and let the ones who care about you help you."

Tears formed in her eyes, as she felt the pent-up emotions from the past twenty-four hours start to release from her. He brought her head down on his chest as the tears flowed from her eyes while she poured out what she had endured during her captivity, holding her, soothing her with words of comfort until she was able to get it all out. She lifted her head, raising her tear reddened eyes to his. "I'm sorry, it seems like all I'm doing lately is crying."

Taking one of the soft cloths from the side of the tub, he gently wiped away her tears. His intense blue eyes gently smiled into hers. "You have nothing to be sorry about," he murmured softly. "You have been under a tremendous amount of stress over the last several weeks." He smiled. "You can cry on me anytime you need to. I'm glad you were able to let it all out." He pressed her sweet body to his, feeling her firm silky breasts against his chest. He closed his eyes and held her close.

It was a few minutes before he let her go. He placed his fingers under her chin, tilting her oval face up so he could place his lips next to hers.

His kiss, soft and gentle, began to stir new sensations inside her. Her hand started caressing his chest, his hand coming up to stop her.

This wasn't the time to make love to her, although he would like nothing more than to caress her tender body till she screamed. He lifted his head, gazing into her amber eyes. "As much as I would like to make love to you," his voice husky, "I need to take a look at that bump on your head."

He stood up, pulling her up next to him. Shutting the jets off, they both came out of the tub. Wrapping a towel around him, he took one of the soft towels and gently dried her skin, from her head to her toes. Watching him, feeling his hands under the soft fabric, made her shiver. When she was dry, he turned her around. She felt his fingers gently separating her hair, the tingles going down her neck.

"The skin's not broken, just some bruising." He went to the cabinet to get some ointment and applied a small amount to the bruise. "This should help with some of the pain." He turned her back around. "I have some pain reliever along with the sandwiches and tea in the bedroom."

"Thank you, I am hungry."

"Good, I'll let you get dressed," his eyes taking her in.

Gazing back into his eyes, she smiled, wanting so badly to tell him how she felt about him. But all she could come up with was, "I'll only be a minute."

He bent down and gave her a sweet kiss before he went into the bedroom to get dressed himself. He quickly finished drying himself with the towel he was wearing, putting on a pair of shorts, leaving his broad chest bare. She joined him at the table that was centered in the bay window. The curtains were pulled back, revealing the beautiful pool lit up in the dark of night. She marveled at the décor of his master suite. The walls were painted with a warm beige color; oil paintings of buildings and landscapes were painted in warm colors to accent the room. The dark mahogany wood that framed his king-size bed, with matching end tables, made the room look very masculine. The soft light from the lamps on the end tables brought intimacy to the room. She sat across from him at the table made of the same mahogany wood, the rich brown leather chair a delight to sit on.

Tammy picked up one of the sandwiches and took a bite. "Hmm, so good," reveling in the taste of roast beef, Swiss cheese, topped with lettuce and mayo.

"You have Mildred to thank for it. She insisted she make something for us before they went home."

That led her to ask, "How has Bethany been?"

"When I came from the bedroom earlier, they were enjoying a game of Monopoly. I joined them for a game and ended up losing. I can never seem to win at that game."

She smiled. "But you certainly can win at poker!" remembering the night he and Detective Williams went out to find Jed Rawlings.

He chuckled. "From my Air Force days. We had a regular poker night, which if we ever got caught, we could have been court-martialed."

She swallowed. "And you still played?"

Still chuckling, he nodded. "Yep. It seemed we had no fear."

She shook her head. "What time did Bethany go down?"

"She fell asleep while we all watched her favorite movie. I put her to bed around nine o'clock, while Mildred made these luscious sandwiches."

"Remind me to thank her when she comes on Monday."

They finished their sandwiches in silence, each in their own thoughts. Mark relieved she wasn't raped at the hands of Morris. And that lowlife of an ex, thinking he could kidnap her in exchange for her daughter! He would make sure they were both put away for a long time.

Tammy, angry that she lost a day with her daughter because of her ex-husband and the trauma he put her through, was missing her. After taking her pain medicine, she finished her tea. She came up from the table, putting the empty dishes on the tray. Mark put his hand out.

"You don't need to do that," he insisted. "Leave them."

Staring into his eyes, he came up from the table beside her. He pulled her into his arms, murmuring softly, "We have this time together, let's enjoy it." He bent to touch his lips to hers in a slow and lazy rhythm.

Before the passion started to consume them, Tammy pulled away, his eyes questioning. "Mark," she whispered, "I haven't seen my daughter in almost two days. I need to go check on her."

Mark traced his finger from her temple, down to the bruise on her soft cheek, his lips gently touching the area. He lifted his head. "Bethany is sound asleep. Morning will be here all too soon," he murmured. She came out of his arms.

"I'll only be a moment. I just need to see her."

He sighed. "Okay. Go. I'll take care of the dishes." He bent and gave her a kiss on the cheek, marveling at her devotion to her daughter. When she left the room, he took the tray of dirty dishes and set them on the counter in the kitchen. He went out into the lanai and stared out at the pool. He hadn't been in it for a while. Stepping out onto the patio, the night air was warm and balmy. With all the pent-up emotions he was feeling, a good workout in the pool was just what he needed. He jumped in, doing as many laps as his lungs would allow.

Tammy entered their room and found her precious daughter all snuggled up with her Mr. Snow Bear. She crept up to the side of her bed, watching her sleep in the soft light from the night lamp beside her bed. *Thank you, Lord, for keeping me and my daughter safe,* she prayed. She wasn't sure if they were completely out of danger yet, but she hoped with the capture of all who were involved last night, they could breathe a little easier. She bent and kissed her soft cheek. Bethany opened her eyes.

Sleepily, she asked, "Hi, Mommy. Are you feeling better?" She smiled down at her daughter.

"Yes, sweetie, I'm feeling much better."

She raised herself up and gave her mom a big hug. "I missed you," her little voice cried. Tammy squeezed her tight.

"I missed you, too." She pulled away and settled her back down on the bed. She came down on her knees. Smiling at her sweet girl, "Tomorrow," she whispered, "we will spend the whole day together."

"Promise?" she asked, her amber eyes questioning.

"I promise. Do you think you can go back to sleep?" She nodded yes. Tammy covered her up and gave her another kiss.

"Goodnight, I love you."

"Love you, too." She sighed as she snuggled up with her bear and closed her eyes.

Softly walking to the door, she turned back, smiling at her daughter, before opening and gently closing the door behind her.

After sleeping all day, she wasn't tired. She went into the kitchen and found the dirty dishes where Mark left them on the counter. She started to put the dishes in the dishwasher when she thought she heard water splashing outside.

Looking out from the lanai, Mark was doing laps in the pool. She watched as his powerful arms push the water back, moving him forward till he reached the end, then turning around and coming back to the other side. She continued to watch him do laps until he walked up the steps and out of the water. Staring at his magnificent body, her eyes feasted on the hard muscles of his broad chest and arms, the beads of water rolling off his skin. She saw him grab a towel off the chair and dry himself, his breathing coming fast from the workout his body endured. She hoped he hadn't over done it. The doctor warned him to take it easy the next couple of days. As he came toward her, their eyes locked through the door of the lanai. He opened the door and came up to her. He took the cap off his head, his breath coming fast.

Full of concern for him, she asked, "How are your lungs?"

He shrugged. "A little sore, but otherwise fine," he assured her. "Was everything all right when you checked in on Bethany?"

She smiled, shaking off the emotions she felt every time he came near her. "Yes. She woke up briefly, but is back to sleep, which I think I'm going to do." She needed to put some distance between them. Even though she wanted to, she didn't want to end up in his bed. It wasn't the impression she wanted to give her daughter. She hoped he would understand. "Goodnight, Mark." She turned to leave, when Mark took her arm, turning her around to face him.

"Hey, I can tell something's bothering you." He had a feeling it wasn't his bed she was going to.

"Mark." Oh, how was she to say this without hurting his feelings. "When I was with Bethany, it made me realize that I can't just sleep with you, wondering if she would come in and find us. That's not me. It would be different if we were..." Her voice trailed off.

"If we were married?" he finished for her. He wasn't sure he wanted marriage yet, but he wanted time for them to get to know each other, but he could see where she was coming from.

Gazing into his eyes, knowing everything that happened in his first marriage, she thought it would be the last thing he would want. She wished she knew how he felt about her. Did he love her, or was it only desire on his part? Not knowing, she sighed and answered, "I think marriage is the last thing either one of us want. Goodnight, Mark."

When she left, he was left with a sense of loss. *Why am I so afraid of telling her that I love her?* He sighed, knowing in his heart he didn't want to go through the hurt if she didn't feel the same. He went to his bedroom and closed the door. He decided after his shower he would work in his study, since he knew the possibility of sleep would elude him.

CHAPTER 23

THE NEXT MORNING, Bethany came running from the bedroom into the kitchen where her mom was making breakfast. "Good morning, Mommy! Is Mr. Mark up yet?"

"Well, good morning, young lady!" she said with a twinkle in her eyes. "And to answer your question, no, Mr. Mark is not up yet."

"What are you making?"

"I thought I would make ham and cheese omelets. How does that sound?"

"That sounds yummy!" She hesitated. In her small voice, she asked, "Can I go wake up Mr. Mark? I can smell the coffee, and I know he really likes coffee, so can I?"

"Uh, I'm not sure when Mr. Mark went to bed last night. Perhaps we should let him sleep." Plus, she didn't know if he slept in the nude. That would be embarrassing.

"Oh, Mom, please! I haven't been able to wake him up since he was at our house. Please?" she pleaded.

"Bethany, I'm not sure it's a good idea…" her voice trailing off when she took off running down the hallway. "Bethany!" she called. She set the pan aside and hurried down the hall after her.

Giggling, her eyes full of mischief, she glanced back at her mom as she opened the door, ran in, and, seeing Mr. Mark was still sleeping, jumped on the bed! Tammy ran in after her. She held her breath when he reared up, with Bethany jumping on his stomach, yelling out his name. She ran up to his bed, taking Bethany off of him. His chest was bare but thank God he was wearing shorts!

"Bethany!" she scolded. "Mommy told you not to wake him!"

Mark lay back down. He finally crashed at five this morning. He tried to work but ending up rehashing the events of the past two days. "What time is it?" yawning and shaking his head as he brought himself back up again.

Bethany giggled. "It's time to get up! Coffee's ready!"

He smiled, catching Tammy's eyes while she struggled to contain her. He held out his arms. Bethany practically jumped into them. He brought her down on the bed and started tickling her!

"Stop!" she laughed. "Stop!" Her laugh was so contagious you couldn't help but laugh with her. Mark brought her up on his lap.

After they were able to catch their breaths, he asked, "Did you say coffee was ready?" She nodded her head yes. His eyes glinted as he touched his finger to her nose. "Then I guess I'd better get up!"

"Yay!" she cried. Jumping off the bed, she ran to the door. She turned around and yelled, "Come on!"

Mark grinned up at her mom, remembering the conversation they had last night before she left to go to bed. He came up and stood next to her, chuckling. "I get it!"

Chuckling with him, "You just never know with her, but I am totally glad you had on a pair of shorts!"

He laughed as he put on a t-shirt and followed them into the kitchen. Bethany took Mark's hand and led him to one of the bar chairs in front of the counter. "You sit here, Mr. Mark, and I'll sit here," she said as she climbed up on the one next to his.

Oh, no, Tammy thought. *She's going into her pretend mode.*

"Now," she instructed, "You be the dad, my mom is your wife, and I'm going to be the demanding daughter!"

There was a glint in his eyes as he glanced up at Tammy and winked. His eyes turned back to Bethany when he asked, "The demanding daughter?"

She nodded. "Uh huh." Pointing, "I tell you and my mom what to do."

"Oh, I see. Okay, what is your first demand?"

"Mom, you are to bring Dad his coffee and me my juice!"

"Oh, yes, ma'am! I'll get right on it!" Tammy poured two cups of coffee and added a little cream to each. She took the juice out of the fridge and poured Her Majesty a glass.

Mark was following her with his eyes, thinking how adorable she looked in her black capris and pink tank top. Her long amber hair was pinned up in a ponytail, with a few tendrils coming down, caressing her cheeks.

When she set the drinks down in front of them, her daughter demanded, "Now, Dad, you need to thank her with a kiss!"

Tammy glanced at her daughter, wondering what had gotten into her. "Bethany," she mused, her eyes turning to Mark. "Mark, you don't have to do this."

He grinned, mischief glowing in his eyes. He threw his hands up. "Your daughter demanded it and I aim to follow orders!" He came around the counter, with Bethany giggling. Mark took the coffee cup she was sipping on out of her hand and set it on the counter. He gazed into her eyes, pulling her close. He slowly lowered his head, touching his lips to hers, when the doorbell rang! They both jumped and backed away.

"Who could that be?" he wondered.

"Let's go see, Mr. Mark!" Going to the door with Bethany right behind him, he opened it. Mike, Jenna, and Peyton with Justice beside him, wagging his tail, stood on the doorstep.

Bethany, staring at the dog, wanted to be picked up. Mark bent down and brought her up into his arms as he greeted his brothers and Jenna. "What do we owe the pleasure?" he asked.

"Have you checked your messages?" asked Mike.

"No, I haven't even looked at my phone."

"I left several messages this morning, along with Zack. He will be here in an hour. He has some important information he wants to share about the case with us."

"Sorry. I left it in my study when I was working last night. We were just about to make breakfast. Have you eaten?" he asked as he stepped aside to let them all in.

"Do you have enough?" asked Mike.

Not really sure, he responded, "I think we can make do."

Jenna went ahead of the men to see what she could do to help. Peyton noticed Bethany's eyes focused on Justice, and wondered if she was a little afraid of him. Peyton smiled at Bethany. He got down on his haunches and petted the top of Justice's head. "Bethany, would you like to meet Justice?" She clung to Mark. He could tell she was apprehensive.

"Hey, sweetie," Mark soothed. "Justice is pretty friendly. Would you like to try and pet him?" She buried her head in his neck, clinging for all she was worth. "Sorry, Peyton. She'll need to get used to him. We'll try a bit later." He carried her into the kitchen, with his brothers following.

Tammy and Jenna were already busy making extra coffee and getting everything ready for ham and cheese omelets. Mark came up to Tammy. "Do we have enough for everyone?" She smiled up at him.

"I think so."

"Bethany is afraid of Justice," he commented.

"Oh, I'm sorry. I'm afraid she hasn't been around very many dogs. Do you want me to take her?"

"No," he murmured, "I've got her. I'll let you get breakfast around."

The sound of the doorbell rang out. Mark, with a puzzled look on his face, wondered who that could be. He wasn't expecting anyone other than Zack this morning, and he wasn't due for an hour.

"Who do you think it is, Mr. Mark?"

"I don't know, sugar. Let's go find out." He opened the door to his ex-wife and his son Cameron holding her hand.

Sherry stared at the little girl in Mark's arms. She could see she was getting attached to him. She thought they would be gone by now with the news reporting on the human-trafficking ring.

"Cameron!" Bethany cried. She slid down Mark and went to greet him. "Come on in!"

Letting go of his mother's hand, he ran in. "Hi, Bethany!" he greeted. "I smell breakfast!"

"My mom and Jenna are making ham and cheese omelets. Let's go see!" They both ran into the kitchen while Sherry came into the house.

"Sorry to barge in like this, but I left you a message on your phone this morning."

With his hands on his hips, he shook his head. It seemed everyone was trying to get ahold of him this morning. "Sorry, I left my phone in the study. I haven't had time to check messages."

"Well, I know you weren't expecting Cameron until this afternoon, but Al's mother has taken ill, and we need to go see her. I hope you don't mind." She paused. "It sounds like you have a houseful."

"Yes, my brothers and Jenna are here, and no, it's fine bringing him this morning. The kids get along, and Peyton brought Justice with him. They will be well entertained. Tell Al I'm sorry about his mom, and I wish her well."

"Thanks, Mark. I appreciate you taking him early. I'm not sure what time we will be back."

"No worries. If he has to stay the night, I'll make sure he gets to school in the morning. Just give me a call."

"Okay, thanks again," she said as she headed out the door to her car.

Mark closed the door and returned to the kitchen where, amazingly, Bethany and Cameron were petting Justice, with Peyton looking on. He grinned up at Mark. He grinned back. "Looks like they're all friends now."

Bethany glanced up, her eyes glistening. "You were right, Mr. Mark! Justice is friendly! Do you want to pet him?"

He chuckled, bending down on his haunches and petting his soft fur. "Justice looks like he's enjoying all the attention you kids are giving him." Smiling, he came back up. His eyes turned to Peyton. "You got this?"

He grinned. "Yeah, I got this. Do you mind if I take them outside until breakfast is ready?"

He shook his head. "No, that would be great, Peyton. Thanks."

Peyton rose up and led the way out through the lanai into the back yard with Justice by his side. Cameron and Bethany followed excitedly behind. Mark went to see if the women and Mike needed any help.

When he was told they had everything under control, he motioned to Mike to follow him back to his study. After they entered, he closed the door. Mark's study consisted of a large oak desk with his computer resting on top. Books of every description lined the wall-to-wall oak bookshelf behind his desk. Across the room was a cream sofa with a patchwork quilt in red, green, and blue tones on a cream background tossed over the back of it. Matching oak end tables were on either side of the sofa. Crystal lamps were set on the tables, giving off a soft light in the evenings when he worked. Two comfortable chairs sat angled on both sides of the end tables, upholstered in a rich blue color, adding to the distinguished appearance.

Mike sat down in one of the chairs, while Mark took the other. Mark crossed his leg as he caught his brother's eyes and asked, "Did Zack give you any indication on what they uncovered from the fire?"

"He didn't give me much, Mark. He wanted to wait until he could sit down with all of us. What I do know is that Roy Gardner never came out of the building. It doesn't look good. There were several shots fired. Chances are he was dead before the fire broke out. We'll know for sure when Zack gets here."

Mark nodded, concerned how Tammy will react if indeed her ex was killed. Mike, watching his brother's reaction, led him to wonder. "How is Tammy doing? She's been through a lot over the last few days, let alone over the past several weeks," he questioned.

"She seems to be holding up well under the circumstances. I was finally able to get her to talk about it." Remembering how distraught she was over Morris's threat, he continued, "Mike, had we not got there when we did, she would have been raped." The anger inside of him at the thought of him with his filthy hands on her left him reeling. Now he knew how Mike felt when Jenna was being attacked by Ralph.

Mike knew this was a sensitive subject, but he had to know. "After all is said and done, are you going to pursue a relationship with her?"

Mark got up from his chair and walked over to the window. Staring out over his manicured yard, he honestly didn't know how to answer him. He was a little irritated that he asked. He loved her, but he wasn't sure he was ready for marriage just yet. And after their conversation last night, he knew she wouldn't just shack up with him. Not with kids involved. He sighed. Turning around, facing Mike, he speculated, "At this point, I don't know what's going to happen. After Zack fills us in, we'll come to a decision about our relationship. And that's all I'm going to say on the matter."

Mike knew he better not push it. He would open up when he was ready. He knew his brother was desperately in love with her. He would let him know it didn't matter about the rules they set up, if that was holding him back. If he wanted to have a relationship with Tammy, it was okay with him.

There was a knock on the door. When Mark went to open the door, Tammy stood there with a downcast expression on her pretty oval face. Fear crept up into his heart. *Did she overhear our conversation?* he wondered.

"Um, I just wanted to let you know that breakfast is on the table." She turned and left before he could say anything.

Mike noticed the look, as well. He walked up beside him and asked, "Do you think she overheard us talking?"

"I don't know, Mike. But I have a feeling she did."

They no sooner sat down when the doorbell rang again! Mark checked his watch. It was a little early for Zack. Irritated, he got up and wondered who in the hell was at his door! He swung it open, to find Zack and Craig standing in front of him.

Zack noticed the surprised look on Mark's face and started to apologize. "Sorry, Mark. I know we are early, but I sent you a message that we were on our way. Is it okay if we step in?"

I guess this was not the day to be without his phone! He stepped back, with a slight smile, and let them in. "We were just sitting down for breakfast. Have you eaten yet?" he asked.

"Yes, thanks." Craig interrupted. "But we would take a cup of coffee, if you have any left."

"Sure, come on in," he invited.

Everyone greeted each other while Mark went to pour each of them a coffee. He set them on the counter where Zack and Craig took a seat. After everyone was seated, Jenna said grace, and everyone dug into the delicious omelets set before them. Trying to listen to the conversations at the table, it seemed to Mark that everyone was talking at once. He kept glancing over at Tammy. When he finally captured her eyes, she quickly turned away. He wondered again if she had overheard him and Mike talking. It was a relief when everyone had finished eating and Tammy and Jenna along with his brothers started to clean up the table. Cameron and Bethany went into the entertainment room, with Justice following close behind. Mark needed something to do, so he went in and made another pot of coffee.

Once the coffee was made and the dishwasher was running, the men gathered around the table. Mark knew Tammy would need to sit in with them, so he came up to Jenna to see if she could help them out. "Hey, Jenna. I hate to ask, but could you keep an eye on the kids?"

She smiled. "No worries, Mark. I brought our swimsuits. I had already planned on taking them out to the pool while you and Tammy sit down and discuss what's happened in the case."

He smiled back. "Jenna, you're a gem!"

She chuckled. "That's what I keep telling Mike!"

Mark grabbed the coffeepot, and when all the cups were filled, he sat down, ready to hear what Zack and Craig had to say.

"Have any of you been listening to the news this morning?" asked Zack. They all shook their heads. "Well, I am happy to inform you that the sting operation that the FBI has been working on brought down one of the biggest human-trafficking rings on the West Coast. Along with our part in it, a total of seventy arrests have been made from here, all the way to Seattle, down through L.A."

As Tammy listened, relief flooded her, knowing that all who were involved were caught. She was desperate to know how the kids were doing, if the little girl made it. "Detective Williams?" she asked.

"Yes, Tammy."

"Can you tell me how the children who were taken to the hospital are, especially the one who was unconscious?"

He smiled. "You'll be happy to know they are all doing fine. The little girl was in critical condition, but as of this morning she was taken out of intensive care and is on the mend. They will all be placed in foster homes, until everything gets sorted out."

"Thank goodness," she breathed. She paused before she asked, "Detective Williams, I need to know. Did you take Roy to jail? I'd like to speak to him, if I may."

For a few moments, Zack hesitated. He was having a hard time with this. He glanced over at Craig. Craig understood and took it from there.

"Tammy." He spoke in a gentle tone. Tammy's eyes shifted to him. The way he spoke her name left her with a feeling of dread inside her. "There were two bodies pulled from the ashes. I'm sorry, there's no easy way of saying this, but one of them was Roy."

Her hands went to her lips as she whispered, "NO!" Tears formed in her eyes as her breathing became rapid, imagining him being trapped in the building, being consumed by fire. She knew what he did was wrong, but she would never have wished this upon him. Tears falling down her cheeks, Mark pulled her close to him, wishing the words would come to him to comfort her. Knowing what he did to her, he couldn't bring himself to feel sorry for him. When she was able to bring her emotions under control, her voice raspy, "Did he die in the fire?" she asked.

"Actually, Tammy, both men died of gunshot wounds to the chest before the warehouse was set on fire," returned Craig.

She nodded, feeling a loss. She didn't love him anymore, but at one time she did, and they'd been happy. She didn't know how to internalize this. "If you'll excuse me, I think I need to be alone for a while." She stood up from the table, Mark coming up beside her. He took her arm.

"Do you need me to come with you?" he murmured.

Glancing up into eyes that held so much concern for her, she shook her head. "No, I'll be fine. I just need some time."

Mark let her go, wishing he could take away all the pain he could see in her amber eyes.

Lying on the bed, Tammy let out all the pent-up emotions she faced over the last few days and was thankful it was finally over. After she was able to pull herself together, she went into the bathroom to rinse her face with cool water, trying to get the redness out of her eyes. She ran a comb through her hair, satisfied she looked presentable. As an afterthought she put on her bathing suit with a matching floral robe, knowing everyone would more than likely be out by the pool. Taking a deep breath, she went to join the others.

When she stepped out onto the patio, seeing the kids laughing and playing in the water, with Justice swimming next to them, brought a smile to her pretty pink lips. Peyton called out to Justice. She watched as he paddled up to the steps. Coming out of the water, he shook his body, spraying her legs. Peyton glanced up, and seeing Tammy, rushed up with a towel to dry Justice. "Sorry, Tammy." He smiled. "I didn't mean for Justice to give you a shower."

She smiled back, bent and petted Justice's head. "It's fine. He looked like he was enjoying the water."

Toweling him down, Peyton responded, "He loves the water. Every chance he gets he's jumping into a lake, or when we walk on the beach, he loves to prance around in the surf."

"I've heard stories from your brother how you and Justice saved victims during a flash flood in Afghanistan."

Rising up after he finished drying Justice off, he affirmed, "Yes, he was very good at finding the Afghan people who needed help.

He's an amazing dog." Still petting his head, she came up and met his eyes.

Smiling she said, "I can see he is very special to you. I'm so glad you were able to adopt him and bring him home."

"Thank you," he returned, meeting her eyes. *If Mark doesn't confess his love for her, it's his loss,* he thought.

Her eyes roamed the patio and found Mark sitting on one of the loungers. Their eyes locked. She gazed intently at him, as he came up off the lounger and up to her. Peyton and Justice moved away, to let them have some privacy. His eyes absorbing every detail of her, he placed a hand along the side of her soft cheek, his thumb caressing the bruise by her chin.

"How are you doing?" his voice like velvet, his eyes still locked with hers.

"I'm okay. It's just a lot to process. I will get through it in time."

With his arm around her, he guided her over to the lounge chair. When he sat down he brought her down on his lap. He took her hands in his. "Tammy." Gazing into her eyes, softly and with sincerity, he spoke. "You don't have to do this alone. I will always be here for you, and for Bethany."

"About that," she murmured. "Now that this human-trafficking ring has been caught, you don't have to feel obligated to keep protecting us." She hated to leave him, but after she overheard him telling Mike that he didn't know if he would have a relationship with her, it left her hurt and confused. One minute they were in a relationship, and the next minute she didn't know. She loved him, but if he wasn't feeling the same… "I've decided Bethany and I are going back home. We both need to get back into our regular schedules, and I need to concentrate on finishing this last semester to graduate. I hope you'll understand if I take tomorrow night off, so I can get everything packed while Bethany is in school and settled in by tomorrow night." She would have to skip Ms. Beret's sessions, but under the circumstances, she was sure it wouldn't be a problem.

Listening, Mark knew this day would come. The thought of them leaving made his pulse quicken and his heart ache. He couldn't bring himself to tell her how he felt. His marriage left scars he couldn't seem to overcome. His eyes still holding hers, "I understand. We did agree that this was only temporary. Take the day, I won't hold you back."

Her heart fell at his words. As she rose from his lap, her thoughts were saddened by the fact he didn't ask if she would stay. Knowing he wasn't in love with her, but only physically attracted to her, made it easier for her to leave. She would get over him in time. She would have to deal with seeing him at work, but after the first of the year, she would never have to see him again.

CHAPTER 24

IN HIS OFFICE, staring at the report in front of him, Mark could only see Tammy packing up and leaving his home. He witnessed the same thing with his first wife, only this time he wasn't there to see it. He told himself that it was okay. They agreed to this arrangement. Only he didn't keep his end of the bargain. He fell hopelessly and madly in love with her. He wasn't sure she felt the same about him. Remembering making love together, they had passion. More than he had ever known with a woman. There was a knock on his door, his thoughts interrupted.

"Come in."

Mike walked in and took a seat in front of his desk.

Is it two o'clock already? he wondered.

Mike, taking in his brother's appearance, looked haggard, his eyes bloodshot from lack of sleep. "What are you doing here, Mark?"

"What do you mean what am I doing here?" he shot back, irritated that he would even ask. "I'm working!"

Mike knew his brother was one stubborn man. Jenna needed that report he'd been working on hours ago. He clearly wasn't focused on his work. "Mark, tell me what's going on."

Staring into his brother's eyes, he finally let go. "She's packing up to go back to her home."

"Are you in love with her?"

"Yes." More than his brother would ever know.

Yesterday, the day started out with laughter, then died like the burning embers in the fire by the end of the day.

"Have you told her?" asked Mike.

"No," he muttered.

"If you love her, why are you waiting?"

Mark sat forward and leaned across his desk. "I don't want to go through with what I went through with Sherry! What if she doesn't feel the same, Mike?"

"I would be willing to bet that she does. You need to go and tell her how you feel. Don't sit here and hash it out in your head. Like Peyton said, she's not Sherry. She's a remarkable woman. I've seen that for myself over the past week. I know without a doubt that she's the kind of woman that would stand with you no matter what. And it doesn't matter that she's an employee of ours. Go to her, before it's too late."

Listening to Mike, he knew if he let his fears get in the way of his love for her, then he had only himself to blame if he lost her. He got up from his desk. "Thanks, Mike. Tell Jenna I'll be back tomorrow morning." He rushed from his office, hoping he could still catch her before she left his house.

Tammy was getting the last box packed up and in her car. She had already made several trips back to her home as her car was too small to fit everything they brought over in it. She decided to take one last look around, to make sure she had everything. Inside, she walked through Mark's home with a feeling of sadness. Through all her misgivings, she loved being here. The memories of their kisses and the passion they shared would stay with her forever.

She checked her watch. It was almost three o'clock. It was a good thing she asked the Langleys to pick up Bethany after school and take her home. She had no idea how Bethany would handle not seeing Mr. Mark again. She had grown very fond of him.

She walked through the lanai and out onto the patio. Gazing at the clear blue water of the kidney-shape pool, she wished she could jump in and feel the water caressing her skin, relieving the tension inside of her. It wasn't long ago she watched him doing laps in the pool, his strong, muscular arms moving the water, pulling him from one end of the pool to the other. She remembered those same arms holding her close. Then his hands would gently move over her body, caressing her, loving her, as he kissed her passionately. She closed her eyes.

"Daydreaming?" a deep, velvety voice murmured behind her. She jumped. Coming out of her trance, she turned around.

"Mark, what are you doing here?" she gasped.

He gazed into her eyes for several moments before he answered her. He closed the gap between them, never taking his eyes off her. Pulling her into his arms, "I came here to say something I should have said days ago." Tammy's heart started beating a wild rhythm inside her chest, anticipating what he was about to say. "Tammy," he whispered, "I love you with all my heart and soul. I've never felt anything so deep in my life. I'm hoping beyond hope you feel the same way." His eyes gazed lovingly into hers, waiting for her response; he held his breath.

Her arms went effortlessly up and around his neck, her heart filling with joy, her eyes glistening. "Mark, I love you, so much," she murmured. "I think I fell in love with you the moment you barged into my home and asked me and Bethany to come live with you."

His eyes full of love, "It was the best question I ever asked," he murmured as he placed his lips next to hers in a kiss that showed all the love he was feeling for her. Her arms tightened around him, returning his kiss in a passion that consumed them both. When they both came up for air, his eyes held a certain curiosity in them. "Weren't you supposed to pick up Bethany from school?"

She smiled. "Um, Mr. and Mrs. Langley are picking her up and taking her home. I told them I didn't know how long I would be."

He cocked an eyebrow. "Oh, you did, did you?"

Smiling, she nodded. He picked her up and carried her back to his bedroom. Closing the door, his voice velvety as he laid her on the bed, "Then I think I will use this time to show you all the ways I love you." She held out her arms, pulling him down beside her, their lips touching, hearts beating wildly as they shared in the love and passion they held for one another.

EPILOGUE

It was New Year's Eve. Mark along with his brother Mike were throwing a formal party for their employees, friends, and family at his home. The bar was set up out on the patio by the pool along with appetizers in the lanai. The festive lights were strung up around different areas around the pool, which gave off an intimate glow as couples conversed around the tables and danced to the music from the band they hired for this special occasion.

Standing at the bar with a scotch in his hand, watching everyone having a good time, Mark reminisced over the last several months since the kidnapping. Tammy, his love, went on to finish her degree and graduated on December 18th, to the cheers of her family and him, along with his brothers, Jenna, and Stacy. Their parents surprised them and came to Hawaii for the holidays. They looked to be enjoying themselves, sitting with Tammy's parents. Peyton, who was dancing with his soon-to-be wife, proposed to Stacy on Christmas Day, and a June wedding was being planned. Cameron was off with some of the kids who came to the party with their parents. Tammy gave her two weeks' notice at the restaurant and would be starting her new job with special needs children next week. Their time together was spent getting to know each other and sharing their homes.

But tonight, he was going to make her permanently his. He had asked her father for her hand in marriage, and he gave him their blessing. She wasn't here yet, and he was getting a little worried if she was going to show up. Mike chose that moment to come up to him.

"You throw a great party, bro. It appears everyone is having a good time."

He nodded. "Yes, but thank Jenna. She came up with the idea."

Mike's eyes gleamed as he thought of the ways he would thank her tonight. "Don't worry. I have plans to thank every inch of her."

Jenna came up beside him. "Are you talking about me?" she chided.

Mike grinned down at his adorable wife. Kissing her on the cheek, he whispered in her ear, "Just all the ways I'm going to make love to you."

She blushed; she couldn't help it. He chuckled. He never got tired of making her blush. Mark chuckled with them. Looking around, his eyes wandered to the lanai. His breath caught.

Tammy stood on the threshold, with Bethany right beside her. Dressed in a long sleeveless gown made of silk, the pale green color shimmered in the soft light, bringing out the color of her light brown hair and amber eyes. The dress hugged her body, and the slit going up to her thigh showed off her beautiful, tanned leg. Bethany looked charming in her silk dress, the color matching her mother's. His eyes locked with Tammy's.

"Excuse me a moment." He set his glass down on the bar and came up to her, in awe of her beauty.

Tammy's heart fluttered when she gazed into the eyes of the ruggedly attractive man, dressed in a black tux, with a stark white shirt and black bow tie, coming toward her. Mark couldn't take his eyes off her. "Hi," she breathed. "I hope you don't mind, the Langleys had other plans tonight, so I had to bring her with me."

He smiled down at Bethany. "You know she is always welcome.

Besides, Cameron is here along with some other kids." Bending down, he picked her up into his strong arms. "You, young lady, look very pretty tonight." She grinned and gave him a big hug.

"Thank you, Mr. Mark! You look quite handsome yourself!" she remarked in her small, little voice. He grinned.

Such big words for such a little one, he thought.

Jenna and Mike came up beside them. "Hello, Tammy. Hello, Bethany," welcomed Mike. "You two look lovely this evening." Tammy smiled.

"Thank you, Mike."

Bethany smiled and asked in her little voice, "Did you say Cameron is here, Mr. Mark?" He grinned.

"I did!"

"Hey, Bethany, would you like to go and find him with me?" asked Jenna.

Smiling, she nodded. Mark put her down. Jenna took her hand and led them into the lanai, with Mike following behind. There was a slow melody playing in the background. With his blue eyes gleaming, he held out his hand, "May I have this dance?"

She couldn't resist. She placed her hand in his as they walked out onto the dance floor. Taking her into his arms, she placed her head on his chest, closing her eyes as they swayed to the music. Bending his head down to her ear, his voice like velvet, "You look exquisite tonight. You take my breath away."

Gazing up into his eyes, she whispered back, "And you are very handsome in your black tux and matching bowtie. I am the envy of all the single women here tonight."

He bent and touched his firm lips to hers in a kiss that sent tingles down her spine, wishing they could be alone at this moment. When the music stopped, he took her hand and led her over to one of the benches on the far side of the pool. When they were seated, he took both of her hands in his. "Sweetheart, these past few months with you have been the best months of my life. You are one strong, confident woman who has stolen my heart, and I can't imagine my life without you and Bethany in it." He came off the bench and went down on one knee. Her breath caught as he pulled a little box out of his suit pocket. Inside, was a single-carat diamond, set in a gold band, dazzling under the light. With her hands to her lips, her eyes moved to his. "Tammy, would you do me the honor of becoming my wife?"

With happy tears forming in her eyes, she nodded her head yes. Coming up from the bench, she threw her arms around him, "Yes, my darling, I will marry you!" They could hear the applause as they kissed. They felt two little ones come in between them as everyone came up to congratulate them. Mark picked up the little invaders and held them in his strong arms.

Bethany grinned as everyone looked on. "Does this mean that Cameron will be my brother and I can call you Dad, Mr. Mark?" she asked innocently.

He chuckled. "That's exactly what it means!"

Cameron giggled. "Yay, now I will have a sister!"

Mark, chuckling, hugging them close, couldn't wait for them to become a family. He smiled down into Tammy's pretty amber eyes with all the love he held for her, knowing she would always be by his side.

Get ready for Sheri Lynne's exciting new historical romance, *Two Hearts, One Quest for Freedom*, coming in 2024!